From Doon With Death

A New Lease of Death

Ruth Rendell

D0610743

arrow books

This edition published by Arrow Books in 2007

Copyright © Kingsmarkham Enterprises Ltd 2007

Ruth Rendell has asserted her right under the
Copyright, Designs and Patents Act, 1988 to be identified
as the author of this work

From Doon With Death copyright © Kingsmarkham Enterprises Ltd 1978
A New Lease of Death © Kingsmarkham Enterprises Ltd 1969

Arrow Books
The Random House Group Limited
20 Vauxhall Bridge Road, London SW1V 2SA

www.randomhouse.co.uk

Addresses for companies within The Random House Group Limited
can be found at:
www.randomhouse.co.uk/offices.htm

The Random House Group Limited Reg. No. 954009

A CIP catalogue record for this book
is available from the British Library

ISBN 9780099524762

The Random House Group Limited makes every effort to ensure
that the papers used in its books are made from trees that
have been legally sourced from well-managed and credibly
certified forests. Our paper procurement policy can be found at:
www.randomhouse.co.uk/paper.htm

Printed and bound in Great Britain by
Cox & Wyman Ltd, Reading, Berkshire

Since her first novel, *From Doon With Death*, published in 1964, Ruth Rendell has won many awards, including the Crime Writers' Association Gold Dagger for 1976's best crime novel with *A Demon in My View*, and the Arts Council National Book Award – genre fiction for *The Lake of Darkness* in 1980.

In 1985 Ruth Rendell received the Silver Dagger for *The Tree of Hands*, and in 1987, writing as Barbara Vine, won her third Edgar from the Mystery Writers of America for *A Dark-Adapted Eye*.

She won the Gold Dagger for *Live Flesh* in 1986, for *King Solomon's Carpet* in 1991 and, as Barbara Vine, a Gold Dagger in 1987 for *A Fatal Inversion*.

Ruth Rendell won the *Sunday Times* Literary Award in 1990, and in 1991 she was awarded the Crime Writers' Association Cartier Diamond Dagger for outstanding contribution to the genre. In 1996 she was awarded the CBE, and in 1997 was made a Life Peer.

Her books have been translated into twenty-five languages and are also published to great acclaim in the United States.

Ruth Rendell has a son and two grandsons, and lives in London.

The verses at the beginning of each chapter and the inscriptions in Minna's books all appear in *The Oxford Book of Victorian Verse*.

FROM DOON WITH DEATH

FOR DON

You have broken my heart. There, I have written it. Not for you to read, Minna, for this letter will never be sent, never shrink and wither under your laughter, little lips prim and pleated, laughter like dulcimer music . . .

Shall I tell you of the Muse who awaited me? I wanted you to walk beside me into her vaulted halls. There were the springs of Helicon! I would furnish you with the food of the soul, the bread that is prose and the wine that is poetry. Ah, the wine, Minna . . . This is the rose-red blood of the troubadour!

Never shall I make that journey, Minna, for when I brought you the wine you returned to me the waters of indifference. I wrapped the bread in gold but you hid my loaves in the crock of contempt.

Truly you have broken my heart and dashed the wine-cup against the wall . . .

Chapter 1

Call once yet,
In a voice that she will know,
'Margaret, Margaret!'

Matthew Arnold, *The Forsaken Merman*

'I think you're getting things a bit out of proportion, Mr Parsons,' Burden said. He was tired and he'd been going to take his wife to the pictures. Besides, the first things he'd noticed when Parsons brought him into the room were the books in the rack by the fireplace. The titles were enough to give the most level-headed man the jitters, quite enough to make a man anxious where no ground for anxiety existed: *Palmer the Poisoner, The Trial of Madeleine Smith, Three Drowned Brides, Famous Trials, Notable British Trials.*

'Don't you think your reading has been preying on your mind?'

'I'm interested in crime,' Parsons said. 'It's a hobby of mine.'

'I can see that.' Burden wasn't going to sit down if he could avoid it. 'Look, you can't say your wife's actually missing. You've been home one and a half hours and she isn't here. That's all. She's probably gone to the pictures. As a matter of fact I'm on my way there now with my wife. I expect we'll meet her coming out.'

'Margaret wouldn't do that, Mr Burden. I know

3

her and you don't. We've been married nearly six years and in all that time I've never come home to an empty house.'

'I'll tell you what I'll do. I'll drop in on my way back. But you can bet your bottom dollar she'll be home by then.' He started moving towards the door. 'Look, get on to the station if you like. It won't do any harm.'

'No, I won't do that. It was just with you living down the road and being an inspector . . .'

And being off duty, Burden thought. If I was a doctor instead of a policeman I'd be able to have private patients on the side. I bet he wouldn't be so keen on my services if there was any question of a fee.

Sitting in the half-empty dark cinema he thought: Well, it is funny. Normal ordinary wives as conventional as Mrs Parsons, wives who always have a meal ready for their husbands on the dot of six, don't suddenly go off without leaving a note.

'I thought you said this was a good film,' he whispered to his wife.

'Well, the critics liked it.'

'Oh, critics,' he said.

Another man, that could be it. But Mrs Parsons? Or it could be an accident. He'd been a bit remiss not getting Parsons to phone the station straight away.

'Look, love,' he said. 'I can't stand this. You stay and see the end. I've got to get back to Parsons.'

'I wish I'd married that reporter who was so keen on me.'

'You must be joking,' Burden said. 'He'd have stayed out all night putting the paper to bed. Or the editor's secretary.'

He charged up Tabard Road, then made himself stroll when he got to the Victorian house where Parsons lived. It was all in darkness, the curtains in

4

the big bay downstairs undrawn. The step was whitened, the brass kerb above it polished. Mrs Parsons must have been a house-proud woman. Must have been? Why not, still was?

Parsons opened the door before he had a chance to knock. He still looked tidy, neatly dressed in an oldish suit, his tie knotted tight. But his face was greenish grey. It reminded Burden of a drowned face he had once seen on a mortuary slab. They had put the glasses back on the spongy nose to help the girl who had come to identify him.

'She hasn't come back,' he said. His voice sounded as if he had a cold coming. But it was probably only fear.

'Let's have a cup of tea,' Burden said. 'Have a cup of tea and talk about it.'

'I keep thinking what could have happened to her. It's so open round here. I suppose it would be, being country.'

'It's those books you read,' Burden said. 'It's not healthy.' He looked again at the shiny paper covers. On the spine of one was a jumble of guns and knives against a blood-red background. 'Not for a layman,' he said. 'Can I use your phone?'

'It's in the front room.'

'I'll get on to the station. There might be something from the hospitals.'

The front room looked as if nobody ever sat in it. With some dismay he noted its polished shabbiness. So far he hadn't seen a stick of furniture that looked less than fifty years old. Burden went into all kinds of houses and he knew antique furniture when he saw it. But this wasn't antique and nobody could have chosen it because it was beautiful or rare. It was just old. Old enough to be cheap, Burden thought, and at the same time young enough not to be expensive. The kettle whistled and he heard Parsons fumbling

5

with china in the kitchen. A cup crashed on the floor. It sounded as if they had kept the old concrete floor. It was enough to give anyone the creeps, he thought again, sitting in these high-ceilinged rooms, hearing unexplained inexplicable creaks from the stairs and the cupboard, reading about poison and hangings and blood.

'I've reported your wife as missing,' he said to Parsons. 'There's nothing from the hospitals.'

Parsons turned on the light in the back room and Burden followed him in. It must have a weak bulb under the parchment lampshade that hung from the centre of the ceiling. About sixty watts, he thought. The shade forced all the light down, leaving the ceiling, with its plaster decorations of bulbous fruit, dark and in the corners blotched with deeper shadow. Parsons put the cups down on the sideboard, a vast mahogany thing more like a fantastic wooden house than a piece of furniture, with its tiers and galleries and jutting beaded shelves. Burden sat down in a chair with wooden arms and seat of brown corduroy. The lino struck cold through the thick soles of his shoes.

'Have you any idea at all where your wife could have gone?'

'I've been trying to think. I've been racking my brains. I can't think of anywhere.'

'What about her friends? Her mother?'

'Her mother's dead. We haven't got any friends here. We only came here six months ago.'

Burden stirred his tea. Outside it had been close, humid. Here in this thick-walled dark place, he supposed, it must always feel like winter.

'Look,' he said, 'I don't like too say this, but somebody's bound to ask you. It might as well be me. Could she have gone out with some man? I'm sorry, but I had to ask.'

'Of course you had to ask. I know, it's all in here.'
He tapped the bookcase. 'Just routine enquiries, isn't
it? But you're wrong. Not Margaret. It's laughable.'
He paused, not laughing. 'Margaret's a good woman.
She's a lay preacher at the Wesleyan place down the
road.'

No point in pursuing it, Burden thought. Others
would ask him, probe into his private life whether he
liked it or not, if she still hadn't got home when the
last train came in and the last bus had rolled into
Kingsmarkham garage.

'I suppose you've looked all over the house?' he
asked. He had driven down this road twice a day for
a year but he couldn't remember whether the house
he was sitting in had two floors or three. His
policeman's brain tried to reassemble the retinal
photograph on his policeman's eye. A bay window
at the bottom, two flat sash windows above it and –
yes, two smaller ones above that under the slated
eyelids of the roof. An ugly house, he thought, ugly
and forbidding.

'I looked in the bedrooms,' Parsons said. He
stopped pacing and hope coloured his cheeks. Fear
whitened them again as he said: 'You think she
might be up in the attics? Fainted or something?'

She would hardly still be there if she'd only
fainted, Burden thought. A brain haemorrhage, yes,
or some sort of accident. 'Obviously we ought to
look,' he said. 'I took it for granted you'd looked.'

'I called out. We hardly ever go up there. The
rooms aren't used.'

'Come on,' Burden said.

The light in the hall was even dimmer than the one
in the dining-room. The little bulb shed a pallid glow
on to a woven pinkish runner, on lino patterned to
look like parquet in dark and lighter brown. Parsons
went first and Burden followed him up the steep

stairs. The house was biggish, but the materials which had been used to build it were poor and the workmanship unskilled. Four doors opened off the first landing and these were panelled but without beading and they looked flimsy. The flat rectangles of plywood in their frames reminded Burden of blind blocked-up windows on the sides of old houses.

'I've looked in the bedrooms,' Parsons said. 'Good heavens, she may be lying helpless up there!'

He pointed up the narrow uncarpeted flight and Burden noticed how he had said 'Good heavens!' and not 'God!' or 'My God!' as some men might have done.

'I've just remembered, there aren't any bulbs in the attic lights.' Parsons went into the front bedroom and unscrewed the bulb from the central lamp fitting. 'Mind how you go,' he said.

It was pitchy dark on the staircase. Burden flung open the door that faced him. By now he was certain they were going to find her sprawled on the floor and he wanted to get the discovery over as soon as possible. All the way up the stairs he'd been anticipating the look on Wexford's face when he told him she'd been there all along.

A dank coldness breathed out of the attic, a chill mingled with the smell of camphor. The room was partly furnished. Burden could just make out the shape of a bed. Parsons stumbled over to it and stood on the cotton counterpane to fit the bulb into the lamp socket. Like the ones downstairs it gave only an unsatisfactory light, which, streaming faintly through a shade punctured all over with tiny holes, patterned the ceiling and the distempered walls with yellowish dots. The window was uncurtained. A bright cold moon swam into the black square and disappeared again under the scalloped edge of a cloud.

'She's not in here,' Parsons said. His shoes had made dusty footprints on the white stuff that covered the bedstead like a shroud.

Burden lifted a corner of it and looked under the bed, the only piece of furniture in the room.

'Try the other room,' he said.

Once more Parsons went through the tedious, maddeningly slow motions of removing the light bulb. Now only the chill radiance from the window lit their way into the second attic. This was smaller and more crowded. Burden opened a cupboard and raised the lids from two trunks. He could see Parsons staring at him, thinking perhaps about what he called his hobby and about the things trunks could contain. But these were full of books, old books of the kind you sometimes see in stands outside second-hand shops.

The cupboard was empty and inside it the paper was peeling from the wall, but there were no spiders. Mrs Parsons was a house-proud woman.

'It's half past ten,' Burden said, squinting at his watch. 'The last train doesn't get in till one. She could be on that.'

Parsons said obstinately, 'She wouldn't go anywhere by train.'

They went downstairs again, pausing to restore the light bulb to the front bedroom. There was something sinister and creepy about the stair-well that could have been so easily dispelled, Burden thought, by white paint and stronger lights. As they descended he reflected momentarily on this woman and the life she lived here, going fussily about her chores, trying to bring a little smartness to the mud-coloured woodwork, the ugly ridged linoleum.

'I don't know what to do,' Parsons said.

Burden didn't want to go back into the little dining-room with the big furniture, the cold tea-dregs in their two cups. By now Jean would be back from the cinema.

'You could try phoning round her friends at the church,' he said, edging towards the front door. If Parsons only knew how many reports they got in of missing women and how few, how tiny a percentage, turned up dead in fields or chopped in trunks . . .

'At this time of night?'

Parsons looked almost shocked, as if the habits of a lifetime, the rule that you never called on anyone after nine o'clock, mustn't be broken even in a crisis.

'Take a couple of aspirins and try to get some sleep,' Burden said. 'If anything comes up you can give me a ring. We've told the station. We can't do anything more. They'll let you know as soon as they hear.'

'What about tomorrow morning?'

If he'd been a woman, Burden thought, he'd beg me to stay. He'd cling to me and say, Don't leave me!

'I'll look in on my way to the station,' he said.

Parsons didn't shut the door until he was half-way up the street. He looked back once and saw the white bewildered face, the faint glow from the hall falling on to the brass step. Then, feeling helpless because he had brought the man no comfort, he raised his hand in a half-wave.

The streets were empty, still with the almost tangible silence of the countryside at night. Perhaps she was at the station now, scuttling guiltily across the platform, down the wooden stairs, gathering together in her mind the threads of the alibi she had concocted. It would have to be good, Burden thought, remembering the man who waited on the knife edge that spanned hope and panic.

It was out of his way, but he went to the corner of

Tabard Road and looked up the High Street. From here he could see right up to the beginning of the Stowerton Road where the last cars were leaving the forecourt of The Olive and Dove. The market place was empty, the only people to be seen a pair of lovers standing on the Kingsbrook Bridge. As he watched the Stowerton bus appeared between the Scotch pines on the horizon. It vanished again in the dip beyond the bridge. Hand in hand, the lovers ran to the stop in the centre of the market place as the bus pulled in close against the dismantled cattle stands. Nobody got off. Burden sighed and went home.

'She hasn't turned up,' he said to his wife.

'It *is* funny, you know, Mike. I should have said she was the last person to go off with some man.'

'Not much to look at?'

'I wouldn't say that exactly,' Jean said. 'She looked so – well, respectable. Flat-heeled shoes, no make-up, tidy sort of perm with hair-grips in it. You know what I mean. You must have seen her.'

'I may have done,' Burden said. 'It didn't register.'

'But I wouldn't call her plain. She's got a funny old-fashioned kind of face, the sort of face you see in family albums. You might not admire it, Mike, but you wouldn't forget her face.'

'Well, I've forgotten it,' Burden said. He dismissed Mrs Parsons to the back of his mind and they talked about the film.

Chapter 2

One forenoon the she-bird crouched not on the nest,
Nor returned that afternoon, nor the next,
Nor ever appeared again.

Walt Whitman, *The Brown Bird*

Burden slept quickly, used to crises. Even here, a market town he had expected to find dull after Brighton, the C.I.D. were seldom idle.

The telephone rang at seven.

'Burden speaking.'

'This is Ronald Parsons. She hasn't come back. And, Mr Burden – she hasn't taken a coat.'

It was the end of May and it had been a squally cold month. A sharp breeze ruffled his bedroom curtains. He sat up.

'Are you sure?' he asked.

'I couldn't sleep. I started going through her clothes and I'm positive she hasn't taken a coat. She's only got three: a raincoat, her winter coat and an old one she does the gardening in.'

Burden suggested a suit.

'She's only got one costume.' Parsons' use of the old-fashioned word was in character. 'It's in her wardrobe. I think she must have been wearing a cotton frock, her new one.' He stopped and cleared his throat. 'She'd just made it,' he said.

'I'll get some things on,' Burden said. 'I'll pick you

up in half an hour and we'll go to the station together.'

Parsons had shaved and dressed. His small eyes were wide with terror. The tea-cups they had used the night before had just been washed and were draining on a home-made rack of wooden dowel rods. Burden marvelled at the ingrained habit of respectability that made this man, at a crisis in his life, spruce himself and put his house in order.

He tried to stop himself staring round the little hole of a kitchen, at the stone copper in the corner, the old gas stove on legs, the table with green American cloth tacked to its top. There was no washing machine, no refrigerator. Because of the peeling paint, the creeping red rust, it looked dirty. It was only by peering closely when Parsons' eyes were not on him that Burden could see it was in fact fanatically, pathetically, clean.

'Are you fit?' he asked. Parsons locked the back door with a huge key. His hand shook against crazed mottled tiles. 'You've got the photograph all right?'

'In my pocket.'

Passing the dining-room he noticed the books again. The titles leapt at him from red and yellow and black covers. Now that the morning had come and she was still missing Burden wondered fantastically if Tabard Road was to join Hilldrop Crescent and Rillington Place in the chronicle of sinister streets.

Would there one day be an account of the disappearance of Margaret Parsons under another such book-jacket with the face of his companion staring from the frontispiece? The face of a murderer is the face of an ordinary man. How much less terrifying if the killer wore the Mark of Cain for all the world to see! But Parsons? He could have killed her, he had been well instructed. His textbooks bore witness to that. Burden thought of the gulf between theory and practice. He shook off fantasy and followed Parsons to the front door.

Kingsmarkham was awake, beginning to bustle. The shops were still closed, but the buses had been running for two hours. Occasionally the sun shone in shafts of watery brilliance, then vanished again under clouds that were white and thick or bluish with rain. The bus queue stretched almost to the bridge; down towards the station men hurried, singly or in pairs, bowler-hatted, armed with cautious umbrellas, through long custom unintimidated by the hour-long commuting to London.

Burden pulled up at the junction and waited for an orange-painted tractor to pass along the major road.

'It all goes on,' Parsons said, 'as if nothing had happened.'

'Just as well.' Burden turned left. 'Helps you keep a sense of proportion.'

The police station stood appropriately at the approach to the town, a guarding bastion or a warning. It was new, white and square like a soap carton, and, rather pointlessly, Burden thought, banded and decorated here and there in a soap carton's colours. Against the tall ancient arcs of elms, only a few yards from the last Regency house, it flaunted its whiteness, its gloss, like a piece of gaudy litter in a pastoral glade.

Its completion and his transfer to Kingsmarkham had coincided, but sometimes the sight of it still shocked him. He watched for Parsons' reaction as they crossed the threshold. Would he show fear or just the ordinary citizen's caution? In fact, he seemed simply awed.

Not for the first time the place irritated Burden. People expected pitch pine and lino, green baize and echoing passages. These were at the same time more

14

quelling to the felon, more comforting to the inno-cent. Here the marble and the tiles, irregularly mottled with a design like stirred oil, the peg-board for the notices, the great black counter that swept in a parabola across half the foyer, suggested that order and a harmony of pattern must reign above all things. It was as if the personal fate of the men and women who came through the swing doors mattered less than Chief Inspector Wexford's impeccable records.

He left Parsons dazed between a rubber plant and a chair shaped like the bowl of a spoon, a spongy spoon, cough-mixture red. It was absurd, he thought, knocking on Wexford's door, to build a concrete box of tricks like this amid the quiet crowded houses of the High Street. Wexford called him to come in and he pushed open the door.

'Mr Parsons is outside, sir.'

'All right.' Wexford looked at his watch. 'I'll see him now.'

He was taller than Burden, thick-set without being fat, fifty-two years old, the very prototype of an actor playing a top-brass policeman. Born up the road in Pomfret, living most of his life in this part of Sussex, he knew most people and he knew the district well enough for the map on the the buttercup-yellow wall to be regarded merely as a decoration.

Parsons came in nervously. He had a furtive cautious look, and there was something defiant about him as if he knew his pride would be wounded and was preparing to defend it.

'Very worrying for you,' Wexford said. He spoke without emphasizing any particular word, his voice level and strong. 'Inspector Burden tells me you haven't seen your wife since yesterday morning.'

'That's right.' He took the snapshot of his wife from his pocket and put it on Wexford's desk. 'That's her, that's Margaret.' He twitched his head at Burden. 'He said you'd want to see it.'

It showed a youngish woman in cotton blouse and dirndl skirt standing stiffly, her arms at her sides, in the Parsonses' garden. She was smiling an unnaturally broad smile straight into the sun and she looked flustered, rather short of breath, as if she had been called away from some mundane household task – the washing-up perhaps – had flung off her apron, dried her hands and run down the path to her husband, waiting with his box camera.

Her eyes were screwed up, her cheeks bunchy; she might really have been saying 'Cheese!' There was nothing here of the delicate cameo Jean's words had suggested.

Wexford looked at it and said, 'Is this the best you can do?'

Parsons covered the picture with his hand as if it had been desecrated.

He looked as if he might flare into rage, but all he said was:

'We're not in the habit of having studio portraits taken.'

'No passport?'

'I can't afford foreign holidays.'

Parsons had spoken bitterly. He glanced quickly at the venetian blinds, the scanty bit of haircord carpet, Wexford's chair with its mauve tweed seat, as if these were signs of a personal affluence rather than the furnishings supplied be a detached authority.

'I'd like a description of your wife, Mr Parsons,' Wexford said. 'Won't you sit down?'

Burden called young Gates in and set him tapping with one finger at the little grey typewriter.

Parsons sat down. He began speaking slowly, shame-facedly, as if he had been asked to uncover his wife's nakedness.

16

'She's got fair hair,' he said. 'Fair curly hair and very light blue eyes. She's pretty.' He looked at Wexford defiantly and Burden wondered if he realized the dowdy impression the photograph had given. 'I think she's pretty. She's got a high sort of forehead.' He touched his own low narrow one. 'She's not very tall, about five feet one or two.'

Wexford went on looking at the picture.

'Thin? Well built?'

Parsons shifted in his chair.

'Well built, I suppose.' An awkward flush tinged the pale face. 'She's thirty. She was thirty a few months ago, in March.'

'What was she wearing?'

'A green and white dress. Well, white with green flowers on it, and a yellow cardigan. Oh, and sandals. She never wears stockings in the summer.'

'Handbag?'

'She never carried a handbag. She doesn't smoke or use make-up, you see. She wouldn't have any use for a handbag. Just her purse and her key.'

'Any distinguishing marks?'

'Appendicitis scar,' Parsons said, flushing again.

Gates ripped the sheet from the typewriter and Wexford looked at it.

'Tell me about yesterday morning, Mr Parsons,' he said. 'How did your wife seem? Excited? Worried?'

Parsons slapped his hands down on to his spread knees. It was a gesture of despair; despair and exasperation.

'She was the same as usual,' he said. 'I didn't notice anything. You see, she wasn't an emotional woman.' He looked down at his shoes and said again, 'She was the same as usual.'

'What did you talk about?'

'I don't know. The weather. We didn't talk much. I have to get off to work at half past eight – I work for

17

the Southern Water Board at Stowerton. I said it was a nice day and she said yes, but it was too bright. It was bound to rain, too good to last. And she was right. It did rain, poured down all the morning.'

'And you went to work. How? Bus, train, car?'

'I don't have a car . . .'

He looked as if he was about to enumerate all the other things he didn't have, so Wexford said quickly:

'Bus then?'

'I always catch the eight-thirty-seven from the market place. I said good-bye to her. She didn't come to the door. But that's nothing. She never did. She was washing up.'

'Did she say what she was going to do with herself during the day?'

'The usual things, I suppose, shopping and the house. You know the sort of things women do.' He paused, then said suddenly: 'Look, she wouldn't kill herself. Don't get any ideas like that. Margaret wouldn't kill herself. She's a religious woman.'

'All right, Mr Parsons. Try to keep calm and don't worry. We'll do everything we can to find her.'

Wexford considered, dissatisfaction in the lines of his face, and Parsons seemed to interpret this characteristically. He sprang to his feet, quivering.

'I know what you're thinking,' he shouted. 'You think I've done away with her. I know how your minds work. I've read it all up.'

Burden said quickly, trying to smooth things down. 'Mr Parsons is by way of being a student of crime, sir.'

'Crime?' Wexford raised his eyebrows. 'What crime?'

'We'll have a car to take you home,' Burden said. 'I should take the day off. Get your doctor to give you something so that you can sleep.'

Parsons went out jerkily, walking like a paraplegic,

and from the window Burden watched him get into the car beside Gates. The shops were opening now and the fruiterer on the opposite side of the street was putting up his sunblind in anticipation of a fine day. If this had been an ordinary Wednesday, a normal weekday, Burden thought, Margaret Parsons might now have been kneeling in the sun, polishing that gleaming step, or opening the windows and letting some air into those musty rooms. Where was she, waking in the arms of her lover or lying in some more final resting place?

'She's bolted, Mike,' Wexford said. 'That's what my old father used to call a woman who eloped. A bolter. Still, better do the usual check-up. You can do it yourself since you knew her by sight.'

Burden picked up the photograph and put it in his pocket. He went first to the station but the ticket-collector and the booking clerks were sure Mrs Parsons hadn't been through.

But the woman serving at the bookstall recognized her at once from the picture.

'That's funny,' she said. 'Mrs Parsons always comes in to pay for her papers on Tuesdays. Yesterday was Tuesday but I'm sure I never saw her. Wait a minute, my husband was on in the afternoon.' She called, 'George, here a sec.!'

The bookstall proprietor came round from the part of the shop that fronted on to the street. He opened his order book and ran a finger down the edge of one of the pages.

'No,' he said. 'She never came. There's two-and-two outstanding.' He looked curiously at Burden, greedy for explanations. 'Peculiar, that,' he said. 'She always pays up, regular as clockwork.'

Burden went back to the High Street to begin on the shops. He marched into the big supermarket and up to the check-out counter. The woman by the till was standing idly, lulled by background music. When Burden showed her the photograph she seemed to jerk back into life.

Yes, she knew Mrs Parsons by name as well as by sight. She was a regular customer and she had been in yesterday as usual.

'About half ten it was,' she said. 'Always the same time.'

'Did she talk to you? Can you remember what she said?'

'Now you are asking something. Wait a minute, I do remember. It's coming back to me. I said it was a problem to know what to give them, and she said, yes, you didn't seem to fancy salad, not when it was raining. She said she'd got some chops, she was going to do them in a batter, and I sort of looked at her things, the things she'd got in her basket. But she said, no, she'd got the chops on Monday.'

'Can you remember what she was wearing? A green cotton frock, yellow cardigan?'

'Oh, no, definitely not. All the customers were in raincoats yesterday morning. Wait a tic, that rings a bell. She said, "Golly, it's pouring." I remember because of the way she said "Golly", like a school-kid. She said, "I'll have to get something to put on my head," so I said, "Why not get one of our rain-hoods in the reduced line?" She said didn't it seem awful to have to buy a rain-hood in May? But she took one. I know that for sure, because I had to check it separately. I'd already checked her goods.'

She left the counter and led Burden to a display of jumbled transparent scarves, pink, blue, apricot and white.

'They wouldn't actually keep the rain out,' she said confidingly. 'Not a downpour, if you know what I mean. But they're prettier than plastic. More

20

glamorous. She had a pink one. I remarked on it. I said it went with her pink jumper.'

'Thank you very much,' Burden said. 'You've been most helpful.'

He checked at the shops between the supermarket and Tabard Road, but no one remembered seeing Mrs Parsons. In Tabard Road itself the neighbours seemed shocked and helpless. Mrs Johnson, Margaret Parsons' next-door neighbour, had seen her go out soon after ten and return at a quarter to eleven. Then, at about twelve, she thought it was, she had been in her kitchen and had seen Mrs Parsons go out into the garden and peg two pairs of socks on to the line. Half an hour later she had heard the Parsonses' front door open and close again softly. But this meant nothing. The milkman always came late, they had complained about it, and she might simply have put her hand out into the porch to take in the bottles.

There had been a sale at the auction rooms on the corner of Tabard Road the previous afternoon. Burden cursed to himself, for this meant that cars had been double parked along the street. Anyone looking out of her downstairs windows during the afternoon would have had her view of the opposite pavement blocked by this row of cars standing nose to tail.

He tried the bus garage, even rather wildly the car-hire firms, and drew a complete blank. Filled with foreboding, he went slowly back to the police station. Suicide now seemed utterly ruled out. You didn't chatter cheerfully about the chops you intended cooking for your husband's dinner if you intended to kill yourself, and you didn't go forth to meet your lover without a coat or a handbag.

Meanwhile Wexford had been through Parsons' house from the ugly little kitchen to the two attics. In a drawer of Mrs Parsons' dressing-table he found two winceyette nightdresses, oldish and faded but neatly folded, one printed cotton nightdress and a fourth, creased and worn perhaps for two nights, under the pillow nearest the wall on the double bed. His wife hadn't any more nightgowns, Parsons said, and her dressing-gown, made of blue woolly material with darker blue braiding, was still hanging on a hook behind the bedroom door. She hadn't a summer dressing-gown and the only pair of slippers she possessed Wexford found neatly packed heel to toe in a cupboard in the dining-room.

It looked as if Parsons had been right about the purse and the key. They were nowhere to be found. In the winter the house was heated solely by two open fires and the water by an immersion heater. Wexford set Gates to examining these fireplaces and to searching the dustbin, last emptied by Kingsmarkham Borough Council on Monday, but there was no trace of ash. A sheet of newspaper had been folded to cover the grate in the dining-room, and this, lightly sprinkled with soot, bore the date April 15th.

Parsons said he had given his wife five pounds housekeeping money on the previous Friday. As far as he knew she had no savings accumulated from previous weeks. Gates, searching the kitchen dresser, found two pound notes rolled up in a cocoa tin on one of the shelves. If Mrs Parsons had received only five pounds on Friday and out of this had bought food for her husband and herself for four or five days, leaving two pounds for the rest of the week, it was apparent that the missing purse could have contained at best a few shillings.

Wexford had hoped to find a diary, an address book or a letter which might give him some help. A brass letter-rack attached to the dining-room wall beside the fireplace contained only a coal bill, a circular from a firm fitting central-heating plant (had

Mrs Parsons, after all, had her dreams?), two soap coupons and an estimate from a contractor for rendering and making good a damp patch on the kitchen wall.

'Your wife didn't have any family at all, Mr Parsons?' Wexford asked.

'Only me. We kept ourselves to ourselves. Margaret didn't ... doesn't make friends easily. I was brought up in a children's home and when she lost her mother Margaret went to live with an aunt. But her aunt died when we were engaged.'

'Where was that, Mr Parsons? Where you met, I mean.'

'In London. Balham. Margaret was teaching in an infants' school and I had digs in her aunt's house.'

Wexford sighed. Balham! The net was widening. Still, you didn't travel forty miles without a coat or a handbag. He decided to abandon Balham for the time being.

'I suppose no one telephoned your wife on Monday night? Did she have any letters yesterday morning?'

'Nobody phoned, nobody came and there weren't any letters.' Parsons seemed proud of his empty life, as if it was evidence of respectability. 'We sat and talked. Margaret was knitting. I think I did a crossword puzzle part of the time.' He opened the cupboard where the slippers were and from the top shelf took a piece of blue knitting on four needles. 'I wonder if it will ever be finished,' he said. His fingers tightened on the ball of wool and he pressed the needles into the palm of his hand.

'Never fear,' Wexford said, hearty with false hope, 'we'll find her.'

'If you've finished in the bedrooms I think I'll go and lie down again. The doctor's given me something to make me sleep.'

23

Wexford sent for all his available men and set them to search the empty houses in Kingsmarkham and its environs, the fields that lay still unspoilt between the High Street and the Kingsbrook Road and, as afternoon came, the Kingsbrook itself. They postponed dragging operations until the shops had closed and the people dispersed, but even so a crowd gathered on the bridge and stood peering over the parapet at the wading men. Wexford, who hated this particular kind of ghoulishness, this lust for dreadful sights thinly disguised under a mask of shocked sympathy, glowered at them and tried to persuade them to leave the bridge, but they drifted back in twos and threes. At last when dusk came, and the men had waded far to the north and the south of the town, he called off the search.

Meanwhile Ronald Parsons, dosed with sodium amytal, had fallen asleep on his lumpy mattress. For the first time in six months dust had begun to settle on the dressing-table, the iron mantelpiece and the linoed floor.

Chapter 3

Ere her limbs frigidly
Stiffen too rigidly,
Decently, kindly,
Smooth and compose them,
And her eyes, close them,
Staring so blindly!

Thomas Hood, *The Bridge of Sighs*

On Thursday morning a baker's roundsman, new to his job, called at a farm owned by a man called Prewett on the main Kingsmarkham-to-Pomfret Road. There was no one about, so he left a large white loaf and a small brown one on a window-ledge and went back to where he had parked his van, leaving the gate open behind him.

Presently a cow nudged against the gate and pushed it wide open. The rest of the herd, about a dozen of them, followed and meandered down the lane. Fortunately for Mr Prewett (for the road to which they were heading was derestricted) their attention was distracted by some clumps of sow thistles on the edge of a small wood. One by one they lumbered across the grass verge, munched at the thistles, and gradually, slowly, penetrated into the thickets. The briars were thick and the wood dim. There were no more thistles, no more wet succulent grass. Trapped and bewildered, they stood still, lowing hopefully.

It was in this wood that Prewett's cowman found them and Mrs Parsons' body at half past one.

By two Wexford and Burden had arrived in Burden's car, while Bryant and Gates brought Dr Crocker and two men with cameras. Prewett and the cowman, Bysouth, primed with knowledge from television serials, had touched nothing, and Margaret Parsons lay as Bysouth had found her, a bundle of damp cotton with a yellow cardigan pulled over her head.

Burden pushed aside the branches to make an arch and he and Wexford came close until they were standing over her. Mrs Parsons was lying against the trunk of a hawthorn tree perhaps eight feet high. The boughs, growing outwards and downwards like the spokes of an umbrella, made an almost enclosed igloo-shaped tent.

Wexford bent down and lifted the cardigan gently. The new dress had a neckline cut lowish at the back. On the skin, running from throat to nape to throat, was a purple circle like a thin ribbon. Burden gazed and the blue eyes seemed to stare back at him. An old-fashioned face, Jean had said, a face you wouldn't forget. But he would forget in time, as he forgot them all. Nobody said anything. The body was photographed from various angles and the doctor examined the neck and the swollen face. Then he closed the eyes and Margaret Parsons looked at them no more.

'Ah, well,' Wexford said. 'Ah, well.' He shook his head slowly. There was, after all, nothing else to say.

After a moment he knelt down and felt among the dead leaves. In the cavern of thin bending branches it was close and unpleasant, but quite scentless. Wexford lifted the arms and turned the body over, looking for a purse and a key. Burden watched him pick something up. It was a used matchstick, half burnt away.

They came out of the the hawthorn tent into comparative light and Wexford said to Bysouth:

'How long have these cows been in here?'

'Be three hour or more, sir.'

Wexford gave Burden a significant look. The wood was badly trampled and the few naked patches of ground were boggy with cattle dung. A marathon wrestling match could have taken place in that wood before breakfast, but Prewett's cows would have obliterated all traces of it by lunchtime; a wrestling match or a struggle between a killer and a terrified woman. Wexford set Bryant and Gates to searching among the maze of gnat-ridden brambles while he and Burden went back to the car with the farmer.

Mr Prewett was what is known as a gentleman farmer and his well-polished riding boots, now somewhat spattered, did no more than pay service to his calling. The leather patches on the elbows of his tobacco-coloured waisted jacket had been stitched there by a bespoke tailor.

'Who uses the lane, sir?'

'I have a Jersey herd pastured on the other side of the Pomfret Road,' Prewett said. He had a county rather than a country accent. 'Bysouth takes them over in the morning and back in the afternoon by way of the lane. Then there is the occasional tractor, you know.'

'What about courting couples?'

'A stray car,' Prewett said distastefully. 'Of course this is a private road. Just as private in fact, Chief Inspector, as your own garage drive, but nobody respects privacy these days. I don't think any of the local lads and lasses come up here on foot. The fields are much more – well, salubrious, shall we say? We do get cars up here. You could stick a car under those overhanging branches and anyone could pass quite close to it at night without even seeing it was there.'

'I was wondering if you'd noticed any unfamiliar tyre marks between now and Tuesday, sir?'

'Oh, come!' Prewett waved a not very horny hand up towards the entrance to the lane and Burden saw what he meant. The lane was all tyre marks; in fact it was the tyre marks that made it into a road. 'The tractors go in and out, the cattle trample it . . .'

'But you have a car, sir. With all this coming and going it's odd nobody saw anything unusual.'

'You must remember it's simply used for coming and going. No one hangs about here. My people have all got a job of work to do. They're good lads and they get on with it. In any case you'll have to discount my wife and myself. We've been in London from Monday until this morning and we mostly use the front entrance anyway. The lane's a short cut, Chief Inspector. It's fine for tractors but my own vehicle gets bogged down.' He stopped, then added sharply, 'When I'm in town I don't care to be taken for a horny-handed son of toil.'

Wexford examined the lane for himself and found only a morass of deeply rutted trenches zig-zagged with the tread marks of tractor tyres and deep round holes made by hoofs. He decided to postpone talking to Prewett's four men and the girl agricultural student until the time of Mrs Parsons' death had been fixed.

Burden went back to Kingsmarkham to break the news to Parsons because he knew him. Parsons opened the door numbly, moving like a sleep-walker. When Burden told him, standing stiffly in the dining-room with the dreadful books, he said nothing, but closed his eyes and swayed.

'I'll fetch Mrs Johnson,' Burden said. 'I'll get her to make you some tea.'

Parsons just nodded. He turned his back and stared out of the window. With something like horror Burden saw that the two pairs of socks were still pegged to the line.

'I'd like to be alone for a bit.'

'Just the same, I'll tell her. She can come in later.' The widower shuffled his feet in khaki-coloured slippers.

'All right,' he said. 'And thanks. You're very good.'

Back at the station Wexford was sitting at his desk looking at the burnt matchstick. He said musingly:

'You know, Mike, it looks as if someone struck this to get a good look at her. That means after dark. Someone held it until it almost burnt his fingers.'

'Bysouth?'

Wexford shook his head.

'It was light, light enough to see – everything. No, whoever struck that match wanted to make sure he hadn't left anything incriminating behind him.' He slipped the piece of charred wood into an envelope. 'How did Parsons take it?' he asked.

'Difficult to say. It's always a shock, even if you're expecting it. He's so doped up on what the doctor's giving him he didn't seem to take it in.'

'Crocker's doing the post-mortem now. Inquest at ten on Saturday.'

'Can Crocker fix the time of death, sir?'

'Some time on Tuesday. I could have told him that. She must have been killed between half twelve and – what time did you say Parsons rang you on Tuesday night?'

'Exactly half past seven. We were going to the pictures and I was keeping an eye on the time.'

'Between half twelve and seven-thirty, then.'

'That brings me to my theory, sir.'

'Let's have it. I haven't got one.'

'Well, Parsons said he got home at six but no one saw him. The first anyone knew he was in the house was when he phoned me at half past seven...'

'Okay, I'm listening. Just stick your head out of the door and get Martin to fetch us some tea.'

Burden shouted for tea and went on:

'Well, suppose Parsons killed her. As far as we know she doesn't know anyone else around here and, as you always say, the husband is the first suspect. Suppose Parsons made a date with his wife to meet him at Kingsmarkham bus garage.'

'What sort of a date?'

'He could have said they'd go and have a meal somewhere in Pomfret, or go for a walk, a picnic ... anything.'

'What about the chops, Mike? She didn't have a date when she was talking to your supermarket woman.'

'They're on the phone. He could have telephoned her during his lunch hour – it had begun to clear up by then – and asked her to pick up the bus at the garage at ten to six, suggested going into Pomfret for a meal. After all, maybe they make a habit of going out to eat. We've only got his word for what they did.'

Martin came in with the tea and Wexford, cup in hand, went over to the window and looked down into the High Street. The bright sun made him screw up his eyes and he pulled at the cord of the blind, half closing the slats.

'The Stowerton bus doesn't go to Pomfret,' he objected. 'Not the five-thirty-five. Kingsmarkham is the terminus.'

Burden took a sheet of paper out of his pocket.

'No, but the five-thirty-two does. Stowerton to Pomfret, via Forby and Kingsmarkham.' He concentrated on the figures he had written. 'Let me put it like this: Parsons phones his wife at lunchtime and asks her to meet the Stowerton bus that gets into Kingsmarkham at five-fifty, two minutes before the other bus, the one that goes into the garage. Now, he could have made that bus if he left a minute or two early.'

'You'll have to check that, Mike.'

'Anyway, Mrs P. catches the bus. It passes through Forby at six-one and reaches Pomfret at six-thirty. When they get to the nearest bus-stop to the wood by Prewett's farm Parsons says it's such a nice evening, let's get off and walk the rest of the way . . .'

'It's a good mile this side of Pomfret. Still, they might be keen on country walks.'

'Parsons says he knows a short cut across the fields to Pomfret . . .'

'Through a practically impenetrable dark wood, thistles, long wet grass?'

'I know, sir. I don't like that bit myself. But they might have seen something in the wood, a deer or a rabbit or something. Anyway, somehow or other Parsons gets her into that wood and strangles her.'

'Oh, marvellous! Mrs Parsons is going out to dinner in a fashionable country pub, but she doesn't object to plunging into the middle of a filthy wet wood after a rabbit. What's she going to do with it when she's caught it, eat it? Her old man follows her and when she's in the thickest part of the wood he says, "Stand still a minute, dear, while I get a bit of rope out of my pocket and strangle you!" God Almighty!'

'He might have killed her in the lane and dragged her body into the bushes. It's a dark lane and there's never anyone walking along the Pomfret Road. He might have carried her – he's a big bloke and you wouldn't see the tracks after those cows had been all over it.'

'True.'

'The bus leaves Pomfret again at six-forty-one, gets to Forby at seven-nine, Kingsmarkham garage seven-twenty. That gives him about fifteen minutes in which to kill his wife and get back to the bus-stop on the other side of the Pomfret Road. The bus gets there at about six-forty-six. He runs up Tabard Road and gets into his own house in five minutes, just in time to phone me at seven-thirty.'

Wexford sat down again in the little swivel chair with the purple cushion.

'He was taking an awful risk, Mike,' he said. 'He might easily have been seen. You'll have to check with the bus people. They can't pick up many passengers at the stop by Prewett's farm. What did he do with her purse and her key?'

'Chucked them in the bushes. There wasn't any point in hiding them, anyway. The thing is, I can't think of a motive.'

'Oh, motive,' Wexford said. 'Any husband's got a motive.'

'I haven't.' Burden was incensed. Someone knocked at the door and Bryant came in.

'I found this on the edge of the wood on the lane side, sir,' Bryant said. He was holding a small gilt cylinder in the tips of his gloved fingers.

'A lipstick,' Wexford said. He took it from Bryant, covering his fingers with a handkerchief, and upended it to expose a circular label on its base. ' "Arctic Sable," ' he read, 'and something that looks like eight-and-six written in violet ink. Anything else?'

'Nothing, sir.'

'All right, Bryant. You and Gates can get over to the Southern Water Board at Stowerton and find out exactly – and I mean precisely to the minute – what time Parsons left work on Tuesday evening.'

'This makes your theory look bloody silly, Mike,' he said when Bryant had gone. 'We'll get the fingerprint boys on it, but, I ask you, is it likely to be Mrs Parsons'? She doesn't take a handbag, she doesn't use make-up and she's as poor as a church mouse (dinner in Pomfret, my foot!), but she takes a lipstick with her in her purse or stuffed down her bosom – an eight-and-sixpenny lipstick, mark you – and when they get to the wood she sees a rabbit. She opens her purse to get out her shotgun, I presume, slings the lipstick into the ditch, runs after the rabbit, striking a match to show her the way, and, when she's in the middle of the wood, sits down and lets her old man strangle her!'

'You sent Bryant off to Stowerton.'

'He's got time on his hands.' Wexford paused, staring at the lipstick. 'By the way,' he said, 'I've checked on the Prewetts. There's no doubt they were in London. Mrs Prewett's mother's seriously ill, and according to University College Hospital they were at her bedside pretty well continuously from before lunch on Tuesday until late that night, and there on and off all day yesterday. The old girl rallied a bit last night and they left their hotel in the Tottenham Court Road after breakfast this morning. So that lets them out.'

He picked up the sheet of paper on which he had placed the Arctic Sable lipstick and held it out for Burden to see. The prints were smudged, but there was a clear one on its domed top.

'It's a new lipstick,' Wexford said. 'It's hardly been used. I want to find the owner of that lipstick, Mike. We'll go over to Prewett's again and talk to that land girl or whatever she calls herself.'

Chapter 4

Thou hast beauty bright and fair,
Manner noble, aspect free,
Eyes that are untouched by care;
What then do we ask of thee?

Bryan Waller Procter, *Hermione*

When Wexford had been told the prints on the lipstick definitely hadn't been made by Mrs Parsons they went back to the farm and questioned each of the men and the land girl (as Wexford called her in his old-fashioned vocabulary) separately. For all but one of them Tuesday afternoon had been busy and, in a very different way from murder, exciting.

Prewett had left the manager, John Draycott, in charge, and on Tuesday morning Draycott had gone to Stowerton market accompanied by a man called Edwards. They had taken a truck and used the front entrance to the farm. This was a long way round, but it was favoured because the lane to the Pomfret Road was narrow and muddy and the week before the truck had got stuck in the ruts.

Bysouth and the man in charge of Prewett's pigs had remained alone at the farm, Miss Sweeting, the land girl, having had the day off on Tuesday to attend a lecture at Sewingbury Agricultural College. At half past twelve they had eaten their dinner in the kitchen, a meal cooked for them, as usual, by Mrs

34

Creavey, who came up to the farm each day from Flagford to cook and clean. After dinner at a quarter past one the pig man, Traynor, had taken Bysouth with him to see a sow that was about to farrow.

At three Draycott and Edwards returned and the manager began immediately on his accounts. Edwards, who included gardening among his duties, went to mow the front lawn. The man hadn't been constantly under his eye, Draycott told Wexford, but for the next hour he had been aware of the sound of the electric mower. At about half past three Draycott was interrupted by Traynor, who came in to tell him he was worried about the condition of the sow. Five piglets had been delivered, but she seemed to be in difficulties and Traynor wanted the manager's consent to call the vet. Draycott had gone to the sties, looked at the sow and talked for a few seconds to Bysouth, who was sitting beside her on a stool, before telephoning for the vet himself. The vet arrived by four and from then until five-thirty the manager, Edwards and Traynor had remained together. During this hour and a half, Traynor said, Bysouth had gone to fetch the cows in and put them in the milking shed. In order to do this he had had to pass the wood twice. Wexford questioned him closely, but he insisted that he had seen nothing out of the way. He had heard no untoward sound and there had been no cars either in the lane itself or parked on the Pomfret Road. According to the other three men he had been even quicker than usual, a haste they attributed to his anxiety as to the outcome of the farrowing.

It was half past six before the whole litter of pigs had been delivered. The vet had gone into the kitchen to wash his hands and they had all had a cup of tea. At seven he left by the same way as he had come, the front entrance, giving a lift to Edwards,

Traynor and Bysouth, who all lived in farm workers' cottages at a hamlet called Clusterwell, some two miles outside Flagford. During the Prewetts' absence Mrs Creavey was staying at the farm overnight. The manager performed his final round at eight and went home to his house about fifty yards down the Clusterwell Road.

Wexford checked with the vet and decided that, apart from mystery story miracles, no one had had time to murder Mrs Parsons and conceal her body in the wood. Only Bysouth had used the lane that passed the wood, and unless he had abandoned his charges dangerously near a derestricted road he was beyond suspicion. To be sure, Mrs Creavey had been alone and out of sight from three-thirty until six-thirty, but she was at least sixty, fat and notoriously arthritic.

Wexford tried to fix the time Bysouth had passed down and then up the lane, but the cowman didn't wear a watch and his life seemed to be governed by the sun. He protested vehemently that his mind had been on the sow's travail and that he had seen no one on the track, in the wood or walking in the fields.

Dorothy Sweeting was the only one of them who might remotely be supposed to have owned the Arctic Sable lipstick. But there is a particularly naked raw look about the face of a woman in an unpainted state when that woman habitually uses make-up. Dorothy Sweeting's face was sunburnt and shiny; it looked as if it had never been protected from the weather by cream and powder. The men were almost derisive when Wexford asked them if they had ever seen lipstick on her mouth.

'You didn't go to the farm all day, Miss Sweeting?'

Dorothy Sweeting laughed a lot. Now she laughed heartily. It seemed that to her the questioning was just like part of a serial or a detective story come to life.

'Not *to* it,' she said, 'but I went near it. Guilty, my lord!' Wexford didn't smile, so she went on: 'I went to see my auntie in Sewingbury after the lecture and it was such a lovely afternoon I got off the bus a mile this side of Pomfret and walked the rest of the way. Old Bysouth was bringing the cows in and I did just stop and have a chat with him.'

'What time would that have been?'

'Fiveish. It was the four-ten bus from Sewingbury.'

'All right, Miss Sweeting. Your prints will be destroyed after the check has been made.'

She roared with laughter. Looking at her big broad hands, her forearms like the village blacksmith's, Burden wondered what she intended to do with her life after she had qualified for whatever branch of bucolic craft she was studying.

'Hang on to them by all means,' she said. 'I'd like to take my place in the rogues' gallery.'

They drove back to Kingsmarkham along the quiet half-empty road. There was still an hour to go before the evening rush began. The sun had dimmed and the mackerel sky thickened until it looked like curds and whey. On the hedges that bordered the road the May blossom still lingered, touched now with brown as if it had been singed by fleeting fire.

Wexford led the way into the police station and they had Miss Sweeting's prints checked with the ones on the lipstick. As Wexford had expected, they didn't match. The student's big pitted fingertips were more like a man's than a woman's.

'I want to find the owner of that lipstick, Mike,' he said again. 'I want every chemist's shop in this place gone over with a small toothcomb. And you'd better do it yourself because it's not going to be easy.'

'Does it have to have any connection with Mrs

Parsons, sir? Couldn't it have been dropped by someone going up the track?'

'Look, Mike, that lipstick wasn't by the road. It was right on the edge of the wood. Apart from the fact that they don't use the lane, Sweeting and Mrs Creavey don't wear lipstick and even if they did they wouldn't be likely to have one in a peculiar shade of pinkish brown like this. You know as well as I do, when a woman only uses lipstick on high days and holidays, for some reason or other, a sense of daring probably, she always picks a bright red. This is a filthy colour, the sort of thing a rich woman might buy if she'd already got a dozen lipsticks and wanted the latest shade for a gimmick.'

Burden knew Kingsmarkham well, but he got the local trade directory to check and found that there were seven chemists in Kingsmarkham High Street, three in side roads and one in a village which had now been absorbed as a suburb into Kingsmarkham itself. Bearing in mind what Wexford had said about a rich woman, he started on the High Street.

The supermarket had a cosmetics counter, but they kept only a limited stock of the more expensive brands. The assistant knew Mrs Parsons by name, having read that she was missing in a newspaper. She also knew her by sight and was agog. Burden didn't tell her the body had been found and he didn't waste any more time on questions when he learnt that, as far as the girl could remember, Mrs Parsons had bought only a tin of cheap talcum powder in the past month.

'That's a new line,' said the assistant in the next shop. 'It's only just come out. It comes in a range of fur shades, sort of soft and subtle, but we don't stock it. We wouldn't have the sale for it, you see.'

He walked up towards the Kingsbrook Bridge past

the Georgian house that was now the Youth Employment Bureau, past the Queen Anne house that was now a solicitor's office, and entered a newly opened shop in a block with maisonettes above it. It was bright and clean, with a dazzling stock of pots and jars and bottles of scent. They kept a large stock of the brand, he was told, but were still awaiting delivery of the fur range.

The waters of the brook had settled and cleared. Burden could see the flat round stones on the bottom. He leaned over the parapet and saw a fish jump. Then he went on, weaving his way between groups of schoolchildren, High School girls in panamas and scarlet blazers, avoiding prams and baskets on wheels. He had called at four shops before he found one that stocked the fur range. But they had only sold one and that in a colour called Mutation Mink, and they didn't put prices on their goods. The girl in the fifth shop, a queenly creature with hair like pineapple candy-floss, said that she was wearing Arctic Sable herself. She lived in a flat above the shop and she went upstairs to fetch the lipstick. It was identical to the one found in the wood except that it had no price written on its base.

'It's a difficult shade to wear,' the girl said. 'We've sold a couple in the other colours but that sort of brownish tint puts the customers off.'

Now there were no more shops on this side of the High Street, only a couple of big houses, the Methodist Church – Mrs Parsons' church – standing back from the road behind a sweep of gravel, a row of cottages, before the fields began. He crossed the street at The Olive and Dove and went into a chemist's shop between a florist's and an estate agent's. Burden had sometimes bought shaving cream in this shop and he knew the man who came out from the dispensary at the back. But he shook his head at once. They didn't stock any cosmetics of that make.

There were only two left: a little poky place with jars of hair cream and toothbrushes in the window, and an elegant emporium, double-fronted, with steps up to the door and a bow window. The vendor of hair cream had never even heard of Arctic Sable. He climbed up a short ladder and took from a shelf a cardboard box of green plastic cylinders.

'Haven't sold a lipstick inside a fortnight,' he said.

Burden opened the door of the double-fronted shop and stepped on to wine-coloured carpet. All the perfumes of Arabia seemed to be assembled on the counters and the gilded tables. Musk and ambergris and new-mown hay assaulted his nostrils. Behind a pyramid of boxes, encrusted with glitter and bound with ribbon, he could see the back of a girl's head, a girl with short blonde curls wearing a primrose sweater. He coughed, the girl turned and he saw that it was a young man.

'Isn't it a delightful shade?' the young man said. 'So young and fresh and innocent. Oh, yes, definitely one of ours. I mark everything with this.' And he picked up a purple ball-point pen from beside the cash register.

'I don't suppose you could tell me who you sold this one to?'

'But I love probing and detecting! Let's be terribly thorough and have a real investigation.'

He opened a drawer with a knob made of cut glass and took out a tray of gilt lipsticks. There were several in each compartment.

'Let me see,' he said. 'Mutation Mink, three gone. I started off with a dozen of each shade. Trinidad Tiger – good heavens, nine gone! Rather a common sort of red, that one. Here we are, Arctic Sable, four gone. Now for my thinking cap.'

Burden said encouragingly that he was being most helpful.

'We do have a regular clientele, what you might call a segment of the affluent society. I don't want to sound snobbish, but I do rather eschew the cheaper lines. I remember now. Miss Clements from the estate agent's had one. No, she had two, one for herself and one for someone's birthday present. Mrs Darrell had another. I do recall that because she took Mutation Mink and changed her mind just as she was going out of the shop. She came back and changed it and while she was making up her mind someone else came in for a pale pink lipstick. Of course, Mrs Missal! She took one look – Mrs Darrell had tried the shade out on her wrist – and she said, "That is absolutely me!" Mrs Missal has exquisite taste because, whatever you may say, Arctic Sable is really intended for red-heads like her.'

'When was this?' Burden asked. 'When did you get the fur range in?'

'Just a tick.' He checked in a delivery book. 'Last Thursday, just a week ago. I sold the two to Miss Clements soon after they came in. Friday, I should say. I wasn't here on Saturday and Monday's always slack. Washing, you know. Tuesday's early closing and I know I didn't sell any yesterday. It must have been Tuesday morning.'

'You've been a great help,' Burden said.

'Not at all. You've brought a little sparkle into my workaday world. By the by, Mrs Missal lives in that rather lovely bijou house opposite the Olive and Dove, and Mrs Darrell has the maisonette with the pink curtains in the new block in Queen Street.'

As luck had it, Miss Clements had both lipsticks in her handbag, her own partly used, and the other one she had bought for a present still wrapped in cellophane paper. As Burden left the estate agent's

41

he glanced at his watch. Half past five. He had just made it before they all closed. He ran Mrs Darrell to earth in the maisonette next to her own. She was having tea with a friend, but she went down the spiral staircase at the back of the block and up the next one, coming back five minutes later with an untouched lipstick, Arctic Sable, marked eight-and-six in violet ink on its base.

The Stowerton-to-Pomfret bus was coming up the hill as he turned out of Queen Street and crossed the forecourt of The Olive and Dove. He checked with his watch and saw that it was gone ten to six. Maybe it had been late leaving Stowerton, maybe it often was. Damn those stupid women and their lipsticks, he thought; Parsons must have done it.

The lovely bijou house was a Queen Anne affair, much done up with white paint, wrought iron and window-boxes. The front door was yellow, flanked with blue lilies in stone urns. Burden struck the ship's bell with a copper clapper that hung on a length of cord. But, as he had expected, no one came. The garage, a converted coach-house, was empty and the doors stood open. He went down the steps again, crossed the road and walked up to the police station, wondering as he went how Bryant had got on with the Southern Water Board.

Wexford seemed pleased about the lipstick. They waited until Bryant had got back from Stowerton before going down to The Olive and Dove for dinner.

'It looks as if this clears Parsons,' Wexford said. 'He left the Water Board at five-thirty or a little after. Certainly not before. He couldn't have caught the five-thirty-two.'

'No,' Burden said reluctantly, 'and there isn't another till six-two.'

They went into the dining-room of The Olive and

Dove and Wexford asked for a window table so that they could watch Mrs Missal's house.

By the time they had finished the roast lamb and started on the gooseberry tart the garage doors were still open and no one had come into or gone out of the house. Burden remained at the table while Wexford went to pay the bill, and just as he was getting up to follow him to the door he saw a blonde girl in a cotton dress enter the High Street from the Sewingbury Road. She walked past the Methodist Church, past the row of cottages, ran up the steps of Mrs Missal's house and let herself in at the front door.

'Come on, Mike,' Wexford said.

He banged at the bell with the clapper.

'Look at that bloody thing,' he said. 'I hate things like that.'

They waited a few seconds. Then the door was opened by the blonde girl.

'Mrs Missal?'

'Mrs Missal, Mr Missal, the children, all are out,' she said. She spoke with a strong foreign accent. 'All are gone to the sea.'

'We're police officers,' Wexford said. 'When do you expect Mrs Missal back?'

'Now is seven.' She glanced behind her at a black grandfather clock. 'Half past seven, eight. I don't know. You come back again in a little while. Then she come.'

'We'll wait, if you don't mind,' Wexford said.

They stepped over the threshold on to velvety blue carpet. It was a square hall, with a staircase running up from the centre at the back and branching at the tenth stair. Through an arch on the right-hand side of this staircase Burden saw a dining-room with a polished floor partly covered by Indian rugs in pale colours. At the far end of this room open french

43

windows gave on to a wide and apparently endless garden. The hall was cool, smelling faintly of rare and subtle flowers.

'Would you mind telling me your name, miss, and what you're doing here?' Wexford asked.

'Inge Wolff. I am nanny for Dymphna and Priscilla.'

Dymphna! Burden thought, aghast. His own children were John and Pat.

'All right, Miss Wolff. If you'll just show us where we can sit down you can go and get on with your work.'

She opened a door on the left side of the hall and Wexford and Burden found themselves in a large drawing-room whose bow windows faced the street. The carpet was green, the chairs and a huge sofa covered in green linen patterned with pink and white rhododendrons. Real rhododendrons, saucer sized heads of blossom on long stems, were massed in two white vases. Burden had the feeling that when rhododendrons went out of season Mrs Missal would fill the vases with delphiniums and change the covers accordingly.

'No shortage of lolly,' Wexford said laconically when the girl had gone. 'This is the sort of set-up I had in mind when I said she might buy Arctic Sable for a gimmick.'

'Cigarette, sir?'

'Have you gone raving mad, Burden? Maybe you'd like to take your tie off. This is Sussex, not Mexico.'

Burden restored the packet and they sat in silence for ten minutes. Then he said, 'I bet she's got that lipstick in her handbag.'

'Look, Mike, four were sold, all marked in violet ink. Right? Miss Clements has two, Mrs Darrell has one. I have the fourth.'

'There could be a chemist in Stowerton or Pomfret or Sewingbury marking lipsticks in violet ink.'

'That's right, Mike. And if Mrs Missal can show me hers you're going straight over to Stowerton first thing in the morning and start on the shops over there.'

But Burden wasn't listening. His chair was facing the window and he craned his neck.

'Car's coming in now,' he said. 'Olive-green Mercedes, nineteen-sixty-two. Registration XPQ189Q.'

'All right, Mike, I don't want to buy it.'

As the wheels crunched on the drive and someone opened one of the nearside doors, Burden ducked his head.

'Blimey,' he said. 'She is something of a dish.'

A woman in white slacks stepped out of the car and strolled to the foot of the steps. The kingfisher-blue and darker-blue patterned silk scarf that held back her red hair matched her shirt. Burden thought she was beautiful, although her face was hard, as if the tanned skin was stretched on a steel frame. He was paid not to admire but to observe. For him the most significant thing about her was that her mouth was painted not brownish pink but a clear golden-red. He turned away from the window and heard her say loudly:

'I am sick to my stomach of bleeding kids! I bet you anything you like, Pete, that lousy little Inge isn't back yet.'

A key was turned in the front-door lock and Burden heard Inge Wolff running along the hall to meet her employers. One of the children was crying.

'Policemen? How many policemen? Oh, I don't believe it, Inge. Where's their car?'

'I suppose they want me, Helen. You know I'm always leaving the Merc outside without lights.'

In the drawing-room Wexford grinned.

The door opened suddenly, bouncing back from one of the flower-vases as if it had been kicked by a petulant foot. The red-haired woman came in first. She was wearing sun-glasses with rhinestone frames, and although the sun had gone and the room was dim, she didn't bother to take them off. Her husband was tall and big, his face bloated and already marked with purple veins. His long shirt-tails hung over his belly like a gross maternity smock. Burden winced at its design of bottles and glasses and plates on a scarlet and white checkerboard.

He and Wexford got up.

'Mrs Missal?'

'Yes, I'm Helen Missal. What the hell do you want?'

'We're police officers, Mrs Missal, making enquiries in connection with the disappearance of Mrs Margaret Parsons.'

Missal stared. His fat lips were already wet, but still he licked them.

'Won't you sit down,' he said. 'I can't imagine why you want to talk to my wife.'

'Neither can I,' Helen Missal said. 'What is this, a police state?'

'I hope not, Mrs Missal. I believe you bought a new lipstick on Tuesday morning?'

'So what? Is it a crime?'

'If you could just show me that lipstick, madam, I shall be quite satisfied and we won't take up any more of your time. I'm sure you must be tired after a day at the seaside.'

'You can say that again.' She smiled. Burden thought she suddenly seemed at the same time more wary and more friendly. 'Have you ever sat on a spearmint ice lolly?' She giggled and pointed to a very faint bluish-green stain on the seat of her trousers. 'Thank God for Inge! I don't want to see those little bastards again tonight.'

'Helen!' Missal said.

'The lipstick, Mrs Missal.'

'Oh, yes, the lipstick. Actually I did buy one, a filthy colour called Arctic something. I lost it in the cinema last night.'

'Are you quite sure you lost it in the cinema? Did you enquire about it? Ask the manager, for instance?'

'What, for an eight-and-sixpenny lipstick? Do I look that poor? I went to the cinema –'

'By yourself, madam?'

'Of course I went by myself.' Burden sensed a certain defensiveness, but the glasses masked her eyes. 'I went to the cinema and when I got back the lipstick wasn't in my bag.'

'Is this it?' Wexford held the lipstick out on his palm, and Mrs Missal extended long fingers with nails lacquered silver like armour-plating. 'I'm afraid I shall have to ask you to come down to the station with me and have your fingerprints taken.'

'Helen, what is this?' Missal put his hand on his wife's arm. She shook it off as if the fingers had left a dirty mark. 'I don't get it, Helen. Has someone pinched your lipstick, someone connected with this woman?'

She continued to look at the lipstick in her hand. Burden wondered if she realized she had already covered it with prints.

'I suppose it is mine,' she said slowly. 'All right, I admit it must be mine. Where did you find it, in the cinema?'

'No, Mrs Missal. It was found on the edge of a wood just off the Pomfret Road.'

'What?' Missal jumped up. He stared at Wexford, then at his wife. 'Take those damn' things off!' he shouted and twitched the sunglasses from her nose.

47

Burden saw that her eyes were green, a very light bluish green flecked with gold. For a second he saw panic there; then she dropped her lids, the only shields that remained to her, and looked down into her lap.

'You went to the pictures,' Missal said. 'You said you went to the pictures. I don't get this about a wood and the Pomfret Road. What the hell's going on?'

Helen Missal said very slowly, as if she was inventing: 'Someone must have found my lipstick in the cinema. Then they must have dropped it. That's it. It's quite simple. I can't understand what all the fuss is about.'

'It so happens,' Wexford said, 'that Mrs Parsons was found strangled in that wood at half past one today.'

She shuddered and gripped the arms of her chair. Burden thought she was making a supreme effort not to cry out. At last she said:

'It's obvious, isn't it? Your murderer, whoever he is, pinched my lipstick and then dropped it at the . . . the scene of the crime.'

'Except,' Wexford said, 'that Mrs Parsons died on Tuesday. I won't detain you any longer, madam. Not just at present. One more thing, though, have you a car of your own?'

'Yes, yes, I have. A red Dauphine. I keep it in the other garage with the entrance in the Kingsbrook Road. Why?'

'Yes, why?' Missal said. 'Why all this? We didn't even know this Mrs Parsons. You're not suggesting my wife . . . ? My God, I wish someone would explain!'

Wexford looked from one to the other. Then he got up.

'I'd just like to have a look at the tyres, sir,' he said.

As he spoke light seemed suddenly to have dawned on Missal. He blushed an even darker brick red and his face crumpled like that of a baby about to cry. There was despair there, despair and the kind of pain Burden felt he should not look upon. Then Missal seemed to pull himself together. He said in a quiet reserved voice that seemed to cover a multitude of unspoken enquiries and accusations:

'I've no objection to your looking at my wife's car but I can't imagine what connection she has with this woman.'

'Neither can I, sir,' Wexford said cheerfully. 'That's what we shall want to find out. I'm as much in the dark as you are.'

'Oh, give him the garage key, Pete,' she said. 'I tell you I don't know any more. It's not my fault if my lipstick was stolen.'

'I'd give a lot to be able to hide behind those rhododendrons and hear what he says to her,' Wexford said as they walked up the Kingsbrook Road to Helen Missal's garage.

'And what she says to him,' Burden said. 'You think it's all right leaving them for the night, sir? She's bound to have a current passport.'

Wexford said innocently: 'I thought that might worry you, Mike, so I'm going to book a room at The Olive and Dove for the night. A little job for Martin. He'll have to sit up all night. My heart bleeds for him.'

The Missals' garden was large and roughly diamond-shaped. On the north side, the side where the angle of the diamond was oblique, the garden was bounded by the Kingsbrook, and on the other a hedge of tamarisk separated it from the Kingsbrook Road. Burden unlocked the cedarwood gates to the garage and made a note of the index number of

Helen Missal's car. Its rear window was almost entirely filled by a toy tiger cub.

'I want a sample taken from those tyres, Mike,' Wexford said. 'We've got a sample from the lane by Prewett's farm. It's a bit of luck for us that the soil's practically solid cow dung.'

'Blimey,' Burden said, wincing as he got to his feet. He re-locked the doors. 'This is millionaires' row, all right.' He put the dried mud into an envelope and pointed towards the houses on the other side of the road: a turreted mansion, a ranch-style bungalow with two double garages and a new house built like a chalet with balconies of dark carved wood.

'Very nice if you can get it,' Wexford said. 'Come on. I'm going to get the car and have another word with Prewett, and, incidentally, the cinema manager. If you'll just drop that key in to Inge, or whatever she calls herself, you can get off home. I shall have to have a word with young Inge tomorrow.'

'When are you going to see Mrs Missal again, sir?'

'Unless I'm very much mistaken,' Wexford said, 'she'll come to me before I can get to her.'

Chapter 5

If she answer thee with No,
Wilt thou bow and let her go?

W. J. Linton, *Faint Heart*

Sergeant Camb was talking to someone on the telephone when Wexford got to the station in the morning. He covered the mouthpiece with his hand and said to the Chief Inspector:

'A Mrs Missal for you, sir. This is the third time she's been on.'

'What does she want?'

'She says she must see you. It's very urgent.' Camb looked embarrassed. 'She wants to know if you can go to her house.'

'She does, does she? Tell her if she wants me she'll have to come here.' He opened the door of his office. 'Oh, and, Sergeant Camb, you can tell her I won't be here after nine-thirty.'

When he had opened the windows and made his desk untidy – the way he liked it – he stuck his head out of the door again and called for tea.

'Where's Martin?'

'Still at The Olive and Dove, sir.'

'God Almighty! Does he think he's on his holidays? Get on to him and tell him he can get off home.'

It was a fine morning, June coming in like a lamb,

and from his desk Wexford could see the gardens of Bury Street and the window-boxes of the Midland Bank full of blown Kaiserskroon tulips. The spring flowers were passing, the summer ones not yet in bud – except for rhododendrons. Just as the first peals of the High School bell began to toll faintly in the distance Sergeant Camb brought in the tea – and Mrs Missal.

'We'll have another cup, please.'

She had done her hair up this morning and left off her glasses. The organdie blouse and the pleated skirt made her look surprisingly demure, and Wexford wondered if she had abandoned her hostile manner with the raffish shirt and trousers.

'I'm afraid I've been rather a silly girl, Chief Inspector,' she said in a confiding voice.

Wexford took a clean piece of paper out of his drawer and began writing on it busily. He couldn't think of anything cogent to put down and as she couldn't see the paper from where she was sitting he just scribbled: *Missal, Parsons; Parsons, Missal.*

'You see I didn't tell you the entire truth.'

'No?' Wexford said.

'I don't mean I actually told lies. I mean I left bits out.'

'Oh, yes?'

'Well, the thing is, I didn't actually go to the pictures by myself. I went with a friend, a man friend.' She smiled as one sophisticate to another. 'There wasn't anything in it, but you know how stuffy husbands are.'

'I should,' Wexford said. 'I am one.'

'Yes, well, when I got home I couldn't find my new lipstick and I think I must have dropped it in my friend's car. Oh, tea for me. How terribly sweet!'

There was a knock at the door and Burden came in.

'Mrs Missal was just telling me about her visit to the cinema on Wednesday night,' Wexford said. He went on writing. By now he had filled half the sheet.

'It was a good picture, wasn't it, Mrs Missal? Unfortunately I had to leave half-way through.' Burden looked for a third tea-cup. 'What happened to that secret-agent character? Did he marry the blonde or the other one?'

'Oh, the other one,' Helen Missal said easily. 'The one who played the violin. She put the message into a sort of musical code and when they got back to London she played it over to M.I.5.'

'It's wonderful what they think of,' Burden said.

'Well, I won't keep you any longer, Mrs Missal . . .'

'No, I must fly. I've got a hair appointment.'

'If you'll just let me have the name of your friend, the one you went to the cinema with . . .'

Helen Missal looked from Wexford to Burden and back from Burden to Wexford. Wexford screwed up the piece of paper and threw it into the wastepaper basket.

'Oh, I couldn't do that. I mean, I couldn't get him involved.'

'I should think it over, madam. Think it over while you're having your hair done.'

Burden held the door open for her and she walked out quickly without looking back.

'I've been talking to a neighbour of mine,' he said to Wexford, 'a Mrs Jones who lives at nine, Tabard Road. You know, she told us about the cars being parked in Tabard Road on Tuesday afternoon. Well, I asked her if she could remember any of the makes or the colours and she said she could remember one car, a bright red one with a tiger in the back. She didn't see the number. She was looking at them from sideways on, you see, and they were parked nose to tail.'

'How long was it there?'

'Mrs Jones didn't know. But she says she first saw at it about three and it was there when the kids got home from school. Of course, she doesn't know if it was there all that time.'

'While Mrs Missal is having her hair done, Mike,' Wexford said, 'I am going to have a word with Inge. As Mrs Missal says, Thank God for Inge!'

There was a tin of polish and a couple of dusters on the dining-room floor and the Indian rugs were spread on the crazy paving outside the windows. Inge Wolff, it seemed, had duties apart from minding Dymphna and Priscilla.

'All I know I will tell you,' she said dramatically. 'What matter if I get the push? Next week, anyhow, I go home to Hanover.'

Maybe, Wexford thought, and, on the other hand, maybe not. The way things were going Inge Wolff might be needed in England for the next few months.

'On Monday Mrs Missal stay at home all the day. Just for shopping in the morning she go out. Also Tuesday she go shopping in the morning, for in the afternoon is closing of all shops.'

'What about Tuesday afternoon, Miss Wolff?'

'Ah, Tuesday afternoon she go out. First we have our dinner. One o'clock. I and Mrs Missal and the children. Ah, next week, only think, no more children! After dinner I wash up and she go up to her bedroom and lie down. When she come down she say, "Inge, I go out with the car," and she take the key and go down the garden to the garage.'

'What time would that be, Miss Wolff?'

'Three, half past two. I don't know.' She shrugged her shoulders. 'Then she come back, five, six.'

'How about Wednesday?'

'Ah, Wednesday. I have half-day off. Very good. Dymphna come home to dinner, go back to school. I go out. Mrs Missal stay home with Priscilla. And when comes the evening she go out, seven, half past seven. I don't know. In this house always are comings and goings. It is like a game.'

Wexford showed her the snapshot of Mrs Parsons.

'Have you ever seen this woman, Miss Wolff? Did she ever come here?'

'Hundreds of women like this in Kingsmarkham. All are alike except rich ones. The ones that come here, they are not like this.' She gave a derisive laugh. 'Oh, no, is funny. I laugh to see this. None come here like this.'

When Wexford got back to the station Helen Missal was sitting in the entrance hall, her red hair done in elaborate scrolls on the top of her head.

'Been thinking things over, Mrs Missal?' He showed her into his office.

'About Wednesday night . . .'

'Frankly, Mrs Missal, I'm not very interested in Wednesday night. Now, Tuesday afternoon . . .'

'Why Tuesday afternoon?'

Wexford put the photograph on his desk where she could see it. Then he dropped the lipstick on top of it. The little gilt cylinder rolled about on the shiny snapshot and came to rest.

'Mrs Parsons was killed on Tuesday afternoon,' he said patiently, 'and we found your lipstick a few yards from her body. So, you see, I'm not very interested in Wednesday night.'

'You can't think . . . Oh, my God! Look, Chief Inspector, I was here on Tuesday afternoon. I went to the pictures.'

'You must just about keep that place going, madam. What a pity you don't live in Pomfret. They had to close the cinema there for lack of custom.'

Helen Missal drew in her breath and let it out

55

again in a deep sigh. She twisted her feet round the metal legs of the chair.

'I suppose I'll have to tell you about it,' she said. 'I mean, I'd better tell the truth.' She spoke as if this was always a last distasteful resort instead of a moral obligation.

'Perhaps it would be best, madam.'

'Well, you see, I only said I went to the pictures on Wednesday to have an alibi. Actually, I went out with a friend.' She smiled winningly. 'Who shall be nameless.'

'For the moment,' Wexford said, un-won.

'I was going out with this friend on Wednesday night, but I couldn't really tell my husband, could I? So I said I was going to the pictures. Actually we just drove around the lanes. Well, I had to see the film, didn't I? Because my husband always ... I mean, he'd obviously ask me about it. So I went to see the film on Tuesday afternoon.'

'In your car, Mrs Missal? You only live about a hundred yards from the cinema.'

'I suppose you've been talking to that bloody little Inge. You see, I had to take the car so that she'd think I'd gone a long way. I mean, I couldn't have gone shopping because it was early closing and I never walk anywhere. She knows that. I thought if I didn't take the car she'd guess I'd gone to the pictures and then she'd think it funny me going again on Wednesday.'

'Servants have their drawbacks,' Wexford said.

'You're not kidding. Well, that's all there is to it. I took the car and stuck it in Tabard Road ... Oh God, that's where that woman lived, isn't it? But I couldn't leave it in the High Street because ...' Again she tried a softening smile. 'Because of your ridiculous rules about parking.'

Wexford snapped sharply:

'Did you know this woman, madam?'

'Oh, you made me jump! Let me see. Oh, no, I don't think so. She's not the sort of person I'd be likely to know, Chief Inspector.'

'Who did you go out with on Wednesday night when you lost your lipstick, Mrs Missal?'

The smiles, the girlish confidences, hadn't worked. She flung back her chair and shouted at him:

'I'm not going to tell you. I won't tell you. You can't make me! You can't keep me here.'

'You came of your own accord, madam,' Wexford said. He swung open the door, smiling genially. 'I'll just look in this evening when your husband's at home and we'll see if we can get everything cleared up.'

The Methodist minister hadn't been much help to Burden. He hadn't seen Mrs Parsons since Sunday and he'd been surprised when she didn't come to the social evening on Tuesday. No, she had made no close friends at the church and he couldn't recall hearing anyone use her Christian name.

Burden checked the bus times at the garage and found that the five-thirty-two had left Stowerton dead on time. Moreover, the conductress on the Kingsmarkham bus, the one that left Stowerton at five-thirty-five, remembered seeing Parsons. He had asked for change for a ten-shilling note and they were nearly in Kingsmarkham before she got enough silver to change it.

'Fun and games with Mrs Bloody Missal,' Wexford said when Burden walked in. 'She's one of those women who tell lies by the light of nature, a natural crook.'

'Where's the motive, sir?'

'Don't ask me. Maybe she was carrying on with Parsons, picked him up at his office on Tuesday

57

afternoon and bribed the entire Southern Water Board to say he didn't leave till after five-thirty. Maybe she'd got another boy friend she goes out with on Wednesdays, one for every day of the week. Or maybe she and Parsons and Mr X, who shall be nameless (God Almighty!), were Russian agents and Mrs Parsons had defected to the West. It's all very wonderful, Mike, and it makes me spew!'

'We haven't even got the thing she was strangled with,' Burden said gloomily. 'Could a woman have done it?'

'Crocker seems to think so. If she was a strong young woman, always sitting about on her backside and feeding her face.'

'Like Mrs Missal.'

'We're going to get down there tonight, Mike, and have the whole thing out again in front of her old man. But not till tonight. I'm going to give her the rest of the day to sweat in. I've got the report from the lab and there's no cow dung on Mrs Missal's tyres. But she didn't have to use her own car. Her husband's a car dealer, got a saleroom in Stowerton. Those people are always chopping and changing their cars. That's another thing we'll have to check up on. The inquest's tomorrow and I want to get somewhere before then.'

Burden drove his own car into Stowerton and pulled into the forecourt of Missal's saleroom. A man in overalls came out from the glass-walled office between the rows of petrol-pumps.

'Two and two shots, please,' Burden said. 'Mr Missal about?'

'He's out with a client.'

'That's a pity,' Burden said. 'I looked in on Tuesday afternoon and he wasn't here . . .'

'Always in and out he is. In and out. I'll just give your windscreen a wipe over.'

'Maybe Mrs Missal?'

'Haven't seen her inside three months. Back in March was the last time. She come in to lend the Merc and bashed the grid in. Women drivers!'

'Had a row, did they? That sounds like Pete.'

'You're not joking. He said, never again. Not the Merc or any of the cars.'

'Well, well,' Burden said. He gave the man a shilling; more would have looked suspicious. 'Marriage is a battlefield when all's said and done.'

'I'll tell him you came in.'

Burden switched on the ignition and put the car in gear.

'Don't trouble,' he said. 'I'm seeing him tonight.'

He drove towards the exit and braked sharply to avoid a yellow convertible that swung sharply in from Maryfield Road. An elderly man was at the wheel; beside him, Peter Missal.

'There he is, if you want to catch him,' the pump attendant shouted.

Burden parked his own car and pushed open the swing doors. He waited beside a Mini-car revolving smoothly on a scarlet roundabout. Outside he could see Missal talking to the driver of the convertible. Apparently the deal was off, for the other man left on foot and Missal came into the saleroom.

'What now?' he said to Burden. 'I don't like being hounded at my place of business.'

'I won't keep you,' Burden said. 'I'm just checking up on Tuesday afternoon. No doubt you were here all day. In and out, that is.'

'It's no business of yours where I was.' Missal flicked a speck of dust from the Mini's wing as it circled past. 'As a matter of fact I went into Kingsmarkham to see a client. And that's all I'm telling you. I respect personal privacy and it's a pity you don't do the same.'

'In a murder case, sir, one's private life isn't always one's own affair. Your wife doesn't seem to have grasped that either.' He went towards the doors.

'My wife . . .' Missal followed him and, looking to either side of him to make sure there was no one about, hissed in an angry half-whisper: 'You can take that heap of scrap metal off my drive-in. It's causing an obstruction.'

Chapter 6

Who was her father?
Who was her mother?
Had she a sister?
Had she a brother?
Or, was there a dearer one
Still, and a nearer one
Yet, than all other?

Thomas Hood, *The Bridge of Sighs*

The murder books had been taken away and the top
shelf of the bookcase was empty. If Parsons was
innocent, a truly bereaved husband, Burden thought,
how dreadfully their covers must have screamed at
him when he came into the shabby dining-room this
morning. Or had he removed them because they had
served their purpose?

'Chief Inspector,' Parsons said, 'I must know. Was
she . . . ? Had she . . . ? Was she just strangled or was
there anything else?' He had aged in the past days or
else he was a consummate actor.

'You can set your mind at rest on that score,'
Wexford said quickly. 'Your wife was certainly
strangled, but I can assure you she wasn't interfered
with in any other way.' He stared at the dull green
curtains, the lino that was frayed at the skirting
board, and said impersonally, 'There was no sexual
assault.'

'Thank God!' Parsons spoke as if he thought there was still a God in some nonconformist heaven and as if he was really thanking Him. 'I couldn't bear it if there had been. I couldn't go on living. It would just about have killed Margaret.' He realized what he had said and put his head in his hands.

Wexford waited until the hands came down and the tearless eyes were once more fixed on his own.

'Mr Parsons, I can tell you that as far as we know there was no struggle. It looks as if your wife was sleeping until just before she was killed. There would have been just a momentary shock, a second's pain – and then nothing.'

Parson's mumbled, turning away his face so that they could catch only the last words, '. . . For though they be punished in the sight of man, yet is their hope full of immortality.'

Wexford got up and went over the the bookcase. He didn't say anything about the missing library of crime, but he took a book out of one of the lower shelves.

'I see this is a guide to the Kingsmarkham district.' He opened it and Burden glimpsed a coloured photograph of the market place. 'It isn't a new book.'

'My wife lived here – well, not here. In Flagford it was – for a couple of years after the end of the war. Her uncle was stationed with the R.A.F. at Flagford and her aunt had a cottage in the village.'

'Tell me about your wife's life.'

'She was born in Balham,' Parsons said. He winced, avoiding the Christian name. 'Her mother and father died when she was a child and she went to live with this aunt. When she was about sixteen she came to live in Flagford, but she didn't like it. Her uncle died – he wasn't killed or anything – he died of heart disease, and her aunt went back to

Balham. My wife went to college in London and started teaching. Then we got married. That's all.'

'Mr Parsons, you told me on Wednesday your wife would have taken her front-door key with her. How many keys did you have between you?'

'Just the two.' Parsons took a plain Yale key from his pocket and held it up to Wexford. 'Mine and – and Margaret's. She kept hers on a ring. The ring has a silver chain with a horseshoe charm on the end of it.' He added simply in a calm voice: 'I gave it to her when we came here. The purse is a brown one, brown plastic with a gilt clip.'

'I want to know if your wife was in the habit of going to Prewett's farm. Did you know the Prewetts or any of the farm workers? There's a girl there called Dorothy Sweeting. Did your wife ever mention her?'

But Parsons had never even heard of the farm until his wife's body had been found there. She hadn't cared much for the country or for country walks and the name Sweeting meant nothing.

'Do you know anyone called Missal?'

'Missal? No, I don't think so.'

'A tall good-looking woman with red hair. Lives in a house opposite The Olive and Dove. Her husband's a car dealer. Big bloke with a big green car.'

'We don't ... we didn't know anyone like that.' His face twisted and he put up a hand to hide his eyes. 'They're a lot of snobs round here. We didn't belong and we should never have come.' His voice died to a whisper. 'If we'd stayed in London,' he said, 'she might still be alive.'

'Why *did* you come, Mr Parsons?'

'It's cheaper living in the country, or you think it's cheaper till you try it.'

'So your coming here didn't have anything to do with the fact that your wife once lived in Flagford?'

'Margaret didn't want to come here, but the job came up. Beggars can't be choosers. She had to work when we were in London. I thought she'd find some peace here.' He coughed and the sound tailed away into a sob. 'And she did, didn't she?'

'I believe there are some books in your attic, Mr Parsons. I'd like to have a good look through them.'

'You can have them,' Parsons said. 'I never want to see another book as long as I live. But there's nothing in them. She never looked at them.'

The dark staircases were familiar now and with familiarity they had lost much of that sinister quality Burden had felt on his first visit. The sun showed up the new dust and in its gentle light the house seemed no longer like the scene of a crime but just a shabby relic. It was very close and Wexford opened the attic window. He blew a film of dust from the surface of the bigger trunk and opened its lid. It was crammed with books and he took the top ones out. They were novels: two by Rhoda Broughton, *Evelina* in the Everyman's Library and Mrs Craik's *John Halifax, Gentleman*. Their fly-leaves were bare and nothing fluttered from the pages when he shook them. Underneath were two bundles of school stories, among them what looked like the complete works of Angela Brazil. Wexford dumped them on the floor and lifted out a stack of expensive-looking volumes, some bound in suède, others in scented leather or watered silk.

The first one he opened was covered in pale green suède, its pages edged with gold. On the fly-leaf someone had printed carefully in ink:

> *If love were what the rose is,*
> *And I were like the leaf,*
> *Our lives would grow together*
> *In sad or singing weather . . .*

And underneath:

Rather sentimental, Minna, but you know what I mean. Happy, happy birthday. All my love, Doon. March 21st, 1950.

Burden looked over Wexford's shoulder.

'Who's Minna?'

'We'll have to ask Parsons,' Wexford said. 'Could be second-hand. It looks expensive. I wonder why she didn't keep it downstairs. God knows, this place needs brightening up.'

'And who's Doon?' Burden asked.

'You're supposed to be a detective. Well, detect.' He put the book on the floor and picked up the next one. This was the *Oxford Book of Victorian Verse*, still in its black and pearl-grey jacket, and Doon had printed another message inside. Wexford read it aloud in an unemotional voice.

'*I know you have set your heart on this, Minna, and I was so happy when I went to Foyle's and found it waiting for me. Joyeux Noel, Doon, Christmas, 1950.*' The next book was even more splendid, red watered silk and black leather. 'Let's have a look at number three,' Wexford said. '*The Poems of Christina Rossetti.* Very nice, gilt lettering and all. What's Doon got to say this time? *An un-birthday present, Minna dear, from Doon who wishes you happy for ever and ever. June 1950.* I wonder if Mrs P. bought the lot cheap from this Minna.'

'I suppose Minna could *be* Mrs P., a sort of nickname.'

'It had just crossed my mind,' Wexford said sarcastically. 'They're such good books, Mike, not the sort of things anyone would give to a church sale, and church sales seem to have been about Mrs Parsons' mark. Look at this lot: *Omar Khayyám;*

Whitman's *Leaves of Grass*; William Morris. Unless I'm much mistaken that *Omar Khayyám* cost three or four pounds. And there's another one here, the *Verses of Walter Savage Landor*. It's an old-fashioned kind of book and the leaves haven't even been cut.' He read the message on the fly-leaf aloud:

> *I promise to bring back with me*
> *What thou with transport will receive,*
> *The only proper gift for thee.*
> *Of which no mortal shall bereave.*

'Rather apt, don't you think, Minna? Love from Doon. March 21st, 1951.'

'It wasn't very apt, was it? And Minna, whoever she is, didn't receive it with transport. She didn't even cut the pages. I'm going to have another word with Parsons, Mike, and then we're going to have all this lot carted down to the station. This attic is giving me the creeps.'

But Parsons didn't know who Minna was and he looked surprised when Wexford mentioned the date, March 21st.

'I never heard anyone call her Minna,' he said distastefully, as if the name was an insult to her memory. 'My wife never spoke about a friend called Doon. I've never even seen those books properly. Margaret and I lived in the house her aunt left her till we moved here and those books have always been in the trunk. We just brought them with us with the furniture. I can't make it out about the date – Margaret's birthday was March 21st.'

'It could mean nothing, it could mean everything,' Wexford said when they were out in the car. 'Doon talks about Foyle's, and Foyle's, in case you don't

66

know, my provincial friend, is in London in the Charing Cross Road.'

'But Mrs P. was sixteen in 1949 and she stayed two years in Flagford. She must have been living only about five miles from here when Doon gave her those books.'

'True. He could have lived here too and gone up to London for the day. I wonder why he printed the messages, Mike. Why didn't he write them? And why did Mrs P. hide the books as if she was ashamed of them?'

'They'd make a better impression on the casual caller than *The Brides in the Bath* or whatever it is,' Burden said. 'This Doon was certainly gone on her.'

Wexford took Mrs Parsons' photograph out of his pocket. Incredible that this woman had ever inspired a passion or fired a line of verse!

'Happy for ever and ever,' he said softly. 'But love isn't what the rose is. I wonder if love could be a dark and tangled wood, a cord twisted and pulled tighter on a meek neck?'

'A cord?' Burden said. 'Why not a scarf, that pink nylon thing? It's not in the house.'

'Could be. You can bet your life that scarf is with the purse and the key. Plenty of women have been strangled with a nylon stocking, Mike. Why not a nylon scarf?'

He had brought the Swinburne and the Christina Rossetti with him. It wasn't much to go on, Burden reflected, a bundle of old books and an elusive boy. Doon, he thought, Doon. If Minna was anything to go by Doon was bound to be a pseudonym too. Doon wouldn't be a boy any more but a man of thirty or thirty-five, a married man with children, perhaps, who had forgotten all about his old love. Burden wondered where Doon was now. Lost, absorbed perhaps into the great labyrinth of London, or still living a mile or two away . . . His heart sank when he recalled the new factory estate at Stowerton, the mazy lanes of Pomfret with a solitary cottage every two hundred yards, and to the north, Sewingbury, where road after road of post-war detached houses pushed outwards like rays from the nucleus of the ancient town. Apart from these, there was Kingmarkham itself and the daughter villages, Flagford, Forby . . .

'I don't suppose that Missal bloke could be Doon,' he said hopefully.

'If he is,' Wexford said, 'he's changed one hell of a lot.'

The river of my years has been sluggish, Minna, flowing slowly to a sea of peace, Ah, long ago how I yearned for the torrent of life!

Then yesternight, yestere'en, Minna, I saw you. Not as I have so often in my dreams, but in life. I followed you, looking for lilies where you trod . . . I saw the gold band on your finger, the shackle of an importunate love, and I cried aloud in my heart, I, I, too have known the terrors of the night!

But withal my feast has ever been the feast of the spirit and to that other dweller in my gates my flesh has been as an unlit candle in a fast-sealed casket. The light in my soul has guttered, shrinking in the harsh wind. But though the casket be atrophied and the flame past resuscitation, yet the wick of the spirit cries, hungering for the hand that holds the taper of companionship, the torch of sweet confidence, the spark of friends reunited.

I shall see you tomorrow and we shall ride together along the silver streets of our youth. Fear not, for reason shall sit upon my bridle and gentle moderation within my reins. Will all not be well, Minna, will all not be pleasant as the warm sun on the faces of little children?

Chapter 7

When she shall unwind
All those wiles she wound about me ...

Francis Thompson, *The Mistress of Vision*

A black Jaguar, not new but well tended, was parked
outside the Missals' house when Wexford and
Burden turned in at the gate at seven o'clock. The
wheels only were soiled, their hub-caps spattered
with dried mud.

'I know that car,' Wexford said. 'I know it but I
can't place it. Must be getting old.'

'Friends for cocktails,' Burden said sententiously.

'I could do with a spot of gracious living myself,'
Wexford grumbled. He rang the ship's bell.

Perhaps Mrs Missal had forgotten they were
coming or Inge hadn't been primed. She looked
surprised yet spitefully pleased. Like her employer's,
her hair was done up on top of her head, but with
less success. In her left hand she held a canister of
paprika.

'All are in,' she said. 'Two come for dinner. What a
man! I tell you it is a waste to have men like him
buried in the English countryside. Mrs Missal say,
"Inge, you must make lasagna." All will be Italian,
paprika, pasta, pimentoes ... Ach, it is just a game!'

'All right, Miss Wolff. We'd like to see Mrs Missal.'

'I show you.' She giggled, opened the drawing-

71

room door and announced with some serendipity, 'Here are the policemen!'

Four people were sitting in the flowered armchairs and there were four glasses of pale dry sherry on the coffee-table. For a moment nobody moved or said anything, but Helen Missal flushed deeply. Then she turned to the man who sat between her and her husband, parted her lips and closed them again.

So that's the character Inge was going on about in the hall, Burden thought. Quadrant! No wonder Wexford recognized the car.

'Good evening, Mr Quadrant,' Wexford said, indicating by a slight edge to his voice that he was surprised to see him in this company.

'Good evening, Chief Inspector, Inspector Burden.'

Burden had long known him as a solicitor he often saw in Kingsmarkham magistrates' court, long known and inexplicably disliked. He nodded to Quadrant and to the woman, presumably Quadrant's wife, who occupied the fourth armchair. They were somewhat alike, these two, both thin and dark with straight noses and curved red lips. Quadrant had the features of a grandee in an El Greco portrait, a grandee or a monk, but as far as Burden knew he was an Englishman. The Latin lips might have first drawn breath in a Cornish town and Quadrant be the descendant of an Armada mariner. His wife was beautifully dressed with the careless elegance of the very rich. Burden thought she made Helen Missal's blue shift look like something from a chain-store sale. Her fingers were heavily be-ringed, vulgarly so, if the stones were false, but Burden didn't think they were false.

'I'm afraid we're intruding again, sir,' Wexford said to Missal, his eyes lingering on Quadrant. 'I'd just like to have a talk with your wife, if you don't mind.'

Missal stood up, his face working with impotent rage. In his light-weight silver-grey suit he looked fatter than ever. Then Quadrant did a strange thing. He took a cigarette out of the box on the table, put it in his mouth and lit the cork tip. Fascinated, Burden watched him choke and drop the cigarette into an ashtray.

'I'm sick and tired of all this,' Missal shouted. 'We can't even have a quiet evening with our friends without being hounded. I'm sick of it. My wife has given you her explanation and that ought to be enough.'

'This is a murder enquiry, sir,' Wexford said.

'We were just going to have dinner.' Helen Missal spoke sulkily. She smoothed her blue skirt and fidgeted with a string of ivory beads. 'I suppose we'd better go into your study, Pete. Inge'll be in and out of the dining-room. God! God damn it all, why can't you leave me in peace?' She turned to Quadrant's wife and said: 'Will you excuse me a moment, Fabia, darling? That is, if you can bear to stay and eat with the criminal classes.'

'You're sure you don't want Douglas to go with you?' Fabia Quadrant sounded amused, and Burden wondered if the Missals had warned them of the impending visit, suggested perhaps that this was to enquire into some parking offence. 'As your solicitor, I mean,' she said. But Wexford had mentioned murder and when he lit that cigarette Quadrant had been frightened.

'Don't be long,' Missal said.

They went into the study and Wexford closed the door.

'I want my lipstick back,' Helen Missal said, 'and I want my dinner.'

Unmoved, Wexford said, 'And I want to know

73

who you went out with when you lost your lipstick, madam.'

'It was just a friend,' she said. She looked coyly up at Wexford, whining like a little girl asking permission to have a playmate to tea. 'Aren't I allowed to have any friends?'

'Mrs Missal, if you continue to refuse to tell me this man's name I shall have no alternative but to question your husband.'

Burden was becoming used to her sudden changes of mood, but still he was not quite prepared for this burst of violence.

'You nasty low-down bastard!' she said.

'I'm not much affected by that sort of abuse, madam. You see, I'm accustomed to moving in circles where such language is among the terms of reference. His name, please. This is a murder enquiry.'

'Well, if you must know it was Douglas Quadrant.'

And that, Burden thought, accounts for the choking act in the other room.

'Inspector Burden,' Wexford said, 'will you just take Mr Quadrant into the dining-room (never mind about Miss Wolff's dinner) and ask him for his version of what happened on Wednesday night? Or was it Tuesday afternoon, Mrs Missal?'

Burden went out and Wexford said with a little sigh, 'Very well, madam, now I'd like to hear about Wednesday night all over again.'

'What's that fellow going to say in front of my husband?'

'Inspector Burden is a very discreet officer. Provided I find everything satisfactory I've no doubt you can convince your husband that Mr Quadrant was consulted simply in his capacity as your solicitor.'

This was the line Burden took when he went back into the drawing-room.

'Is there some difficulty about Mrs Missal, then, Inspector?' Fabia Quadrant asked. She might have been asking some minion if he had attended to the wants of a guest. 'I expect my husband can sort it out.'

Quadrant got up lazily. Burden was surprised that he offered no resistance. They went into the dining-room and Burden pulled out two chairs from the side of the table. It was laid with place mats, tall smoky purple glasses, knives and forks in Swedish steel and napkins folded into the shape of water-lilies.

'A man must live,' Quadrant said easily when Burden asked him about his drive with Helen Missal. 'Mrs Missal is perfectly happily married. So am I. We just like to do a little dangerous living together from time to time. A drive, a drink . . . No harm done and everyone the happier for it.' He was being disarmingly frank.

Burden wondered why. It didn't seem to tie up with his manner when they had first arrived. Everyone the happier for it? Missal didn't look happy . . . and the woman with the rings? She had her money to console her. But what had all this to do with Mrs Parsons?

'We drove to the lane,' Quadrant said, 'parked the car and stood on the edge of the wood to have a cigarette. You know how smoky it gets inside a car, Inspector.' Burden was to be brought in as another man of the world. 'I'm afraid I know nothing about the lipstick. Mrs Missal is rather a happy-go-lucky girl. She tends to be careless about unconsidered trifles.' He smiled. 'Perhaps that's what I like about her.'

Had he seen him? Part of the time, yes, but he certainly hadn't had Quadrant under his eye all day.

'I suppose all this did happen on Wednesday,' Burden said, 'not Tuesday afternoon?'

'Now, come, Inspector. I was in court all day Tuesday. You saw me yourself.'

'We'd like to have a look at your car tyres, sir.' But as he said it Burden knew it was hopeless. Quadrant admitted visiting the lane on Wednesday.

In the study Wexford was getting much the same story from Helen Missal.

'We didn't go into the wood,' she said. 'We just stood under the trees. I took my handbag with me because it had got quite a bit of money in it and I think I must have dropped my lipstick when I opened the bag to get my hanky out.'

'You never went out of sight of the car?'

The net was spread and she fell in it.

'We never went out of sight of the car,' she said. 'We just stood under the trees and talked.'

'What a nervous person you must be, Mrs Missal, nervous and extremely cautious. You had Mr Quadrant with you and you were in sight of the car, but you were afraid someone might try to steal your handbag under your very eyes.'

She was frightened now and Wexford was sure she hadn't told him everything.

'Well, that's how it happened. I can't be expected to account for everything I do.'

'I'm afraid you can, madam. I suppose you've kept your cinema ticket?'

'Oh, my God! Can't you give me any peace? Of course I don't keep cinema tickets.'

'You don't show much foresight, madam. It would have been prudent to have kept it in case your husband wanted to see it. Perhaps you'll have a look for that ticket and when you've found it I'd like you to bring it down to the station. The tickets are numbered and it will be simple to determine whether yours was issued on Tuesday or Wednesday.'

Quadrant was waiting for him in the dining-room, standing by the sideboard now and reading the labels on two bottles of white wine. Burden still sat at the table.

'Ah, Chief Inspector,' Quadrant said in the tone he used for melting the hearts of lay magistrates. ' "What a tangled web we weave when first we practise to deceive"!'

'I wish you could convince Mrs Missal of the truth of that maxim, sir. Very unfortunate for you that you happened to choose that particular lane for your ... your talk with her on Wednesday night.'

'May I assure you, Chief Inspector, that it was merely a matter of misfortune.' He continued to look at the bottles of Barsac, misted and ice-cold. 'Had I been aware of the presence of Mrs Parsons' body in the wood I should naturally have come straight to you. In my position, my peculiar position, I always take it upon myself to give every possible assistance to you good people.'

'It is a peculiar position, isn't it, sir? What I should call a stroke of malignant fate.'

In the drawing-room Missal and Mrs Quadrant were sitting in silence. They looked, Burden thought, as if they had little in common. Helen Missal and the solicitor filed in, smiling brightly, as if they had all been playing some party game. The charade had been acted, the word discovered. Now they could all have their dinner.

'Perhaps we can all have our dinner now,' Missal said.

Wexford looked at him.

'I believe you were in Kingsmarkham on Tuesday

afternoon, Mr Missal? Perhaps you'll be good enough to tell me where you were exactly and if anyone saw you.'

'No, I won't,' Missal said. 'I'm damned if I do. You send your henchman –'

'Oh, Peter,' Fabia Quadrant interrupted. 'Henchman! What a word.'

Burden stood woodenly, waiting.

'You send your underling to show me up in front of my clients and my staff. You persecute my wife. I'm damned if I tell you what I do with every minute of my time!'

'Well, I had to,' Helen Missal said. She seemed pleased with herself, delighted that the focus of attention had shifted from herself to her husband.

'I'd like a sample from your car tyres,' Wexford said, and Burden wondered despairingly if they were going to have to scrape mud from the wheels of every car in Kingsmarkham.

'The Merc's in the garage,' Missal said. 'Make yourself at home. You do inside, so why not make free with the grounds? Maybe you'd like to borrow the lawn for the police sports.'

Fabia Quadrant smiled slightly and her husband pursed his lips and looked down. But Helen Missal didn't laugh. She glanced quickly at Quadrant and Burden thought she gave the ghost of a shiver. Then she lifted her glass and drained the sherry at a single gulp.

Wexford sat at his desk, doodling on a piece of paper. It was time to go home, long past time, but they still had the events of the day, the stray remarks, the evasive answers, to sift through and discuss. Burden saw that the Chief Inspector was writing, apparently aimlessly, the pair of names he had scribbled that morning when Mrs Missal had first come to him: *Missal, Parsons; Parsons, Missal.*

'But what's the connection, Mike? There must be a connection.' Wexford sighed and drew a thick black line through the names. 'You know, sometimes I wish this *was* Mexico. Then we could keep a crate of hooch in here. Tequila or some damn' thing. This everlasting tea is making me spew.'

'Quadrant and Mrs Missal . . .' Burden began slowly.

'They're having a real humdingin' affair,' Wexford interrupted, 'knocking it off in the back of his Jag.'

Burden was shocked.

'A woman like that?' he said. 'Why wouldn't they go to an hotel?'

'The best bedroom at The Olive and Dove? Be your age. He can't go near her place because of Inge and she can't go to his because of his wife.'

'Where does he live?'

'You know where Mrs Missal keeps her car? Well, up on the other side, on the corner of what our brothers in the uniformed branch call the junction with the Upper Kingsbrook Road. That place with the turrets. She couldn't go there because of darling Fabia. My guess is they went to that lane because Dougie Q. knows it well, takes all his bits of stuff there. It's quiet, it's dark and it's nasty. Just the job for him and Mrs M. When they've had their fun and games in the back of the car they go into the wood . . .'

'Perhaps Mrs Missal saw a rabbit, sir,' Burden said innocently.

'Oh, for God's sake!' Wexford roared. 'I don't know why they went into the wood, but Mrs Missal might well fancy having a bit more under the bushes in God's sweet air. Maybe they saw the body . . .'

'Quadrant would have come to us.'

'Not if Mrs Missal persuaded him not to, not if she said it would mean her Peter and his Fabia finding out about them. She got to work on him and our courteous Dougie, whom ne'er the word of No woman heard speak – I *can* read, Mike – our courteous Dougie agrees to say nothing about it.'

Burden looked puzzled. Finally he said: 'Quadrant was scared, sir. He was scared stiff when we came in.'

'I suppose he guessed it was going to come out. His wife was there. That's quite natural.'

'Then wouldn't you have expected him to have been more cagey about it all? But he wasn't. He was almost too open about it.'

'Perhaps,' Wexford said, 'he wasn't scared we were going to ask about it. He was scared of *what* we were going to ask.'

'Or of what Mrs Missal might say.'

'Whatever it was, we didn't ask it or she gave the right answer. The right answer from his point of view, I mean.'

'I asked him about Tuesday. He said he was in court all day. Says I saw him there. I did, too, off and on.'

Wexford groaned. 'Likewise,' he said. 'I saw him but I wasn't keeping a watch on him and that makes a mighty lot of difference. I was up in Court One. He was defending in that drunk driving case downstairs. Let me think. They adjourned at one, went back at two.'

'We went into the Carousel for lunch . . .'

'So did he. I saw him. But we went upstairs, Mike. He may have done too. I don't know. He was back in court by two and he didn't have the car. He walks when he's that near home.'

'Missal could do with taking a leaf out of his book,' Burden said. 'Get his weight down. He's a nasty piece of work, sir. Henchman!' he added in disgust.

'Underling, Mike,' Wexford grinned.

'What's stopping him telling us where he was on Tuesday?'

'God knows, but those tyres were as clean as a whistle.'

'He could have left the car on the Pomfret Road.'

'True.'

'I suppose Mrs Missal could have got some idea into her head that Quadrant was carrying on with Mrs P. –'

Wexford had begun to look fretful. 'Oh, come off it,' he said. 'Dougie Q. and Mrs P.? He's been knocking it off on the side for years. It's common knowledge. But have you seen the sort of things his taste runs to? I tell you, on Saturday mornings the High Street is littered with his discards, consoling themselves for their broken maidenheads or their broken marriages by showing off their new Mini-Minors. Mrs P. just wasn't his style. Anyway, Mrs Missal wouldn't have done murder for him. He was just a different way of passing a dull evening, one degree up on the telly.'

'I thought it was only men who looked at it that way.' Burden was always startled by his chief's occasional outbursts of graphic frankness. Wexford, who was always intuitive, sometimes even lyrical, could also be coarse. 'She was risking a lot for a casual affair.'

'You want to buck your ideas up, Mike,' Wexford snapped. 'Minna's *Oxford Book of Victorian Verse* is just about your mark. I'm going to lend it to you for your bedtime reading.'

Burden took the book and flicked through the pages: Walter Savage Landor, Coventry Patmore, Caroline Elizabeth Sarah Norton … The names seemed to come from far away, the poets long dust. What possible connection could they have with dead, draggled Minna, with the strident Missals? Love, sin, pain – these were the words that sprang from almost every verse. After Quadrant's flippancies they sounded like ridiculous anachronisms.

'A connecting link, Mike,' Wexford said. 'That's what we want, a connection.'

But there was none to be found that night. Wexford took three of the other books ('Just in case our Mr Doon underlined anything or put in any fancy little ticks') and they walked out into the evening air. Beyond the bridge Quadrant's car still waited.

Chapter 8

One of my cousins long ago,
A little thing the mirror said...

James Thomson, *In the Room*

A bird was singing outside Wexford's office window; a blackbird, Burden supposed. He had always rather liked listening to it until one day Wexford said it sang the opening bars of 'The Thunder and Lightning Polka', and after that its daily reiteration annoyed him. He wanted it to go on with the tune or else vary a note or two. Besides, this morning he had had enough of blackbirds and larks and nightingales, enough of castle-bound maidens dying young and anaemic swains serenading them with lute and tabor. He had sat up half the night reading the Oxford Book and he was by no means convinced that it had had anything to do with Mrs Parsons' death.

It was going to be a beautiful day, too beautiful for an inquest. When Burden walked in Wexford was already at his desk, turning the pages of the suède-covered Swinburne. The rest of the Doon books had been removed from the house in Tabard Road and dumped on Wexford's filing cabinet.

'Did you get anything, sir?' Burden asked.

'Not so's you'd notice,' Wexford said, 'but I did have an idea. I'll tell you about it when you've read the report from Balham. It's just come in.'

The report was typed on a couple of sheets of foolscap. Burden sat down and began to go through it:

Margaret Iris Parsons (he read) was born Margaret Iris Godfrey to Arthur Godfrey, male nurse, and his wife, Iris Drusilla Godfrey, at 213 Holderness Road, Balham, on March 21st, 1933. Margaret Godfrey attended Holderness Road Infants' School from 1938 until 1940 and Holderness Road Junior School from 1940 until 1944. Both parents killed as a result of enemy action, Balham, 1942, after which Margaret resided with her maternal aunt and legal guardian, Mrs Ethel Mary Ives, wife of Leading Aircraftman Geoffrey Ives, a member of the regular Air Force, at 42 St John's Road, Balham. At this time the household included Anne Mary Ives, daughter of the above, birth registered at Balham, February 1st, 1932.

Leading Aircraftman Ives was transferred to Flagford, Sussex, R.A.F. Station during September 1949 (date not known). Mrs Ives, Anne Ives and Margaret Godfrey left Balham at this time, Mrs Ives having let her house in St John's Road, and took up residence in Flagford.

On the death of Geoffrey Ives from coronary thrombosis (Sewingbury R.A.F. Hospital, July 1951) Mrs Ives, her daughter and Margaret Godfrey returned to Balham and lived together at 42 St John's Road. From September 1951 until July 1953 Margaret Godfrey was a student at Albert Lake Training College for Women, Stoke Newington, London.

On August 15th, 1952, Anne Ives married Private Wilbur Stobart Katz, U.S. Army, at Balham Methodist Chapel, and left the United Kingdom for the United States with Private Katz in October 1952 (date not known).

Margaret Godfrey joined staff of Holderness Road Infants' School, Balham, September 1953.

Ronald Parsons (clerk) aged twenty-seven, became a lodger at 42 St John's Road, in April 1954. Death of Mrs Ethel Ives from cancer (Guy's Hospital, London), registered at Balham by Margaret Godfrey, May 1957. Margaret Godfrey and Ronald Parsons married at Balham Methodist Chapel, August 1957, and took up residence at 42 St John's Road, the house having been left jointly to Mrs Parsons and Mrs Wilbur Katz under the will of Mrs Ives.

42 St John's Road was purchased compulsorily by Balham Council, November 1962, whereupon Mr and Mrs Parsons removed to Kingsmarkham, Sussex, Mrs Parsons having resigned from the staff of Holderness Road School.

(Refs: Registrar of Births and Deaths, Balham; Rev. Albert Derwent, Minister, Methodist Chapel, Balham; Royal Air Force Records; United States Air Force Records; London County Council Education Dept.; Guy's Hospital; Balham Borough Council.)

'I wonder where Mrs Wilbur Katz is now?' Burden said.

'You got any cousins in America, Mike?' Wexford asked in a quiet, deceptively gentle voice.

'I believe I have.'

'So've I and so have half the people I've ever met. But nobody ever does know where they are or even if they're alive or dead.'

'You said you'd had an idea, sir?'

Wexford picked up the report and stabbed at the second paragraph with his thick forefinger.

'It came to me in the night,' he said, 'in the interval between Whitman and Rossetti – sound like a couple of gangsters, don't they? Sweet Christ, Mike, I ought to have thought of it before! Parsons said his wife came here when she was sixteen and even then it didn't click. I assumed, backwoods copper that I am, that Mrs Parsons had left school by then. But, Mike, she was a teacher, she went to a training college. When she was in Flagford she must have gone to school! I reckon they came to Flagford just after she'd taken her School Cert., or whatever they call it these days, and when she got here she went right on going to school.'

'There are only two girls' schools around here,' Burden said. 'The Kingsmarkham County High and that convent place in Sewingbury. St Catherine's.'

'Well, she wouldn't have gone there. She was a Methodist and, as far as we know, her aunt was too. Her daughter got married in a Methodist chapel at any rate. It's just our luck that's it's Saturday and the school's shut.

'I want you to root out the head – you can dip out on the inquest, I'll be there. The head's a Miss Fowler and she lives in York Road. See what you can dig up. They must keep records. What we want is a list of the girls who were in Margaret Godfrey's class between September 1949 and July 1951.'

'It'll be a job tracing them, sir.'

'I know that, Mike, but somehow or other we've got to have a break. This just might be it. We know all about Margaret Parsons' life in Balham, and by the look of it it was mighty dull. Only two sensational things ever happened to her as far as I can see. Love and death, Mike, love and death. The thing is they both happened here in my district. Somebody loved her here and when she came back somebody killed her. One of those girls may remember a boy friend, a possessive boy friend with a long memory.'

'I wish,' Burden said, 'I wish some decent public-spirited cop-loving citizen would walk in here and just tell us he knew Mrs P., just tell us he'd taken her out in 1950 or even seen her in a shop last week.' He brooded for a second over the Balham report. 'They were an unhealthy lot, weren't they, sir? Cancer, coronary thrombosis . . .'

Wexford said slowly: 'When Parsons was telling us a bit of his wife's history I did just wonder why he said, "Her uncle died, he wasn't killed." It's a small point, but I see it now. Her parents *were* killed, but not in the way we mean when we talk about killing.'

After he had gone across the courthouse behind the police station Burden telephoned Miss Fowler. A deep cultured voice answered, carefully enunciating the name of the exchange and the number. Burden began to explain but Miss Fowler interrupted him. Yes, Margaret had been at the High School, although she could scarcely remember her from that time. However, she had seen her recently in Kingsmarkham and had recognized her as the murdered woman from a newspaper photograph.

'Honestly, Inspector,' she said, 'what a very shocking thing!' She spoke as if the killing had offended rather than distressed her, or, Burden thought, as if the education meted out at her school should automatically have exempted any pupil from falling victim to a murderer.

He apologized for troubling her and asked if she could let him have the list Wexford wanted.

'I'll just give our school secretary, Mrs Mortlock, a ring,' Miss Fowler said. 'I'll get her to nip along to school and have a look through the records. If you could call on me about lunchtime, Inspector?'

Burden said he was most grateful.

'Not at all. It's no trouble,' Miss Fowler said. 'Honestly.'

The inquest was over in half an hour and Dr Crocker's evidence occupied ten minutes of that time. Death, he said, was caused by strangulation by means of a ligature; a scarf possibly or a piece of cloth. Mrs Parsons' body was otherwise unbruised and there had been no sexual assault. She had been a healthy woman, slightly overweight for her height. In his evidence Wexford gave his opinion that it was impossible to say whether or not there had been a struggle as the wood had been heavily trampled by Prewett's cows. The doctor was recalled and said that he had found a few superficial scratches on the dead woman's legs. These were so slight that he would not care to say whether they had been made before or after death.

A verdict was returned of murder by person or persons unknown.

Ronald Parsons had sat quietly throughout the inquest, twisting a handkerchief in his lap. He kept his head bowed as the coroner offered some perfunctory expressions of sympathy and indicated that he heard only by a slight movement, a tiny nod. He seemed so stunned with misery that Wexford was surprised when he caught up with him as he was crossing the flagged courtyard and touched him on the sleeve.

Without preamble he said, 'A letter came for Margaret this morning.'

'What d'you mean, a letter?' Wexford stopped. He had seen some of Mrs Parsons' letters; advertisements and coal bills.

'From her cousin in the States,' Parsons said. He took a deep breath and shivered in the warm sun.

Looking at him, Wexford realized that he was no longer stupefied. Some fresh bitterness was affecting him.

'I opened it.'

He spoke with a kind of guilt. She was dead and they had plundered her possessions. Now even her letters, letters posthumously received, were to be picked over, their words dissected as meticulously as her own body had been examined and exposed.

'I don't know . . . I can't think,' he said, 'but there's something in it about someone called Doon.'

'Have you got it with you?' Wexford asked sharply.

'In my pocket.'

'We'll go into my office.'

If Parsons noticed his wife's books spread about the room he gave no sign. He sat down and handed an envelope to Wexford. On the flap, just beneath the ragged slit Parsons had made, was a handwritten address: *From Mrs Wilbur S. Katz, 1183 Sunflower Park, Slate City, Colorado, U.S.A.*

'That would be Miss Anne Ives,' Wexford said. 'Did your wife correspond with her regularly?'

Parsons looked surprised at the name.

'Not to say regularly,' he said. 'She'd write once or twice a year. I've never met Mrs Katz.'

'Did your wife write to her recently, since you came here?'

'I wouldn't know, Chief Inspector. To tell you the truth, I didn't care for what I knew of Mrs Katz. She used to write and tell Margaret all about the things she'd got – cars, washing machines, that sort of thing . . . I don't know whether it upset Margaret. She'd been very fond of her cousin and she never said she minded hearing about all those things. But I made it plain what I thought and she stopped showing me the letters.'

'Mr Parsons, I understand Mrs Ives' house was left jointly to your wife and Mrs Katz. Surely –?'

Parsons interrupted bitterly: 'We bought our share off her, Chief Inspector. Every penny of seven hundred pounds we paid – through a bank in London. My wife had to work full-time so that we could do it, and when we'd paid the lot, just paid off the lot, the council bought the place off us for nine hundred. They had a sort of order.'

'A compulsory-purchase order,' Wexford said. 'I see.' He stuck his head round the door. 'Sergeant Camb! Tea, please, and an extra cup. I'll just read that letter, if you don't mind, Mr Parsons.'

It was written on thin blue paper and Mrs Katz had found plenty to tell her cousin. The first two pages were entirely taken up with an account of a holiday Mr and Mrs Katz and their three children had spent in Florida; Mrs Katz's new car; a barbecue her husband had bought her. Mr and Mrs Parsons were invited to come to Slate City for a holiday. Wexford began to see what Parsons had meant.

The last page was more interesting.

Gee, Meg (Mrs Katz had written), *I sure was amazed to see you and Ron had moved to Kingsmarkham. I'll bet that was Ron's idea, not yours. And you have met up with Doon again, have you? I sure would like to know who Doon is. You've got to tell me, not keep dropping hints.*

Still, I can't see why you should be scared of Doon. What of, for the Lord's sake? There was never anything in that. (You know what I mean, Meg.) I can't believe Doon is still keen. You always had a suspicious mind!!! But if meeting Doon means trips in the car and a few free meals I wouldn't be too scrupulous.

When are you and Ron going to get a car of your own? Wil says he just doesn't know how you make out . . .

There was some more in the same vein, sprinkled with exclamation marks and heavily underlined. The letter ended:

. . . Regards to Ron and remind him there's a big welcome waiting for you both in Sunflower Park whenever you feel like hitting Colorado, U.S.A. Love

from Nan. Greg, Joanna and Kim send hugs to their Auntie Meg.

'This could be very important, Mr Parsons,' Wexford said. 'I'd like to hang on to it.'

Parsons got up, leaving his tea untasted.

'I wish it hadn't come,' he said. 'I wanted to remember Margaret as I knew her. I thought she was different. Now I know she was just like the rest, carrying on with another man for what she could get out of him.'

Wexford said quietly: 'I'm afraid it looks like that. Tell me, didn't you have any idea that your wife might be going out with this man, this Doon? It looks very much as if Doon knew her when she lived in Flagford and took up with her again when she came back. She must have gone to school here, Mr Parsons. Didn't you know that?'

Did Parsons look furtive, or was it just a desire to hold on to some remnants of his private life, his marriage broken both by infidelity and by death, that made him flush and fidget?

'She wasn't happy in Flagford. She didn't want to talk about it and I stopped asking her. I reckon it was because they were such a lot of snobs. I respected her reticence, Chief Inspector.'

'Did she talk to you about her boy friends?'

'That was a closed book,' Parsons said, 'a closed book for both of us. I didn't *want* to know, you see.' He walked to the window and peered out as if it was night instead of bright day. 'We weren't those kind of people. We weren't the kind of people who have love affairs.' He stopped, remembering the letter. 'I can't believe it. I can't believe that of Margaret. She was a good woman, Chief Inspector, a good loving woman. I can't help thinking that Katz woman was

91

making up a lot of things that just weren't true, making them up out of her own head.'

'We shall know a bit more when we hear from Colorado,' Wexford said. 'I'm hoping to get hold of the last letter your wife wrote to Mrs Katz. There's no reason why it shouldn't be made available to you.'

'Thank you for nothing,' Parsons said. He hesitated, touched the green cover of Swinburne's verses and walked quickly from the room.

It was some sort of a break, Wexford thought, some sort of a break at last. He picked up the telephone and told the switchboard girl he wanted to make a call to the United States. This had been a strange woman, he reflected as he waited, a strange secretive woman leading a double life. To her husband and the unobservant world she had been a sensible prudent housewife in sandals and a cotton frock, an infants' teacher who polished the front step with Brasso and went to church socials. But someone, someone generous and romantic and passionate, had been tantalized and maddened by her for twelve long years.

Chapter 9

Sometimes a troop of damsels glad . . .

Tennyson, *The Lady of Shalott*

Miss Fowler's was an unacademic bookless flat. Burden, who was aware of his own failing of cataloguing people in types, had tried not to expect old-maidishness. But this was what he found. The room into which Miss Fowler showed him was full of hand-made things. The cushion covers had been carefully embroidered, the amateurish water-colours obviously executed with patience, the ceramics bold. It looked as if Miss Fowler could hardly bear to reject the gift of an old scholar, but the collection was neither restful nor pleasing.

'Poor, poor Margaret,' she said. Burden sat down and Miss Fowler perched herself in a rocking chair opposite him, her feet on a petit-point footstool. 'What a very shocking thing all this is! That poor man too. I've got the list you wanted.'

Burden glanced at the neatly typed row of names.

'Tell me about her,' he said.

Miss Fowler laughed self-consciously, then bit her lip as if she thought this was no occasion for laughter.

'Honestly, Inspector,' she said, 'I can't remember. You see, there are so many girls . . . Of course, we don't forget them all, but naturally it's the ones who achieve something, get Firsts or find really spectacular posts, those are the ones we remember. Hers wasn't a very distinguished year. There was plenty of promise, but none of it came to very much. I saw her, you know, after she came back.'

'Here? In Kingsmarkham?'

'It must have been about a month ago.' She took a packet of Weights from the mantelpiece, offered one to Burden, and puffed bravely at her own as he held a match to it.

They never really grow up, he thought.

'I was in the High Street,' she went on. 'It was just after school and she was coming out of a shop. She said, "Good afternoon, Miss Fowler." Honestly, I hadn't the faintest idea who she was. Then she said she was Margaret Godfrey. You see, they expect you to remember them, Inspector.'

'Then how did you . . . ?'

'How did I connect her with Mrs Parsons? When I saw the photograph. You know, I felt sorry we hadn't talked, but I'm always seeing old girls, but I honestly couldn't tell you who they are or their ages, come to that. They might be eighteen or thirty. You know how it is, you can't tell the ages of people younger than yourself.' She looked up at Burden and smiled. 'But you *are* young,' she said.

Again he returned to the list. The names were in alphabetical order. He read aloud slowly, waiting for Miss Fowler's reactions:

'*Lyn Annesley, Joan Bertram, Clare Clarke, Wendy Ditcham, Margaret Dolan, Margaret Godfrey, Mary Henshaw, Jillian Ingram, Anne Kelly, Helen Laird, Marjorie Miller, Hilda Pensteman, Janet Probyn, Fabia Rogers, Deirdre Sachs, Diana Stevens, Winifred Thomas, Gwen Williams, Yvonne Young.*'

Under the names Mrs Morpeth had written with an air of triumph: *Miss Clare Clarke is a member of the High School teaching staff!!!*

'I'd like to talk to Miss Clarke,' he said.

'She lives at Nectarine Cottage down the first lane on the left on the Stowerton Road,' Miss Fowler said.

Burden said slowly, 'Fabia is a very unusual name.'

Miss Fowler shrugged. She patted her stiffly waved grey hair. 'Not a particularly unusual type,' she said. 'Just one of those very promising people I was telling you about who never amounted to much. She lives here somewhere. She and her husband are quite well known in what I believe are called social circles. Helen Laird was another one. Very lovely, very self-confident. Always in trouble. Boys, you know. Honestly, so silly! I thought she'd go on the stage, but she didn't, she just got married. And then Miss Clarke, of course . . .'

Burden had the impression she had been about to include Miss Clarke among the failures, but that loyalty to her staff prevented her. He didn't pursue it. She had given him a more disturbing lead.

'What did you say happened to Helen Laird?'

'I really know nothing, Inspector. Mrs Morpeth said something about her having married a car sales-man. Such a waste!' She stubbed out her cigarette into an ashtray that was daubed with poster paint and obviously home-baked. When she went on her voice sounded faintly sad. 'They leave, you know, and we forget them, and then about fifteen years later a little tot turns up in the first form and you think, I've seen that face before somewhere! Of course you have – her mother's.'

Dymphna and Priscilla, Burden thought, nearly sure. Not long now, and Dymphna's face, the same red hair perhaps, would revive in Miss Fowler's memory some long-lost chord.

'Still,' she said, as if reading his thoughts, 'there's a limit to everything and I retire in two years' time.'

He thanked her for the list and left. As soon as he got to the station Wexford showed him the Katz letter.

'It all points to Doon being the killer, sir,' Burden said, 'whoever he is. What do we do now, wait to hear from Colorado?'

'No, Mike, we'll have to press on. Clearly Mrs Katz doesn't know who Doon is and the best we can hope for is to get some of the background from her and the last letter Mrs P. sent her before she died. Doon is probably going to turn out to be a boy friend Mrs P. had when she was at school here. Let's hope she didn't have too many.'

'I've been wondering about that,' Burden said, 'because honestly – as Miss Fowler would say – those messages in Minna's books don't look like the work of a boy at all, not unless he was a very mature boy. They're too polished, too smooth. Doon could be an older man who got interested in her.'

'I thought of that,' Wexford said, 'and I've been checking up on Prewett and his men. Prewett bought that farm in 1949 when he was twenty-eight. He's an educated person and quite capable of writing those messages, but he was in London on Tuesday. There's no doubt about it, unless he was involved in a conspiracy with two doctors, an eminent heart specialist, a sister, God knows how many nurses and his own wife.

'Draycott's only been in the district two years and he was in Australia from 1947 to 1953. Bysouth can scarcely write his own name, let alone dig up suitable bits of poetry to send to a lady love, and much the same goes for Traynor. Edwards was in the

Army throughout 1950 and 1951, and Dorothy Sweeting can't possibly know what was going on in Minna's love life twelve years ago. She was only seven.'

'Then it looks as if we'll have to ferret out what we can from the list,' Burden said. 'I think you'll be interested when you see some of the names, sir.'

Wexford took the list and when he came to Helen Laird and Fabia Rogers he swore fiercely. Burden had pencilled in *Missal* and *Quadrant*, following each surname with a question mark.

'Somebody's trying to be clever,' Wexford said, 'and that I won't have. Rogers. Her people are old man Rogers and his missus at Pomfret Hall. They're loaded. All made out of paint. There's no reason why she should have told us she knew Mrs P. When we talked to Dougie this Doon angle didn't seem that important. But Mrs Missal . . . Not know Mrs P. indeed, and they were in the same class!'

He had grown red with anger. Burden knew how he hated being taken for a ride.

'I was going to forget all about that cinema ticket, Mike, but now I'm not so sure. I'm going to have it all out again with Mrs Missal now.' He stabbed at the list. 'While I'm gone you can start contacting these women.'

'It would have to be a girls' school,' Burden grumbled. 'Women change their names, men don't.'

'Can't be helped,' Wexford said snappily. 'Mr Griswold's been on twice already since the inquest, breathing down my neck.'

Griswold was the Chief Constable. Burden saw what Wexford meant.

'You know him, Mike. The least hint of difficulty and he's screaming for the Yard,' Wexford said, and went out, leaving Burden with the list and the letter.

Before embarking on his womanhunt Burden read

the letter again. It surprised him because it gave an insight into Mrs Parsons' character, revealing a side he had not really previously suspected. She was turning out to be a lot less pure than anyone had thought.

... If meeting Doon means rides in the car and a few free meals I wouldn't be too scrupulous, Mrs Katz had written. But at the same time she didn't know who Doon was. Mrs Parsons had been strangely secretive, enigmatic, hiding the identity of a boy friend from a cousin who had also been an intimate friend.

A strange woman, Burden thought, and a strange boy friend. It was a funny sort of relationship she had with this Doon, he said to himself. Mrs Katz says, *I can't see why you should be scared,* and later on, *there was never anything in that.* What did she mean, anything in that? But Mrs P. was *scared.* What of, sexual advances? Mrs Katz says she had a suspicious mind. Fair enough, he reflected. Any virtuous woman would be scared and suspicious of a man who paid her a lot of attention. But at the same time there was never anything in it. Mrs P. mustn't be too scrupulous.

Burden groped vainly. The letter, like its recipient, was a puzzle. As he put it down and turned to the telephone he was certain of only two facts: Doon hadn't been making advances; he wanted something else, something that frightened Mrs Parsons but which was so innocuous in the estimation of her cousin that it would be showing excessive suspicion to be scrupulous about it. He shook his head like a man who has been flummoxed by an intricate riddle, and began to dial.

He tried Bertram first because there was no Annesley in the book – and, incidentally, no Penste-man and no Sachs. But the Mr Bertram who answered said he was over eighty and a bachelor.

Next he rang the number of the only Ditchams he could find, but although he listened to the steady ringing past all reason, there was no reply.

Mrs Dolan's number was engaged. He waited five minutes and tried again. This time she answered. Yes, she was Margaret Dolan's mother, but Margaret was now Mrs Heath and had gone to live in Edinburgh. In any case, Margaret had never brought anyone called Godfrey to the house. Her particular friends had been Janet Probyn and Deirdre Sachs, and Mrs Dolan remembered them as having been a little shut-in clique on their own.

Mary Henshaw's mother was dead. Burden spoke to her father. His daughter was still in Kingsmarkham. Married? Burden asked. Mr Henshaw roared with laughter while Burden waited as patiently as he could. He recovered and said his daughter was indeed married. She was Mrs Hedley and she was in the county hospital.

'I'd like to talk to her,' Burden said.

'You can't do that,' Henshaw said, hugely amused. 'Not unless you put a white coat on. She's having a baby, her fourth. I thought you were them, bringing me the glad news.'

Through Mrs Ingram he was put on to Jillian Ingram, now Mrs Bloomfield. But she knew nothing of Margaret Parsons except that at school she had been pretty and prim, fond of reading, rather shy.

'Pretty, did you say?'

'Yes, she was pretty, attractive in a sort of way. Oh, I know, I've seen the papers. Looks don't necessarily last, you know.'

Burden knew, but still he was surprised.

Anne Kelly had gone to Australia, Marjorie Miller . . .

'My daughter was killed in a car crash,' said a

harsh voice, full of awakened pain. 'I should have thought the police of all people would know that.'

Burden sighed. Pensteman, Probyn, Rogers, Sachs . . . all were accounted for. In the local directory alone he found twenty-six Stevenses, forty Thomases, fifty-two Williamses, twelve Youngs.

To track them all down would take best part of the afternoon and evening. Clare Clarke might be able to help him. He closed the directory and set off for Nectarine Cottage.

The french windows were open when Inge Wolff let Wexford into the hall and he heard the screams of quarrelling children. He followed her across the lawn and at first saw nobody but the two little girls: the elder a sharp miniature fascimile of her mother, bright-eyed, red-headed; the younger fat and fair with a freckle-blotched face. They were fighting for possession of a swing-boat, a red and yellow fairground thing with a rabbit for a figurehead.

Inge rushed over to them, shouting.

'Are you little girls that play so, or rough boys? Here is one policeman come to lock you up!'

But the children only clung more tightly to the ropes, and Dymphna, who was standing up, began to kick her sister in the back.

'If he's a policeman,' she asked, 'where's his uniform?'

Someone laughed and Wexford turned sharply. Helen Missal was in a hammock slung between a mulberry tree and the wall of a summerhouse and she was drinking milk-less tea from a glass. At first he could see only her face and a honey-coloured arm dangling over the edge of the canvas. Then, as he came closer, he saw that she was dressed for sunbathing. She wore only a bikini, an ice-white figure of eight and a triangle against her golden skin.

100

Wexford was embarrassed and his embarrassment fanned his anger into rage.

'Not again!' she said. 'Now I know how the fox feels. He doesn't enjoy it.'

Missal was nowhere about, but from behind a dark green barrier of macrocarpa Wexford could hear the hum of a motor mower.

'Can we go indoors, Mrs Missal?'

She hesitated for a moment. Wexford thought she was listening, perhaps to the sounds from the other side of the hedge. The noise of the mower ceased, then, as she seemed to hold her breath, started again. She swung her legs over the hammock and he saw that her left ankle was encircled by a thin gold chain.

'I suppose so,' she said. 'I don't have any choice, do I?'

She went before him through the open doors, across the cool dining-room where Quadrant had looked on the wine, and into the rhododendron room. She sat down and said:

'Well, what is it now?'

There was something outrageous and at the same time spiteful about the way she spread her nakedness against the pink and green chintz. Wexford turned away his eyes. She was in her own home and he could hardly tell her to go and put some clothes on. Instead he took the photograph from his pocket and held it out to her.

'Why did you tell me you didn't know this woman?'

Fear left her eyes and they flared with surprise.

'I didn't know her.'

'You were at school with her, Mrs Missal.'

She snatched the photograph and stared at it.

'I was not.' Her hair fell over her shoulders, bright copper like a new penny. 'At least, I don't think I was. I mean, she was years older than me by the look of this. She may have been in the sixth when I was in the first form. I just wouldn't know.'

Wexford said severely: 'Mrs Parsons was thirty, the same age as yourself. Her maiden name was Godfrey.'

'I adore "maiden name". It's such a charitable way of putting it, isn't it? All right, Chief Inspector, I do remember now. But she's aged, she's different . . .' Suddenly she smiled, a smile of pure delighted triumph, and Wexford marvelled that this woman was the same age as the pathetic dead thing they had found in the wood.

'It's very unfortunate you couldn't remember on Thursday evening, Mrs Missal. You've put yourself in a most unpleasant light, firstly by deliberately lying to Inspector Burden and myself and secondly by concealment of important facts. Mr Quadrant will tell you that I'm quite within my rights if I charge you with being an accessary –'

Helen Missal interrupted sulkily. 'Why pick on me? Fabia knew her too, and . . . Oh, there must be lots and lots of other people.'

'I'm asking you,' he said. 'Tell me about her.'

'If I do,' she said, 'will you promise to go away and not come back?'

'Just tell me the truth, madam, and I will gladly go away. I'm a very busy man.'

She crossed her legs and smoothed her knees. Helen Missal's knees were like a little girl's, a little girl who has never climbed a tree or missed a bath.

'I didn't like school,' she said confidingly. 'It was so restricting, if you know what I mean. I just begged and begged Daddy to take me away at the end of my first term in the sixth –'

'Margaret Godfrey, Mrs Missal.'

'Oh, yes, Margaret Godfrey. Well she was a sort of cipher – isn't that a lovely word? I got it out of a book. A sort of cipher. She was one of the fringe people, not very clever or nice-looking or anything.' She glanced once more at the picture. 'Margaret Godfrey. D'you know, I can hardly believe it. I should have said she was the last girl to get herself murdered.'

'And who would be the first, Mrs Missal?'

'Well, someone like me,' she said, and giggled.

'Who were her friends, the people she went around with?'

'Let me think. There was Anne Kelly and a feeble spotty bitch called Bertram and Diana Something . . . '

'That would be Diana Stevens.'

'My God, you know it all, don't you?'

'I meant boy friends.'

'I wouldn't know. I was rather busy in that direction myself.' She looked at him, pouting provocatively, and Wexford wondered, with the first flicker of pity he had felt for her, if her coyness would increase as her beauty declined until in age she became grotesque.

'Anne Kelly,' he said, 'Diana Stevens, a girl called Bertram. What about Clare Clarke, what about Mrs Quadrant? Would they remember?'

She had said that she hated school, but as she began to speak her voice was softer than he had ever known it and her expression gentler. For a moment he forgot his anger, her lies, the provocative costume she wore, and listened.

'It's funny,' she said, 'but thinking of those names has sort of brought it back to me. We used to sit in a kind of garden, a wild old place. Fabia and me and a girl called Clarke – I see her around sometimes – and Jill Ingram and that Kelly girl and – and Margaret Godfrey. We were supposed to be working but we didn't much. We used to talk about . . . Oh, I don't know . . .'

'About your boy friends, Mrs Missal?' As soon as the words were out Wexford knew he had been obtuse.

'Oh, no,' she said sharply. 'You've got it wrong. Not then, not in the garden. It was a wilderness, an old pond, bushes, a seat. We used to talk about . . . well, about our dreams, what we wanted to do, what we were going to make of our lives.' She stopped and Wexford could see in a sudden flash of vision a wild green place, the girls with their books and hear with his mind's ear the laughter, the gasp of dizzy ambition. Then he almost jumped at the change in her voice. She whispered savagely, as if she had forgotten he was there: 'I wanted to act! They wouldn't let me, my father and my mother. They made me stay at home and it all went. It sort of dissolved into nothing.' She shook back her hair and smoothed with the tips of two fingers the creases that had appeared between her eyebrows. 'I met Pete,' she said, 'and we got married.' Her nose wrinkled. 'The story of my life.'

'You can't have everything,' Wexford said.

'No,' she said, 'I wasn't the only one . . .'

She hesitated and Wexford held his breath. He had an intuitive conviction that he was about to hear something of enormous significance, something that would iron out the whole case, wrap it up and tie it ready to hand to Mr Griswold. The green eyes widened and lit up; then suddenly the incandescence died and they became almost opaque. Outside in the hall a floorboard squeaked and Wexford heard the squashy sound of a rubber sole on thick carpet. Helen Missal's face became quite white.

'Oh God!' she said. 'Please, please don't ask about the cinema ticket. Please don't!'

Wexford cursed inwardly as the door opened and Missal came in. He was sweating and there were damp patches on the underarms of his singlet. He stared at his wife and in his eyes was a strange mixture of disgust and concupiscence.

'Put something on,' he shouted. 'Go on, put some clothes on.'

She got up awkwardly and Wexford had the illusion that her husband's words were scrawled across her body like the obscene scribble on a pin-up picture.

'I was sunbathing,' she said.

Missal wheeled round on Wexford.

'Come to see the peep-show, have you?' His face was crimson with exertion and with jealousy. 'What the copper saw.'

Wexford wanted to be angry, to match the other man's rage with his own colder kind, but he could feel only pity.

All he said was, 'Your wife has been able to help me.'

'I'll bet she has.' Missal held the door open and almost pushed her through. 'Been kind, has she? That's a speciality of hers, being kind to every Tom, Dick and Harry.' He fingered his wet shirt as if his body disgusted him. 'Go on,' he said, 'start on me now. What were you doing in Kingsmarkham on Tuesday afternoon, Mr Missal? The name of the client, Mr Missal. Your car was seen in the Kingsbrook Road, Mr Missal. Well, go on. Don't you want to know?'

Wexford got up and walked a few paces towards the door. The heavy blossoms, pink, puce and white, brushed against his legs. Missal stood staring at him like an overfed, under-exercised dog longing to let out an uninhibited howl.

'Don't you want to know? Nobody saw me. I

105

could have been strangling that woman. Don't you want to know what I was doing? Don't you?'

Wexford didn't look at him. He had seen too many men's souls stripped to relish an unnecessary spiritual skinning.

'I know what you were doing,' he said, skipping the name, the 'sir'. 'You told me yourself, just now in this room.' He opened the door. 'If not in so many words.'

Douglas Quadrant's house was much larger and far less pleasing to the eye than the Missals'. It stood on an eminence amid shrubby grounds some fifty feet back from the road. A huge cedar softened to some extent its austere aspect, but when he was half-way up the path Wexford recalled similar houses he had seen in the north of Scotland, granite-built, vaguely gothic and set at each end with steeple-roofed towers.

There was something odd about the garden, but it was a few minutes before he realized in what its strangeness consisted. The lawns were smooth, the shrubs conventionally chosen, but about it all was a sombre air. There were no flowers. Douglas Quadrant's garden presented a Monet-like landscape of grey and brown and many-shaded green.

After Mrs Missal's blue lilies, the rhododendrons real and artificial in her drawing-room, this stately drabness should have been restful. Instead it was hideously depressing. Undoubtedly no flowers could bloom because none had been planted, but the effect was rather that the soil was barren or the air inclement.

Wexford mounted the shallow flight of broad steps under the blank eyes of windows hung with olive and burgundy and pigeon grey, and pressed the bell. Presently the door was opened by a woman

106

of about seventy dressed amazingly in a brown frock with a beige cap and apron. She was what was once known, Wexford thought, as 'an elderly body'. Here, he was sure, there would be no frivolous Teutonic blondes.

She in her turn looked as if she would designate him as 'a person', a creature not far removed from a tradesman, who should have known better than to present himself at the front door. He asked for Mrs Quadrant and produced his card.

'Madam is having her tea,' she said, unimpressed by Wexford's bulk, his air of justice incarnate. 'I'll see if she can speak to you.'

'Just tell her Chief Inspector Wexford would like a word with her.' Affected by the atmosphere, he added, 'If you please.'

He stepped over the threshold and into the hall. It was as big as a large room and, surprisingly enough, the tapestries of hunting scenes stretched on frames and attached to the walls did nothing to diminish its size. Again there was the same absence of colour, but not quite a total absence. Worked into the coats of the huntsmen, the palfreys of their mounts, Wexford caught the gleam of dull gold, ox-blood red and a hint of heraldic murrey.

The old woman looked defiantly at him as if she was prepared to argue it out, but as Wexford closed the front door firmly behind him someone called out:

'Who is it, Nanny?'

He recognized Mrs Quadrant's voice and remembered how the night before she had smiled at Missal's crude joke.

Nanny just got to the double doors before him. She opened them in a way he had only seen done in films and, incongruously, grotesquely, there rose before his eyes a shot, ridiculous and immensely funny,

107

from a Marx Brothers picture. The vision fled and he entered the room.

Douglas and Fabia Quadrant were sitting alone at either end of a low table covered by a lace cloth. Tea had apparently only just been brought in because the book Mrs Quadrant had been reading was lying open and face-upwards on the arm of her chair. The soft old silver of the teapot, the cream jug and the sugar bowl was so brightly polished that it reflected her long hands against the sombre colours of the room. It was forty years since Wexford had seen a brass kettle like this one boiling gently over a spirit flame.

Quadrant was eating bread and butter, just plain bread and butter but crustless and cut thin as a wafer.

'This is an unexpected pleasure,' he said, rising to his feet. This time there were no clumsy incidents with cigarettes. He restored his cup almost gracefully to the table and waved Wexford into an armchair.

'Of course, you know my wife?' He was like a cat, Wexford thought, a slim detached tom-cat who purred by day and went out on the tiles at night. And this room, the silver, the china, the long wine-coloured curtains like blood transmuted into velvet! And amidst it all Mrs Quadrant, dark-haired, elegant in black, was feeding cream to her cat. But when the lamps were lit he stole away to take his feline pleasures under the bushes in the creeping dark.

Tea, Chief Inspector?' She poured a driblet of water into the pot.

'Not for me, thank you.' She had come a long way, Wexford thought, since those days in the wilderness garden, or perhaps, even then, her gym tunic had been of a more expensive make, her hair more expertly cut than the other girls'. She's beautiful, he thought, but she looks old, much older than Helen

Missal. No children, plenty of money, nothing to do all day but feed cream to a ranging cat. Did she mind his infidelity, did she even know about it? Wexford wondered curiously if the jealousy that had reddened Missal had blanched and aged Quadrant's wife.

'And what can I do for you?' Quadrant asked. 'I half expected a visit this morning. I gather from the newspapers that you aren't making a great deal of headway.' Lining himself up on the side of the law, he added, 'An elusive killer this time, am I right?'

'Things are sorting themselves out,' Wexford said heavily. 'As a matter of fact it was your wife I wanted to speak to.'

'To me?' Fabia Quadrant touched one of her platinum ear-rings and Wexford noticed that her wrists were thin and her arms already corded like a much older woman's. 'Oh, I see. Because I knew Margaret, you mean. We were never very close, Chief Inspector. There must be dozens of people who could tell you more about her than I can.'

Possibly, Wexford thought, if I only knew where to find them.

'I didn't see her at all after her family moved away from Flagford until just a few weeks ago. We met in the High Street and had coffee. We discovered we'd gone our separate ways and – well!'

And that, Wexford said to himself, contrasting Tabard Road with the house he was in, must be the understatement of the case. For a second, building his impressions as he always did in a series of pictures, he glimpsed that meeting: Mrs Quadrant with her rings, her elaborately straight hair, and Margaret Parsons awkward in the cardigan and sandals that had seemed so comfortable until she came upon her old companion. What had they in common, what had they talked about?

'What did she talk about, Mrs Quadrant?'

'Oh, the changes in the place, people we'd known at school, that sort of thing.' The governess and the lady of the manor. Wexford sighed within himself.

'Did you ever meet anyone called Anne Ives?'

'You mean Margaret's cousin? No, I never met her. She wasn't at school with us. She was a typist or a clerk or something.'

Just another of the hoi-polloi, Wexford thought, the despised majority, the bottom seventy-five per cent.

Quadrant sat listening, swinging one elegant leg. His wife's condescension seemed to amuse him. He finished his tea, crumpled his napkin and helped himself to a cigarette. Wexford watched him take a box of matches from his pocket and strike one. Matches! That was odd. Surely if he had behaved consistently Quadrant would have used a lighter, one of these table lighters that look like a Georgian teapot, Wexford thought, his imagination working. There had been a single matchstick beside Mrs Parsons' body, a single matchstick half burnt away . . .

'Now, Margaret Godfrey's boy friends, Mrs Quadrant. Can you remember anyone at all?'

He leant forward, trying to impress her with the urgency of his question. A tiny flash of something that might have been malice or simply recollection darted into her eyes and was gone. Quadrant exhaled deeply.

'There was a boy,' she said.

'Try to remember, Mrs Quadrant.'

'I ought to remember,' she said, and Wexford was sure she could, certain she was only stalling for effect. 'It was like a theatre, a London theatre.'

'Palladium, Globe, Haymarket?' Quadrant was enjoying himself. 'Prince of Wales?'

Fabia Quadrant giggled softly. It was an unkind titter, sympathetic towards her husband, faintly hostile to the Chief Inspector. For all his infidelity Quadrant and his wife shared something, something stronger, Wexford guessed, than ordinary marital trust.

'I know, it was Drury. Dudley Drury. He used to live in Flagford.'

'Thank you, Mrs Quadrant. It had just crossed my mind that your husband might have known her.'

'I?' As he spoke the monosyllable Quadrant's voice was almost hysterically incredulous. Then he began to rock with laughter. It was a soundless cruel mirth that seemed to send an evil wind through the room. He made no noise, but Wexford felt scorn leap out of the laughing man like a springing animal, scorn and contempt and the wrath that is one of the deadly sins. 'I, know *her*? In that sort of way? I assure you, dear Chief Inspector, that I most emphatically knew her not!'

Sickened, Wexford turned away. Mrs Quadrant was looking down into her lap. It was as if she had withdrawn into a sort of shame.

'This Drury,' Wexford said, 'do you know if she ever called him Doon?'

Was it his imagination or was it simply coincidence that at that moment Quadrant's laughter was switched off like a wrenched tap?

'Doon?' his wife said. 'Oh, no, I never heard her call anyone Doon.'

She didn't get up when Wexford rose to go, but gave him a dismissive nod and reached for the book she had been reading. Quadrant let him out briskly, closing the door before he reached the bottom of the steps as if he had been selling brushes or reading the meter. Dougie Q! If there was ever a fellow who could strangle one woman and then make love to

111

another a dozen yards away ... But why? Deep in thought, he walked down the Kingsbrook Road, crossed to the opposite side of the road and would have passed Helen Missal's garage unseeing but for the voice that hailed him.

'Did you see Douglas?' Her tone was wistful but she had cheered up since he had last seen her. The bikini had been changed for a printed silk dress, high-heeled shoes and a big hat.

The question was beneath Wexford's dignity.

'Mrs Quadrant was able to fill in a few gaps,' he said.

'Fabia was? You amaze me. She's very discreet. Just as well, Douglas being what he is.' For a moment her pretty face was swollen with sensuality. 'He's magnificent, isn't he? He's splendid.' Shaking herself, she drew her hand across the face and when she withdrew it Wexford saw that the lust had been wiped away. 'My Christ,' she said, once more cheerful and outrageous, 'some people don't know when they're well off!' She unlocked the garage doors, opened the boot of the red Dauphine and took out a pair of flatter shoes.

'I had the impression,' Wexford said, 'that there was something else you wanted to tell me.' He paused. 'When your husband interrupted us.'

'Perhaps there was and perhaps there wasn't. I don't think I will now.' The shoes changed, she danced up to the car and swung the door open.

'Off to the cinema?' Wexford asked.

She banged the door and switched on the ignition.

'Damn you!' Wexford heard her shout above the roar of the engine.

Chapter 10

We were young, we were merry, we were very very wise,
And the door stood open at our feast ...

Mary Coleridge, *Unwelcome*

Nectarine Cottage lay in a damp hollow, a bramble-filled basin behind the Stowerton Road. The approach down a winding path was hazardous and Miss Clarke was taking no chances. Notices pencilled on lined paper greeted Burden at intervals as he descended. The first on the gate had commanded *Lift and push hard*; the second, some ten feet down the path, *Mind barbed wire*. Presently the brambles gave place to faint traces of cultivation. This was of a strictly utilitarian kind, rows of sad cabbages among the weeds, a splendid marrow plant protected from the thistles by a home-made cloche. Someone had pinned a sheet of paper to its roof, *Do not remove glass*. Evidently Miss Clarke had clumsy friends or was the victim of trespassers. This Burden could understand, for there was nothing to indicate habitation but the vegetables and the notices, and the cottage only came into view when he was almost upon it at the end of the path.

The door stood wide open and from within came rich gurgling giggles. For a moment he thought that, although there were no other houses in the lane, he had come to the wrong place. He rapped on the

113

door, the giggles rose to a gale and someone called out:

'Is that you, Dodo? We'd almost given you up.'

Dodo might be a man or a woman, probably a woman. Burden gave a very masculine cough.

'Oh, gosh, it isn't,' said the voice. 'I tell you what, Di. It must be old Fanny Fowler's cop, a coughing cop.'

Burden felt uncommonly foolish. The voice seemed to come from behind a closed door at the end of the passage.

He called loudly, 'Inspector Burden, madam!'

The door was immediately flung open and a woman came out dressed like a Tyrolean peasant. Her fair hair was drawn tightly back and twisted round her head in plaits.

'Oh, gosh,' she said again. 'I didn't realize the front door was still open. I was only kidding about you being Miss Fowler's cop. She rang up and said you might come.'

'Miss Clarke?'

'Who else?' Burden thought she looked very odd, a grown woman dressed up as Humperdinck's Gretel. 'Come and pig it along with Di and me in the dungeon,' she said.

Burden followed her into the kitchen. *Mind the steps*, said another notice pinned to the door and he saw it just in time to stop himself crashing down the three steep steps to the slate-flagged floor. The kitchen was even nastier than Mrs Parsons' and much less clean. But outside the window the sun was shining and a red rose pressed against the diamond panes.

There was nothing odd about the woman Miss Clarke had called Di. It might have been Mrs Parsons' double sitting at the table eating toast, only this woman's hair was black and she wore glasses.

114

'Di Plunkett, Inspector Burden,' Clare Clarke said. 'Sit down, Inspector – not that stool. It's got fat on it – and have a cup of tea.'

Burden refused the tea and sat on a wooden chair that looked fairly clean.

'I've no objection if you talk while I eat,' said Miss Clarke, bursting once more into giggles. She peered at a tin of jam and said crossly to her companion: 'Confound it! South African. I know I shan't fancy it now.' She pouted and said dramatically, 'Ashes on my tongue!' But Burden noticed that she helped herself generously and spread the jam on to a doorstep of bread. With her mouth full she said to him: 'Fire away. I'm all ears.'

'All I really want to know is if you can tell me the names of any of Mrs Parsons' boy friends when she was Margaret Godfrey, when you knew her.'

Miss Clarke smacked her lips.

'You've come to the right shop,' she said. 'I've got a memory like an elephant.'

'You can say that again,' said Di Plunkett, 'and it's not only your memory.' They both laughed, Miss Clarke with great good humour.

'I remember Margaret Godfrey perfectly,' she said. 'Second-class brain, anaemic looks, personality both prim and dim. Still, *de mortuis* and all that jazz, you know. (Prang that fly, Di. There's a squeegy-weegy sprayer thing on the shelf behind your great bonce.) Not a very social type, Margaret, no community spirit. Went around with a female called Bertram, vanished now into the mists of obscurity. (Got him, Di!) Chummed up with one Fabia Rogers for a while – Fabia, forsooth! not to mention Diana Stevens of sinister memory –'

Miss or Mrs Plunkett broke in with a scream of laughter and waving the fly-killer made as if to fire a

115

stream of liquid at Miss Clarke's head. Burden shifted his chair out of range.

Ducking and giggling, Clare Clarke went on: '. . . Now notorious in the Stowerton rural district as Mrs William Plunkett, one of this one-eyed burg's most illustrious sons!'

'You are a scream, Clare,' Mrs Plunkett gasped. 'Really, I envy those lucky members of the upper fourth. When I think of what we had to put up with –'

'What about boy friends, Miss Clarke?'

'*Cherchez l'homme*, eh? I said you'd come to the right shop. D'you remember, Di, when she went out with him the first time and we sat behind them in the pictures? Oh, gosh, I'll never forget that to my dying day.'

'Talk about sloppy,' said Mrs Plunkett. '"Do you mind if I hold your hand, Margaret?" I thought you were going to burst a blood-vessel, Clare.'

'What was his name?' Burden was bored and at the same time angry. He thought the years had toughened him, but now the picture of the green and white bundle in the wood swam before his eyes; that and Parsons' face. He realized that of all the people they had interviewed he hadn't liked a single one. Was there no pity in any of them, no common mercy?

'What was his name?' he said again wearily.

'Dudley Drury. On my sacred oath, Dudley Drury.'

'What a name to go to bed with,' Mrs Plunkett said.

Clare Clarke whispered in her ear, but loud enough for Burden to hear: 'She never did! Not on your sweet life.'

Mrs Plunkett saw his face and looked a little

116

ashamed. She said defensively in a belated effort to help:

'He's still around if you want to trace him. He lives down by Stowerton Station. Surely you don't think he killed Meg Godfrey?'

Clare Clarke said suddenly: 'She was quite pretty. He was very keen on her. She didn't look like that then, you know, not like that ghastly mockery in the paper. I think I've got a snap somewhere. All girls together.'

Burden had got what he wanted. Now he wanted to go. It was a bit late in the day for snaps. If they could have seen one on Thursday it might have helped but that was all.

'Thank you, Miss Clarke,' he said, 'Mrs Plunkett. Good afternoon.'

'Well, cheeri-bye. It's been nice meeting you.' She giggled. 'It's not often we see a man in here, is it, Di?'

Half-way down the overgrown path he stopped in his tracks. A woman in jodhpurs and open-necked shirt was coming up towards the cottage, whistling. It was Dorothy Sweeting.

Dodo, he thought. They'd mistaken him for some-one called Dodo and Dodo was Dorothy Sweeting. From long experience Burden knew that whatever may happen in detective fiction, coincidence is more common than conspiracy in real life.

'Good afternoon, Miss Sweeting.'

She grinned at him with cheerful innocence.

'Oh, hallo,' she said, 'fancy seeing you. I've just come from the farm. There's a blinking great crowd like a Cup Final in that wood. You ought to see them.'

Still not inured to man's inhuman curiosity, Burden sighed.

'You know that bush where they found her?' Dorothy Sweeting went on excitedly. 'Well, Jimmy

117

Traynor's flogging twigs off it at a bob a time. I told Mr Prewett he ought to charge half a crown admittance.'

'I hope he's not thinking of taking your advice, miss,' Burden said in a repressive voice.

'There's nothing wrong in it. I knew a fellow who had a plane crash on his land and he turned a whole field into a car park he had so many sightseers.'

Burden flattened himself against the hedge to let her pass.

'Your tea will be getting cold, Miss Sweeting,' he said.

'Whatever next?' Wexford said. 'If we don't look sharp they'll have every stick in that wood uprooted and taken home for souvenirs.'

'Shall I have a couple of the lads go over there, sir?' Burden asked.

'You do that, and go and get the street directory. We'll go and see this Drury character together.'

'You aren't going to wait to hear from Colorado, then?'

'Drury's a big possibility, Mike. He could well be Doon. I can't help feeling that whatever Parsons says about his wife's chastity, when she came back here she met up with Doon again and succumbed to his charms. As to why he should have killed her – well, all I can say is, men *do* strangle women they're having affairs with, and Mrs P. may have accepted the car rides and the meals without being willing to pay for services rendered.

'The way I see it, Mike, Doon had been seeing Mrs P. and asked her out on Tuesday afternoon with a view to persuading her to become his mistress. They couldn't meet at her home because of the risks and Doon was going to pick her up on the Pomfret Road. She took the rain-hood with her because the weather had been wet and she didn't bank on being in the car all the time. Even if she didn't want Doon for her lover she wouldn't want him to see her with wet hair.'

The time factor was bothering Burden and he said so.

'If she was killed early in the afternoon, sir, why did Doon strike a match to look at her? And if she was killed later, why didn't she pay for her papers before she went out with him and why didn't she explain to Parsons that she was going to be late?'

Wexford shrugged. 'Search me,' he said. 'Dougie Q. uses matches, carries them in his pocket. So do most men. He's behaving in a very funny way, Mike. Sometimes he's co-operative, sometimes he's actively hostile. We haven't finished with him yet. Mrs Missal knows more than she's saying –'

'Then there's Missal himself,' Burden interrupted.

Wexford looked thoughtful. He rubbed his chin and said: 'I don't think there's any mystery about what he was doing on Tuesday. He's as jealous as hell of that wife of his and not without reason as we know. I'm willing to take a bet that he keeps tabs on her when he can. He probably suspects Quadrant and when she told him she was going out on Tuesday afternoon he nipped back to Kingsmarkham on the off-chance, watched her go out, satisfied himself that she didn't go to Quadrant's office and went back to Stowerton. He'd know she'd dress herself up to the nines if she was meeting Dougie. When he saw her go off in the car along the Kingsbrook Road in the same clothes she was wearing that morning he'd bank on her going shopping in Pomfret – they don't close on Tuesdays – and he'd be able to set his mind at rest. I'm certain that's what happened.'

119

'It sounds like him,' Burden agreed. 'It fits. Was Quadrant here twelve years ago, sir?'

'Oh, yes, lived here all his life, apart from three years at Cambridge and, anyway, he came down in 1949. Still, Mrs P. was hardly his style. I asked him if he knew her and he just laughed, but it was the way he laughed. I'm not kidding, Mike, it made my blood run cold.'

Burden looked at his chief with respect. It must have been quite a display, he thought, to chill Wexford.

'I suppose the others could have been just – well, playthings as it were, and Mrs P. a life-long love.'

'Christ!' Wexford roared. 'I should never have let you read that book. Playthings, life-long love! You make me puke. For pity's sake find out where Drury lives and we'll get over there.'

According to the directory, Drury, Dudley J. and Drury, Kathleen lived at 14 Sparta Grove, Stowerton. Burden knew it as a street of tiny pre-war semi-detached houses, not far from where Peter Missal had his garage. It was not the kind of background he had visualized for Doon. He and Wexford had a couple of rounds of sandwiches from the Carousel and got to Stowerton by seven.

Drury's house had a yellow front door with a lot of neatly tied climbing roses on the trellis round the porch. In the middle of the lawn was a small pond made from a plastic bath and on its rim stood a plaster gnome with a fishing rod. Someone had evidently been polishing the Ford Popular on the garage drive. As a vehicle for clandestine touring Mrs Katz would probably have despised it, but it was certainly shiny enough to have dazzled Margaret Parsons.

The door-knocker was a cast-iron lion's head with a ring in its mouth. Wexford banged it hard, but no

120

one came, so he pushed open the side gate and they entered the back garden. On a vegetable plot by the rear fence a man was digging potatoes.

Wexford coughed and the man turned round. He had a red glistening face, and although it was warm, the cuffs of his long-sleeved shirt were buttoned. His sandy hair and the whiteness of his wrists confirmed Wexford's opinion that he was probably sensitive to sunburn. Not the sort of man, Burden thought, to be fond of poetry and send snippets of verse to the girl he loved, surely not the sort of man to buy expensive books and write delicate whimsical messages in their fly-leaves.

'Mr Drury?' Wexford asked quietly.

Drury looked startled, almost frightened, but this could simply be alarm at the invasion of his garden by two men much larger than himself. There was sweat on his upper lip, again probably only the result of manual toil.

'Who are you?'

It was a thin highish voice that sounded as if its development towards a greater resonance had been arrested in puberty.

'Chief Inspector Wexford, sir, and Inspector Burden. County Police.'

Drury had looked after his garden. Apart from a couple of square yards from which potatoes had been lifted, there were various freshly turned patches all over the flower-beds. He stuck the prongs of the fork into the ground and wiped his hands on his trousers.

'Is this something to do with Margaret?' he asked.

'I think we'd better go into the house, Mr Drury.'

He took them in through a pair of french windows, considerably less elegant than Mrs Missal's, and into a tiny room crowded with post-war utility furniture.

Someone had just eaten a solitary meal. The cloth

121

was still on the table and the dirty plates had been half-heartedly stacked.

'My wife's away,' Drury said. 'She took the kids to the seaside this morning. What can I do for you?'

He sat down on a dining chair, offered another to Burden and, observant of protocol, left the only armchair to Wexford.

'Why did you ask if it was something to do with Margaret, Mr Drury?'

'I recognized her photograph in the paper. It gave me a bit of a turn. Then I went to a do at the chapel last night and they were all talking about it. It made me feel a bit queer, I can tell you, on account of me meeting Margaret through the chapel.'

That would have been Flagford Methodist Church, Burden reflected. He recalled a maroon-painted hut with a corrugated-iron roof on the north side of the village green.

Drury didn't look scared any longer, only sad. Burden was struck by his resemblance to Ronald Parsons, not only a physical likeness but a similarity of phrase and manner. As well as the undistinguished features, the thin sandy hair, this man had the same defensiveness, the same humdrum turn of speech. A muscle twitched at the corner of his mouth. Anyone less like Douglas Quadrant would have been difficult to imagine.

'Tell me about your relationship with Margaret Godfrey,' Wexford said.

Drury looked startled.

'It wasn't a relationship,' he said.

What did he think he was being accused of? Burden wondered.

'She was one of my girl friends. She was just a kid at school. I met her at chapel and took her out ... what, a dozen times.'

'When did you first take her out, Mr Drury?'

122

'It's a long time ago. Twelve years, thirteen years ... I can't remember.' He looked at his hands on which the crusts of earth were drying. 'Will you excuse me if I go and have a bit of a wash?'

He went out of the room. Through the open serving hatch Burden saw him run the hot tap and swill his hands under it. Wexford moved out of Drury's line of vision and towards the bookcase. Among the Penguins and the *Reader's Digests* was a volume covered in navy-blue suède. Wexford took it out quickly, read the inscription and handed it to Burden.

It was the same printing, the same breathless loving style. Above the title – *The Picture of Dorian Gray* – Burden read:

Man cannot live on wine alone, Minna, but this is the very best bread and butter. Farewell. Doon, July, 1951.

Chapter 11

They out-talked thee, hissed thee, tore thee,
Better men fared thus before thee.

Matthew Arnold, *The Last Word*

Drury came back, smiling cautiously. He had rolled up his sleeves and his hands were pink. When he saw the book Wexford was holding the smile faded and he said aggressively:

'I think you're taking a liberty.'

'Where did you get this book, Mr Drury?'

Drury peered at the printing, looked at Wexford and blushed. The tic returned, pumping his chin.

'Oh dear,' he said, 'she gave it me. I'd forgotten I'd got it.'

Wexford had become stern. His thick lower lip stood out, giving him a prognathous look.

'Look here, she gave me that book when I was taking her out. It says July here and that's when it must have been. July, that's right.' The blush faded and he went white. He sat down heavily. 'You don't believe me, do you? My wife'll tell you. It's been there ever since we got married.'

'Why did Mrs Parsons give it to you, Mr Drury?'

'I'd been taking her out for a few weeks.' He stared at Wexford with eyes like a hare's caught in the beam of headlights. 'It was the summer of – I don't know. What does it say there? Fifty-one. We were in her

124

aunt's house. A parcel came for Margaret and she opened it. She looked sort of mad and she just chucked it down, chucked it on the floor, you see, but I picked it up. I'd heard of it and I thought ... well, I thought it was a smutty book if you must know, and I wanted to read it. She said, "Here, you can have it, if you like." Something like that. I can't remember the details of what she said. It was a long time ago. Minna had got fed up with this Doon and I thought she was sort of ashamed of him ...'

'Minna?'

'I started calling her Minna then because of the name in the book. What have I said? For God's sake, don't look at me like that!'

Wexford stuck the book in his pocket.

'When did you last see her?'

Drury picked at the cord that bound the seat of his chair. He began pulling out little shreds of red cotton. At last he said:

'She went away in the August. Her uncle had died ...'

'No, no. I mean recently.'

'I saw her last week. That isn't a crime, is it, seeing somebody you used to know? I was in the car and I recognized her. She was in the High Street, in Kingsmarkham. I stopped for a minute and asked her how she was, that sort of thing ...'

'Go on. I want all the details.'

'She said she was married and I said so was I. She said she'd come to live in Tabard Road and I said we must get together sometime with her husband and Kathleen. Kathleen's my wife. Anyway, I said I'd give her a ring, and that was all.'

'She told you her married name?'

'Of course she did. Why shouldn't she?'

'Mr Drury, you said you recognized her photograph. Didn't you recognize her name?'

'Her name, her face, what's the odds? I'm not in court. I can't watch every word I say.'

'Just tell the truth and you won't have to watch your words. Did you telephone her?'

'Of course I didn't. I was going to, but then I read she was dead.'

'Where were you on Tuesday between twelve-thirty and seven?'

'I was at work. I work in my uncle's hardware shop in Pomfret. Ask him, he'll tell you I was there all day.'

'What time does the shop close?'

'Half past five, but I always try to get away early on Tuesdays. Look, you won't believe me.'

'Try me, Mr Drury.'

'I know you won't believe me, but my wife'll tell you, my uncle'll tell you. I always go to Flagford on Tuesdays to collect my wife's vegetable order. There's a nursery there, see, on the Clusterwell Road. You have to get there by half five otherwise they're closed. Well, we were busy last Tuesday and I was late. I try to get away by five, but it was all of a quarter past. When I got to Spellman's there wasn't anybody about. I went round the back of the greenhouses and I called out, but they'd gone.'

'So you went home without the vegetables?'

'No, I didn't. Well, I did, but not straight away. I'd had a hard day and I was fed up about the place being closed, so I went into The Swan and had a drink. A girl served me. I've never seen her before. Look, does my wife have to know about that? I'm a Methodist, see? I'm a member of the chapel. I'm not supposed to drink.'

Burden drew in his breath. A murder enquiry and he was worrying about his clandestine pint!

'You drove to Flagford along the main Pomfret Road?'

'Yes, I did. I drove right past that wood where they found her.' Drury got up and fumbled in vain along the mantelpiece for cigarettes. 'But I never stopped. I drove straight to Flagford. I was in a hurry to get the order ... Look, Chief Inspector, I wouldn't have done anything to Minna. She was a nice kid. I was fond of her. I wouldn't do a thing like that, kill someone!'

'Who else called her Minna apart from you?'

'Only this Doon fellow as far as I know. She never told me his real name. I got the impression she was sort of ashamed of him. Goodness knows why. He was rich and he was clever too. She said he was clever.' He drew himself up and looked at them belligerently. 'She preferred me,' he said.

He got up suddenly and stared at the chair he had mutilated. Among the dirty plates was a milk bottle, half full, with yellow curds sticking to its rim. He tipped the bottle into an empty tea-cup and drank from it, slopping a puddle into the saucer.

'I should sit down if I were you,' Wexford said.

He went into the hall and beckoned to Burden. They stood close together in the narrow passage. The carpet was frayed by the kitchen door and one of Drury's children had scribbled on the wallpaper with a blue crayon.

'Get on to The Swan, Mike,' he said. He thought he heard Drury's chair shift and, remembering the open french windows, turned swiftly. But Drury was still sitting at the table, his head buried in his hands.

The walls were thin and he could hear Burden's voice in the front room, then a faint trill as the receiver went back into its rest. Burden's feet thumped across the floor, entered the hall and stopped. There was utter silence and Wexford edged out of the door, keeping his eye on Drury through the crack.

Burden was standing by the front door. On the wall at the foot of the narrow staircase was a coat-rack, a zig-zag metal affair with gaudily coloured knobs instead of hooks. A man's sports jacket and a child's plastic mac hung on two of the knobs and on the one nearest to the stairs was a transparent pink nylon hood.

'It won't take prints,' Wexford said. 'Get back on that phone, Mike. I shall want some help. Bryant and Gates should be coming on about now.'

He unhooked the hood, covered the diminutive hall in three strides, and showed his find to Drury.

'Where did you get this, Mr Drury?'

'It must be my wife's,' Drury said. Suddenly assertive, he added pugnaciously, 'It's no business of yours!'

'Mrs Parsons bought a hood like this one on Tuesday morning.' Wexford watched him crumple once more in sick despair. 'I want your permission to search this house, Drury. Make no mistake about it, I can get a warrant, but it'll take a little longer.'

Drury looked as if he was going to cry.

'Oh, do what you like,' he said. 'Only, can I have a cigarette? I've left mine in the kitchen.'

'Inspector Burden will get them when he comes off the phone,' Wexford said.

They began to search, and within half an hour were joined by Gates and Bryant. Then Wexford told Burden to contact Drury's uncle at Pomfret, Spellman's nursery and the manager of the supermarket.

'The girl at The Swan isn't on tonight,' Burden said, 'but she lives in Flagford at 3 Cross Roads Cottages. No phone. Her name's Janet Tipping.'

'We'll get Martin over there straight away. Try and get a phone number out of Drury where we can get hold of his wife. If she's not gone far away – Brighton or Eastbourne – you can get down there tonight.

128

When I've turned the place over I'm going to have another word with Mrs Quadrant. She admits she was "friendly" with Mrs P. and she's practically the only person who does, apart from our friend in the next room.'

Burden stretched the pink scarf taut, testing its strength.

'You really think he's Doon?' he asked incredulously.

Wexford went on opening drawers, feeling among a mêlée of coloured pencils, Snap cards, reels of cotton, scraps of paper covered with children's scribble. Mrs Drury wasn't a tidy housewife and all the cupboards and drawers were in a mess.

'I don't know,' he said. 'At the moment it looks like it, but it leaves an awful lot of loose ends. It doesn't fit in with my fancies, Mike, and since we can't afford to go by fancies . . .'

He looked through every book in the house – there were not more than two or three dozen – but he found no more from Doon to Minna. There was no Victorian poetry and the only novels apart from *The Picture of Dorian Gray* were paperback thrillers.

On a hook in the kitchen cabinet Bryant found a bunch of keys. One fitted the front door lock, another the strong box in Drury's bedroom, two more the dining-room and front-room doors, and a fifth the garage. The ignition keys to Drury's car were in his jacket on the coat-rack and the key to the back door was in the lock. Wexford, looking for purses, found only one, a green and white plastic thing in the shape of a cat's face. It was empty and labelled on the inside: *Susan Mary Drury*. Drury's daughter had taken her savings with her to the seaside.

The loft was approached by a hatch in the landing ceiling. Wexford told Bryant to get Drury's steps from the garage and investigate this loft. He left

Gates downstairs with Drury and went out to his car. On the way he scraped some dust from the tyres of the blue Ford.

A thin drizzle was falling. It was ten o'clock and dark for a midsummer evening. If Drury had killed her at half past five, he thought, it would still have been broad daylight, much too early to need the light of a match flame. It would have to be a match they had found. Of all the things to leave behind a matchstick was surely the least incriminating! And why hadn't she paid for her papers, what had she done with herself during the long hours between the time she left the house and the time she met Doon? But Drury was terribly frightened ... Wexford too had observed the resemblance between him and Ronald Parsons. It was reasonable to suppose, he argued, that this type of personality attracted Margaret Parsons and that she had chosen her husband because he reminded her of her old lover.

He switched on his headlights, pulled the windscreen wiper button, and started back towards Kingsmarkham.

Chapter 12

Were you and she whom I met at dinner last week,
With eyes and hair of the Ptolemy black?

Sir Edwin Arnold, *To a Pair of Egyptian Slippers*

The house looked forbidding at night. In Wexford's headlights the rough grey granite glittered and the leaves of the flowerless wistaria which clung to it showed up a livid yellowish green.

Someone was dining with the Quadrants. Wexford pulled up beside the black Daimler and went up the steps to the front door. He rang the bell several times; then the door was opened, smoothly, almost offensively slowly, by Quadrant himself.

For dining with Helen Missal he had worn a lounge suit. At home, with his wife and guests, he ascended to evening dress. But there was nothing vulgar about Quadrant, no fancy waistcoat, no flirtation with midnight blue. The dinner jacket was black and faultless, the shirt – Wexford liked to hit on an apt quotation himself when he could – 'whiter than new snow on a raven's back'.

He said nothing but seemed to stare right through Wexford at the shadowy garden beyond. There was an insolent majesty about him which the tapestries that framed his figure did nothing to dispel. Then Wexford told himself sharply that this man was, after all, only a provincial solicitor.

131

'I'd like another word with your wife, Mr Quadrant.'

'At this hour?'

Wexford looked at his watch and at the same time Quadrant lifted his own cuff – links of silver and onyx glinted in the muted lights – raised his eyebrow at the square platinum dial on his wrist and said:

'It's extremely inconvenient.' He made no move to let Wexford enter. 'My wife isn't a particularly strong woman and we do happen to have my parents-in-law dining with us . . .'

Old man Rogers and his missus, Pomfret Hall, Wexford thought vulgarly. He stood stolidly, not smiling.

'Oh, very well,' Quadrant said, 'but keep it brief, will you?'

There was a faint movement in the hall behind him. A brown dress, a wisp of coffee-coloured stuff, appeared for an instant against the embroidered trees on the hangings, then Mrs Quadrant's nanny scuttled away.

'You'd better go into the library.' Quadrant showed him into a room furnished with blue leather chairs. 'I won't offer you a drink since you're on duty.' The words were a little offensive. Then Quadrant gave his quick cat-like smile. 'Excuse me,' he said, 'while I fetch my wife.' He turned with the slow graceful movement of a dance measure, paused briefly and closed the door behind him, shutting Wexford in.

So he wasn't going to let him bust in on any family party, Wexford thought. The man was nervous, hiding some nebulous fear in the manner of men of his kind, under a massive self-control.

As he waited he looked about him at the books. There were hundreds here, tier upon tier of them on every wall. Plenty of Victorian poetry and plenty of

Victorian novels, but just as much verse from the seventeenth and eighteenth centuries. Wexford shrugged. Kingsmarkham was surrounded by such houses as this one, a bastion of affluence, houses with libraries, libraries with books . . .

Fabia Quadrant came in almost soundlessly. Her long dress was black and he remembered that black was not a colour but just a total absorption of light. Her face was gay, a little hectic, and she greeted him cheerfully.

'Hallo again, Chief Inspector.'

'I won't keep you long, Mrs Quadrant.'

'Won't you sit down?'

'Thank you. Just for a moment.' He watched her sit down and fold her hands in her lap. The diamond on her left hand burned in the dark nest between her knees. 'I want you to tell me everything you can remember about Dudley Drury,' he said.

'Well, it was my last term at school,' she said. 'Margaret told me she'd got a boy friend – her first, perhaps. I don't know. It's only twelve years ago, Chief Inspector, but we weren't like the adolescents of today. It wasn't remarkable to be without a boy friend at eighteen. Do you understand?' She spoke clearly and slowly, as if she were instructing a child. Something about her manner angered Wexford and he wondered if she had ever had to hurry in her life, ever had to snatch a meal standing up or run to catch a train. 'It was a little unusual, perhaps, but not odd, not remarkable. Margaret didn't introduce me to her friend but I remember his name because it was like Drury Lane and I had never heard it before as a surname.'

Wexford tried to crush his impatience.

'What did she tell you about him, Mrs Quadrant?'

'Very little.' She paused and looked at him as if she was anxious not to betray a man in danger. 'There was only one thing. She said he was jealous, jealous to the point of fanaticism.'

'I see.'

'He didn't care for her to have any other friends. I had the impression that he was very emotional and possessive.'

Traits you would hardly understand, Wexford thought, or would you? He remembered Quadrant's inconstancies and wondered again. Her voice, uncharacteristically sharp and censorious, interrupted his reverie.

'He was very upset that she was moving back to London. She said he was in a terrible state, his life wouldn't be worth living without her. You can imagine the sort of thing.'

'But he'd only known her a few weeks.'

'I'm simply telling you what she said, Chief Inspector.' She smiled as if she was an immense distance from Drury and Margaret Godfrey, light years, an infinity of space. 'She didn't seem to care. Margaret wasn't a sensitive person.'

Soft footsteps sounded in the hall and behind Wexford the door opened.

'Oh, there you are,' Fabia Quadrant said. 'Chief Inspector Wexford and I have been talking about young love. It all seems to me rather like the expense of spirit in a waste of shame.'

But that wasn't young love, Wexford thought, trying to place the quotation. It was much more like what he had seen on Helen Missal's face that afternoon.

'Just one small point, Mrs Quadrant,' he said. 'Mrs Parsons seems to have been interested in Victorian poetry during the two years she lived in Flagford. I've wondered if there was any special significance behind that.'

'Nothing sinister, if that's what you mean,' she

said. 'Nineteenth century verse was part of the Advanced English syllabus for Higher School Certificate when we took it in 1951. I believe they call it "A" Levels now.'

Then Quadrant did a strange thing. Crossing the library between Wexford and his wife, he took a book out of the shelves. He put his hand on it without hesitation. Wexford had the impression he could have picked it out blindfold or in the dark.

'Oh, Douglas,' Mrs Quadrant said, 'he doesn't want to see that.'

'Look.'

Wexford looked and read from an ornate label that had been pasted inside the cover:

Presented to Fabia Rogers for distinguished results in Higher School Certificate, 1951.

In his job it didn't do to be at a loss for words, but now he could find no phrase to foster the pride on Quadrant's dark face, or mitigate the embarrassment on his wife's.

I'll be going now,' he said at last.

Quadrant put the book back abruptly and took his wife's arm. She rested her fingers firmly on his jacket sleeve. Suddenly they seemed very close, but, for all that, it was a strangely sexless communion. Brother and sister, Wexford thought, a Ptolemy and a Cleopatra.

'Good night, Mrs Quadrant. You've been most co-operative. I apologize for troubling you . . .' He looked again at his watch. 'At this hour,' he said, savouring Quadrant's enmity.

'No trouble, Chief Inspector.' She laughed deprecatingly, confidently, as if she was really a happy wife with a devoted husband.

Together they showed him out. Quadrant was

urbane, once more courteous, but the hand beneath the sleeve where his wife's fingers lay was clenched and the knuckles showed like white flints under the brown skin.

A bicycle was propped against the police-station wall, a bicycle with a basket, practical-looking lights and a bulging tool bag. Wexford walked into the foyer and almost collided with a fat fair woman wearing a leather windcheater over a dirndl skirt.

'I beg your pardon.'

'That's all right,' she said. 'No bones broken. I suppose you wouldn't be him, this Chief Inspector bod?'

Behind the desk the sergeant grinned slightly, changed the grin to a cough, and covered his mouth with his hand.

'I am Chief Inspector Wexford. Can I help you?'

She fished something out of her shoulder bag.

'Actually,' she said, 'I'm supposed to be helping you. One of your blokes came to my cottage . . .'

'Miss Clarke,' Wexford said. 'Won't you come into my office?'

His hopes had suddenly risen unaccountably. It made a change for someone to come to him. Then they fell again when he saw what she had in her hand. It was only another photograph.

'I found it,' she said, 'among a lot of other junk. If you're sort of scouring the joint for people who knew Margaret it might help.'

The picture was an enlarged snapshot. It showed a dozen girls disposed in two rows and it was obviously not an official photograph.

'Di took it,' Miss Clarke said. 'Di Stevens that was. Best part of the sixth form are there.' She looked at him and made a face as if she was afraid that by bringing it she had done something silly. 'You can keep it if it's any use.'

Wexford put it in his pocket, intending to look at it later, although he doubted whether it would be needed now. As he was showing Miss Clarke out he met Sergeant Martin coming back from his interview with the manager of the supermarket. No records had been kept of the number of pink hoods sold during the week, only the total sale of hoods in all colours. The stock had come in on Monday and Saturday night twenty-six hoods had been sold. The manager thought that about twenty-five per cent of the stock had been pink and on a very rough estimate he guessed that about six pink ones had been sold.

Wexford sent Martin over to Flagford in search of Janet Tipping. Then he rang Drury's number. Burden answered. They hadn't found anything in the house. Mrs Drury was staying with her sister in Hastings, but the sister had no telephone.

'Martin'll have to get down there,' Wexford said. 'I can't spare you. What did Spellman say?'

'They closed at five-thirty sharp on Tuesday. Drury collected his wife's vegetable order on Wednesday.'

'What's he buying vegetables for, anyway? He grows them in the garden.'

'The order was for tomatoes, a cucumber and a marrow, sir.'

'That's fruit, not vegetables. Talking of gardening, I'm going to get some lights over to you and they can start digging. I reckon that purse and that key could be interred with Drury's potatoes.'

Dudley Drury was in a pitiful state when Wexford got back to Sparta Grove. He was pacing up and down but he looked weak at the knees.

'He's been sick, sir,' Gates said.

'Hard cheese,' Wexford said. 'What d'you think I am, a health visitor?'

The search of the house had been completed and the place looked a lot tidier than it had before they began. When the lighting equipment arrived Bryant and Gates started digging over the potato patch. White-faced, Drury watched from the dining-room windows as the clods of earth were lifted and turned. This man, Wexford thought, had once said life would be unlivable without Margaret Parsons. Had he really meant it would be unendurable, if another possessed her?

I'd like you to come down to the station now, Drury.'

'Are you going to arrest me?'

'I'd just like to ask you a few more questions,' Wexford said. 'Just a few more questions.'

Meanwhile Burden had driven over to Pomfret, awakened the ironmonger and checked his nephew's alibi.

'Dud always gets off early on Tuesdays,' he grumbled. 'Gets earlier and earlier every week, it does. More like five than a quarter past.'

'So you'd say he left around five last Tuesday?'

'I wouldn't like to say five. Ten past, a quarter past. I was busy in the shop. Dud came in and said, "I'm off now, Uncle." I'd no call to go checking up on him, had I?'

'It might have been ten past or a quarter past?'

'It might have been twenty past for all I know.'

It was still raining softly. The main road was black and stickily gleaming. Whatever Miss Sweeting may have seen in the afternoon, the lane and the wood were deserted now. The top branches of the trees moved in the wind. Burden slowed down, thinking how strange it was that an uninteresting corner of the countryside should suddenly have become,

138

because of the use to which someone had put it, a sinister and dreadful hiding place, the focal point of curious eyes and the goal, perhaps for years to come, of half the visitors to the neighbourhood. From henceforth Flagford Castle would take second place to Prewett's wood in the guide book of the ghoulish.

He met Martin on the forecourt of the police station. Janet Tipping couldn't be found. As usual on Saturday night she had gone out with her boy friend, and her mother had told Martin with a show of aggressive indifference that it was nothing for her to return as late as one or two o'clock. The cottage was dirty and the mother a slattern. She didn't know where her daughter was and, on being asked to hazard a guess, said that Janet and her friend had probably gone for a spin to the coast on his motorbike.

Burden knocked on Wexford's door and the Chief Inspector shouted to him to come in.

Drury and Wexford sat facing each other.

'Let's go over Tuesday evening again,' Wexford was saying. Burden moved silently into one of the steel and tweed chairs. The clock on the wall, between the filing cabinet where Doon's books still lay and the map of Kingsmarkham, said that it was ten minutes to midnight.

'I left the shop at a quarter past five and I drove straight to Flagford. When I got to Spellman's they were closed so I went down the side and looked round the greenhouses. I called out a couple of times but they'd all gone. Look, I've told you all this.'

Wexford said quietly, 'All right, Drury. Let's say I've got a bad memory.'

Drury's voice had become very high and strained. He took out his handkerchief and wiped his forehead.

'I had a look round to see if the order was

139

anywhere about, but it wasn't.' He cleared his throat. 'I was a bit fed-up on account of my wife wanting the vegetables for tea. I drove slowly through the village because I thought I might see Mr Spellman and get him to let me have the order, but I didn't see him.'

'Did you see anybody you know, anybody you used to know when you lived in Flagford?'

'There were some kids,' Drury said. 'I don't know who they were. Look, I've told you the rest. I went into The Swan and this girl served me . . .'

'What did you have to drink?'

'A half of bitter.' He blushed. At the lie, Burden wondered, or at the breach of faith? 'The place was empty. I coughed and after a bit this girl came out from behind the back. I ordered the bitter and paid for it. She's bound to remember.'

'Don't worry, we'll ask her.'

'She didn't stay in the bar. I was all alone. When I'd finished my drink I went back to Spellman's to see if there was anyone about. I didn't see anyone and I went home.'

Drury jumped up and gripped the edge of the desk. Wexford's papers quivered and the telephone receiver rattled in its rest.

'Look,' he shouted, 'I've told you. I wouldn't have laid a finger on Margaret.'

'Sit down,' Wexford said and Drury crouched back, his face twitching. 'You were very jealous of her, weren't you?' His tone had become conversational, understanding. 'You didn't want her to have any friends but you.'

'That's not true.' He tried to shout but his voice was out of control. 'She was just a girl friend. I don't know what you mean, jealous. Of course I didn't want her going about with other boys when she was with me.'

140

'Were you her lover, Drury?'

'No, I was not.' He flushed again at the affront. 'You've got no business to ask me things like that. I was only eighteen.'

'You gave her a lot of presents, didn't you, a lot of books?'

'Doon gave her those books, not me. She'd finished with Doon when she came out with me. I never gave her anything. I couldn't afford it.'

'Where's Foyle's, Drury?'

'It's in London. It's a bookshop.'

'Did you ever buy any books there and give them to Margaret Godfrey?'

'I tell you I never gave her any books.'

'What about *The Picture of Dorian Gray*? You didn't give her that one. Why did you keep it? Because you thought it would shock her?'

Drury said dully, 'I've given you a specimen of my printing.'

'Printing changes a lot in twelve years. Tell me about the book.'

'I have told you. We were in her aunt's cottage and the book came in a parcel. She opened it and when she saw who'd sent it she said I could have it.'

At last they left him to sit in silence with the sergeant. Together they went outside.

'I've sent Drury's printing over to that handwriting bloke in St Mary's Road,' Wexford said. 'But printing, Mike, and twelve years ago! It looks as if whoever printed those inscriptions did so because his handwriting was poor or difficult to read. Drury's writing is very round and clear. I got the feeling he doesn't write much and his writing's never matured.'

'He's the only person we've talked to who called Mrs P. Minna,' Burden said, 'and who knew about Doon. He had one of those hood things in his house

141

and while it could be one of the other five it could be Mrs P.'s. If he left his uncle's at five-ten or five-fifteen even he could have been at Prewett's by twenty past and by then Bysouth had had those cows in for nearly half an hour.'

The telephones had been silent for a long time now, an unusually long time for the busy police station. What had happened to the call they had been awaiting since lunchtime? Wexford seemed to read his thoughts almost uncannily.

'We ought to hear from Colorado any minute,' he said. 'Calculating roughly that they're about seven hours behind us in time, suppose Mrs Katz was out for the day, she'd be getting home just about now. It's half past twelve here and that makes it between five and six in the West of the United States. Mrs Katz has got little kids. I reckon she and her family have been out for the day and they haven't been able to get hold of her. But she ought to be coming home about now and I hope they won't be too long.'

Burden jumped as the bell pealed. He lifted the receiver and gave it to Wexford. As soon as he spoke Burden could tell it was just another bit of negative evidence.

'Yes,' Wexford said. 'Yes, thank you very much. I see. Can't be helped . . . Yes, good night.'

He turned back to Burden. 'That was Egham, the handwriting fellow. He says Drury could have printed those inscriptions. There's no question of the printing being disguised, but he says it was very mature for a boy of eighteen and if it's Drury's he would have expected a much greater development than Drury's present specimen shows.

'Moreover, there's another point in his favour. I took a sample from the treads of his tyres and although they haven't finished with it, the lab boys are pretty certain that car hadn't been parked in a

142

muddy lane since it was new. The stuff I got was mostly sand and dust. Let's have some tea, Mike.'

Burden cocked his thumb at the door.

'A cup for him, sir?'

'My God, yes,' Wexford said. 'How many times do I have to tell you? This isn't Mexico.'

Chapter 13

And I am sometimes proud and sometimes meek,
And sometimes I remember days of old . . .

Christina Rossetti, *Aloof*

Margaret Godfrey was one of five girls on the stone seat and she sat in the middle of the row. Those who stood behind rested their hands on the shoulders of the seated. Wexford counted twelve faces. The snapshot Diana Stevens had taken was very sharp and clear and the likenesses, even after so long, were good. He re-created in his mind the face he had seen on the damp ground, then stared with awakened curiosity at the face in the sun.

The others were all smiling, all but Margaret Godfrey, and her face was in repose. The white forehead was very high, the eyes wide and expressionless; her lips were folded, the corners tilted very slightly upwards, and she was looking at the camera very much as the Gioconda had looked at Leonardo. Secrecy vied with something else in those serene features. This girl, Wexford thought, looked as if she had undergone an experience most of her fellows could never have fathomed, and it had marked her not with suffering or shame but simply with smug tranquillity.

The gym tunic was an incongruity. She could have worn a high-necked dress with puffy sleeves. Her hair, soft then, not crimped and waved as it had been later, skimmed her cheek-bones and lay across her temples in two shining arcs.

Wexford glanced across to the silent Drury, now sitting some five yards from him. Then, screening it once more with his hands, he looked long at the photograph. When Burden came in he was still gazing and his tea had grown cold.

It was almost three o'clock.

'Miss Tipping is here,' Burden said.

Wexford came out of the sunny garden, covered the snapshot with a file and said:

'Let's have her in, then.'

Janet Tipping was a plump healthy-looking girl with a cone of lacquered hair above a stupid suspicious face. When she saw Drury her expression, vacuous and uncomprehending, was unaltered.

'Well, I can't say,' she said. 'I mean, it was a long time ago.'

Not twelve years, Burden thought, only four days.

'I could have served him. I mean, I serve hundreds of fellows with bitter . . .' Drury stared at her, round-eyed, as if he was trying to drive recognition into her dim, tired consciousness. 'Look here,' she said, 'I don't want to get anybody hung.'

She came closer, peering, in the manner of one attracted by a monstrosity in a museum. Then she retreated, shaking her head.

'You must remember me,' Drury shouted. 'You've got to remember. I'll do anything, I'll give you anything if you'll only remember. You don't realize, this means everything to me . . .'

'Oh, do me a favour,' the girl said, frightened now. 'I've racked my brains and I don't remember.' She looked at Wexford and said, 'Can I go now?'

The telephone rang as Burden showed her out. He lifted the receiver and handed it to Wexford.

145

'Yes ... yes, of course I want her brought back,' Wexford said. 'That was Martin,' he said to Burden outside. 'Mrs Drury said she bought that rain-hood on Monday afternoon.'

'That doesn't necessarily mean –' Burden began.

'No, and Drury got in after six-thirty on Tuesday. She remembers because she was waiting for the tomatoes. She wanted to put them in a salad for their tea. If he wasn't killing Mrs P., Mike, that was a hell of a long drink he had. For an innocent man he's practically crazy with terror.'

Again Burden said, 'That doesn't necessarily mean –'

'I know, I know. Mrs Parsons liked them green and goosey, didn't she?'

'I suppose there wasn't anything in the garden, was there, sir?'

'Five nails, about a hundredweight of broken bricks and a Dinky Toy Rolls-Royce,' Wexford said. 'He ought to thank us. It won't need digging in the autumn.' He paused and added, 'If he's still here in the autumn.'

They went back into the office. Drury was sitting utterly immobile, his face lard-coloured like a peeled nut.

'That was a mighty long drink, Drury,' Wexford said. 'You didn't get home till after six-thirty.'

Drury mumbled, his lips scarcely moving: 'I wanted the order. I hung about. There's a lot of traffic about at six. I'm not used to drink and I didn't dare to drive for a bit. I wanted to find Mr Spellman.'

Half a pint, Burden thought, and he didn't dare to drive?

'When did you first resume your relationship with Mrs Parsons?'

'I tell you there wasn't a relationship. I never saw

146

her for twelve years. Then I was driving through the High Street and I stopped and spoke to her . . .'

'You were jealous of Mr Parsons, weren't you?'

'I never met Parsons.'

'You would have been jealous of anyone Mrs Parsons had married. You didn't have to see him. I suggest you'd been meeting Mrs Parsons, taking her out in your car. She got tired of it and threatened to tell your wife.'

'Ask my wife, ask her. She'll tell you I've never been unfaithful to her. I'm happily married.'

'Your wife's on her way here, Drury. We'll ask her.'

Drury had jumped each time the telephone rang. Now as it sounded again after a long lull, a great shudder passed through him and he gave a little moan. Wexford, for hours on tenterhooks, only nodded to Burden.

'I'll take it outside,' he said.

Bryant's shorthand covered the sheet of paper in swift spidery hieroglyphics. Wexford had spoken to the Colorado police chief, but now as he stood behind Bryant he could hear nothing of that thick drawl through the headphones, only watch the words fall on to paper in a tangled code.

By four it had been transcribed. His face still phlegmatic, but to Burden vital with latent excitement, Wexford read the letter again. The dead words, now coldly typed on official paper, seemed still to have the force of life, a busy bustling life led by a woman in a country backwater. Here in the depths of the night, among the office furniture and the green steel filing cabinets, Mrs Parsons was for a moment – one of the few moments in the whole case – resurrected and become a real person. There was no drama in her words and only the whisper of a small tragedy, but because of her fate the letter was a dreadful document, the only existing recorded fragment of her inner life.

Dear Nan (Wexford read),

I can picture your surprise when you read my new address. Yes, we have come back here and are living a stone's throw from school and only a few miles from the dear old cottage. We had to sell auntie's house and lost quite a bit on it, so when Ron got the chance of a job out here we thought this might be the answer. It is supposed to be cheaper living in the country, but we have not noticed it yet, I can tell you.

In spite of what you all thought, I quite liked living in Flagford. It was only you-know-what that turned me off it. Believe me, Nan, I was really scared over that Doon business, so you can imagine I wasn't too pleased to run slap bang up against Doon again a couple of weeks after we moved in. Although I'm a lot older I still feel frightened and a bit revolted. I said it was better to let things rest but Doon will not have this. I must say it is quite pleasant to get a few rides in a nice comfortable car and get taken out for meals in hotels.

Believe me, Nan, it is as it has always been, just friendship. When Doon and I were younger I really don't think we knew it could be anything else. At least, I didn't. Of course the very thought disgusts me. Doon only wants companionship but it is a bit creepy.

So you are going to get another new car. I wish we could afford one but at present it is beyond our wildest dreams. I was sorry to hear about Kim having chicken pox so soon after measles. I suppose having a family has its drawbacks and its worries as well as its advantages. It does not look as if Ron and I will have the anxiety or the happiness now as I have not even had a false alarm for two years.

Still, I always say if you have a really happy marriage as

148

we have, you should not need children to keep it together. Perhaps this is just sour grapes. Anyway, we are happy, and Ron seems much more relaxed now we are away from town. I never will understand, Nan, why people like Doon can't be content with what they have and not keep crying for the moon.

Well, I must close now. This is quite a big house really and not exactly filled with mod. cons.! Remember me to Wil and your offspring. Regards from Ron.

Love from Meg

A happy marriage? Could a marriage be happy, rocking uneasily on a sea of deceit and subterfuge? Burden put the letter down, then picked it up and read it again. Wexford told him of his conversation with the police chief and his face cleared a little.

'We'll never prove it,' Burden said.

'One thing, you can go and tell Drury Gates'll take him home now. If he wants to sue us I daresay Dougie Q. will be nothing loth to lend a hand. Only don't tell him that and don't let me see him. He's upsetting my liver.'

It was beginning to grow light. The sky was grey and misty and the streets were drying. Wexford, stiff and cramped with sitting, decided to leave his car and walk home.

He liked the dawn without usually being sufficiently strong-minded to seek it unless he must. It helped him to think. No one was about. The market place seemed much larger than it did by day and a shallow puddle lay in the gutter where the buses pulled in. On the bridge he met a dog, going purposefully about its mysterious business, trotting quickly, head high, as if making for some definite goal. Wexford stopped for a second and looked down into the water. The big grey figure stared back at him until the wind disturbed the surface and broke up the reflection.

Past Mrs Missal's house, past the cottages ... He was nearly home. On the Methodist church notice-board he could just make out the red-painted letters in the increasing light: 'God needs you for his friend.' Wexford came closer and read the words on another notice pinned beneath it. 'Mr R. Parsons invites all church members and friends to a service in memory of his wife, Margaret, who died so tragically this week, to be held here on Sunday at ten a.m.'

So today, for the first time since she had died, the house in Tabard Road would be empty ... No, Wexford thought, Parsons was at the inquest. But, then ... His thoughts returned to certain events of the afternoon, to laughter shut off in full spate, to a book, a fierce transposition of emotion, to a woman dressed for an assignation.

'We'll never prove it,' Burden had said.

But they could go to Tabard Road in the morning, and they could try.

My demands were modest, Minna. I wanted so little, but a few hours out of the scores of hours that make a week, infinitesimal eddies in the great ocean of eternity.

I wanted to talk, Minna, to spread at your feet the pains and sorrows, the anguish of a decade of despair. Time, I thought, time that planes out the rough edge of cruelty, that dulls the cutting blade of contempt, that trims the frayed fringe of criticism, time will have softened her eye and made tender her ear.

It was a quiet wood we went to, a lane where we had walked long ago, but you had forgotten the flowers we had gathered, the waxen diadem of the Traveller's Joy.

I talked softly, thinking you were pondering. All the while I thought you listening and at last I paused, hungry for your gentle praise, your love at last. Yes, Minna, love. Is that so bad, so evil, if it treads in the pure garments of companionship?

I gazed, I touched your hair. Your eyes were closed for you found dull sleep more salutary than my words and I knew it was too late. Too late for love, too late for friendship, too late for anything but death . . .

Chapter 14

Such closets to search, such alcoves to importune.

Robert Browning, *Love in a Life*.

Parsons was dressed in a dark suit. His black tie, not new and worn perhaps on previous mourning occasions, showed the shiny marks of a too-hot, inexpertly handled iron. Sewn to his left sleeve was a diamond-shaped patch of black cotton.

'We'd like to go over the house again,' Burden said, 'if you wouldn't mind leaving me the key.'

'I don't care what you do,' Parsons said. 'The minister's asked me to Sunday dinner. I shan't be back till this afternoon.' He began to clear his breakfast things from the table, putting the teapot, the marmalade jar away carefully in the places the dead woman had appointed for them. Burden watched him pick up the Sunday paper, unopened and unread, and tip his toast crusts on it before depositing it in a bucket beneath the sink. 'I'm selling this place as soon as I can,' he said.

'My wife thought of going along to the service,' Burden said.

Parsons kept his back turned to him. He poured water from a kettle over the single cup, the saucer, the plate.

'I'm glad,' he said. 'I thought people might like to come, people who won't be able to get along to the funeral tomorrow.' The sink was stained with brown now; crumbs and tea-leaves clung along a greasy tide-mark. 'I suppose you haven't got a lead yet? On the killer, I mean.' It was grotesque. Then Burden remembered what this man had read while his wife knitted.

'Not yet.'

He dried the crockery, then his hands, on the tea towel.

'It doesn't matter,' he said wearily. 'It won't bring her back.'

It was going to be a hot day, the first really hot day of the summer. In the High Street the heat was already making water mirages, lakes that sparkled and then vanished as Burden approached; in the road where actual water had lain the night before phantom water gleamed on the tar. Cars were beginning the nose-to-tail pilgrimage to the coast and at the junction Gates was directing the traffic, his arms flailing in blue shirt sleeves. Burden felt the weight of his own jacket.

Wexford was waiting for him in his office. In spite of the open windows the air was still.

'The air conditioning works better when they're shut,' Burden suggested.

Wexford walked up and down, sniffing the sunlight.

'It feels better this way,' he said. 'We'll wait till eleven. Then we'll go.'

They found the car Wexford had expected to see, parked discreetly in a lane off the Kingsbrook Road near where it joined the top end of Tabard Road.

'Thank God,' Wexford said almost piously. 'So far so good.'

Parsons had given them the back-door key and they let themselves silently into the kitchen. Burden

154

had thought this house would always be cold, but now, in the heat of the day, it felt stuffy and smelt of stale food and frowsty unwashed linen.

The silence was absolute. Wexford went into the hall, Burden following. They trod carefully lest the old boards should betray them. Parsons' jacket and raincoat hung on the hallstand, and on the little square table among a pile of circulars, a dirty handkerchief and a heap of slit envelopes, something gleamed. Burden came closer and stared, knowing better than to touch it. He pushed the other things aside and together they looked at a key with a horseshoe charm on the end of a silver chain.

'In here,' Wexford whispered, mouthing the words and making no sound.

Mrs Parsons' drawing-room was hot and dusty, but nothing was out of place. Wexford's searchers had replaced everything as they had found it, even to the vase of plastic roses that screened the grate. The sun, streaming through closed windows, showed a myriad dance of dust particles in its shafts. Otherwise all was still.

Wexford and Burden stood behind the door, waiting. It seemed like an age before anything happened at all. Then, when it did, Burden could hardly believe his eyes.

The bay window revealed a segment of deserted street, bright grey in the strong light and sharply cut by the short shadows of trees in the gardens opposite. There was no colour apart from this grey and sunlit green. Then, from the right-hand side, as if into a film shot, a woman appeared walking quickly. She was as gaudy as a kingfisher, a technicolor queen in orange and jade. Her hair, a shade darker than her shirt, swung across her face like heavy drapery. She pushed open the gate, her nails ten garnets on the peeling wood, and scuttled out of sight towards the back door. Helen Missal had come at last to her schoolfellow's house.

Wexford laid his finger unnecessarily to his lips. He gazed upwards at the ornate ceiling. From high above them came a faint footfall. Someone else had heard the high heels of their visitor.

Through the crack between the door and its frame, a quarter-inch-wide slit, Burden could see a knife-edge section of staircase. Up till now it had been empty, a vertical line of wallpaper above wooden banister. He felt the sweat start in his armpits. A stair squeaked and at the same moment a hinge gave a soft moan as the back door swung open.

Burden kept his eyes on the bright, sword-like line. He tensed, scarcely daring to breathe, as the wallpaper and the wood were for a second obscured by a flash of black hair, dark cheek, white shirt shadowed with blue. Then, no more. He was not even certain where the two met, but it was not far from where he stood, and he felt rather than heard their meeting, so heavy and so desperate had the silence become.

Four people alone in the heat. Burden found himself praying that he could keep as still and at the same time as alert as Wexford. At last the heels tapped again. They had moved into the dining-room.

It was the man who spoke first and Burden had to strain to hear what he said. His voice was low and held under taut control.

'You should never have come here,' Douglas Quadrant said.

'I had to see you.' She spoke with loud urgency. 'You said you'd meet me yesterday, but you never came. You could have come, Douglas.'

'I couldn't get away. I was going to, but Wexford came.' His voice died away and the rest of the sentence went unheard.

'Afterwards you could. I know, I met him.'

In the drawing-room Wexford made a small movement of satisfaction as another loose end was tied.

'I thought . . .' They heard her give a nervous laugh, 'I thought I'd said too much. I almost did . . .'

'You shouldn't have said anything.'

'I didn't. I stopped myself. Douglas, you're hurting me!'

His reply was something savage, something they couldn't hear.

Helen Missal was taking no pains to keep her voice down and Burden wondered why one of them should show so much caution, the other hardly any.

'Why have you come here? What are you looking for?'

'You knew I would come. When you telephoned me last night and told me Parsons would be out, you knew it . . .'

They heard her moving about the room and Burden imagined the little straight nose curling in disgust, the fingers outstretched to the shabby cushions, drawing lines in the dust on the galleried sideboard. Her laughter, disdainful and quite humourless, was a surprise.

'Have you ever seen such a horrible house? Fancy, she lived here, she actually lived here. Little Meg Godfrey . . .'

It was then that his control snapped and, caution forgotten, he shouted aloud.

'I hated her! My God, Helen, how I hated her! I never saw her, not till this week, but it was she who made my life what it was.' The ornaments on the tiered shelves rattled and Burden guessed that Quadrant was leaning against the sideboard, near enough for him to touch him but for the intervening wall. 'I didn't want her to die, but I'm glad she's dead!'

'Darling!' They heard nothing, but Burden knew as if he could see her that she was clinging to Quadrant now, her arms around his neck. 'Let's go away now. Please. There's nothing here for you.'

He had shaken her off violently. The little cry she gave told them that, and the slithering sound of a chair skidding across lino.

'I'm going back upstairs,' Quadrant said, 'and you must go. Now, Helen. You're as conspicuous in that get-up as...' They heard him pause, picking a metaphor, '... as a parrot in a dovecote.'

She seemed to stagger out, crippled both by her heels and his rejection. Burden, catching momentary sight of flame and blue through the door crack, made a tiny movement, but Wexford's fingers closed on his arm. Above them in the silent house someone was impatient with waiting. The books crashing to the floor two storeys up sounded like thunder when the storm is directly overhead.

Douglas Quadrant heard it too. He leapt for the stairs, but Wexford reached them first, and they confronted each other in the hall. Helen Missal screamed and flung her arm across her mouth.

'Oh God!' she cried, 'Why wouldn't you come when I told you?'

'No one is going anywhere, Mrs Missal,' Wexford said, 'except upstairs.' He picked up the key in his handkerchief.

Quadrant was immobile now, arm raised, for all the world, Burden thought, like a fencer in his white shirt, a hunter hunted and snared. His face was blank. He stared at Wexford for a moment and closed his eyes.

At last he said, 'Shall we go, then?'

They ascended slowly, Wexford leading, Burden at the rear. It was a ridiculous procession, Burden thought. Taking their time, hands to the banister,

158

they were like a troop of house hunters with an order to view or relatives bidden upstairs to visit the bedridden.

At the first turn Wexford said:

'I think we will all go into the room where Minna kept her books, the books that Doon gave her. The case began here in this house and perhaps there will be some kind of poetic justice in ending it here. But the poetry books have gone, Mr Quadrant. As Mrs Missal said, there is nothing here for you.'

He said no more, but the sounds from above had grown louder. Then, as Wexford put his hand to the door of the little room where he and Burden had read the poetry aloud, a faint sigh came from the other side.

The attic floor was littered with books, some open and slammed face-downwards, others on their spines, their pages spread in fans and their covers ripped. One had come to rest against a wall as if it had been flung there and had fallen open at an illustration of a pigtailed girl with a hockey stick. Quadrant's wife knelt among the chaos, clutching a fistful of crumpled coloured paper.

When the door opened and she saw Wexford she seemed to make an immense effort to behave as if this were her home, as if she was hunting in her own attic and the four who entered were unexpected guests. For a second Burden had the fantastic notion that she would attempt to shake hands. But no words came and her hands seemed paralysed. She began to back away from them and towards the window, gradually raising her arms and pressing her be-ringed fingers against her cheeks. As she moved her heels caught one of the scattered books, a girls' annual, and she stumbled, half falling across the larger of the two trunks. A star-shaped mark showed on her cheek-bone where a ring had dug into the flesh.

She lay where she had fallen until Quadrant stepped forward and lifted her against him. Then she moaned softly and turned her face, hiding it in his shoulder.

In the doorway Helen Missal stamped and said, 'I want to go home!'

'Will you close the door, Inspector Burden?' Wexford went to the tiny window and unlatched it as calmly as if he was in his own office. 'I think we'll have some air,' he said.

It was a tiny shoe-box of a room and khaki-coloured like the interior of a shoe-box. There was no breeze but the casement swung open to let in a more wholesome heat.

'I'm afraid there isn't much room,' Wexford said like an apologetic host. 'Inspector Burden and I will stand and you, Mrs Missal, can sit on the other trunk.'

To Burden's astonishment she obeyed him. He saw that she was keeping her eyes on the Chief Inspector's face like a subject under hypnosis. She had grown very white and suddenly looked much more than her actual age. The red hair might have been a wig bedizening a middle-aged woman.

Quadrant had been silent, nursing his wife as if she were a fractious child. Now he said with something of his former scorn:

'Sûreté methods, Chief Inspector? How very melodramatic.'

Wexford ignored him. He stood by the window, his face outlined against clear blue.

'I'm going to tell you a love story,' he said, 'the story of Doon and Minna.' Nobody moved but Quadrant. He reached for his jacket on the trunk where Helen Missal sat, took a gold case from the pocket and lit a cigarette with a match. 'When Margaret Godfrey first came here,' Wexford began, 'she was sixteen. She'd been brought up by old-fashioned people and as a result she appeared prim and shockable. Far from being the London girl come to startle the provinces, she was a suburban orphan thrown on the sophisticated county. Isn't that so, Mrs Missal?'

'You can put it that way if you like.'

'In order to hide her gaucheness she put on a curious manner, a manner compounded of secretive-ness, remoteness, primness. To a lover these can make up a fascinating mixture. They fascinated Doon.

'Doon was rich and clever and good-looking. I don't doubt that for a time Minna – that's the name Doon gave her and I shall refer to her by it – Minna was bowled over. Doon could give her things she could never have afforded to buy and so for a time Doon could buy her love or rather her companion-ship; for this was a love of the mind and nothing physical entered into it.'

Quadrant smoked fiercely. He inhaled deeply and the cigarette end glowed.

'I have said Doon was clever,' Wexford went on. 'Perhaps I should add that brilliance of intellect doesn't always go with self-sufficiency. So it was with Doon. Success, the flowering of ambition, actual achievement depended in this case on close contact with the chosen one – Minna. But Minna was only waiting, biding her time. Because, you see . . .' He looked at the three people slowly and severally. '. . . You *know* that Doon, in spite of the wealth, the intellect, the good looks, had one insurmountable disadvantage, a disadvantage greater than any deformity, particularly to a woman of Minna's background, that no amount of time or changed circumstances could alter.'

Helen Missal nodded sharply, her eyes alight with memory. Leaning against her husband, Fabia Quadrant was crying softly.

'So when Dudley Drury came along she dropped Doon without a backward glance. All the expensive books Doon had given her she hid in a trunk and she never looked at them again. Drury was dull and ordinary – callow is the word, isn't it, Mrs Quadrant? Not passionate or possessive. Those are the adjectives I would apply to Doon. But Drury was without Doon's disadvantage, so Drury won.'

'She preferred me!' Burden remembered Drury's exultant cry in the middle of his interrogation.

Wexford continued:

'When Minna withdrew her love, or willingness to be loved, if you like, Doon's life was broken. To other people it had seemed just an adolescent crush, but it was real all right. At that moment, July 1951, a neurosis was set up which, though quiescent for years, flared again when she returned. With it came hope. They were no longer teenagers but mature. At last Minna might listen and befriend. But she didn't and so she had to die.'

Wexford stepped forward, coming closer to the seated man.

'So we come to you, Mr Quadrant.'

'If it wasn't for the fact that you're upsetting my wife,' Quadrant said, 'I should say that this is a splendid way of livening up a dull Sunday morning.' His voice was light and supercilious, but he flung his cigarette from him across the room and out of the open window past Burden's ear. 'Please go on.'

'When we discovered that Minna was missing – you knew we had. Your office is by the bridge and you must have seen us dragging the brook – you

162

realized that the mud from that lane could be found in your car tyres. In order to cover yourself, for in your "peculiar position" (I quote) you knew our methods, and you had to take your car back to the lane on some legitimate pretext. It would hardly have been safe to go there during the day, but that evening you were meeting Mrs Missal –'

Helen Missal jumped up and cried, 'No, it isn't true!'

'Sit down,' Wexford said. 'Do you imagine she doesn't know about it? D'you think she didn't know about you and all the others?' He turned back to Quadrant. 'You're an arrogant man, Mr Quadrant,' he said, 'and you didn't in the least mind our knowing about your affair with Mrs Missal. If we ever connected you with the crime at all and examined your car, you could bluster a little but your reason for going to the lane was so obviously clandestine that any lies or evasions would be put down to that.

'But when you came to the wood you had to look and see, you had to make sure. I don't know what excuse you made for going into the wood . . .'

'He said he saw a Peeping Tom,' Helen Missal said bitterly.

'. . . but you did go in and because it was dark by then you struck a match to look more closely at the body. You were fascinated as well you might be and you held the match until it burnt down and Mrs Missal called out to you.

'Then you drove home. You had done what you came to do and with any luck nobody would ever connect you with Mrs Parsons. But later when I mentioned the name Doon to you – it was yesterday afternoon, wasn't it? – you remembered the books. Perhaps there were letters too – it was all so long ago. As soon as you knew Parsons would be out of

163

the house you used the dead woman's missing key to get in, and so we found you searching for what Doon might have left behind.'

'It's all very plausible,' Quadrant said. He smoothed his wife's dishevelled hair and drew his arm more tightly around her. 'Of course, there isn't the remotest chance of your getting a conviction on that evidence, but we'll try it if you like.' He spoke as if they were about to embark on some small stratagem, the means of getting home when the car has broken down or a way of getting tactfully out of a party invitation.

'No, Mr Quadrant,' Wexford said, 'we won't waste our time on it. You can go if you wish, but I'd prefer you to stay. You see, Doon *loved* Minna, and although there might have been hatred too, there would never have been contempt. Yesterday afternoon when I asked you if you had ever known her you laughed. That laughter was one of the few sincere responses I got out of you and I knew then that although Doon might have killed Minna, passion would never have turned into ridicule.

'Moreover, at four o'clock this morning I learnt something else. I read a letter and I knew then that you couldn't be Doon and Drury couldn't be Doon. I learnt exactly what was the nature of Doon's disadvantage.'

Burden knew what was coming but still he held his breath.

'Doon is a woman,' Wexford said.

Chapter 15

Love not, love not! The thing you love may change,
The rosy lip may cease to smile on you;
The kindly beaming eye grow cold and strange;
The heart still warmly beat, yet not be true.

Caroline Norton, Love Not

He would have let them arrest him, would have gone with them, Burden thought, like a lamb. Now, assured of his immunity, his aplomb had gone and panic, the last emotion Burden would have associated with Quadrant, showed in his eyes.

His wife pulled herself away from him and sat up. During Wexford's long speeches she had been sobbing and her lips and eyelids were swollen. Her tears, perhaps because crying is a weakness of the young, made her look like a girl. She was wearing a yellow dress made of some expensive creaseless fabric that fell straight and smooth like a tunic. So far she had said nothing. Now she looked elated, breathless with unspoken words.

'When I knew that Doon was a woman,' Wexford said, 'almost everything fell into place. It explained so much of Mrs Parsons' secrecy, why she deceived her husband and yet could feel she wasn't deceiving him; why Drury thought she was ashamed of Doon; why in self-disgust she hid the books...'

And why Mrs Katz, knowing Doon's sex but not

her name, was so curious, Burden thought. It explained the letter that had puzzled them the day before. *I don't know why you should be scared. There was never anything in that* . . . The cousin, the confidante, had known all along. For her it was no secret but a fact of which she had so long been aware that she had thought it unnecessary to tell the Colorado police chief until he had probed. Then it had come out as an artless postscript to the interview.

'Say, what is this?' he had said to Wexford. 'You figured it was a guy?'

Helen Missal had moved back into the shade. The trunk she sat on was against the wall and the sun made a brighter splash on her bright blue skirt, leaving her face in shadow. Her hands twitched in her lap and the window was reflected ten times in her mirror-like nails.

'Your behaviour was peculiar, Mrs Missal,' Wexford said. 'Firstly you lied to me in saying you didn't know Mrs Parsons. Perhaps you really didn't recognize her from the photograph. But with people like you it's so difficult to tell. You cry Wolf! so often that in the end we can only find out what actually happened from the conversation of others or by things you let slip accidentally.'

She gave him a savage glance.

'For God's sake give me one of those cigarettes, Douglas,' she said.

'I'd made up my mind that you were of no significance in this case,' Wexford went on, 'until something happened on Friday night. I came into your drawing-room and told your husband I wanted to speak to his wife. You were only annoyed but Mr Quadrant was terrified. He did something very awkward then and I could see that he was nervous. I assumed when you told me that you'd been out with him that he didn't want us to find out about it. But not a bit of it. He was almost embarrassingly forthcoming.

'So I thought and I thought and at last I realized that I'd been looking at that little scene from upside down. I remembered the exact words I'd used and who I'd been looking at . . . but we'll leave that now and pass on.

'Your old headmistress remembered you, Mrs Missal. Everyone thought you'd go on the stage, she said. And you said the same thing. "I wanted to act!" you said. You weren't lying then. That was in 1951, the year Minna left Doon for Drury. I was working on the assumption that Doon was ambitious and her separation from Minna frustrated that ambition. If I was looking for a spoiled life I didn't have to go any further.

'In late adolescence Doon had been changed from a clever, passionate, hopeful girl into someone bitter and disillusioned. You fitted into that pattern. Your gaiety was really very brittle. Oh, yes, you had your affairs, but wasn't that consistent too? Wasn't that a way of consoling yourself for something real and true you couldn't have?'

She interrupted him then and shouted defiantly:

'So what?' She stood up and kicked one of the books so that it skimmed across the floor and struck the wall at Wexford's feet. 'You must be mad if you think I'm Doon. I wouldn't have a disgusting . . . a revolting thing like that for another woman!' Flinging back her shoulders, projecting her sex at them, she denied perversion as if it would show in some deformity of her body. 'I hate that sort of thing. It makes me feel sick! I hated it at school. I saw it all along, all the time . . .'

Wexford picked up the book she had kicked and took another from his pocket. The bloom on the pale green suède looked like dust.

'This was love,' he said quietly. Helen Missal breathed deeply. 'It wasn't disgusting or revolting. To Doon it was beautiful. Minna had only to listen and be gentle, only to be kind.' He looked out of the window as if engrossed by a flock of birds flying in leaf-shaped formation. 'Minna was only asked to go out with Doon, have lunch with her, drive around the lanes where they'd walked when they were young, listen when Doon talked about the dreams which never came to anything. Listen,' he said. 'It was like this.' His finger was in the book, in its centre. He let it fall open at the marked page and began to read:

> 'If love were what the rose is;
> And I were like the leaf,
> Our lives would grow together
> In sad or singing weather . . .'

Fabia Quadrant moved and spoke. Her voice seemed to come from far away, adding to the stanza out of old memory:

> 'Blown fields or flowerful closes,
> Green pleasure or grey grief . . .'

They were the first words she had uttered. Her husband seized her wrist, clamping his fingers to the thin bones. If he had only dared, Burden thought, he would have covered her mouth.

> 'If love were what the rose is,' she said,
> 'And I were like the leaf.'

She stopped on a high note, a child waiting for the applause that should have come twelve years before and now would never come. Wexford had listened, fanning himself rhythmically with the book. He took the dream from her gently and said:

'But Minna didn't listen. She was bored.' To the woman who had capped his verse he said earnestly, 'She wasn't Minna any more, you see. She was a housewife, an ex-teacher who would have liked to talk about cooking and knitting patterns with someone of her own kind.

'I'm sure you remember,' he said conversationally, 'how close it got on Tuesday afternoon. It must have been very warm in the car. Doon and Minna had had their lunch, a much bigger lunch than Minna would have had here . . . She was bored and she fell asleep.' His voice rose but not in anger. 'I don't say she deserved to die then, but she asked for death!'

Fabia Quadrant shook off her husband's hand and came towards Wexford. She moved with dignity to the only one who had ever understood. Her husband had protected her, Burden thought, her friends had recoiled, the one she loved had only been bored. Neither laughing nor flinching, a country policeman had understood.

'She did deserve to die! She did!' She took hold of the lapels of Wexford's coat and stroked the stuff. 'I loved her so. May I tell you about it because you understand? You see, I had only my letters.' Her face was pensive now, her voice soft and unsteady. 'No books to write.' She shook her head slowly, a child rejecting a hard lesson. 'No poems. But Douglas let me write my letters, didn't you, Douglas? He was so frightened . . .' Emotion came bubbling up, flooding across her face till her cheeks burned, and the heat from the window bathed her.

'There was nothing to be frightened of!' The words were notes in a crescendo, the last a scream. 'If only they'd let me love her . . . love her, love her . . .' She

169

took her hands away and tore them through the crest of hair. 'Love her, love her ...'

'Oh God!' Quadrant said, crouching on the trunk. 'Oh God!'

'Love her, love her ... green pleasure or grey grief ...' She fell against Wexford and gasped into his shoulder. He put his arm around her hard, forgetting the rules, and closed the window.

Still holding her, he said to Burden: 'You can take Mrs Missal away now. See she gets home all right.'

Helen Missal drooped, a battered flower. She kept her eyes down and Burden edged her through the door, out on to the landing and down the hot dark stair. Now was not the time, but he knew Wexford must soon begin:

'Fabia Quadrant, I must tell you that you are not obliged to say anything in answer to the charge but that anything you do say ...'

The love story was ended and the last verse of the poem recited.

Chapter 16

The truth is great and shall prevail.

Coventry Patmore, *Magna est Veritas*

Doon had written precisely a hundred and thirty-four letters to Minna. Not one had ever been sent or even left the Quadrants' library where, in the drawer of a writing-desk, Wexford found them that Sunday afternoon. They were wrapped in a pink scarf and beside them was a brown purse with a gilt clip. He had stood on this very spot the night before, all unknowing, his hand within inches of the scarf, the purse and these wild letters.

Scanning them quickly, Burden understood now why Doon had printed the inscriptions in Minna's books. The handwriting daunted him. It was spidery and difficult to decipher.

'Better take them away, I suppose,' he said. 'Are we going to have to read them all, sir?'

Wexford had looked more closely, sifting the significant from the more obviously insane.

'Only the first one and the last two, I fancy,' he said. 'Poor Quadrant. What a hell of a life! We'll take all this lot down to the office, Mike. I've got an uneasy feeling Nanny's listening outside the door.'

Outside, the heat and the bright light had robbed the house of character. It was like a steel engraving. Who would buy it, knowing what it had sheltered? It could become a school, Burden supposed, or an hotel or an old people's home. The aged might not care, chatting, reminiscing, watching television in the room where Fabia Quadrant had written to the woman she killed.

They crossed the lawn to their car.

' "Green pleasure and grey grief",' Wexford said. 'That just about sums this place up.'

He got into the passenger seat and they drove away.

At the police station they were all talking about it, loitering in the foyer. It was an excitement that had come just at the right moment, just when they were growing tired of remarking on the heat-wave. A murderer and a woman at that . . . In Brighton it was one thing, Burden thought, but here! For Sergeant Camb it was making Sunday duty bearable; for green young Gates, who had almost decided to resign, it had tipped the scales in favour of his staying.

As Wexford came in, setting the doors swinging and creating a breeze out of the sultry air, they dispersed. It was as if each had suddenly been summoned to urgent business.

'Feeling the heat?' Wexford snapped. He banged into his office.

The windows had all been left open but not a paper on the desk had stirred.

'Blinds, Mike. Pull down the blinds!' Wexford threw his jacket on to a chair. 'Who in hell left the windows open? It upsets the air conditioning.'

Burden shrugged and pulled down the yellow slats. He could see that the gossip he hated had shaken Wexford into impatient rage. Tomorrow the whole town would seethe with speculation, with wisdom after the event. Somehow in the morning they were going to have to get her into the special court . . . But it was his day off. He brightened as he thought that he would take Jean to the sea.

Wexford had sat down and put the letters, thick as the manuscript of a long novel or an autobiography, Doon's autobiography, on the desk. It was shady in the office now, thin strips of light seeping through the blinds.

'D'you think he knew about it when he married her?' Burden asked. He began to sort through the letters, picking here and there on a legible phrase. He read in a kind of embarrassed wonder, '"Truly you have broken my heart and dashed the wine cup against the wall . . ." '

Cooler now in temperature and temper, Wexford swivelled round in his purple chair.

'God knows,' he said. 'I reckon he always thought he was God's gift to women and marrying him would make her forget all about Minna.' He stabbed at one of the letters with his forefinger. 'I doubt whether the marriage was ever consummated.' Burden looked a little sick, but Wexford went on. '"Even to that other dweller in my gates my flesh has been as an unlit candle . . ." ' He looked at Burden. 'Et cetera, et cetera. All right, Mike, it is a bit repulsive.' If it had been less hot he would have brought his fist down on the desk. Fiercely he added, 'They're going to gobble it up at the Assizes.'

'It must have been terrible for Quadrant,' Burden said. 'Hence Mrs Missal and Co.'

'I was wrong about her. Mrs Missal, I mean. She was really gone on Quadrant, mad for him. When she realized who Mrs P. was and remembered what had happened at school, she thought Quadrant had killed her. Then, of course, she connected it with his behaviour in the wood. Can't you see her, Mike? . . .' Wexford was intent yet far away. 'Can't you imagine her thinking fast when I told her who Mrs P. was? She'd have remembered how Quadrant insisted on going to that lane, how he left her in the car and when he was gone a long time she followed him, saw the match flame under the bushes, called to him perhaps. I bet he was as white as a sheet when he got back to her.

'Then I talked to her yesterday and I caught her unawares. For a split second she was going to tell me about Fabia, about all her ambitions going to pot. She would have told me, too, only Missal came in. She telephoned Quadrant, then, in the five minutes it took me to get to his house and she went out to meet him. I asked her if she was going to the cinema! He didn't turn up. Coping with Fabia, probably. She phoned him again in the evening and told him she knew Fabia was Doon, knew she had had a school-girl crush on Mrs P. Then he must have said he wanted to get into Parsons' house and get hold of the books, just in case we'd overlooked them. Remember, he'd never seen them – he didn't know what was in them. Mrs Missal had seen the church notice-board. It's just by her house. She told Quadrant Parsons would be out . . .'

'And Fabia had a key to Parsons' house,' Burden said. 'The key Mrs P. left in the car before she was killed.'

'Quadrant had to protect Fabia,' Wexford said. 'He couldn't be a husband but he could be a guardian. He had to make sure no one found out what things were really like for him and her. She was mad, Mike, really crazy, and his whole livelihood would have gone up in smoke if it was known. Besides, she had the money. It's only cat's meat what he makes out of his practice compared with what she's got.

'But it's no wonder he was always sneaking off in the evenings. Apart from the fact that he's obviously

174

highly sexed, anything was preferable to listening to interminable stories about Minna. It must have been almost intolerable.'

He stopped for a moment, recalling his two visits to the house. How long had they been married? Nine years, ten? First the hints and the apologies; then the storms of passion, the memories that refused to be crushed, the bitter resentment of a chance infatuation that had warped a life.

With terrible finesse, worse than any clumsiness, Quadrant must have tried to break the spell. Wexford wrenched his thoughts away from those attempts, feeling again the convulsions of the woman in the attic, her heart beating against his chest.

Burden, whose knowledge of the Quadrants was less personal, sensed his chief's withdrawal. He said practically:

'Then Minna came back as Mrs P. Fabia met her and they went driving together in Quadrant's car. He didn't have it on Tuesday, but she did. When she got home on Tuesday night Fabia told him she'd killed Mrs P. What he'd always been afraid of, that her mental state would lead to violence, had actually happened. His first thought must have been to keep her out of it. She told him where the body was and he thought of the car tyres.'

'Exactly,' Wexford said, caught up once more in circumstantial detail. 'Everything I said to him in Parsons' attic was true. He went to get fresh mud in the tyres and to look at the body. Not out of curiosity or sadism – although he must have felt sadistic towards Mrs P. and curious, by God! – but simply to satisfy himself that she *was* there. For all we know Fabia wasn't always lucid. Then Mrs Missal dropped her lipstick. She's what Quadrant calls a happy-go-lucky girl and that was just carelessness.

'He hoped we wouldn't get around to questioning

Fabia, not for some time, at any rate. When I walked into Mrs Missal's drawing-room on Friday night –'

'You spoke to Missal,' Burden interrupted, 'but you were looking at Quadrant because we were both surprised to see him there. You said, "I'd like a word with your wife," and Quadrant thought you were speaking to him.'

'I was suspicious of him until yesterday afternoon,' Wexford said. 'Then when I asked him if he'd known Mrs P. and he laughed I knew he wasn't Doon. I said his laughter made me go cold and no wonder. There was a lot in that laugh, Mike. He'd seen Mrs P. dead and he'd seen her photograph in the paper. He must have felt pretty bitter when he thought of what it was that had driven his wife out of her mind and wrecked his marriage.'

'He said he'd never seen her alive,' Burden said. 'I wonder why not? I wonder why he didn't try to see her.'

Wexford reflected. He folded the scarf and put it away with the purse and the key. In the drawer his fingers touched something smooth and shiny.

'Perhaps he didn't dare,' he said. 'Perhaps he was afraid of what he might do . . .' He took the photograph out, but Burden was preoccupied, looking at another, the one Parsons had given them.

'They say love is blind,' Burden said. 'What did Fabia ever see in her?'

'She wasn't always like that,' Wexford said. 'Can't you imagine that a rich, clever, beautiful girl like Fabia was, might have found just the foil she was looking for in that . . .' He changed the pictures over, subtracting twelve years. 'Your pal, Miss Clarke, brought me this,' he said. 'It gave me a few ideas before we ever heard from Colorado.'

Margaret Godfrey was one of five girls on the stone seat and she sat in the middle of the row. Those who stood behind rested their hands on the shoulders of the seated. Burden counted twelve faces. The others were all smiling but her face was in repose. The white forehead was very high, the eyes wide and expressionless. Her lips were folded, the corners tilted very slightly upwards, and she was looking at the camera very much as the Gioconda had looked at Leonardo . . .

Burden picked out Helen Missal, her hair in outmoded sausage curls; Clare Clarke with plaits. All except Fabia Quadrant were staring at the camera. She stood behind the girl she had loved, looking down at a palm turned uppermost, at a hand dropping, pulled away from her own. She too was smiling but her brows had drawn together and the hand that had held and caressed hung barren against her friend's sleeve. Burden gazed, aware that chance had furnished them with a record of the first cloud on the face of love.

'Just one more thing,' he said. 'When you saw Mrs Quadrant yesterday you said she was reading. I wondered if . . . I wondered what the book was.'

Wexford grinned, breaking the mood. 'Science fiction,' he said. 'People are inconsistent.'

Then they pulled their chairs closer to the desk, spread the letters before them and began to read.

A New Lease of Death

For
MY FATHER AND SIMON

All the chapter heading quotations are extracts from
The Book of Common Prayer

Chapter 1

The laws of the Realm may punish Christian men
with death for heinous and grievous offences.

The Thirty-nine Articles.

It was five in the morning. Inspector Burden had
seen more dawns than most men, but he had never
quite become jaundiced by them, especially summer
dawns. He liked the stillness, the sight of the little
country town in a depopulated state, the hard blue
light that was of the same shade and intensity as the
light at dusk but without dusk's melancholy.

The two men they had been questioning about last
night's fight in one of Kingsmarkham's cafés had
confessed separately and almost simultaneously just
a quarter of an hour before. Now they were locked
into two stark white cells on the ground floor of this
incongruously modern police station. Burden stood
by the window in Wexford's office, looking at the
sky which had the peculiar greenish tint of aqua-
marine. A flock of birds flying in dense formation
crossed it. They reminded Burden of his childhood
when, as at dawn, everything had seemed bigger,
clearer and of more significance than it did today.
Tired and a little sickened, he opened the window to
get rid of cigarette smoke and the sweaty smell of
youths who wore leather jackets in the height of
summer.

Outside in the corridor he could hear Wexford
saying good night – or good morning – to Colonel
Griswold, the Chief Constable. Burden wondered if
Griswold had guessed when he arrived just before
ten with a long spiel about stamping out hooliganism

1

that he was in for an all-night session. That, he thought unfairly, was where meddling got you.

The heavy front door clanged and Griswold's car started. Burden watched it move off the forecourt, past the great stone urns filled with pink geraniums and into Kingsmarkham High Street. The Chief Constable was driving himself. Burden saw with approval and grudging amusement that Griswold drove at just about twenty-eight miles per hour until he reached the black and white derestriction sign. Then the car gathered speed and flashed away out of sight along the empty country road that led to Pomfret.

He turned round when he heard Wexford come in. The Chief Inspector's heavy grey face was a little greyer than usual, but he showed no other sign of tiredness and his eyes, dark and hard as basalt, showed a gleam of triumph. He was a big man with big features and a big intimidating voice. His grey suit – one of a series of low fastening, double-breasted affairs – appeared more shabby and wrinkled than ever today. But it suited Wexford, being not unlike an extension of his furrowed pachydermatous skin.

'Another job jobbed,' he said, 'as the old woman said when she jobbed the old man's eye out.'

Burden bore with such vulgarisms stoically. He knew that they were meant to horrify him; they always succeeded. He made his thin lips crease into a tight smile. Wexford handed him a blue envelope and he was glad of the diversion to hide his slight embarrassment.

'Griswold's just given me this,' Wexford said. 'At five in the morning. No sense of timing.'

Burden glanced at the Essex postmark.

'Is that the man he was on about earlier, sir?'

'Well, I don't have fanmail from beautiful olde

2

worlde Thringford as a general rule, do I, Mike? This is the Rev. Mr Archery all right, taking advantage of the Old Pals' Act.' He lowered himself into one of the rather flimsy chairs and it gave the usual protesting creak. Wexford had what his junior called a love-hate relationship with those chairs and indeed with all the aggressively modern furnishings of his office. The glossy block floor, the square of nylon carpet, the chairs with their sleek chrome legs, the primrose venetian blinds – all these in Wexford's estimation were not 'serviceable', they were dust-traps and they were 'chichi'. At the same time he took in them an enormous half-secret pride. They had their effect. They served to impress visiting strangers such as the writer of this letter Wexford was now taking from its envelope.

It too was written on rather thick blue paper. In a painfully authentic upper-class accent, the Chief Inspector said affectedly, 'May as well get on to the Chief Constable of Mid-Sussex, my dear. We were up at Oxford together, don't you know?' He squeezed his face into a kind of snarling grin. 'All among the bloody dreaming spires,' he said. 'I hate that sort of thing.'

'Were they?'

'Were they what?'

'At Oxford together?'

'I don't know. Something like that. It may have been the playing fields of Eton. All Griswold said was, "Now we've got those villains wrapped up, I'd like you to have a look at a letter from a very good friend of mine called Archery. Excellent fellow, one of the best. This enclosure's for you. I'd like you to give him all the help you can. I've a notion it's got something to do with that scoundrel Painter."'

'Who's Painter?'

'Villain who got the chop about fifteen or sixteen

years ago,' said Wexford laconically. 'Let's see what the parson has to say, shall we?'

Burden looked over his shoulder. The letter was headed St Columba's Vicarage, Thringford, Essex. The Greek e's awakened in him a small hostility. Wexford read it aloud.

'"Dear sir, I hope you will forgive me for taking up your valuable time . . ." Don't have much choice, do I? ". . . but I regard this matter as being of some urgency. Col. Griswold, the Chief Constable of blah blah blah and so on, has very kindly told me you are the gentleman who may be able to assist me in this problem so I am taking the liberty, having first consulted him, of writing to you."' He cleared his throat and loosened his crumpled grey tie. 'Takes a hell of a time coming to the point, I must say. Ah, here we go. "You will remember the case of Herbert Arthur Painter . . ." I *will*. "I understand you were in charge of it. I therefore supposed I should come to you before pursuing certain enquiries which, much against my will, I am compelled to make."'

'Compelled?'

'That's what the man says. Doesn't say why. The rest's a load of compliments and can he come and see me tomorrow – no, today. He's going to phone this morning, but he "anticipates my willingness to meet him".' He glanced at the window to where the sun was coming up over York Street and with one of his distorted quotations, said, 'I suppose he's sleeping in Elysium at this moment, crammed with distressful cold mutton or whatever parsons go to bed on.'

'What's it all about?'

'O God, Mike, it's obvious, isn't it? You don't want to take any notice of this "being compelled" and "against his will" stuff. I don't suppose his stipend amounts to much. He probably writes true crime

4

stories in between early Communion and the Mothers' Meeting. He must be getting desperate if he reckons on titillating the mass appetite by resurrecting Painter.'

Burden said thoughtfully, 'I seem to remember the case. I'd just left school . . .'

'And it inspired your choice of a career, did it?' Wexford mocked. '"What are you going to be, son?" "I'm going to be a detective, Dad." '

In his five years as Wexford's right hand man, Burden had grown immune to his teasing. He knew he was a kind of safety valve, the stooge perhaps on whom Wexford could vent his violent and sometimes shocking sense of humour. The people of this little town, indiscriminately referred to by Wexford as 'our customers', had, unless suspected of felony, to be spared. Burden was there to take the overflow of his chief's rage, ridicule and satire. Now he was cast as the sponge to soak up the scorn that was rightly the due of Griswold and Griswold's friend.

He looked shrewdly at Wexford. After a trying, frustrating day and night, this letter was the last straw. Wexford was suddenly tense with irritation, his skin more deeply wrinkled than usual, his whole body flexed with the anger that would not suffer fools gladly. That tension must find release.

'This Painter thing,' Burden said slyly, slipping into his role of therapist, 'a bit run of the mill, wasn't it? I followed it in the papers because it was the big local sensation. I don't remember it was remarkable in any other way.'

Wexford slipped the letter back into its envelope and put it in a drawer. His movements were precise and under a tight control. One wrong word, Burden thought, and he'd have torn it up, chucked the pieces on the floor and left them to the mercy of the cleaner. His words had apparently been as right as possible under the circumstances for Wexford said in a sharp cool voice, 'It was remarkable to me.'

'Because you handled it?'

'Because it was the first murder case I ever handled on my own. It was remarkable to Painter because it hanged him and to his widow, I daresay. I suppose it shook her a bit as far as anything could shake that girl.'

Rather nervously Burden watched him observe the cigarette burn one of the men they had been interviewing had made in the lemon-coloured leather of a chair seat. He waited for the explosion. Instead Wexford said indifferently:

'Haven't you got a home to go to?'

'Too late now,' said Burden, stifling a yawn that threatened. 'Besides, my wife's away at the seaside.'

A strongly uxorious man, he found his bungalow like a morgue when Jean and the children were absent. This was a side of his character that afforded Wexford many opportunities for quips and snide remarks, this coupled with his comparative youth, his stolid stick-in-the-mud nature and a certain primness of outlook. But all Wexford said was, 'I forgot.'

He was good at his job. The big ugly man respected him for that. Although he might deride, Wexford appreciated the advantage of having a deputy whose grave good looks were attractive to women. Seated opposite that ascetic face, warmed by a compassion Wexford called 'softness', they were more inclined to open their hearts than to a majestic fifty-five-year-old heavyweight. His personality, however, was not strong and his superior effaced him. Now, in order to channel off that sharp-edged vitality, he was going to have to risk a rebuke for stupidity.

He risked it. 'If you're going to have to argue the

toss with this Archery, wouldn't it be a good idea if we had a re-cap of the facts?'

'We?'

'Well, you then, sir. You must be a bit rusty yourself on the case after so long.'

The outburst came with an undercurrent of laughter. 'God Almighty! D'you think I can't see your brain working? When I want a psychiatrist I'll hire a professional.' He paused and the laughter became a wry grin. 'O.K. it might help me . . .' But Burden had made the mistake of relaxing too soon. 'To get the facts straight for Mr Bloody Archery, I mean,' Wexford snapped. 'But there's no mystery, you know, no cunning little red herrings. Painter did it all right.' He pointed eastwards out of the window. The broad Sussex sky was becoming suffused with rose and gold, bands of soft creamy pink like strokes from a watercolour brush. 'That's as sure as the sun's rising now,' he said. 'There never was any doubt. Herbert Arthur Painter killed his ninety-year-old employer by hitting her over the head with an axe and he did it for two hundred pounds. He was a brutal savage moron. I read in the paper the other day that the Russians call anti-social people "unpersons" and that just about describes him. Funny sort of character for a parson to champion.'

'If he's championing him.'

'We shall see,' said Wexford.

They stood in front of the map that was attached to the yellow 'cracked ice' wallpaper.

'She was killed in her own home, wasn't she?' Burden asked. 'One of those big houses off the Stowerton Road?'

The map showed the whole of this rather sleepy country district. Kingsmarkham, a market town of some twelve thousand inhabitants, lay in the centre,

7

its streets coloured in brown and white, its pastoral environs green with the blotches of dark veridian that denoted woodland. Roads ran from it as from the meshy heart of a spider's web, one leading to Pomfret in the South, another to Sewingbury in the North-east. The scattered villages, Flagford, Clusterwell and Forby, were tiny flies on this web.

'The house is called Victor's Piece,' said Wexford. 'Funny sort of name. Some general built it for himself after the Ashanti Wars.'

'And it's just about here.' Burden put his finger on a vertical strand of the web that led from Kingsmarkham to Stowerton, lying due north. He pondered and light dawned. 'I think I know it,' he said. 'Hideous dump with a lot of green woodwork all over it. It was an old people's home up until last year. I suppose they'll pull it down.'

'I daresay. There are a couple of acres of land to it. If you've got the picture we may as well sit down.'

Burden had moved his chair to the window. There was something consoling and at the same time rejuvenating in watching the unfolding of what was going to be a lovely day. On the fields tree shadows lay long and densely blue and bright new light glinted on the slate roofs of ancient houses. Pity he hadn't been able to get away with Jean. The sunlight and the fresh heady air turned his thoughts towards holidays and prevented him from recalling details of this case that had long ago shocked Kingsmarkham. He searched his memory and found to his shame that he could not even remember the murdered woman's name.

'What was she called?' he asked Wexford. 'A foreign name, wasn't it? Porto or Primo something?'

'Primero. Rose Isabel Primero. That was her married name. Far from being foreign, she'd been

8

brought up at Forby Hall. Her people were by way of being squires of Forby.'

Burden knew Forby well. What tourists there were in this agricultural country with neither seaside nor downs, castles nor cathedrals, made a point of going to Forby. The guide books listed it absurdly as the fifth prettiest village in England. Every local news-agent's contained postcards of its church. Burden himself regarded it with a certain affection because its inhabitants had shown themselves almost totally devoid of criminal tendencies.

'This Archery could be a relative,' he suggested. 'Maybe he wants some gen for his family archives.'

'I doubt it,' Wexford said, basking in the sun like a huge grey cat. 'The only relatives she had were her three grandchildren. Roger Primero, the grandson, lives at Forby Hall now. Didn't inherit it, had to buy it. I don't know the details.'

'There used to be a family called Kynaston at Forby Hall, or so Jean's mother says. Mind you, that was years and years ago.'

'That's right,' Wexford said with a hint of impa-tience in his rumbling bass voice. 'Mrs Primero was born a Kynaston and she was going on for forty when she married Dr Ralph Primero. I imagine her people looked on it a bit askance – this was at the turn of the century, remember.'

'What was he, a G.P.?'

'Some sort of specialist, I think. It was when he retired that they came to live at Victor's Piece. They weren't all that well-off, you know. When the doctor died in the thirties Mrs Primero was left with about ten thousand pounds to live on. There was one child of the marriage, a son, but he'd died soon after his father.'

'D'you mean she was living alone in that great place? At her age?'

Wexford pursed his lips, reminiscing. Burden knew his chief's almost supernatural memory. When he was sufficiently interested he had the nearest thing to total recall. 'She had one maid,' Wexford said. 'Her name was – is, she's still alive – her name was Alice Flower. She was a good bit younger than her employer, seventy odd, and she'd been with Mrs Primero for about fifty years. A real ancient retainer of the old school. Living like that, you might think they'd have become friends rather than mistress and servant, but Alice kept to her place and they were "Madam" and "Alice" to each other till the day Mrs Primero died. I knew Alice by sight. She was quite a local character when she came into town to do their shopping, particularly when Painter started bringing her in in Mrs Primero's Daimler. D'you remember how nursemaids used to look? No, you wouldn't. You're too young. Well, Alice always wore a long navy coat and what's called a "decent" navy felt hat. She and Painter were both servants, but Alice put herself miles above him. She'd pull her rank on him and give him his orders just like Mrs Primero herself. He was Bert to his wife and his cronies but Alice called him "Beast". Not to his face, mind. She wouldn't have quite dared that.'

'You mean she was frightened of him?'

'In a way. She hated him and resented his being there. I wonder if I've still got that cutting.' Wexford opened the bottom drawer of his desk, the one where he kept personal, semi-official things, grotesqueries that had interested him. He hadn't much hope of finding what he sought. At the time of Mrs Primero's murder Kingsmarkham police had been housed in an old yellow brick building in the centre of the town. That had been pulled down four or five years ago and replaced by this block of startling modernity on the outskirts. The cutting had very probably got lost

10

in the move from the high pitch pine desk to this one of lacquered rosewood. He leafed through notes, letters, odd little souvenirs, finally surfacing with a grin of triumph.

'There you are, the "unperson" himself. Good-looking if you like the type. Herbert Arthur Painter, late of the Fourteenth Army in Burma. Twenty-five years old, engaged by Mrs Primero as chauffeur, gardener and odd-job man.'

The cutting was from the *Sunday Planet*, several columns of type surrounding a double-column block. It was a clear photograph and Painter's eyes were staring straight at the camera.

'Funny, that,' said Wexford. 'He always looked you straight in the eye. Supposed to denote honesty, if you've ever heard such a load of rubbish.'

Burden must have seen the picture before, but he had entirely forgotten it. It was a large well-made face with a straight though fleshy nose, spread at the nostrils. Painter had the thick curved lips that on a man are a coarse parody of a woman's mouth, a flat high brow and short tightly waving hair. The waves were so tightly crimped that they looked as if they must have pulled the skin and pained the scalp.

'He was tall and well-built,' Wexford went on. 'Face like a handsome overgrown pug, don't you think? He'd been in the Far East during the war, but if the heat and the privation had taken it out of him it didn't show by then. He had a sort of glistening good health about him like a shire horse. Sorry to use all these animal metaphors, but Painter was like an animal.'

'How did Mrs Primero come to take him on?'

Wexford took the cutting from him, looked at it for a moment and folded it up.

'From the time the doctor died,' he said, 'until 1947 Mrs Primero and Alice Flower struggled to keep the

11

place going, pulling up a few weeds here and there, getting a man in when they wanted a shelf fixed. You can imagine the kind of thing. They had a succession of women up from Kingsmarkham to help with the housework but sooner or later they all left to go into the factories. The place started going to rack and ruin. Not surprising when you think that by the end of the war Mrs Primero was in her middle eighties and Alice nearly seventy. Besides, leaving her age out of it, Mrs Primero never touched the place as far as housework went. She hadn't been brought up to it and she wouldn't have known a duster from an antimacassar.'

'Bit of a tartar, was she?'

'She was what God and her background had made her,' Wexford said gravely but with the faintest suspicion of irony in his voice. 'I never saw her till she was dead. She was stubborn, a bit mean, what nowadays is called "reactionary", inclined to be an autocrat and very much monarch of all she surveyed. I'll give you a couple of examples. When her son died he left his wife and kids very badly off. I don't know the ins and outs of it, but Mrs Primero was quite willing to help financially provided it was on her terms. The family was to come and live with her and so on. Still, I daresay she couldn't afford to keep up two establishments. The other thing was that she'd been a very keen churchwoman. When she got too old to go she insisted on Alice going in her place. Like a sort of whipping boy. But she had her affections. She adored the grandson, Roger, and she had one close friend. We'll come to that later.

'As you know, there was an acute housing short-age after the war and a hell of a servant problem too. Mrs Primero was an intelligent old woman and she got to thinking how she could use one to solve the other. In the grounds of Victor's Piece was a coach house with a sort of loft over the top of it. The place for the coach was used to house the aforesaid Daimler. No one had driven it since the doctor died – Mrs Primero couldn't drive and, needless to say, Alice couldn't either. There was precious little petrol about but you could get your ration, enough to do the shopping and take a couple of old dears for a weekly jaunt around the lanes.'

'So Alice was that much of a friend?' Burden put in.

Wexford said solemnly, 'A lady can be accompanied by her maid when she goes driving. Anyway, Mrs Primero put an advert in the Kingsmarkham *Chronicle* for a young able-bodied man, willing to do the garden, perform odd jobs, maintain and drive the car in exchange for a flat and three pounds a week.'

'*Three pounds?*' Burden was a non-smoker and no lover of extravagant living, but he knew from doing his wife's weekend shopping what a little way three pounds went.

'Well, it was worth a good bit more in those days, Mike,' Wexford said almost apologetically. 'Mrs Primero had the loft painted up, divided into three rooms and piped for water. It wasn't Dolphin Square but, God, people were glad of one room back in 1947! She got a lot of answers but for some reason – God knows *what* reason – she picked Painter. At the trial Alice said she thought the fact that he had a wife and a baby daughter would keep him steady. Depends what you mean by steady, doesn't it?'

Burden shifted his chair out of the sun. 'Was the wife employed by Mrs Primero too?'

'No, just Painter. She'd got this little kid, you see. She was only about two when they came. If she'd worked up at the house she'd have had to bring the child with her. Mrs Primero would never have stood for that. As far as she was concerned between her

13

and the Painters there was a great gulf fixed. I
gathered she'd hardly exchanged more than a couple
of words with Mrs Painter all the time Painter was
there and as for the little girl – her name was
Theresa, I think – she barely knew of her existence.'

'She doesn't sound a very nice sort of woman,'
Burden said doubtfully.

'She was typical of her age and class,' Wexford
said tolerantly. 'Don't forget she was a daughter of
the lord of the manor when lords of the manor still
counted for something. To her Mrs Painter was
comparable to a tenant's wife. I've no doubt that if
Mrs Painter had been ill she'd have sent old Alice
over with a bowl of soup and some blankets. Besides,
Mrs Painter kept herself to herself. She was very
pretty, very quiet and with a sort of deadly respectability about her. She was a bit scared of Painter
which wasn't hard to understand, she being so small
and Painter such a great hulking brute. When I
talked to her after the murder I noticed she'd got
bruises on her arm, too many bruises for her just to
have got them through the usual kitchen accidents,
and I wouldn't mind betting her husband used to
knock her about.'

'So, in fact,' Burden said, 'they were two completely separate units. Mrs Primero and her maid
living alone at Victor's Piece, the Painter family in
their own home at the bottom of the garden.'

'I don't know about "bottom of the garden". The
coach house was about a hundred feet from the back
door of the big house. Painter only went up there to
carry in the coal and receive his instructions.'

'Ah,' said Burden, 'there was some complicated
business about coal, I seem to remember. Wasn't it
more or less the crux of the whole thing?'

'Painter was supposed to chop wood and carry
coal,' Wexford continued. 'Alice was past carrying

14

coal and Painter was supposed to bring a scuttleful at mid-day – they never lit a fire before that – and another one at six-thirty. Now, he never objected to the gardening or the car maintenance, but for some reason he drew the line at the coal. He did it – apart from frequent lapses – but he was always grumbling about it. The mid-day duty cut across his dinner time, he said, and he didn't like turning out on winter evenings. Couldn't he bring two scuttles at eleven? But Mrs Primero wouldn't have that. She said she wasn't going to have her drawing room turned into a railway yard.'

Burden smiled. His tiredness had almost worn off. Given breakfast, a shave and a shower down, he would be a new man. He glanced at his watch, then across the High Street to where the blinds were going up on the Carousel Café.

'I could do with a cup of coffee,' he said.

'Two minds with but a single thought. Root someone out and send them over.'

Wexford stood up and stretched, tightened his tie and smoothed back the hair that was too sparse to become untidy. The coffee arrived in wax cups with plastic spoons and little cubes of wrapped sugar.

'That's better,' said Wexford. 'D'you want me to go on?' Burden nodded.

'By September 1950 Painter had been working for Mrs Primero for three years. The arrangement appeared to work pretty well apart from the difficulties Painter made about the coal. He never brought it in without complaining and he was always asking for a rise.'

'I suppose he thought she was rolling in money?'

'Of course, he couldn't have known what she'd got in the bank or in shares or whatever it was. On the other hand it was an open secret she kept money in the house.'

'In a safe, d'you mean?'

'Not on your life. You know these old girls. Some of it was in drawers stuffed into paper bags, some of it in old handbags.'

With a feat of memory Burden said suddenly, 'And one of those handbags contained *the* two hundred pounds?'

'It did,' Wexford said grimly. 'Whatever she might have been able to afford, Mrs Primero refused to raise Painter's wages. If he didn't like the set-up he could go, but that would mean giving up the flat.

'Being a very old woman, Mrs Primero felt the cold and she liked to start fires in September. Painter thought this unnecessary and he made the usual fuss about it . . .'

He stopped as the telephone rang and he took the receiver himself. Burden had no idea from Wexford's reiterated, 'Yes, yes . . . all right,' who it could be. He finished his coffee with some distaste. The rim of the wax cup had become soggy. Wexford dropped the phone.

'My wife,' he said. 'Am I dead? Have I forgotten I've got a home of my own? She's run out of house-keeping and she can't find the cheque book.' He chuckled, felt in his pocket and produced it. 'No wonder. I'll have to nip back.' He added with sudden kindness, 'Go home and have a bit of shut-eye, why don't you?'

'I don't like being left in the air,' Burden grumbled. 'Now I know how my kids feel when I break off in the middle of a bedtime story.'

Wexford began bundling things into his briefcase.

'Leaving out all the circumstantial stuff,' he said, 'there isn't much more. I told you it was straight-forward. It was the evening of September 24th it happened, a cold wet Sunday. Mrs Primero had sent Alice off to church. She went at about a quarter past

16

six, Painter being due to bring the coal at half past. He brought it all right and departed two hundred pounds to the good.'

'I'd like to hear the circumstantial stuff,' Burden said.

Wexford was at the door now.

'To be continued in our next.' He grinned. 'You can't say I'm leaving you in suspense.' The grin faded and his face hardened. 'Mrs Primero was found at seven. She was in the drawing room lying on the floor by the fireplace in a great pool of blood. There was blood on the walls and on her armchair, and in the hearth was a blood-stained wood chopper.'

Chapter 2

When sentence is given upon him let him be
condemned ... let his children be fatherless and his
wife a widow.

Psalm 109, appointed for the 22nd Day.

The nap Wexford had prescribed for him would
have been attractive on a dull day, but not this
morning when the sky was blue and cloudless and
the sun promised tropical heat by mid-day. Moreover, Burden remembered that he had not made his
bed for three days. Better have that shower and that
shave instead.

After a canteen breakfast of two eggs and a couple
of rashers of the greenback he liked, he had made up
his mind what he was going to do. An hour could
easily be spared. He drove northwards along the
High Street with all the car windows down, past the
shops, over the Kingsbrook Bridge, past the Olive
and Dove and out on to the Stowerton Road. Apart
from a new house here and there, a supermarket on
the site of the old police station, and aggressive road
signs all over the place, things had not changed
much in sixteen years. The meadows, the tall trees
burdened with the heavy foliage of July, the little
weatherboard cottages were much the same as when
Alice Flower had seen them on her shopping trips in
the Daimler. There would have been less traffic, then,
he thought. He braked, pulled in and raised his
eyebrows at the youth on a motor-bike who, overtak-
ing the oncoming stream, had missed him by inches.

The lane where Victor's Piece was must be somewhere about here. Those circumstantial details Wex-

18

ford had been so tantalising about were coming back
to him from his own memory. Surely he had read
about a bus stop and a telephone box at the end of
the lane? Would these be the meadows he remembered reading that Painter had crossed, desperate to
conceal a bundle of blood-stained clothing?

Here was the phone box now. He indicated left
and turned slowly into the lane. For a short way its
surface was metalled, then it petered out into a track
ending in a gate. There were only three houses: a
white-plastered semi-detached pair and opposite them
the late Victorian pile he had described as 'a hideous
dump'.

He had never been as near to it as this before, but
he saw nothing to make him change his opinion. The
roof of grey slates had been constructed – tortured
almost – into a number of steep gables. Two of these
dominated the front of the house, but there was a
third on the right hand side and out of it grew
another smaller one that apparently overlooked the
back. Each gable was criss-crossed with timbering,
some of it inexpertly carved into chevrons and all
painted a dull bottle green. In places the plaster
between the wood had fallen away, exposing rough
pinkish brickwork. Ivy, of the same shade of green,
spread its flat leaves and its rope-like grey tendrils
from the foot of the downstairs windows to the
highest gable where a lattice flapped open. There it
had crept and burrowed into the mealy wall, prising
the window frame away from the bricks.

Burden observed the garden with a countryman's
eye. Never had he seen such a fine selection of
weeds. The fertile black soil, cultivated and tended
for many years, now nourished docks with leaves as
thick and glossy as rubber plants, puce-headed
thistles, nettles four feet tall. The gravel paths were
choked with grass and mildewed groundsel. Only

the clarity of the air and the soft brilliance of sunlight prevented the place from being actually sinister.

The front door was locked. No doubt this window beside it belonged to the drawing room. Burden could not help wondering with a certain wry humour what insensitive administrator had decreed that this scene of an old woman's murder should be for years the home – indeed the last refuge – of other old women. But they were gone now. The place looked as if it had been empty for years.

Through the window he could see a large shadowy room. In the grate of the amber-coloured marble fireplace someone had prudently placed crumpled newspaper to catch the drifts of soot. Wexford had said there had been blood all over that fireplace. There, just in front of the copper kerb, was where the body must have lain.

He made his way round the side, pushing through a shrubbery where elders and strong little birches were threatening to oust the lilac. The panes in the kitchen casement were blurred with dirt and there was no kitchen door, only a back door that apparently opened off the end of the central passage. The Victorians, he reflected, were not too hot on design. Two doors with a straight passage between them! The draught would be appalling.

By now he was in the back garden but he literally could not see the wood for the trees. Nature had gone berserk at Victor's Piece and the coach house itself was almost totally obscured by creeper. He strolled across the shady flagged yard, made cool by the jutting walls of the house, and found himself skirting a conservatory, attached apparently to a kind of morning or breakfast room. It housed a vine, long dead and quite leafless.

So that was Victor's Piece. Pity he couldn't get

inside, but he would, in any case, have to get back. Out of long habit – and partly to set a good example – he had closed all the windows of his car and locked the doors. Inside it was like an oven. He drove out of the broken gateway, into the lane and joined the traffic stream on the Stowerton road.

A greater contrast between the building he had left and the building he entered could hardly have been found. Fine weather suited Kingsmarkham Police Station. Wexford sometimes said that the architect of this new building must have designed it while holidaying in the South of France. It was white, boxy, unnecessarily vast and ornamented here and there with frescoes that owed something to the Elgin marbles.

On this July morning its whiteness glared and glistened. But if its façade seemed to welcome and bask in the sun its occupants did not. There was far too much glass. All right, said Wexford, for hothouse plants or tropical fish, but a mixed blessing for an elderly Anglo-Saxon policeman with high blood pressure and a low resistance to heat. The telephone receiver slid about in his large hand and when he had finished talking to Henry Archery he pulled down the venetian blinds.

'Heat wave's coming,' he said to Burden. 'I reckon your wife's picked a good week.'

Burden looked up from the statement he had begun to read. Lean as a greyhound, his face thin and acute, he often had the hound's instinct for scenting the unusual, coupled with a man's eager imagination.

'Things always seem to happen in a heat wave,' he said. 'Our sort of things. I mean.'

'Get away,' said Wexford. 'Things are always

21

happening around here.' He raised his spiky tooth-brush brows. 'What's happening today,' he said, 'is Archery. He's coming at two.'

'Did he say what it's all about?'

'He's leaving that for this afternoon. Very la-di-da manner he's got with him. All part of the mystique of how to be a gentleman on nothing a year. One thing, he's got a transcript of the trial so I shan't have to go through the whole thing again.'

'That'll have cost him something. He must be keen.'

Wexford looked at his watch and rose. 'Got to get over to the court,' he said. 'Polish off those villains who lost me my night's sleep. Look, Mike, I reckon we deserve a bit of gracious living and I don't fancy the Carousel's steak pie for my lunch. What about popping into the Olive and booking a table for one sharp?'

Burden smiled. It suited him well enough. Once in a blue moon Wexford would insist on their lunching or even dining in comparative style.

'It shall be done,' he said.

The Olive and Dove is the best hostelry in Kingsmarkham that can properly be called an hotel. By a stretch of the imagination the Queen's Head might be described as an inn, but the Dragon and the Crusader cannot claim to be more than pubs. The Olive, as locals invariably call it, is situated in the High Street at the Stowerton end of Kingsmarkham, facing the exquisite Georgian residence of Mr Missal, the Stowerton car dealer. It is partly Georgian itself, but it is a hybrid structure with lingering relics of Tudor and a wing that claims to be pre-Tudor. In every respect it conforms to what nice middle-class people mean when they talk about a 'nice' hotel. There are always three waiters, the chambermaids are staid and often elderly, the bath water is hot, the food as well as can be expected and the A.A. Guide has given it two stars.

Burden had booked his table by phone. When he walked into the dining room just before one he saw to his satisfaction that he had been placed by the High Street window. Here it was just out of the sun and the geraniums in the window box looked fresh and even dewy. Girls waiting on the other side of the street for the Pomfret bus wore cotton frocks and sandals.

Wexford marched in at five past. 'I don't know why he can't get up at half twelve like they do in Sewingbury,' he grumbled. 'He' Burden knew, meant the chairman of the Kingsmarkham bench. 'God, it was hot in court. What are we going to eat?'

'Roast duck,' said Burden firmly.

'All right, if you twist my arm. As long as they don't mix a lot of rubbish up with it. You know what I mean, sweet corn and bananas.' He took the menu, scowling. 'Look at that, Polynesian chicken. What do they think we are, aborigines?'

'I went and had a look at Victor's Piece this morning,' said Burden while they waited for the duck to come.

'Did you now? I see it's up for sale. There's a card in the agent's window with a highly misleading photograph. They're asking six thousand. Bit steep when you think Roger Primero got less than two for it in 1951.'

'I suppose it's changed hands several times since then?'

'Once or twice before the old folks moved in. Thanks,' he said to the waiter. 'No we don't want any wine. Two halves of bitter.' He spread his napkin over his capacious lap and to Burden's controlled distaste sprinkled wing and orange sauce liberally with pepper.

'Was Roger Primero the heir?'

'One of the heirs. Mrs Primero died intestate. Remember I told you she'd only got ten thousand to leave and that was divided equally between Roger and his two younger sisters. He's a rich man now, but however he got his money it wasn't from his grandmother. All kinds of pies he's got his finger in – oil, property development, shipping – he's a real tycoon.'

'I've seen him around, I think.'

'You must have. He's very conscious of his status as a landowner since he bought Forby Hall. Goes out with the Pomfret hounds and all that.'

'How old is he?' Burden asked.

'Well, he was twenty-two when his grandmother was killed. That makes him about thirty-eight now. The sisters were much younger. Angela was ten and Isabel nine.'

'I seem to remember he gave evidence at the trial.'

Wexford pushed his plate away, signalled rather imperiously to the waiter and ordered two portions of apple pie. Burden knew that his chief's notion of gracious living was somewhat limited.

'Roger Primero had been visiting his grandmother that Sunday,' Wexford said. 'He was working in a solicitor's office in Sewingbury at the time and he used to make quite a habit of having Sunday tea at Victor's Piece. Maybe he had his eye on a share of the loot when Mrs Primero went – God knows he hadn't a bean in those days – but he seemed genuinely fond of her. It's certainly a fact that after we'd seen the body and sent for him from Sewingbury as next of kin, we had to restrain him forcibly from going over to the coach house and laying violent hands on Painter. I daresay his grandmother and Alice made a lot of him, you know, buttered him up and waited on him. I told you Mrs Primero had her affections.

There'd been a family quarrel but apparently it didn't extend to the grandchildren. Once or twice Roger had taken his little sisters down to Victor's Piece and they'd all got on very well together.'

'Old people usually do get on well with kids,' said Burden.

'They had to be the right kind of children, Mike. Angela and Isabel, yes, and she had a very soft spot for young Liz Crilling.'

Burden put down his spoon and stared at the Chief Inspector.

'I thought you said you'd read all this up at the time?' Wexford said suspiciously. 'Don't say it was a long time ago. My customers are always saying that to me and it makes me see red. If you read the account of that trial you must remember that Elizabeth Crilling, aged precisely five at the time, found Mrs Primero's body.'

'I assure you I can't remember, sir.' That must have been the day he'd missed, the day he hadn't bothered with the papers because he'd been nervous about an interview. 'She didn't appear at the trial, surely?'

'Not at that age – there are limits. Besides, although she was actually the first to go into the drawing room and come upon the body, her mother was with her.'

'Digressing a little,' Burden said, 'I don't quite get this stuff about the right kind of children. Mrs Crilling lives over there in Glebe Road.' He turned to the window and waved his hand in the direction of the least attractive part of Kingsmarkham where long streets of small terraced brown houses had sprung up between the wars. 'She and the girl live in half a house, they haven't a penny to bless themselves with . . .'

'They've come down a lot,' said Wexford. 'In

25

September 1950 Crilling himself was still alive – he died of T.B. soon after – and they lived opposite Victor's Piece.'

'In one of those white semi-detached places?'

'That's right. A Mrs White and her son lived next door. Mrs Crilling was about thirty at the time, little bit over thirty.'

'You're joking,' said Burden derisively. 'That makes her only in her late forties now.'

'Look, Mike, people can say what they like about hard work and childbearing and all that. I tell you there's nothing like mental illness to make a woman look old before her time. And you know as well as I do Mrs Crilling's been in and out of mental hospitals for years.' He paused as their coffee came and pursed his lips censoriously at the anaemic brown liquid.

'You did say black, sir?' the waiter asked.

Wexford gave a sort of grunt. The church clock struck the last quarter. As the reverberation died away, he said to Burden:

'Shall I keep the parson waiting ten minutes?'

Burden said neutrally, 'That's up to you, sir. You were going to tell me how Mrs Primero and the Crilling woman became friends. I suppose they were friends?'

'Not a doubt of it. Mrs Crilling was ladylike enough in those days and she had a way with her, sycophantic, sucking up, *you* know. Besides, Crilling had been an accountant or something, just enough of a professional man, anyway, in Mrs Primero's eyes to make his wife a lady. Mrs Crilling was always popping over to Victor's Piece and she always took the child with her. God knows, they must have been pretty close. Elizabeth called Mrs Primero "Granny Rose" just as Roger and his sisters did.'

'So she "popped over" that Sunday night and found Granny Rose dead?' Burden hazarded.

It wasn't as simple as that. Mrs Crilling had been making the kid a party frock. She finished it by about six, dressed Elizabeth up and wanted to take her over and show her off to Mrs Primero. Mind you, she and Alice Flower were always at loggerheads. There was a good bit of jealousy there, spheres of influence and so on. So Mrs Crilling waited until Alice had gone off to church and went over alone, intending to go back and fetch the child if Mrs Primero was awake. She dozed a good bit, you see, being so old.

'That first time – it was about twenty past six – Mrs Primero *was* asleep and Mrs Crilling didn't go in. She just tapped on the drawing room window. When the old woman didn't stir she went back and returned again later. By the way, she saw the empty scuttle through the window so she knew Painter hadn't yet been in with the coal.'

'You mean that Painter came in and did the deed between Mrs Crilling's visits?' Burden asked.

'She didn't go back again till seven. The back door had to be left unlocked for Painter, so she and the child went in, called out "yoo-hoo" or some damn' thing, and marched into the drawing room when they didn't get an answer. Elizabeth went first – more's the pity – and Bob's your uncle!'

'Blimey,' said Burden, 'that poor kid!'

'Yes,' Wexford murmured, 'yes . . . Well, much as I should like to while away the rest of the afternoon, reminiscing over the coffee cups, I do have to see this clerical bloke.'

They both got up. Wexford paid the bill, leaving a rather obviously exact ten per cent for a tip.

'I can't see where the parson comes into it at all,' Burden said when they were in the car.

'He can't be an abolitionist because they've done

away with the death penalty. As I say, he's writing a book, expects to make a big thing out of it and that's why he's laid out good money on a transcript.'

'Or he's a prospective buyer of Victor's Piece. He's a haunted house merchant and he thinks he's got another Borley Rectory.'

An unfamiliar car stood on the forecourt of the police station. The numberplate was not local and beside it was a little metal label that bore the name Essex with the country coat of arms of three scimitars on a red field.

'We shall soon know,' said Wexford.

Chapter 3

There are false witnesses risen up against me and
such as speak wrong.

Psalm 27, appointed for the 5th Day.

In general Wexford disliked the clergy. To him the
dog collar was like a slipped halo, indicating a false
saintliness, probable hypocrisy and massive self-
regard. As he saw it vicars were not vicarious
enough. Most of them expected you to worship God
in them.

He did not associate them with good looks and
charm. Henry Archery, therefore, caused him slight
surprise. He was possibly not much younger than
Wexford himself, but he was still slim and exceed-
ingly good-looking, and he was wearing an ordinary
rather light-coloured suit and an ordinary collar and
tie. His hair was thick enough and fair enough for
the grey not to show much, his skin was tanned and
his features had a pure evenly cut regularity.

During the first preliminary small-talk remarks
Wexford had noticed the beauty of his voice. You felt
it would be a pleasure to hear him read aloud. As he
showed him to a chair and sat down opposite him,
Wexford chuckled to himself. He was picturing a
group of tired ageing female parishioners working
their fingers to the bone for the pitiful reward of this
man's smile. Archery was not smiling now and he
looked anything but relaxed.

'I'm familiar with the case, Chief Inspector,' he
began. 'I've read the official transcript of the trial and
I've discussed the whole thing with Colonel Griswold.'

'What exactly do you want to know, then?' Wexford asked in his blunt way.

Archery took a deep breath and said rather too quickly:

'I want you to tell me that somewhere in your mind there is just the faintest doubt, the shadow of a doubt, of Painter's guilt.'

So that was it, or part of it. Burden with his theories that the parson was a Primero relative or seeking to buy the Primero house couldn't have been more wrong. This man, whatever axe he might be grinding, was bent on whitewashing Painter.

Wexford frowned and after a moment said, 'Can't be done. Painter did it all right.' He set his jaw stubbornly. 'If you want to quote me in your book you're quite welcome. You can say that after sixteen years Wexford still maintains that Painter was guilty beyond the shadow of a doubt.'

'What book is this?' Archery inclined his handsome head courteously. His eyes were brown and now they looked bewildered. Then he laughed. It was a nice laugh and it was the first time Wexford had heard it. 'I don't write books,' he said. 'Well, I did once contribute a chapter to a work on Abyssinian cats but that hardly . . .'

Abyssinian cats. Bloody great red cats, thought Wexford. Whatever next? 'Why are you interested in Painter, Mr Archery?'

Archery hesitated. The sun showed up lines on his face that Wexford had not realised were there. Funny, he thought ruefully, how dark women age slower than fair ones but the reverse was true of men.

'My reasons are very personal, Chief Inspector. I can't suppose that they would interest you. But I can assure you that there's no possibility of my publishing anything you tell me.'

30

Well, he had promised Griswold – as to that, he didn't have much choice. Hadn't he, in any case, already resigned himself to giving up most of the afternoon to this clergyman? Weariness was at last beginning to gain a hold on him. He might be equal to reminiscing, going over past familiar words and scenes; on this hot afternoon he was quite unequal to anything more exacting. Probably the personal reasons – and he confessed mentally to an almost childish curiosity about them – would emerge in due course. There was something frank and boyish in his visitor's face which made Wexford think he would not be particularly discreet.

'What d'you want me to tell you?' he asked.

'Why you are so determined Painter was guilty. Of course I don't know any more about this sort of thing than the average layman, but it seems to me there were a good many gaps in the evidence. There were other people involved, people who had quite definite interests in Mrs Primero's death.'

Wexford said coldly, 'I'm fully prepared to go over any points with you, sir.'

'Now?'

'Certainly now. Have you got that transcript with you?'

Archery produced it from a very battered leather briefcase. His hands were long and thin but not womanish. They reminded Wexford of saints' hands in what he called 'churchy' paintings. For five minutes or so he scanned the papers in silence, refreshing his memory on tiny points. Then he put them down and raised his eyes to Archery's face.

'We have to go back to Saturday, September 23rd,' he said, 'the day before the murder. Painter didn't appear with the coal at all that evening. The two old women waited until nearly eight o'clock when the fire was almost out, and Mrs Primero said she would

31

go to bed. Alice Flower was incensed at this and went out to get what she called "a few lumps".'

'That was when she hurt her leg,' Archery said eagerly.

'It wasn't a serious injury but it made Mrs Primero angry and she blamed Painter. At about ten on the following morning she sent Alice down to the coach house to tell Painter she wanted to see him at eleven thirty sharp. He came up ten minutes late, Alice showed him into the drawing room and afterwards she heard him and Mrs Primero quarrelling.'

'This brings me to the first point I want to raise,' Archery said. He flipped through the transcript and, putting his finger at the beginning of a paragraph, passed it to Wexford. 'This, as you know, is part of Painter's own evidence. He doesn't deny the quarrel. He admits that Mrs Primero threatened him with dismissal. He also says here that Mrs Primero finally came round to see his point of view. She refused to give him a rise because she said that would put ideas into his head and he would only ask for another increase in a few months' time. Instead she'd give him what she understood was called a bonus.'

'I remember all that well,' Wexford said impatiently. 'He said she told him to go upstairs and into her bedroom where he'd find a handbag in her wardrobe. He was to bring that handbag down to her and this, he said, he did. There was about two hundred pounds in the handbag and this he could have, take it away in the handbag and look upon it as a bonus on condition he was absolutely circumspect about bringing the coal at the required times.' He coughed. 'I never believed a word of it and neither did the jury.'

'Why not?' Archery asked quietly.

God, thought Wexford, this was going to be a long session.

'Firstly, because the stairs at Victor's Piece run up between the drawing room and the kitchen. Alice Flower was in the kitchen cooking the lunch. She had remarkably good hearing for her age, but she never heard Painter go up those stairs. And, believe me, he was a big heavy lout if ever there was one.' Archery winced faintly at this but Wexford went on, 'Secondly, Mrs Primero would never have sent the gardener upstairs to poke about in her bedroom. Not unless I'm very mistaken in her character. She would have got Alice to have fetched the money on some pretext or other.'

'She might not have wanted Alice to know about it.'

'That's for sure,' Wexford retorted sharply. 'She wouldn't have. I said on some pretext or other.' That made the parson draw in his horns. Wexford said very confidently, 'In the third place Mrs Primero had a reputation for being rather mean. Alice had been with her for half a century but she'd never given Alice anything bar her wages and an extra pound at Christmas.' He jabbed at the page. 'Look, she says so here in black and white. We know Painter wanted money. The night before when he hadn't brought the coal he'd been drinking up at the Dragon with a pal of his from Stowerton. The pal had a motor-bike to sell and he'd offered it to Painter for a bit less than two hundred pounds. Apparently Painter hadn't a hope of getting the money but he asked his friend to hold on to the bike for a couple of days and he'd contact him the minute anything came up. You're saying he got the money before noon on Sunday. I say he stole it after he brutally murdered his employer in the evening. If you're right, why didn't he get in touch with his friend on Sunday afternoon? There's a phone box at the bottom of the lane. We checked with the pal, he didn't move out of his house all day and the phone never rang.'

It was a very tempest of fact and Archery yielded, or appeared to yield, before it. He said only:

'You're saying, I think, that Painter went to the wardrobe after he'd killed Mrs Primero in the evening. There was no blood on the inside of the wardrobe.'

'For one thing he wore rubber gloves to do the deed. Anyway, the prosecution's case was that he stunned her with the flat side of the axe blade, took the money, and when he came downstairs, finished her off in a panic.'

Archery gave a slight shiver. 'Doesn't it strike you as odd,' he then said, 'that if Painter did it he should have been so transparent about it?'

'Some are. They're stupid, you see.' Wexford said it derisively, his mouth curling. He still had no notion what Archery's interest in Painter might be, but that he was pro-Painter was apparent. 'Stupid,' he said again, intent on flicking the clergyman on the raw. Another wince from Archery rewarded him. 'They think you'll believe them. All they've got to say is it must have been a tramp or a burglar and you'll go away satisfied. Painter was one of those. That old tramp thing,' he said. 'When did you last *see* a tramp? More than sixteen years ago, I'll bet.'

'Let's come to the murder itself,' Archery said quietly.

'By all means.' Again Wexford took the transcript, gathering with a quick glance the information he needed. 'Now, then,' he began, 'Painter said he went over to fetch the coal at half six. He remembered the time – twenty-five past six when he left the coach house – because his wife said five minutes to go before the child's bedtime. The time's not all that important, anyway. We know it was between twenty

34

past six and seven o'clock that she was killed. Painter went over, chopped some wood and cut his finger. Or so he said. He certainly did cut his finger – cut it deliberately.'

Archery ignored this last. 'He and Mrs Primero belonged to the same blood group,' he said.

'They were both Group O. They weren't quite so accurate about the minute grouping of blood sixteen years ago as they are now. It was handy for Painter, that. But it didn't do him any real good.'

The clergyman crossed his legs and leaned back. Wexford could see he was trying to appear relaxed and making a poor job of it. 'I believe you personally went to interview Painter after the crime was discovered?'

'We were round at the coach house by a quarter to eight. Painter was out. I asked Mrs Painter where he was and she said he'd come back from the big house some time after six-thirty, washed his hands and gone straight out again. He'd told her he was going to Stowerton to see his friend. We'd only been there about ten minutes when he came in. His story didn't stand up, there was far too much blood around to have come from a cut finger and – well, you know the rest. It's all down there. I charged him on the spot.'

The transcript fluttered a little in Archery's hand. He could not keep his fingers quite steady. 'In evidence,' he said, speaking slowly and evenly, 'Painter said he hadn't been to Stowerton. "I waited at the bus stop at the end of the lane, but the bus never came. I saw the police cars turn into the lane and I wondered what was up. Presently I felt a bit faint on account of my finger bleeding a lot. I came back to my flat. I thought my wife might know what it was all about."' After a pause, he added with a kind of pleading eagerness, 'That doesn't sound like

35

the evidence of the complete moron you make him out to be.'

Wexford answered him patiently as if he were talking to a precocious teenager. 'They edit these things, Mr Archery. They condense them, make them sound coherent. Believe me. You weren't in court and I was. As to the truth of that statement, I was in one of those police cars and I was keeping my eyes open. We overtook the Stowerton bus and turned left into the lane. There wasn't anyone waiting at that bus stop.'

'I imagine you mean that while he said he was at the bus stop he was in fact hiding some clothes.'

'Of course he was hiding the clothes! When he was working he habitually wore a raincoat. You'll see that in Mrs Crilling's evidence and in Alice's. Sometimes it hung in the coach house and sometimes on a hook behind the back door of Victor's Piece. Painter said he had worn it that evening and had left it hanging on the back door. That raincoat couldn't be found. Both Alice and Roger Primero said they remembered having seen it on the back door that afternoon, but Mrs Crilling was certain it wasn't there when she brought Elizabeth in at seven.'

'You finally found the raincoat rolled up in a ball under a hedge two fields away from the bus stop.'

'The raincoat plus a pullover,' Wexford retorted, 'and a pair of rubber gloves. The lot was sodden with blood.'

'But anyone could have worn the raincoat and you couldn't identify the pullover.'

'Alice Flower went so far as to say it looked like one Painter sometimes wore.'

Archery gave a deep sigh. For a time he had been firing questions and statements briskly at Wexford, but suddenly he had fallen silent. Little more than indecision showed on his face. Wexford waited. At last, he thought, Archery had reached a point where it was going to become necessary to reveal those 'personal reasons'. A struggle was going on within him and he said in an artificial tone:

'What about Painter's wife?'

'A wife cannot be compelled to give evidence against her husband. As you know, she didn't appear at the trial. She and the child went off somewhere and a couple of years later I heard she'd married again.'

He stared at Archery, raising his eyebrows. Something he had said had made the clergyman's mind up for him. A slight flush coloured Archery's even tan. The brown eyes were very bright as he leaned forward, tense again.

'That child . . .'

'What of her? She was asleep in her cot when we searched Painter's bedroom and that's the only time I saw her. She was four or five.'

Archery said jerkily, 'She's twenty-one now and she's a very beautiful young woman.'

'I'm not surprised. Painter was a nice enough looking fellow if you like the type, and Mrs Painter was pretty.' Wexford stopped. Archery was a clergyman. Had Painter's daughter taken after her father and somehow come into his care as a result of her transgressions? Archery could be a prison visitor. It was right up his street, Wexford thought nastily. Anger rose in his throat as he wondered if all this sparring discussion had been engineered merely because Archery wanted his help in getting the right psychological approach to a convicted thief or confidence woman. 'What about her?' he snapped. Griswold could go to hell! 'Now come on, sir, you'd better tell me and have done.'

'I have a son, Chief Inspector, an only child. He also is twenty-one . . .'

'Well?'

Obviously the clergyman had difficulty in framing the words. He hesitated and pressed his long hands together. At last he said diffidently and in a low voice, 'He wishes to marry Miss Painter.' When Wexford started and stared at him, he added, 'Or Miss Kershaw, as her legal name now is.'

Wexford was all at sea. He was astonished, a rare thing for him, and he felt a sharp-edged excitement. But he had shown all the surprise he thought consistent with policy and now he spoke soberly.

'You must excuse me, Mr Archery, but I can't see how your son, the son of an Anglican clergyman, came to meet a girl in Miss Painter's – er, Miss Kershaw's – position.'

'They met at Oxford,' Archery said easily.

'At the *university*?'

'That is so. Miss Kershaw is quite an intelligent young woman.' Archery gave a slight smile. 'She's reading Modern Greats. Tipped for a First, I'm told.'

Chapter 4

If any of you know cause or just impediment why these two persons should not be joined together in holy matrimony, ye are to declare it.

The Banns of Marriage.

If he had been asked to predict the future of such a one as Theresa Painter, what would he have foreseen for her? Children like her, Wexford reflected as he recovered from his second shock, children like Painter's little girl started life with a liability and a stain. The surviving parent, well-meaning relatives and cruel schoolfellows often made matters worse. He had hardly thought about the fate of the child until today. Now, thinking quickly, he supposed he would have counted her lucky to have become an anonymous manual worker with perhaps already a couple of petty convictions.

Instead to Theresa Painter had apparently come the greatest blessings of civilised life: brains, advanced education, beauty, friendship with people like this vicar, an engagement to this vicar's son.

Wexford cast his mind back to the first of only three encounters with Mrs Painter. A quarter to eight it had been on that Sunday in September. He and the sergeant with him had knocked on the door at the foot of the coach house stairs and Mrs Painter had come down to let them in. Whatever might have been fashionable in London at that time, the young women of Kingsmarkham were still doing their hair in a big pile on the forehead with tight curls falling to the shoulders. Mrs Painter was no exception. Hers was naturally fair, her face was powdered and her mouth painted diffidently red. Respectable provincial matrons did not go in for eye make-up in 1950 and Mrs Painter was of all things respectable. There seemed to be very little else to her. On her dry fine skin lines had already begun to form, little indentations which marked a regular prudish pursing of the lips, a setting of the chin that accompanied an outraged flounce.

She had the same attitude to the police as others might have to bugs or mice. When they came upstairs she alternated her replies to their questions with reiterated remarks that it was a disgrace to have them in the house. She had the blankest, most obtuse blue eyes he had ever seen on anyone. At no time, even when they were about to take Painter away, did she show the least pity or the least horror, only this fixated dread of what people would think if they found the police had been questioning her husband.

Perhaps she had not been so stupid as he had thought. Somewhere in that pretty respectable mouse and that great hunk of sub-humanity, her husband, must have been the spring from which their daughter drew her intelligence. 'Quite an intelligent girl,' Archery had said casually. Good God, thought Wexford, remembering how he had boasted when his own daughter got eight O Level passes. Good God! What were Modern Greats, anyway? Were they the same as Mods and did that mean Modern Languages? He had a vague idea that this might be the esoteric and deliberately deceptive name given to Philosophy and Political Economy. He wouldn't show his ignorance to Archery. Philosophy! He almost whistled. Painter's daughter reading – yes, that was the term, reading – philosophy! It made you think all right. Why, it made you doubt . . .

'Mr Archery,' he said, 'you're quite sure this *is* Herbert Arthur Painter's girl?'

'Of course I'm sure, Chief Inspector. She told me.' He looked almost defiantly at Wexford. Perhaps he thought the policeman would laugh at his next words. 'She is as good as she is beautiful,' he said. Wexford's expression remained unaltered. 'She came to stay with us at Whitsun. It was the first time we'd seen her, though naturally our son had written to us and told us about her. We took to her at once.

'Chief Inspector, times have changed since I was at college. I had to face the possibility that my son would meet some girl at Oxford, perhaps want to marry her at an age when I'd thought of myself as still a boy and when Orders were a lifetime away. I'd see my friends' children marry at twenty-one and I was prepared to try and manage something for him, give him something to start life on. All I hoped was that the girl would be someone we could like and understand.

'Miss Kershaw – I'll use that name if you don't mind – is just what I would have chosen for him myself, beautiful, graceful, well-mannered, easy to talk to. Oh, she does her best to hide her looks in the uniform they all wear nowadays, long shaggy hair, trousers, great black duffel coat – you know the kind of thing. But they all dress like that. The point is she can't hide them.

'My wife is a little impulsive. She was hinting about the wedding before Theresa had been with us for twenty-four hours. I found it hard to understand why the young people were so diffident about it. Charles's letters had been paeans of praise and I could see they were deeply in love. Then she told us. She came out with it quite baldly. She said – I remember the very words – "I think you ought to know something about me, Mrs Archery. My father's name was Painter and he was hanged for killing an old woman."

'At first my wife didn't believe it. She thought it was some sort of a game. Charles said, "It's true. It doesn't matter. People are what they are, not what their parents did." Then Theresa – we call her Tess – said, "It would matter if he had done it, only he didn't. I told you *why* he was hanged. I didn't mean he'd done it." Then she began to cry.'

'Why does she call herself Kershaw?'

'It's her stepfather's name. He must be a very remarkable man, Chief Inspector. He's an electrical engineer, but ...' You needn't come that rude mechanicals stuff with me, thought Wexford crossly. '... but he must be a most intelligent, perceptive and kind person. The Kershaws have two children of their own, but as far as I can gather, Mr Kershaw has treated Tess with no less affection than his own son and daughter. She says it was his love that helped her to bear – well, what I can only call the stigma of her father's crime when she learnt about it at the age of twelve. He followed her progress at school, encouraged her in every way and fostered her wish to get a County Major Scholarship.'

'You mentioned "the stigma of her father's crime". I thought you said she thinks he didn't do it?'

'My dear Chief Inspector, she *knows he didn't do it*.'

'Wexford said slowly, 'Mr Archery, I'm sure I don't have to tell a man like yourself that when we talk of somebody *knowing* something we mean that what they know is a fact, something that's true beyond a reasonable doubt. We mean that the majority of other people *know* it too. In other words, it's history, it's written down in books, it's common knowledge.' He paused. 'Now I and the Law Lords and the official records and what your son means when he talks about the Establishment, know beyond any reasonable doubt, that Painter did kill Mrs Rose Primero.'

'Her mother told her so,' said Archery. 'She told her that she had absolute irrefutable personal knowledge that Tess's father did not kill Mrs Primero.'

Wexford shrugged and smiled. 'People believe what they want to believe. The mother thought it was the best thing for her daughter. If I'd been in her shoes I daresay I'd have said the same.'

'I don't think it was like that,' Archery said stubbornly. 'Tess says her mother is a very unemotional woman. She never talks about Painter, never discusses him at all. She just says quite calmly, "Your father never killed anybody" and beyond that she won't say any more.'

'Because she can't say any more. Look, sir, I think you're taking a rather romantic view of this. You're visualising the Painters as a devoted couple, kind of merry peasants, love in a cottage and all that. It wasn't like that. Believe me, Painter was no loss to her. I'm certain in my own mind he was in the habit of striking her just when the fancy took him. As far as he was concerned, she was just his woman, someone to cook his meals, wash his clothes and – well,' he added brutally, 'someone to go to bed with.'

Archery said stiffly, 'I don't see that any of that's material.'

'Don't you? You're picturing some sort of declaration of innocence plus incontrovertible proof made to the one person he loved and whom he knew would believe in him. Forgive me, but that's a load of rubbish. Apart from the few minutes when he came back to the coach house to wash his hands – and incidentally hide the money – he was never alone with her. And he couldn't have told her then. He wasn't supposed to know about it. D'you understand me? He could have told her he had done it, he couldn't have told her he had *not*.

'Then we came. We found blood flecks in the sink

and faint blood marks on the kitchen wall where he'd stripped off that pullover. As soon as he came back he took the bandage off his hand to show us the cut and he handed the bandage to his wife. But he didn't speak to her, didn't even appeal to her for support. He made just one reference to her ...'

'Yes?'

'We found the handbag with the money in it under the mattress in their double bed. Why hadn't Painter told his wife if he'd been given that money in the morning? Here it is, find it in your transcript. "I knew the wife would want to get her hooks on it. She was always nagging me to buy things for the flat." That's all he said and he didn't even look at her. We charged him and he said, "O.K., but you're making a big mistake. It was a tramp done it." He came straight down the stairs with us. He didn't kiss his wife and he didn't ask to go in and see his child.'

'She must have seen him in prison?'

'With a prison officer present. Look, sir, you appear to be satisfied and so do all the parties concerned. Surely that's the main thing. You must forgive me if I can't agree with you.'

Silently Archery took a snapshot from his wallet and laid it on the desk. Wexford picked it up. Presumably it had been taken in the vicarage garden. There was a great magnolia tree in the background, a tree as tall as the house it partly concealed. It was covered with waxen cup flowers. Under its branches stood a boy and a girl, their arms round each other. The boy was tall and fair. He was smiling and he was plainly Archery's son. Wexford wasn't particularly interested in him.

The girl's face was in sad repose. She was looking into the camera with large steady eyes. Light-coloured hair fell over her forehead in a fringe and down to the shoulders of a typical under-graduate's

44

shirtwaister, faded, tightly belted and with a crumpled skirt. Her waist was tiny, her bust full. Wexford saw the mother again, only this girl was holding a boy's hand instead of a bloody rag.

'Very charming,' he said dryly. 'I hope she'll make your son happy.' He handed the photograph back. 'No reason why she shouldn't.'

A mixture of emotions, anger, pain, resentment, flared in the clergyman's eyes. Interestedly, Wexford watched him.

'I do not know what or whom to believe,' Archery said unhappily, 'and while I'm in this state of uncertainty, Chief Inspector, I'm not in favour of the marriage. No, that's putting it too coolly.' He shook his head vehemently. 'I'm bitterly, bitterly against it,' he said.

'And the girl, Painter's daughter?'

'She believed – perhaps accepts is the better word – in her father's innocence, but she realises others may not. When it comes to it, I don't think she would marry my son while his mother and I feel as we do.'

'What are you afraid of, Mr Archery?'

'Heredity.'

'A very chancy thing, heredity.'

'Have you children, Chief Inspector?'

'I've got two girls.'

'Are they married?'

'One is.'

'And who is her father-in-law?'

For the first time Wexford felt superior to this clergyman. A kind of *schadenfreude* possessed him. 'He's an architect, as a matter of fact, Tory councillor for the North Ward here.'

'I see.' Archery bowed his head. 'And do your grandchildren already build palaces with wooden bricks, Mr Wexford?' Wexford said nothing. The only sign of his first grandchild's existence was so far envinced in its mother's morning sickness. 'I shall watch mine from their cradle, waiting to see them drawn towards objects with sharp edges.'

'You said if you objected she wouldn't marry him.'

'They're in love with each other. I can't . . .'

'Who's going to know? Palm Kershaw off as her father.'

'I shall know,' said Archery. 'Already I can see Painter when I look at her. Instead of her mouth and her eyes I can see his thick lips and his bloodlust. It's the same blood, Chief Inspector, the blood that mingled with Mrs Primero's, on the floor, on the clothes, down the water pipes. That blood will be in my grandchild.' He seemed to realise that he had allowed himself to be carried away, for he stopped suddenly, blushed, and shut his eyes briefly as if wincing at the sight he had described.

Wexford said gently, 'I wish I could help you, Mr Archery, but the case is close, over, finished. There is nothing more I can do.'

Archery shrugged and quoted softly, almost as if he could not stop himself, '"He took water and washed his hands before the multitude, saying, I am innocent of the blood of this just person . . ."' Then he jumped up, his expression suddenly contrite. 'Forgive me, Chief Inspector. That was an appalling thing to say. May I tell you what I intend to do?'

'Pontius Pilate, that's me,' said Wexford. 'So see you show more respect in future.'

Burden grinned. 'What exactly did he want, sir?'

'Firstly to tell him Painter may have been unjustly executed, which I can't. Damn it all, it would be tantamount to saying I didn't know my job. It was my first murder case, Mike, and it was fortunate for me it was so straightforward. Archery's going to do a spot of enquiry on his own. Hopeless after sixteen years but it's useless telling him. Secondly, he wanted my permission to go around hunting up all the witnesses. Wanted my support if they come round here, complaining and foaming at the mouth.'

'And all he's got to go on,' said Burden thoughtfully, 'is Mrs Painter's sentimental belief in her husband's innocence?'

'Aah, that's nothing! That's a load of hooey. If you got the chop, wouldn't Jean tell John and Pat you were innocent? Wouldn't my wife tell the girls? It's natural. Painter didn't make any last-minute confessions – you know what the prison authorities are like for watching out for things like that. No, she dreamed it up and convinced herself.'

'Has Archery ever met her?'

'Not yet, but he's making a day of it. She and her second husband live in Purley and he's got himself an invite for tea.'

'You say the girl told him at Whitsun. Why has he waited so long? It must be a couple of months.'

'I asked him that. He said that for the first couple of weeks he and his wife just let it ride. They thought the son might see reason. But he wouldn't. He got his father to get hold of a transcript of the trial, nagged him into working on Griswold. Of course he's an only child and as spoilt as they come. The upshot was that Archery promised to start poking his nose into it as soon as he got his fortnight's holiday.'

'So he'll be back?'

'That will depend on Mrs Painter,' said Wexford.

Chapter 5

... That they may see their children christianly and
virtuously brought up.

The Solemnisation of Matrimony.

The Kershaws' house was about a mile from the
town centre, separated from shops, station, cinema
and churches by thousands of other large suburban
villas. For number 20 Craig Hill was large, half-
heartedly Georgian and built of raspberry red brick.
The garden was planted with annuals, the lawn was
cloverfree and the dead heads had been nipped off
the standard rose bushes. On the concrete drive a
boy of about twelve was washing down a large white
Ford.

Archery parked his car at the kerb. Unlike Wexford he had not yet seen the coach house at Victor's
Piece, but he had read about it and it seemed to him
that Mrs Kershaw had climbed high. Sweat started
on his forehead and his upper lip as he got out of the
car. He told himself that it was unusually hot and
that he had always been prone to feel the heat.

'This is Mr Kershaw's house, isn't it?' he asked the
boy.

'That's right.' He was very like Tess, but his hair
was fairer and his nose was freckled. 'The front
door's open. Shall I give him a shout?'

'My name is Archery,' said the clergyman and he
held out his hand.

The boy wiped his hands on his jeans. 'Hallo,' he
said.

By now a little wrinkled man had come down the
porch steps. The bright hot air seemed to hang

between them. Archery tried not to feel disappointment. What had he expected? Certainly not someone so small, so unfinished looking and so wizened as this scrawny creature in old flannels and tieless knitted shirt. Then Kershaw smiled and the years fell from him. His eyes were a bright sparkling blue and his uneven teeth white and clean.

'How do you do?'

'Good afternoon, Mr Archery. I'm very happy to meet you. As a matter of fact I've been sitting in the window, looking out for you.'

In this man's presence it was impossible not to feel hope, cheerfulness almost. Archery detected at once a rare quality in him, a quality he had come upon perhaps only half a dozen times in his life. This was a man who was interested in all things. Energy and enthusiasm radiated from him. On a winter's day he would warm the air. Today, in this heat, his vitality was overwhelming.

'Come inside and meet my wife.' His voice was a hot breeze, a cockney voice that suggested fish and chips, eels and mash and East end pubs. Following him into the square panelled hall, Archery wondered how old he was. Perhaps no more than forty-five. Drive, the fire of life, lack of sleep because sleep wasted time, could prematurely have burnt away his youth. 'We're in the lounge,' he said, pushing open a reeded glass door. 'That's what I like about a day like this. When I get home from work I like to sit by the french windows for ten minutes and look at the garden. Makes you feel all that slogging in the winter was worthwhile.'

'To sit in the shade and look upon verdure?' After the words were out Archery was sorry he had spoken. He didn't want to put this suburban engineer in a false position.

Kershaw gave him a quick glance. Then he smiled

and said easily, 'Miss Austen certainly knew what she was talking about, didn't she?' Archery was overcome. He went into the room and held out his hand to the woman who had got up from an armchair.

'My wife. This is Mr Archery, Rene.'

'How do you do?'

Irene Kershaw said nothing, but holding out her hand, smiled a tight bright smile. Her face was Tess's face as it would be when time had hardened it and finished it. In her youth she had been blonde. Now her hair, evidently set that day and perhaps in his honour, was dyed a dull leaf-brown and arranged in unreal feathery wisps about her forehead and ears.

'Sit down, Mr Archery,' said Kershaw. 'We won't keep you a minute for your tea. Kettle's on, isn't it, Renee?'

Archery sat in an armchair by the window. Kershaw's garden was full of experimental rose pergolas, eruptions of rockery and stone sporting geraniums. He gave the room a quick glance, noting at once its cleanliness and the enormous mass of things which had to be kept clean. Books abounded, Readers' Digests, encyclopaedias, dictionaries, works on astronomy, deep sea fishing, European history. There was a tank of tropical fish on a corner table, several model aircraft on the mantelpiece; stacks of sheet music covered the grand piano, and on an easel was a half-finished, rather charming, portrait in oils of a young girl. It was a large room, conventionally furnished with Wilton carpet and chintz covers, but it expressed the personality of the master of the house.

'We've had the pleasure of meeting your Charlie,' said Kershaw. 'A nice unassuming boy. I liked him.' Charlie! Archery sat very still, trying not to feel affronted. Charles's eligibility, after all, was not in question.

Quite suddenly Renee Kershaw spoke. 'We all like him,' she said. Her accent was just the same as Wexford's. 'But I'm sure I don't know how they plan to manage, what with everything being such an awful price – the cost of living, you know – and Charles not having a job in line ...' Archery felt amazement. Was she really concerned with this trivia? He began to wonder how he would broach the subject that had brought him to Purley. 'I mean where will they live?' Mrs Kershaw asked primly. 'They're just babies really. I mean, you've got to have a home of your own, haven't you? You've got to get a mortgage and ...'

'I think I can hear the kettle, Renee,' said her husband.

She got up, holding her skirt modestly down to cover her knees. It was a very suburban skirt of some permanently pleated material banded in muted blue and heather pink and of dead sexless respectability. With it she wore a short-sleeved pink jumper and around her neck a single string of cultured pearls. If cultured meant tended and nurtured, Archery thought he had never seen such obviously cultured pearls. Each night, he was sure, they were wrapped in tissue and put away in the dark. Mrs Kershaw smelt of talcum powder, some of which lingered in the lines of her neck.

'I don't think we've got to the mortgage stage yet,' said Kershaw when she had gone. Archery gave a wry smile. 'Believe me, Mr Archery, I know you haven't come here just for an in-laws' get-together over the tea cups.'

'I'm finding it more awkward than I thought possible.'

Kershaw chuckled. 'I daresay. I can't tell you

51

anything about Tess's father that isn't common knowledge, that wasn't in the papers at the time. You know that?'

'But her mother?'

'You can try. At times like this women see things through a cloud of orange blossom. She's never been very keen on Tess being an educated woman. She wants to see her married and she'll do her best to see nothing stands in her way.'

'And you, what do you want?'

'Me? Oh, I want to see her happy. Happiness doesn't necessarily begin at the altar.' Suddenly he was brisk and forthright. 'Frankly, Mr Archery, I'm not sure if she can be happy with a man who suspects her of homicidal tendencies before she's even engaged to him.'

'It isn't like that!' Archery hadn't expected the other man to put him on the defensive. 'Your stepdaughter is perfect in my son's eyes. I'm making the inquiries, Mr Kershaw. My son knows that, he wants it for Tess's sake, but he doesn't even know I'm here. Put yourself in my position ...'

'But I *was* in your position. Tess was only six when I married her mother.' He looked quickly at the door, then leaned closer to Archery. 'D'you think I didn't watch her, look out for the disturbance to show itself? When my own daughter was born Tess was very jealous. She resented the baby and one day I found her leaning over Jill's pram striking her on the head with a celluloid toy. Luckily, it *was* a celluloid toy.'

'But, good heavens ...!' Archery felt the pallor drawing at his face muscles.

'What could I do? I had to go to work and leave the children. I had to trust my wife. Then we had a son – I think you bumped into him outside cleaning the car – and Jill resented him in just the same way

52

and with just the same violence. All children behave like this, that's the point.'

'You never saw any more – any more of these tendencies?'

'Tendencies? A personality isn't made by heredity, Mr Archery, but by environment. I wanted Tess to have the best sort of environment and I think I can say, with all due modesty, that she has.'

The garden shimmered in the heat haze. Archery saw things he hadn't noticed at first, chalk lines on the lawn, where, regardless of herbaceous borders, the grass had been marked out for a tennis court; a shambles of rabbit hutches attached to the garage wall; an ancient swing. Behind him on the mantelpiece he saw propped against ornaments two party invitations. A framed photograph above it showed three children in shirts and jeans sprawled on a haystack. Yes, this had been the best of all possible environments for the murderer's orphan.

The door was pushed open and the girl in the portrait came in pushing a tea trolley. Archery who was too hot and troubled to feel hungry, saw with dismay that it was laden with home-baked pastries, strawberries in glass dishes, fairy cakes in paper cases. The girl looked about fourteen. She was not so beautiful as Tess and she wore a bunchy school tunic, but her father's vitality illumined her face.

'This is my daughter Jill.'

Jill sprawled in a chair, showing a lot of long leg.

'Now, sit nicely, dear,' said Mrs Kershaw sharply. She gave the girl a repressive look and began to pour tea, holding the pot with curled fingers. 'They don't realise they're young women at thirteen these days, Mr Archery.' Archery was embarrassed but the girl didn't seem to care. 'You must have one of these cakes. Jill made them.' Unwillingly he took a pastry. 'That's right. I've always said to both my girls, schooling is all very well in its way, but algebra won't cook the Sunday dinner. Tess and Jill are both good plain cooks . . .'

'Mummy! I'm not plain and Tess certainly isn't.'

'You know what I mean. Now don't take me up on everything. When they get married their husbands won't be ashamed to have anybody for a meal.'

'This is my managing director, darling,' said Jill pertly. 'Just cut a slice off him and put it under the grill, will you?'

Kershaw roared with laughter. Then he took his wife's hand. 'You leave Mummy alone.' All this jollity and family intimacy was making Archery nervous. He forced a smile and knew it looked forced.

'What I really mean is, Mr Archery,' said Mrs Kershaw earnestly, 'is that even if your Charlie and my Tessie have their ups and downs at first, Tess hasn't been brought up to be an idle wife. She'll put a happy home before luxuries.'

'I'm sure she will.' Archery looked helplessly at the lounging girl, firmly entrenched in her chair and devouring strawberries and cream. It was now or never. 'Mrs Kershaw, I don't doubt Theresa's suitability as a wife . . .' No, that wasn't right. That was just what he did doubt. He floundered. 'I wanted to talk to you about . . .' Surely Kershaw would help him? Jill's brows drew together in a small frown and her grey eyes stared steadily at him. Desperately he said, 'I wanted to speak to you alone.'

Irene Kershaw seemed to shrink. She put down her cup, laid her knife delicately across her plate and, folding her hands in her lap, looked down at them. They were poor hands, stubby and worn, and she wore just one ring, her second wedding ring.

'Haven't you got any homework to do, Jill?' she asked in a whisper. Kershaw got up, wiping his mouth.

'I can do it in the train,' said Jill.

Archery had begun to dislike Kershaw, but he could not help admiring him. 'Jill, you know all about Tess,' Kershaw said, 'what happened when she was little. Mummy has to discuss it with Mr Archery. Just by themselves. We have to go because, although we're involved, it's not quite our business. Not like it is theirs. O.K.?'

'O.K.,' said Jill. Her father put his arm round her and took her into the garden.

He had to begin, but he was hot and stiff with awkwardness. Outside the window Jill had found a tennis racquet and was practising shots against the garage wall. Mrs Kershaw picked up a napkin and dabbed at the corners of her mouth. She looked at him, their eyes met, and she looked away. Archery felt suddenly that they were not alone, that their thoughts concentrated on the past, had summoned from its prison grave a presence of brute strength that stood behind their chairs, laying a bloody hand on their shoulders and listening for judgment.

'Tess says you have something to tell me,' he said quietly. 'About your first husband.' She was rolling the napkin now, squashing it, until it was like a golf-ball. 'Mrs Kershaw, I think you ought to tell me.'

The paper ball was tipped soundlessly on to an empty plate. She put her hand up to her pearls.

'I never speak of him, Mr Archery. I prefer to let the past be the past.'

'I know it's painful – it must be. But if we could discuss it just once and get it over, I promise I'll never raise the subject again.' He realised that he was speaking as if they would meet again and often, as if they were already connected by marriage. He was also speaking as if he had confidence in her word. 'I've been to Kingsmarkham today and . . .'

She clutched at the straw. 'I suppose they've built it all up and spoiled it.'

'Not really,' he said. Please God, don't let her digress!

'I was born near there,' she said. He tried to stifle a sigh. 'A funny little sleepy place it was, my village. I reckon I thought I'd live and die there. You can't tell what life will bring forth, can you?'

'Tell me about Tess's father.'

She dropped her hands from fidgeting with the pearls and rested them in her respectable blue lap. When she turned to him her face was dignified, almost ridiculously prim and shuttered. She might have been a mayoress, taking the chair at some parochial function, clearing her throat preparatory to addressing the Townswomen's Guild. 'Madam chairman, ladies . . .' she should have begun. Instead she said:

'The past is the past, Mr Archery.' He knew then that it was hopeless. 'I appreciate your difficulty, but I really can't speak of it. He was no murderer, you'll have to take my word. He was a good kind man who wouldn't have harmed a fly.' It was curious, he thought, how she jumbled together old village phrases with platform jargon. He waited, then burst out:

'But how do you know? How *can* you know? Mrs Kershaw, did you see something or hear something . . . ?'

The pearls had gone up to her mouth and her teeth closed over the string. As it snapped pearls sprayed off in all directions, into her lap, across the tea things, on to the carpet. She gave a small refined laugh, petulant and apologetic. 'Look what I've done now!' In an instant she was on her knees, retrieving the scattered beads and dropping them into a saucer.

'I'm very keen on a white wedding.' Her face

56

bounced up from behind the tea trolley. Politeness demanded that he too should get on his knees and help in the hunt. 'Get your wife to back me up, will you? Oh, thanks so much. Look, there's another one, just by your left foot.' He scrambled round after her on all fours. Her eyes met his under the overhanging cloth. 'My Tess is quite capable of getting married in jeans if the fancy takes her. And would you mind if we had the reception here? It's such a nice big room.'

Archery got up and handed her three more pearls. When the tennis ball struck the window he jumped. The sound had been like a pistol shot.

'Now, that's quite enough, Jill,' said Mrs Kershaw sharply. Still holding the saucer full of pearls, she opened the window. 'If I've told you once, I've told you fifty times, I don't want any more breakages.'

Archery looked at her. She was annoyed, affronted, even slightly outraged. He wondered suddenly if this was how she had looked on that Sunday night long ago when the police had invaded her domain at the coach house. Was she capable of any emotion greater than this, of mere irritation at disturbance of her personal peace?

'You just can't settle to a quiet discussion with children about, can you?' she said.

Within an instant, as if at a cue, the whole family was upon them, Jill truculent and protesting, the boy he had encountered on the drive now demanding tea, and Kershaw himself, vibrant as ever, his little lined face showing a certain dry acuteness.

'Now, you're to come straight out and give me a hand with these dishes, Jill.' The saucer was transferred to the mantelpiece and stuck between an Oxfam collecting box and a card inviting Mrs Kershaw to a coffee morning in aid of Cancer Relief. 'I'll say good-bye now, Mr Archery.' She held out her hand. 'You've such a long way to go, I know you'll want to be on your way.' It was almost rude, yet it was queenly. 'If we don't meet again before the great day – well, I'll see you in church.'

The door closed. Archery remained standing.

'What am I to do?' he said simply.

'What did you expect?' Kershaw countered. 'Some sort of incontrovertible evidence, an alibi that only she can prove?'

'Do *you* believe her?' Archery cared.

'Ah, that's another matter. I don't care, you see. I don't care one way or the other. It's so easy *not* to ask, Mr Archery, just to do nothing and accept.'

'But I care,' said Archery. 'If Charles goes ahead and marries your stepdaughter, I shall have to leave the church. I don't think you realise the sort of place I live in, the sort of people . . .'

'Aah!' Kershaw wrinkled up his mouth and spread his hands angrily fanwise. 'I've no patience with that sort of out-dated rubbish. Who's to know? Everybody round here thinks she's my kid.'

'I shall know.'

'Why the hell did she have to tell you? Why couldn't she keep her mouth shut?'

'Are you condemning her for her honesty, Kershaw?'

'Yes, by God I am!' Archery winced at the oath and shut his eyes against the light. He saw a red haze. It was only eyelid membrane, but to him it seemed like a lake of blood. 'It's discretion, not honesty, that's the best policy. What are you worrying about, anyway? You know damn' well she won't marry him if you don't want it.'

Archery snapped back, 'And what sort of a relationship should I have with my son after that?' He controlled himself, softened his voice and his expression. 'I shall have to try to find a way. Your wife is so sure?'

'She's never weakened.'

'Then I shall go back to Kingsmarkham. It's rather a forlorn hope, isn't it?' He added with an absurdity he realised after the words had come, 'Thanks for trying to help and – and for an excellent tea.'

Chapter 6

Yet, forasmuch as in all appearance the time of his
dissolution draweth near, so fit and prepare him ...
against the hour of death.

The Visitation of the Sick.

The man lay on his back in the middle of the zebra
crossing. Inspector Burden, getting out of the police
car, had no need to ask where he was or to be taken
to the scene of the accident. It was all there before his
eyes like a horrible still from a Ministry of Transport
warning film, the kind of thing that makes women
shudder and turn quickly to the other channel.

An ambulance was waiting, but nobody was
making any attempt to move the man. Inexorably
and with a kind of indifference the twin yellow
beacons went on winking rhythmically. Up-ended,
with its blunt nose poking into the crushed head of a
bollard, was a white Mini.

'Can't you get him away?' asked Burden.

The doctor was laconic. 'He's had it.' He knelt
down, felt the left wrist and got up again, wiping
blood from his fingers. 'I'd hazard a guess the spine's
gone and he's ruptured his liver. The thing is he's
still more or less conscious and it'd be hell's own
agony to try to shift him.'

'Poor devil. What happened? Did anybody see it?'

His eye roved across the knot of middle-aged
women in cotton dresses, late homegoing commuters
and courting couples on their evening stroll. The last
of the sun smiled gently on their faces and on the
blood that gilded the black and white crossing.
Burden knew that Mini. He knew the stupid sign in

the rear window that showed a skull and the words: *You have been Mini-ed*. It had never been funny and now it was outrageous, cruel in the way it mocked the man in the road.

A girl lay sprawled over the steering wheel. Her hair was short, black and spiky, and she had thrust her fingers through it in despair or remorse. The long red nails stuck out like bright feathers.

'Don't worry about her,' said the doctor contemptuously. 'She's not hurt.'

'You, madam . . .' Burden picked out the calmest and least excited looking of the bystanders. 'Did you happen to see the accident?'

'Ooh, it was awful! Like a beast she was, the little bitch. Must have been doing a hundred miles an hour.'

Picked a right one there, thought Burden. He turned to a white-faced man holding a sealyham on a lead.

'Perhaps you can help me, sir?'

The lead was jerked and the sealyham sat down at the kerb.

'That gentleman . . .' Blanching afresh, he pointed towards the crumpled thing lying on the stripes. 'He looked right and left like you're supposed to. But there was nothing coming. You can't see all that well on account of the bridge.'

'Yes, yes. I get the picture.'

'Well, he started to cross to the island like, when that white car came up out of nowhere. Going like a mad thing she was. Well, not a hundred, but sixty, I reckon. Those Minis can go at a terrible lick when they've had their engines hotted up. He sort of hesitated and then he tried to go back. You know, it was all in a flash. I can't rightly go into details.'

'You're doing very well.'

'Then the car got him. Oh, the driver slammed on

her brakes for all she was worth. I'll never forget the noise to my dying day, what with the brakes screaming and him screaming too, and sort of throwing up his arms and going down like a ninepin.'

Burden set a constable to take names and addresses, turned away and took a step in the direction of the white car. A woman touched his arm.

'Here,' she said, 'he wants a priest or something. He kept on asking before you came. Get me Father Chiverton, he says, like he knew he was going.'

'That right?' said Burden sharply to Dr Crocker.

Crocker nodded. The dying man was covered now, a folded mac under his head, two policemen's jackets across his body. 'Father Chiverton is what he said. Frankly, I was more concerned for his physical than his spiritual welfare.'

'R.C. then, is he?'

'God, no. Bunch of atheists, you cops are. Chiverton's the new vicar here. Don't you ever read the local rag?'

'*Father?*'

'He's very high. Genuflecting and Sung Eucharist and all that jazz.' The doctor coughed. 'I'm a Congregationalist myself.'

Burden walked over to the crossing. The man's face was blanched a yellowish ivory, but his eyes were open and they stared back. With a little shock Burden realised he was young, perhaps no more than twenty.

'Anything you want, old chap?' He knew the doctor had given him a pain-killing injection. With his own bent body he shielded him from the watchers. 'We'll get you away from here in a minute,' he lied. 'Anything we can get you?'

'Father Chiverton . . .' It was a toneless whisper, as detached and inhuman as a puff of wind. 'Father

Chiverton ...' A spasm crossed the waning face. 'Confess ... atone ... spare Thou them which are penitent.'

'Bloody religion,' said the doctor. 'Can't even let a man die in peace.'

'You must be an asset to the Congregationalists,' Burden snapped. He got up, sighing. 'He obviously wants to confess. I suppose they do have confession in the Church of England?'

'You can have it if you want it but you needn't if you don't fancy it. That's the beauty of the C of E.' When Burden looked murderous, he added, 'Don't get in a tiz with me. We've been on to Chiverton, but he and his curate are off at some conference.'

'Constable Gates!' Burden beckoned impatiently to the man noting down addresses. 'Nip into Stowerton and fetch me a – a vicar.'

'We've tried Stowerton, sir.'

'O God,' said Burden quietly.

'Excuse me, sir, but there's a clergyman got an appointment with the Chief Inspector now. I could get on to the station and ...'

Burden raised his eyebrows. Kingsmarkham Police Station had apparently become the battleground of the Church Militant.

'You do that, and quick ...'

He murmured something useless to the boy, and moved towards the girl who had begun to sob.

She was not crying because of what she had done, but because of what she had seen two hours before. It was two or three years now since she had what she called a waking nightmare – though at one time they were more real than reality – and she was crying because the nightmares were going to begin again and the remedy she had tried had not erased the picture from her mind.

She had seen it in the estate agent's window when she was coming home from work. It was a photograph of a house, but not as it was now, dirty and weathered, set in a tangled wilderness. The estate agents deceived you, they meant you to think it was like it had once been long ago ... You? As soon as she found she was addressing herself as 'You' she knew it was beginning again, the re-telling of the nightmare. So she had got into the Mini and driven to Flagford, away from associations and memories and the hateful You voice, to drink and drink and try to send it away.

But it would not go away and you were back in the big house, listening to the voices that went on coaxing, cajoling, arguing until you were bored, so bored until you went out into the garden and met the little girl.

You went up to her and you said, 'Do you like my dress?'

'It's pretty,' she said, and she didn't seem to mind that it was much nicer than her own.

She was playing with a heap of sand, making pies in an old cup without a handle. You stayed and played and after that you came to the sand every day, down there out of sight of the big windows. The sand was warm and nice and you could understand it. You could understand the little girl too, even though she was the only little girl you had ever known. You knew a lot of grown ups, but you could not understand them, nor the ugly words and the funny wheedling way the talk was always about money, so that you seemed to see coins dropping out of wriggling lips and sliding dirtily through twitching fingers.

The little girl had some magic about her, for she lived in a tree. Of course it was not really a tree but a house inside a kind of bush all shivering with leaves.

The sand was not dry like the desert you lived in now, but warm and moist, like beach sand washed by a tepid sea. It was dirty too and you were afraid of what would happen if you got it on your dress ...

You cried and stamped your foot, but you never cried as you were crying now as the good-looking inspector came up to the car, his eyes full of anger.

Did he seriously imagine he was going to find anything new after so long? Archery considered Wexford's question. It was, he decided, more a matter of faith than of any real belief in Painter's innocence. But faith in what? Not, surely, in Mrs Kershaw. Perhaps it was just a childlike certainty that such things could not happen to anyone connected with him, Archery. The child of a murderer could not be as Tess was, Kershaw would not have loved her, Charles would not want to marry her.

'It can't do any harm to see Alice Flower,' he said. He felt he was pleading, and pleading weakly. 'I'd like to talk to the Primero grandchildren, particularly the grandson.'

For a moment Wexford said nothing. He had heard of faith moving mountains, but this was simply absurd. To him it was almost as ridiculous as if some crank had come to him with the suggestion that Dr Crippen was the innocent victim of circumstances. From bitter experience he knew how difficult it was to hunt a killer when only a week had elapsed between a murder and the beginning of an investigation. Archery was proposing to open an enquiry a decade and a half too late and Archery had no experience at all.

'I ought to put you off,' he said at last. 'You don't know what you're attempting.' It's pathetic, he thought, it's laughable. Aloud he said, 'Alice Flower's in the geriatric ward at Stowerton Infirmary.

She's paralysed. I don't even know if she could make herself understood.'

It occurred to him that Archery must be totally ignorant of the geography of the place. He got up and lumbered over to the wall map.

'Stowerton's there,' he said, pointing with the sheathed tip of a ballpoint pen, 'and Victor's Piece is about here, between Stowerton and Kingsmarkham.'

'Where can I find Mrs Crilling?'

Wexford made a wry face. 'In Glebe Road. I can't recall the number off-hand, but I'll get it looked up or you could find it on the electoral register.' He turned round ponderously and fixed Archery with a grey glare. 'You're wasting your time, of course. I'm sure I don't have to tell you to be very careful when it comes to throwing out a lot of unfounded accusations.'

Under those cold eyes it was difficult for Archery not to drop his own. 'Chief Inspector, I don't want to find someone else guilty, just prove that Painter was innocent.'

Wexford said briskly, 'I'm afraid you may find the former consequent upon the latter. It would be a wrong conclusion, of course – I don't want trouble.' At a knock on the door he spun round testily. 'Yes, what is it?'

Sergeant Martin's bland face appeared. 'That fatal on the zebra in the High Street, sir?'

'What of it? It's hardly my province.'

'Gates has just been on, sir. A white Mini, LMB 12M, that we've had our eye on – it was in collision with a pedestrian. It appears they want a clergyman and Gates recalled that Mr Archery was ...'

Wexford's lips twitched. Archery was in for a surprise. In the courtly manner he sometimes assumed, he said to the vicar of Thringford, 'It looks as if the secular arm needs some spiritual assistance, sir. Would you be so good ... ?'

'Of course I will.' Archery looked at the sergeant. 'Someone has been knocked down and is – is *dying*?'

'Unfortunately, yes, sir,' said Martin grimly.

'I think I'll come with you,' said Wexford.

As a priest of the Anglican Church Archery was obliged to hear confession if a confessor was needed. Until now, however, his only experience of this mystery concerned a Miss Baylis, an elderly female parishioner of his who, having been (according to Mrs Archery) for many years in love with him, demanded that he should listen to a small spate of domestic sins mumbled out each Friday morning. Hers was a masochistic, self-abasing need, very different from the yearning of the boy who lay in the road.

Wexford shepherded him across the black and white lines to the island. Diversion notices had been placed in the road, directing the traffic around Queen Street, and the crowd had been induced to go home. There were several policemen buzzing and pacing. For the first time in his life Archery realised the aptness of the term 'bluebottles'. He glanced at the Mini and averted his eyes hastily from the bright bumper with its ribbon of blood.

The boy looked at him doubtfully. He had perhaps five minutes to live. Archery dropped to his knees and put his ear to the white lips. At first he felt only fluttering breath, then out of the soft sighing vibration came something that sounded like 'Holy orders ...', with the second word rising on a high note of enquiry. He bent closer as the confession began to flow out, jerky, toneless, spasmodic, like the gulping of a sluggish stream. It was something about a girl, but it was utterly incoherent. He could make nothing of it. We fly unto Thee for succour, he thought, in behalf of this Thy servant, here lying under Thy hand in great weakness of body ...

The Anglican Church provides no order quite comparable to that of Extreme Unction. Archery found himself saying urgently over and over again, 'It will be all right, it will be all right.' The boy's throat rattled and a stream of blood welled out of his mouth, splashing Archery's folded hands. 'We humbly commend the soul of this Thy servant, our dear brother, into Thy hands ...' He was tired and his voice broke with compassion and with horror. 'Most humbly beseeching Thee that it may be precious in Thy sight ...'

It was the doctor's hand that appeared, mopping with a handkerchief at Archery's fingers, then feeling a still heart and an inert pulse. Wexford looked at the doctor, gave an infinitesimal shrug. Nobody spoke. Across the silence came the sound of brakes, a horn braying and an oath as a car, taking the diversion too late, veered into Queen Street. Wexford pulled the coat up over the dead face.

Archery was shattered and cold in the evening heat. He got up stiffly, feeling an utter loneliness and a terrible desire to weep. The only thing to lean on now the bollard was gone was the rear of that lethal white car. He leaned on it, feeling sick.

Presently he opened his eyes and moved slowly along the body of the car to where Wexford stood contemplating a girl's shaggy black head. This was no business of his, Archery's. He wanted no hand in it, only to ask Wexford where he could find an hotel for the night.

Something in the other man's expression made him hesitate. The big Chief Inspector's face was a study in irony. He watched Wexford tap on the glass.

The window was slid back and the girl inside lifted to them a face drowned in tears.

'This is a bad business,' he heard Wexford say, 'a very bad business, Miss Crilling.'

'God moves in a mysterious way,' said Wexford as he and Archery walked over the bridge, 'His wonders to perform.' He hummed the old hymn tune, apparently liking the sound of his rather rusty baritone.

'That's true,' said Archery very seriously. He stopped, rested his hand on the granite parapet and looked down into the brown water. A swan sailed out from under the bridge, dipping its long neck into the drifting weed. 'And that is really the girl who found Mrs Primero's body?'

'That's Elizabeth Crilling, yes. One of the wild young things of Kingsmarkham. A boy friend – a very *close* friend, I may add – gave her the Mini for her twenty-first and she's been a menace in it ever since.'

Archery was silent. Tess Kershaw and Elizabeth Crilling were the same age. Their lives had begun together, almost side by side. Each must have walked with her mother along the grass verges of the Stowerton Road, played in the fields behind Victor's Piece. The Crillings had been comfortably off, middle-class people; the Painters miserably poor. In his mind's eye he saw again that tear-wrecked face down which grease and mascara ran in rivulets, and he heard again the ugly words she had used to Wexford. Another face superimposed itself on Elizabeth Crilling's, a fair aquiline face with steady intelligent eyes under a page-boy's blonde fringe. Wexford interrupted his thoughts.

'She's been spoilt, of course, made too much of. Your Mrs Primero had her over with her every day, stuffing her with sweets and what-have-you, by all accounts. After the murder Mrs Crilling was always taking her to psychiatrists, wouldn't let her go to school till they had the kid-catcher down on her. God knows how many schools she *has* been to. She was what you might call the female lead in the juvenile court here.'

But it was Tess whose father had been a murderer, Tess who might have been expected to grow up like that. 'God knows how many schools she's been to . . .' Tess had been to one school and to one ancient, distinguished university. Yet the daughter of the innocent friend had become a delinquent; the killer's child a paragon. Certainly God moved in a mysterious way.

'Chief Inspector, I want very much to talk to Mrs Crilling.'

'If you care to attend the special court in the morning, sir, she'll in all likelihood be there. Knowing Mrs Crilling, I'd say you might again be called upon in your professional capacity and then, who knows?'

Archery frowned as they walked on. 'I'd rather it was all above-board. I don't want to do anything underhand.'

'Look, sir,' said Wexford in a burst of impatience, 'if you're coming in on this lark you'll have to be underhand. You've no real authority to ask questions of innocent people and if they complain I can't protect you.'

'I'll explain everything frankly to her. May I talk to her?'

Wexford cleared his throat. 'Are you familiar with *Henry the Fourth*, Part One, sir?'

Slightly puzzled, Archery nodded. Wexford stopped under the arch that led to the coaching yard of the Olive and Dove. 'The quotation I had in mind is

Hotspur's reply to Mortimer when he says he can call spirits from the vasty deep.' Startled by Wexford's deep voice, a little cloud of pigeons flew out from the beams, fluttering rusty grey wings. 'I've found that reply very useful to me in my work when I've been a bit too optimistic.' He cleared his throat and quoted, '"And so can I and so can any man. But will they come when you do call to them?" Good night, sir. I hope you find the Olive comfortable.'

Chapter 7

Into how high a dignity ... ye are called, that is to say to be Messengers, Watchmen and Stewards ...

The Ordering of Priests.

Two people sat in the public gallery of Kingsmarkham court, Archery and a woman with sharp, wasted features. Her long grey hair, oddly fashionable through carelessness rather than intent, and the cape she wore gave her a medieval look. Presumably she was the mother of this girl who had just been charged with manslaughter, the girl whom the clerk had named as Elizabeth Anthea Crilling, of 24A Glebe Road, Kingsmarkham in the County of Sussex. She had a look of her mother and they kept glancing at each other, Mrs Crilling's eyes flicking over her daughter's string-thin body or coming to rest with maudlin watery affection on the girl's face. It was a well-made face, though gaunt but for the full mouth. Sometimes it seemed to become all staring dark eyes as a word or a telling phrase awakened emotion, sometimes blank and shuttered like that of a retarded child with an inner life of goblins and things that reach out in the dark. An invisible thread held mother and daughter together but whether it was composed of love or hatred Archery could not tell. Both were ill-dressed, dirty-looking, a prey, he felt, to cheap emotion, but there was some quality each had – passion? Imagination? Seething memory? – that set them apart and dwarfed the other occupants of the court.

He had just enough knowledge of the law to know that this court could do no more than commit the girl to the Assizes for trial. The evidence that was being laboriously taken down on a typewriter was all against her. Elizabeth Crilling, according to the licensee of the Swan at Flagford, had been drinking in his saloon bar since six-thirty. He had served her with seven double whiskies and when he had refused to let her have another, she had abused him until he had threatened to call the police.

'No alternative but to commit you for trial at the Assizes at Lewes,' the chairman was saying. '. . . Nothing to hope for from any promise of favour, and nothing to fear from any threat which may be . . .'

A shriek came from the public gallery. 'What are you going to do to her?' Mrs Crilling had sprung up, the tent-like cape she wore billowing out and making a breeze run through the court. 'You're not going to put her in prison?'

Hardly knowing why he did so, Archery moved swiftly along the form until he was at her side. At the same time Sergeant Martin took half a dozen rapid strides towards her, glaring at the clergyman.

'Now, madam, you'd far better come outside.'

She flung herself away from him, pulling the cape around her as if it were cold instead of suffocatingly hot.

'You're not going to put my baby in gaol!' She pushed at the sergeant who stood between her and her view of the bench. 'Get away from me, you dirty sadist!'

'Take that woman outside,' said the magistrate with icy calm. Mrs Crilling spun round to face Archery and seized his hands. 'You've got a kind face. Are you my friend?'

Archery was horribly embarrassed. 'You can ask for bail, I think,' he muttered.

The policewoman who stood by the dock came over to them. 'Come along now, Mrs Crilling . . .'

'Bail, I want bail! This gentleman is an old friend of mine and he says I can have bail. I want my rights for my baby!'

'We really can't have this sort of thing.' The magistrate cast an icy scornful look upon Archery who sat down, wrenching his hands from Mrs Crilling's. 'Do I understand you wish to ask for bail?' He turned his eyes on Elizabeth who nodded defiantly.

'A nice cup of tea, Mrs Crilling,' said the policewoman. 'Come along now.' She shepherded the demented woman out, her arm supporting her waist. The magistrate went into conference with the clerk and bail was granted to Elizabeth Crilling in her own recognisance of five hundred pounds and that of her mother for a similar sum.

'Rise, please!' said the warrant officer. It was over.

On the other side of the court Wexford shovelled his papers into his briefcase.

'A friend in need, that one,' he said to Burden, glancing in Archery's direction. 'You mark my words, he'll have a job getting out of old Mother Crilling's clutches. Remember when we had to cart her off to the mental unit at Stowerton that time? You were her friend then. Tried to kiss you, didn't she?'

'Don't remind me,' said Burden.

'Funny affair altogether last night, wasn't it? Him being on hand, I mean, to show that poor kid his way to heaven.'

'It was lucky.'

'I only remember that happening once before, except in the case of R.C.s, of course.' He turned as Archery slipped between the wooden forms and came up to them. 'Good morning, sir. I hope you slept well. I was just saying to the inspector, there was a fellow killed out Forby way soon after I came here. Must be all of twenty years. I've never forgotten it. He was just a kid too and got it in the neck from an army lorry. But he wasn't quiet, he was screaming. All about a girl and a kid it was.' He paused. 'Did you speak, sir? Sorry, I thought you did. He wanted a clergyman, too.'

'I hope and trust he got what he wanted.'

'Well, no he didn't as a matter of fact. He died – unshriven is the word, I think. The vicar's car broke down on the way. Funny, I've never forgotten it. Grace was his name, John Grace. Shall we go?'

The Crillings had departed. As they came out into the sunshine, the policewoman came up to Wexford.

'Mrs Crilling left a note with me, sir. She asked me to give it to a Mr Archery.'

'Take my advice,' said Wexford. 'Tear it up. She's as mad as a hatter.' But Archery had already slit open the envelope.

Dear Sir, he read.

They tell me that you are a man of God. Blessed is he that sitteth not in the seat of the scornful. God has sent you to me and my baby. I will be at home this afternoon, waiting to thank you in person.

Your affectionate friend, Josephine Crilling

Archery's bedroom combined charmingly the best of old and new. The ceiling was beamed, the walls painted pink and decorated with a tooled design of chevrons, but there was also a fitted carpet, an abundance of lights on walls and bedhead and a telephone. He rinsed his hands at the pink washbasin (a private bathroom he felt to be an unwarranted extravagance), lifted the receiver and asked for a call to Thringford in Essex.

'Darling?'

'Henry! Thank heaven you've phoned. I've been trying over and over again to get you at that Olive Branch place or whatever it's called.'

'Why, what's the matter?'

'I've had a dreadful letter from Charles. Apparently poor darling Tess phoned her people late yesterday afternoon and now she's told Charles the engagement's definitely off. She says it wouldn't be fair on him or us.'

'And ...?'

'And Charles says if Tess won't marry him he's going to come down from Oxford and go out to Africa to fight for Zimbabwe.'

'How utterly ridiculous!'

'He says if you try and stop him he'll do something dreadful and get sent down.'

'Is that all?'

'Oh, no. There's lots and lots of it. Let me see. I've got the letter here. "... What's the use of Father always ballsing on" – sorry, darling, does that mean something awful? – "on about faith and taking things on trust if he won't take Tess's word and her mother's? I've been into the whole fiasco of the case myself and it's full of holes. I think Father could get the Home Secretary to have the case re-opened if he would only make some sort of effort. For one thing there was an inheritance involved but it never came up at the trial. Three people inherited vast sums and at least one of them was buzzing around the place the day Mrs Primero died ..."'

'All right,' said Archery wearily. 'If you remember, Mary, I have a transcript of the trial myself and it cost me two hundred pounds. How are things apart from that?'

'Mr Sims is behaving rather oddly.' Mr Sims was Archery's curate. 'Miss Bayliss says he keeps the

76

communion bread in his pocket, and this morning she got a long blonde hair in her mouth.'

Archery smiled. This parish chit-chat was more in his wife's line than solving murders. It brought her to him visually, a handsome strong woman who minded the lines on her face that he never noticed. He was beginning to miss her mentally and physically.

'Now, listen, darling. Write back to Charles – be diplomatic. Tell him how well Tess is behaving and say I'm having some very interesting talks with the police. If there's the slightest chance of getting the case re-opened I'll write to the Home Secretary.'

'That's wonderful, Henry. Oh, there go your second lot of pips. I'll ring off. By the way, Rusty caught a mouse this morning and left it in the bath. He and Tawny are missing you.'

'Give them my love,' said Archery to please her.

He went downstairs into the dark cool dining room, ordered something called a *Navarin d'agneau*, and in a burst of recklessness, a half-bottle of Anjou. All the windows were open but on some of them the green shutters had been closed. A table in one of these embrasures reminded him with its white cloth, its tilted cane chairs and its vaseful of sweet peas of a Dufy that hung on the walls of his study at home. Filtered sunlight lay in primrose-pale bars across the cloth and the two places laid with silver.

But for himself and half a dozen elderly residents, the dining room was deserted, but presently the door from the bar opened and the head waiter ushered in a man and a woman. Archery wondered if the management would object to the apricot poodle the woman fondled in her arms. But the head waiter was smiling deferentially and Archery saw him pat the tiny woolly head.

The man was small and dark and would have been

good-looking but for his glassy, red-rimmed eyes. Archery thought he might be wearing contact lenses. He sat down at the Dufy table, ripped open a packet of Peter Stuyvesant and poured the contents into a gold cigarette case. In spite of the man's obvious polish – his sleek hair, svelte suit, taut bone-smooth skin – there was something savage in the way his white fingers tore the paper. A wedding ring and a big bold signet gleamed in the soft light as he tossed the mutilated packet on to the cloth. Archery was amused to see how much jewellery he wore, a sapphire tie pin and a watch as well as the rings.

By contrast the woman wore none. She was plainly dressed in a cream silk suit that matched her hair, and everything about her from the gauzy hat and hair to her crossed ankles was the colour of faint sunlight, so that she seemed to glow with a pale radiance. Outside the cinema and the pictures in Mary's magazines, she was the most beautiful woman he had seen for years. Compared to her Tess Painter was just a pretty girl. Archery was reminded of an ivory orchid or a tea rose which, when lifted from the florist's cube of cellophane, still retains its patina of dew.

He gave himself a little shake and applied himself determinedly to his *Navarin*. It had turned out to be two lamb chops in a brown sauce.

Between Kingsmarkham High Street and the Kingsbrook Road lies an estate of ugly terraced houses covered with that mixture of mortar and grit builders call pebble dashing. On a hot day when the roads are dusty and flickering with heat mirage these rows of dun-coloured houses look as if they have been fashioned out of sand. A giant's child might have built them, using his crude tools unimaginatively.

Archery found Glebe Road by the simple and

78

traditional expedient of asking a policeman. He was getting into the habit of asking policemen and this one was low in the hierarchy, a young constable directing traffic at the crossroads.

Glebe Road might have been designed by the Romans, it was so straight, so long and so uncompromising. The sand houses had no woodwork about them. Their window frames were of metal and their porch canopies excrescences of pebbly plaster. After every fourth house an arch in the façade led into the back and through these arches sheds, coal bunkers and dustbins could be seen.

The street was numbered from the Kingsbrook Road end and Archery walked nearly half a mile before he found twenty-four. The hot pavements running with melted tar made his feet burn. He pushed open the gate and saw that the canopy covered not one front door but two. The house had been converted into two surely tiny flatlets. He tapped the chromium knocker on the door marked 24A and waited.

When nothing happened he tapped again. There was a grinding trundling sound and a boy on roller skates came out from under the arch. He took no notice at all of the clergyman. Could Mrs Crilling be asleep? It was hot enough for a siesta and Archery felt languid himself.

He stepped back and looked through the arch. Then he heard the door open and slam shut. So somebody was at home. He rounded the sandy wall and came face to face with Elizabeth Crilling.

At once he sensed that she had not answered, nor probably even heard, his knock. Evidently she was going out. The black dress had been changed for a short blue cotton shift that showed the outlines of her prominent hip bones. She wore backless white mules and carried a huge white and gilt handbag.

'What d'you want?' It was obvious she had no idea who he was. He thought she looked old, finished, as if somehow she had been used and wrecked. 'If you're selling something,' she said, 'you've come to the wrong shop.'

'I saw your mother in court this morning,' Archery said. 'She asked me to come and see her.'

He thought she had rather a charming smile, for her mouth was well-shaped and her teeth good. But the smile was too brief.

'That,' she said, 'was this morning.'

'Is she at home?' He looked helplessly at the doors. 'I – er – which one is it, which flat?'

'Are you kidding? It's bad enough sharing a house with her. Only a stone-deaf paralytic could stick living *underneath* her.'

'I'll go in, shall I?'

'Suit yourself. She's not likely to come out here.' The bag strap was hoisted on to the right shoulder, pulling the blue stuff tight across her breasts. Without knowing why, Archery remembered the exquisite woman in the dining room of the Olive and Dove, her petal skin and her easy grace.

Elizabeth Crilling's face was greasy. In the bright afternoon light the skin had the texture of lemon peel. 'Well, go on in,' she said sharply, unlocking the door. She pushed it open and turned away, her mules flapping and clacking down the path. 'She won't bite you,' she said over her shoulder. 'At least, I shouldn't think so. She bit me once, but there were – well, extenuating circumstances.'

Archery went into the hall. Three doors led off it but they were all closed. He coughed and said tentatively, 'Mrs Crilling?' The place was stuffy and silent. He hesitated for a moment, then opened the first of the doors. Inside was a bedroom divided into two by a hardboard partition. He had been wondering how the two women managed. Now he knew. The middle room must be where they lived. He tapped on the door and opened it.

Although the french windows were ajar the air was thick with smoke and the two ashtrays on a gateleg table were filled with stubs. Every surface was covered with papers and debris and the debris with dust. As he entered a blue budgerigar in a tiny cage broke into a stream of high brittle chatter. The cage swung furiously.

Mrs Crilling wore a pink nylon dressing gown that looked as if it had once been designed for a bride. The honeymoon, Archery thought, was long over, for the dressing gown was stained and torn and hideous. She was sitting in an armchair looking through the window at a fenced-in piece of land at the back. It could hardly be called a garden for nothing grew in it but nettles, three feet high, rose-pink fireweed, and brambles that covered everything with fly-infested tendrils.

'You hadn't forgotten I was coming, Mrs Crilling?'

The face that appeared round the wing of the chair was enough to intimidate anyone. The whites of the eyes showed all the way round the black pupils. Every muscle looked tense, taut and corrugated as if from some inner agony. Her white hair, fringed and styled like a teenager's, curtained the sharp cheekbones.

'Who are you?' She dragged herself up, clinging to the chair arm and came slowly round to face him. The vee at the dressing gown front showed a ridged and withered valley like the bed of a long-dried stream.

'We met in court this morning. You wrote to me...'

He stopped. She had thrust her face within inches

81

of his and seemed to be scrutinising it. Then she stepped back and gave a long chattering laugh which the budgerigar echoed.

'Mrs Crilling, are you all right? Is there anything I can do?'

She clutched her throat and the laugh died away in a rising wheeze. 'Tablets . . . asthma . . .' she gasped. He was puzzled and shocked, but he reached behind him for the bottle of tablets on the littered mantelpiece. 'Give me my tablets and then you can . . . you can get out!'

'I'm sorry if I've done anything to distress you.'

She made no attempt to take a tablet but held the bottle up against her quaking chest. The movement made the tablets rattle and the bird, fluttering its wings and beating against the bars, began a frenzied crescendo, half song and half pain.

'Where's my baby?' Did she mean Elizabeth? She must mean Elizabeth.

'She's gone out. I met her in the porch. Mrs Crilling, can I get you a glass of water? Can I make you a cup of tea?'

'Tea? What do I want with tea? That's what she said this morning, that police girl. Come and have a cup of tea, Mrs Crilling.' A terrible spasm shook her and she fell back against the chair, fighting for breath. 'You . . . my baby . . . I thought you were my friend . . . Aaah!'

Archery was really frightened now. He plunged from the room into the dirty kitchen and filled a cup with water. The window ledge was stacked with empty chemist's bottles and there was a filthy hypodermic beside an equally dirty eye dropper. When he came back she was still wheezing and jerking. Should he make her take the tablets, dare he? On the bottle label were the words: *Mrs F. Crilling. Take two when needed*. He rattled two into his hand

and, supporting her with his other arm, forced them into her mouth. It was all he could do to suppress the shudder of distaste when she dribbled and choked over the water.

'Filthy ... nasty,' she mumbled. He half-eased, half-rolled her into the chair and pulled together the gaping edges of the dressing gown. Moved with pity and with horror, he knelt down beside her.

'I will be your friend if you want me to be,' he said soothingly.

The words had the opposite effect. She made a tremendous effort to draw breath. Her lips split open and he could see her tongue rising and quivering against the roof of her mouth.

'Not my friend ... enemy ... police friend! Take my baby away ... I saw you with them ... I watched you come out with them.' He drew back from her, rising. Never would he have believed her capable of screaming after that spasm and when the scream came, as clear and ear-splitting as a child's, he felt his hands go up to his face. '... Not let them get her in there! Not in the prison! They'll find it out in there. She'll tell them ... my baby ... She'll have to tell them!' With a sudden galvanic jerk she reared up, her mouth open and her arms flailing. 'They'll find it all out. I'll kill her first, kill her ... D'you hear?'

The french windows stood open. Archery staggered back into the sun against a stinging prickling wall of weeds. Mrs Crilling's incoherent gasps had swollen into a stream of obscenity. There was a gate in the wire netting fence. He unlatched it, wiping the sweat from his forehead, and stepped into the cool dark cave of the sand-walled arch.

'Good afternoon, sir. You don't look very well. Heat affecting you?'

Archery had been leaning over the bridge parapet,

breathing deeply, when the detective inspector's face appeared beside him.

'Inspector Burden, isn't it?' He shook himself, blinking his eyes. There was comfort in this man's steady gaze and in the shoppers who flowed languidly across the bridge. 'I've just come from Mrs Crilling's and . . .'

'Say no more, sir. I quite understand.'

'I left her in the throes of an asthma attack. Perhaps I should have got a doctor or an ambulance. Frankly, I hardly knew what to do.'

There was a crumb of stony bread on the wall. Burden flicked it into the water and a swan dived for it.

'It's mostly in the mind with her, Mr Archery. I should have warned you what to expect. Threw one of her scenes on you, did she?' Archery nodded. 'Next time you see her I daresay she'll be as nice as pie. That's the way it takes her, up one minute, down the next. Manic-depressive is the term. I was just going into the Carousel for a cup of tea. Why don't you join me?'

They walked up the High Street together. Some of the shops sported faded striped sunblinds. The shadows were as black as night, the light cruelly bright under a Mediterranean blue sky. Inside the Carousel it was darkish and stuffy and it smelt of aerosol fly spray.

'Two teas, please,' said Burden.

'Tell me about the Crillings.'

'There's plenty to tell, Mr Archery. Mrs Crilling's husband died and left her without a penny, so she moved into town and got a job. The kid, Elizabeth, was always difficult and Mrs Crilling made her worse. She took her to psychiatrists – don't ask me where the money came from – and then when they made her send her to school it was one school after another. She was in St Catherine's, Sewingbury for a bit but she got expelled. When she was about fourteen she came up before the juvenile court here as being in need of care and protection and she was taken away from her mother. But she went back eventually. They usually do.'

'Do you think all this came about because she found Mrs Primero's body?'

'Could be.' Burden looked up and smiled as the waitress brought the tea. 'Thanks very much, miss. Sugar, Mr Archery? No, I don't either.' He cleared his throat and went on, 'I reckon it would have made a difference if she'd had a decent home background, but Mrs Crilling was always unstable. In and out of jobs, by all accounts, until she ended up working in a shop. I think some relative used to give them financial assistance. Mrs Crilling used to take days off from work ostensibly on account of the asthma but really it was because she was crazy.'

'Isn't she certifiable?'

'You'd be surprised how difficult it is to get anyone certified, sir. The doctor did say that if ever he saw her in one of her tantrums he could get an urgency order, but they're cunning, you see. By the time the doctor gets there she's as normal as you or me. She's been into Stowerton once or twice as a voluntary patient. About four years ago she got herself a man friend. The whole place was buzzing with it. Elizabeth was training to be a physiotherapist at the time. Anyway, the upshot of it all was that the boy friend preferred young Liz.'

'*Mater pulchra, filia pulchrior*,' Archery murmured.

'Just as you say, sir. She gave up her training and went to live with him. Mrs Crilling went off her rocker again and spent six months in Stowerton. When she came out she wouldn't leave the happy couple alone, letters, phone calls, personal appearances, the lot. Liz couldn't stand it so eventually she went back to mother. The boy friend was in the car trade and he gave her that Mini.'

Archery sighed. 'I don't know if I ought to tell you this, but you've been very kind to me, you and Mr Wexford ...' Burden felt the stirring of guilt. It wasn't what he would call kind. 'Mrs Crilling said that if Elizabeth – she calls her her baby – went to prison ... it might mean prison, mightn't it?'

'It might well.'

'Then she'd tell you something, you or the prison authorities. I got the impression she'd feel compelled to give you some information Mrs Crilling wanted kept secret.'

'Thank you very much, sir. We shall have to wait and see what time brings forth.'

Archery finished his tea. Suddenly he felt like a traitor. Had he betrayed Mrs Crilling because he wanted to keep in with the police?

'I wondered,' he said, justifying himself, 'if it could have anything to do with Mrs Primero's murder. I don't see why Mrs Crilling couldn't have worn the raincoat and hidden it. You admit yourself she's unbalanced. She was there, she had just as much opportunity as Painter.'

Burden shook his head. 'What was the motive?'

'Mad people have motives which seem very thin to normal men.'

'But she dotes on her daughter in her funny way. She wouldn't have taken the kid with her.'

Archery said slowly, 'At the trial she said she went over the first time at twenty-five past six. But we've only her word for it. Suppose instead she went at twenty to seven when *Painter had already been and gone*. Then she took the child back later because no-one would believe a killer would wittingly let a child discover a body she knew was there.'

'You've missed your vocation, sir,' said Burden, getting up. 'You should have come in on our lark. You'd have been a superintendent by now.'

'I'm letting my fancy run away with me,' Archery said. To avoid a repetition of the gentle teasing, he added quickly, changing the subject, 'Do you happen to know the visiting times at Stowerton Infirmary?'

'Alice Flower's next on your list, is she? I'd give the matron a ring first, if I were you. Visiting's seven till seven-thirty.'

Chapter 8

The days of our age are threescore years and ten; and though men be so strong that they come to fourscore years, yet is their strength then but labour and sorrow.

Psalm 90. *The Burial of the Dead.*

Alice Flower was eighty-seven, almost as old as her employer had been at the time of her death. A series of strokes had battered her old frame as tempests batter an ancient house, but the house was strong and sturdily built. No gimcrack refinements of decoration or delicacy had ever belonged to it. It had been made to endure wind and weather.

She lay in a narrow high bed in a ward called Honeysuckle. The ward was full of similar old women in similar beds. They had clean pink faces and white hair through which patches of rose-pink scalp showed. Every bed trolley held at least two vases of flowers, the sops to conscience, Archery supposed, of visiting relatives who only had to sit and chat instead of handing bedpans and tending bed-sores.

'A visitor for you, Alice,' said the sister. 'It's no use trying to shake hands with her. She can't move her hands but her hearing's perfectly good and she'll talk the hind leg off a donkey.'

A most un-Christian hatred flared in Archery's eyes. If she saw it the sister took no notice.

'Like a good gossip, don't you, Alice? This is the Reverend Archery.' He winced at that, approached the bed.

'Good evening, sir.'

Her face was square with deeply ridged rough skin. One corner of her mouth had been drawn down by the paralysis of the motor nerves, causing her lower jaw to protrude and reveal large false teeth. The sister bustled about the bed, pulling the old servant's nightgown higher about her neck and arranging on the coverlet her two useless hands. It was terrible to Archery to have to look at those hands. Work had distorted them beyond hope of beauty, but disease and oedema had smoothed and whitened the skin so that they were like the hands of a misshapen baby. The emotion and the feel for the language of 1611 that was with him always welled in a fount of pity. Well done, thou good and faithful servant, he thought. Thou hast been faithful over a few things, I will make thee ruler over many things . . .

'Would it upset you to talk to me about Mrs Primero, Miss Flower?' he asked gently, easing himself into a bentwood chair.

'Of course it wouldn't,' said the sister, 'she loves it.'

Archery could bear no more. 'This is rather a private matter, if you don't mind.'

'Private! It's the whole ward's bedtime story, believe me.' She flounced away, a crackling navy and white robot.

Alice Flower's voice was cracked and harsh. The strokes had affected her throat muscles or her vocal cords. But her accent was pleasant and correct, learnt, Archery supposed, in the kitchens and nurseries of educated people.

'What was it you wanted to know, sir?'

'First tell me about the Primero family.'

'Oh, I can do that. I always took an interest.' She gave a small rattling cough and turned her head to hide the twisted side of her mouth. 'I went to Mrs Primero when the boy was born . . .'

'The boy?'

'Mr Edward, her only child he was.'

Ah, thought Archery, the father of rich Roger and his sisters.

'He was a lovely boy and we always got on a treat, him and me. I reckon it really aged me and his poor mother when he died, sir. But he'd got a family of his own by then, thanks be to God, and Mr Roger was the living spit of his father.'

'I suppose Mr Edward left him pretty well off, did he?'

'Oh, no, sir, that was the pity of it. You see, old Dr Primero left his money to madam, being as Mr Edward was doing so well at the time. But he lost everything on something in the city and when he was taken Mrs Edward and the three kiddies were quite badly off.' She coughed again, making Archery wince. He fancied he could see a terrible vain effort to raise those hands and cover the rattling lips. 'Madam offered to help – not that she had more than she needed – but Mrs Edward was that proud, she wouldn't take a penny from her mother-in-law. I never shall know how she managed. There was the three of them, you see. Mr Roger, he was the eldest, and then there was the two little mites, ever so much younger than their brother, but close together if you take my meaning. No more than eighteen months between them.'

She rested her head back on the pillows and bit at her lip as if trying to pull it back into place. 'Angela was the oldest. Time flies so I reckon she'd be twenty-six now. Then there was Isabel, named after madam. They was just babies when their Daddy died and it was years before we saw them.

'It was a bitter blow to madam, I can tell you, not

knowing what had become of Mr Roger. Then one day just out of the blue he turned up at Victor's Piece. Fancy, he was living in digs just over at Sewingbury, studying to be a solicitor with a very good firm. Somebody Mrs Edward knew had got him in. He hadn't no idea his granny was still alive, let alone in Kingsmarkham, but he was looking up somebody in the phone book, in the line of business, sir, and there it was: Mrs Rose Primero, Victor's Piece. Once he'd come over there was no stopping him. Not that we wanted to stop him, sir. Pretty nearly every Sunday he came and once or twice he fetched his little sisters all the way from London and brought them with him. Good as gold they were.

'Mr Roger and madam, they used to have some laughs together. All the old photographs they'd have out and the tales she used to tell him!' She stopped suddenly and Archery watched the old face swell and grow purple. 'It was a change for us to have a nice gentlemanlike young fellow about the place after that Painter.' Her voice changed to a shrill whistling shriek. 'That dirty murdering beast!'

Across the ward another old woman in a bed like Alice Flower's smiled a toothless smile as of one hearing a familiar tale retold. The ward's bedtime story, the sister had said.

Archery leant towards her. 'That was a dreadful day, Miss Flower,' he said, 'the day Mrs Primero died.' The fierce eyes flickered, red and spongey blue. 'I expect you feel you'll never forget it ...'

'Not to my dying day,' said Alice Flower. Perhaps she thought of the now useless body that had once been so fine an instrument and was already three-quarters dead.

'Will you tell me about it?'

As soon as she began he realised how often she must have told it before. It was likely that some of

91

these other old women were not absolutely bedridden, that sometimes in the evenings they got up and gathered round Alice Flower's bed. A tale, he thought, paraphrasing, to draw children from play and old women from the chimney corner.

'He was a devil,' she said, 'a terror. I was scared of him but I never let him know it. Take all and give nothing, that was his motto. Six pounds a year, that was all I got when I first went out into service. Him, he had his home and his wages, a lovely motor to drive. There's some folks want the moon. You'd think a big strong young fellow like that'd be only too glad to fetch the coal in for an old lady, but not Mr Bert Painter. Beast Painter was what I called him.

'That Saturday night when he never come and he never come madam had to sit all by herself in the icy cold. Let me go over and speak to him, madam, I said, but she wouldn't have it. The morning's time enough, Alice, she said. I've said to myself over and over again, if he'd come that night I'd have been in there with them. He wouldn't have been able to tell no lies then.'

'But he did come the next morning, Miss Flower . . .'

'She told him off good and proper. I could hear her giving him a dressing down.'

'What were you doing?'

'Me? When he come in first I was doing the vegetables for madam's lunch, then I popped on the oven and put in the meat tin. They asked me all that at the court in London, the Old Bailey it was.' She paused and there was suspicion in the look she gave him. 'You writing a book about it all, are you, sir?'

'Something like that,' said Archery.

'They wanted to know if I was sure I could hear all right. My hearing's better than that judge's, I can tell you. Just as well it is. If I'd been hard of hearing we might have all gone up in smoke that morning.'

'How was that?'

'Beast Painter was in the drawing room with madam and I'd gone into the larder to get the vinegar for the mint sauce, when all of a sudden I heard a kind of a plop and sizzle. That's that funny old oven, I said, and sure enough it was. I popped back quick and opened the oven door. One of the potatoes had kind of spat out, sir, and fallen on the gas. All in flames it was and sizzling and roaring like a steam engine. I turned it off quick and then I did a silly thing. Poured water on it. Ought to have known better at my age. Ooh, the racket and the smoke! You couldn't hear yourself think.'

There had been nothing about that in the trial transcript. Archery caught his breath in the excitement. 'You couldn't hear yourself think . . .' While you were choked with smoke and deafened by hissing you might not hear a man go upstairs, search a bedroom and come down again. Alice's evidence in this matter had been one of the most important features of the case. For if Painter had been offered and had taken the two hundred pounds in Mrs Primero's presence in the morning, what motive could he have had for killing her in the evening?

'Well, we had our lunch and Mr Roger came. My poor old leg was aching from where I'd bruised it the night before getting a few lumps in on account of Beast Painter being out on the tiles. Mr Roger was ever so nice about it, kept asking me if there was anything he could do, wash up or anything. But that isn't man's work and I always say it's better to keep going while you can.

'It must have been half past five when Mr Roger said he'd have to go. I was up to my neck what with the dishes and worrying if Beast would turn up like he'd promised. "I'll let myself out, Alice," Mr Roger said, and he come down to the kitchen to say goodbye to me. Madam was having a little snooze in the drawing room, God rest her. It was the last she had before her long sleep.' Aghast, Archery watched two tears well into her eyes and flow unchecked down the ridged sunken cheeks. 'I called out, "Cheeri-by, Mr Roger dear, see you next Sunday", and then I heard him shut the front door. Madam was sleeping like a child, not knowing that ravening wolf was lying in wait for her.'

'Try not to upset yourself, Miss Flower.' Doubtful as to what he should do – the right thing is the kind thing, he thought – he pulled out his own clean white handkerchief and gently wiped the wet cheeks.

'Thank you, sir. I'll be all right now. You do feel a proper fool not being able to dry your own tears.' The ghastly cracked smile was almost more painful to witness than the weeping. 'Where was I? Oh, yes. Off I went to church and as soon as I was out of the way along comes Madam Crilling, poking her nose in . . .'

'I know what happened next, Miss Flower,' Archery said very kindly and quietly. 'Tell me about Mrs Crilling. Does she ever come to see you in here?'

Alice Flower gave a kind of snort that would have been comical in a fit person. 'Not she. She's kept out of my way ever since the trial, sir. I know too much about her for her liking. Madam's best friend, my foot! She'd got one interest in madam and one only. She wormed that child of hers into madam's good books on account of she thought madam might leave her something when she went.'

Archery moved closer, praying that the bell for the end of visiting would not ring yet.

'But Mrs Primero didn't make a will.'

'Oh, no, sir, that's what worried Mrs Clever

94

Crilling. She'd come out into my kitchen when madam was sleeping. "Alice," she'd say, "we ought to get dear Mrs Primero to make her last will and testament. It's our duty, Alice, it says so in the Prayer Book."'

'Does it?'

Alice looked both shocked and smug. 'Yes, it does, sir. It says, "But men should often be put in remembrance to take order for the settling of their temporal estates whilst they are in health." Still I don't hold with everything that's in the Prayer Book not when it comes to downright interference – saving your presence, sir. "It's in your interest too, Alice," she says. "You'll be turned out into the streets when she goes."

'But madam wouldn't have it, anyway. Everything was to go to her natural heirs, she said, them being Mr Roger and the little girls. It'd be theirs automati-cally, you see, without any nonsense about wills and lawyers.'

'Mr Roger didn't try to get her to make a will?'

'He's a lovely person is Mr Roger. When Beast Painter had done his murdering work and poor madam was dead Mr Roger got his bit of money – three thousand it was and a bit more. "I'll take care of you, Alice," he said, and so he did. He got me a nice room in Kingsmarkham and gave me two pounds a week on top of my pension. He was in business on his own then and he said he wouldn't give me a lump sum. An allowance, he called it, bless his heart, out of his profits.'

'Business? I thought he was a solicitor.'

'He always wanted to go into business on his own, sir. I don't know the ins and outs of it, but he came to madam one day – must have been two or three weeks before she died – and he said a pal of his would take him in with him if he could put up ten thousand pounds. "I know I haven't got a hope," he said, speaking ever so nice. "It's just a castle in the air, Granny Rose." "Well, it's no good looking at me," says madam. "Ten thousand is all I've got for me and Alice to live on and that's tucked away in Woolworth's shares. You'll get your share when I'm gone." I don't mind telling you, sir, I thought then, if Mr Roger liked to do his little sisters down he could try getting round madam to make that will and leave him the lot. But he never did, never mentioned it again, and he'd always made a point of bringing the two mites just whenever he could. Then Beast Painter killed madam and the money went like she said it would, to the three of them.

'Mr Roger's doing very well now, sir, very well indeed, and he comes to see me regular. I reckon he got the ten thousand from somewhere or maybe another pal came up with something else. It wasn't for me to ask, you see.'

A nice man, Archery thought, a man who had needed money perhaps desperately, but would do nothing underhand to get it; a man who provided for his dead grandmother's domestic while he was struggling to get a business going, who still visited her and who doubtless listened patiently over and over again to the tale Archery had just heard. A very nice man. If love, praise and devotion could reward such a man, he had his reward.

'If you should see Mr Roger, sir, if you want to see him about the story you're writing, would you give him my best respects?'

'I won't forget, Miss Flower.' He put his hand over her dead one and pressed it. 'Good-bye and thank you.' Well done, thou good and faithful servant.

It was gone eight when he got back to the Olive and Dove. The head waiter glared at him when he walked into the dining room at a quarter past. Archery stared about him at the empty room, the chairs arranged against the walls.

'Dance on tonight, sir. We did make a point of asking residents to take their dinner at seven sharp, but I expect we can find you something. In here, if you please.'

Archery followed him into the smaller of the two lounges that led off the dining room. The tables had been crammed in and people were hastily gobbling their meal. He ordered, and through the glass doors, watched the band take its place on the dais.

How was he to spend this long hot summer evening? The dancing would probably go on until half-past twelve or one and the hotel would be unbearable. A quiet stroll was the obvious thing. Or he could take the car and go and look at Victor's Piece. The waiter came back with the braised beef he had ordered, and Archery, resolutely economical, asked for a glass of water.

He was quite alone in his alcove, at least two yards from the next table, and he jumped when he felt something soft and fluffy brush against his leg. Drawing back, he put his hand down, lifted the cloth and met a pair of bright eyes set in a golden woolly skull.

'Hallo, dog,' he said.

'Oh I'm so sorry. Is he being a nuisance?'

He looked up and saw her standing beside him. They had evidently just come in, she, the man with the glassy eyes and another couple.

'Not a bit.' Archery's poise deserted him and he found himself almost stammering. 'I don't mind, really. I'm fond of animals.'

'You were here at lunch, weren't you? I expect he recognised you. Come out, Dog. He doesn't have a name. We just call him Dog because he is one and it's

just as good a name as Jock or Gyp or something.
When you said, "Hallo, dog," he thought you were a
personal friend. He's very intelligent.'

'I'm sure he is.'

She gathered the poodle up in her arms and held
him against the creamy lace of her dress. Now that
she wore no hat he could see the perfect shape of her
head and the high unshadowed brow. The head
waiter minced over, no longer harassed.

'Back again, Louis, like the proverbial bad pen-
nies,' said the glassy-eyed man heartily. 'My wife
took a fancy to come to your hop, but we must have
a spot of dinner first.' So they were married, these
two. Why hadn't it occurred to him before, what
business was it of his and, above all, why should it
cause him this faint distress? 'Our friends here have a
train to catch, so if you can go all out with the old
speed we'll be eternally grateful.'

They all sat down. The poodle mooched between
diners' legs, scavenging for crumbs. Archery was
faintly amused to see how quickly their dinner was
brought to them. They had all ordered different
dishes, but there was little delay and at the same
time little hustle. Archery lingered over his coffee
and his bit of cheese. Surely he was no bother to
anyone in his small corner. People were coming in to
dance now, passing his table and leaving in their
wake the faint scent of cigars and floral perfume. In
the dining room, a ballroom, now, the garden doors
had been opened and couples stood on the terrace
listening to the music in the tranquillity of the
summer night.

The poodle sat on the threshold, bored, watching
the dancers.

'Come here, Dog,' said his owner. Her husband
got up.

'I'll take you to the station, George,' he said.

'We've only got ten minutes, so get a wiggle on, will you?' He seemed to have a variety of expressions to imply the making of haste. 'You don't have to come, darling. Finish your coffee.'

The table was veiled in smoke. They had smoked throughout the courses. He would be gone perhaps only half an hour but he bent over and kissed his wife. She smiled at him, lit another cigarette. When they had gone, she and Archery were alone. She moved into her husband's chair from where she could watch the dancers, many of whom she seemed to know, for she waved occasionally and nodded as if promising she would soon join them.

Archery suddenly felt lonely. He knew no one in this place except two rather hostile policemen. His stay might be for the whole fortnight. Why hadn't he asked Mary to join him? It would be a holiday for her, a change, and – heaven knew – she needed a change. In a minute, when he had finished his second cup, he would go upstairs and telephone her.

The girl's voice startled him. 'Do you mind if I have your ashtray? Ours are all full.'

'Of course not, take it.' He lifted the heavy glass plate and as he handed it to her the tips of her cool dry fingers touched his own. The hand was small, childlike, with short unpainted nails. 'I don't smoke,' he added rather foolishly.

'Are you staying here long?' Her voice was light and soft, yet mature.

'Just a few days.'

'I asked,' she said, 'because we come here so often and I hadn't seen you before today. Most of the people are regulars.' She put out the cigarette carefully, stubbing it until the last red spark was dead. 'They have these dances once a month and we always come. I love dancing.'

Afterwards Archery wondered what on earth had

induced him, a country vicar neary fifty years old, to say what he did. Perhaps it was the mingled scents, the descending twilight or just that he was alone and out of his environment, out of his identity almost.

'Would you like to dance?'

It was a waltz they were playing. He was sure he could waltz. They waltzed at church socials. You simply had to make your feet go one, two, three in a sort of triangle. And yet, for all that, he felt himself blush. What would she think of him at his age? She might suppose he was doing what Charles called 'picking her up'.

'I'd love to,' she said.

Apart from Mary and Mary's sister, she was the only woman he had danced with in twenty years. He was so shy and so overcome by the enormity of what he was doing, that for a moment he was deaf to the music and blind to the hundred or so other people who circled the floor. Then she was in his arms, a light creature of scent and lace whose body so incongruously touching his had the fluidity and the tenuousness of a summer mist. He felt that he was dreaming and because of this, this utter unreality, he forgot about his feet and what he must make them do, and simply moved with her as if he and she and the music were one.

'I'm not very good at this sort of thing,' he said when he found his voice. 'You'll have to overlook my mistakes.' He was so much taller than she that she had to lift her face up to him.

She smiled. 'Hard to make conversation when you're dancing, isn't it? I never know what to say but one must say something.'

'Like "Don't you think this is a good floor?"' Strange, he remembered that one from undergraduate days.

'Or "Do you reverse?" It's absurd really. Here we

100

are dancing together and I don't even know your name.' She gave a little deprecating laugh. 'It's almost immoral.'

'My name's Archery. Henry Archery.'

'How do you do, Henry Archery?' she said gravely. Then as they moved into a pool of sunset light, she looked steadily at him, the glowing colour falling on her face. 'You really don't recognise me, do you?' He shook his head, wondering if he had made some terrible *faux pas*. She gave a mock sigh. 'Such is fame! Imogen Ide. Doesn't it ring a bell?'

'I'm awfully sorry.'

'Frankly, you don't look as if you spend your leisure perusing the glossy magazines. Before I married I was what they call a top model. The most photographed face in Britain.'

He hardly knew what to say. The things that came to mind all had some reference to her extraordinary beauty and to speak them aloud would have been impertinent. Sensing his predicament, she burst out laughing, but it was a companionable laugh, warm and kind.

He smiled down at her. Then over her shoulder he caught sight of a familiar face. Chief Inspector Wexford had come on to the floor with a stout pleasant-looking woman and a young couple. His wife, his daughter and the architect's son, Archery supposed, feeling a sudden pang. He watched them sit down and just as he was about to avert his eyes, Wexford's met his. The smiles they exchanged were slightly antagonistic and Archery felt hot with awkwardness. Wexford's expression held a mocking quality as if to say that dancing was a frivolity quite out of keeping with Archery's quest. Abruptly he looked away and back to his partner.

'I'm afraid I only read *The Times*,' he said, feeling

the snobbishness of the remark as soon as the words were out.

'I was in *The Times* once,' she said. 'Oh, not my picture. I was in the High Court bit. Somebody mentioned my name in a case and the judge said, "Who is Imogen Ide?"'

'That really is fame.'

'I've kept the cutting to this day.'

The music that had been so liquid and lullaby-like suddenly jerked into a frightening tempo with a stormy undertone of drums.

'I haven't a hope of doing this one,' Archery said helplessly.

He released her quickly, there in the middle of the floor.

'Never mind. Thank you very much, anyway. I've enjoyed it.'

'So have I, very much indeed.'

They began to thread their way between couples who were shuddering and bounding about like savages. She was holding his hand and he could hardly withdraw it without rudeness.

'Here's my husband back,' she said. 'Won't you join us for the evening if you've nothing better to do?'

The man called Ide was coming up to them, smiling. His evenly olive face, dead black hair and almost feminine standard of grooming gave him the look of a waxwork. Archery had the absurd notion that if you came upon him at Madame Tussaud's the old joke of the naive spectator mistaking a model for a flesh and blood attendant would be reversed. In this case you would pass the real man by, thinking him a figure in wax.

'This is Mr Archery, darling. I've been telling him he ought to stay. It's such a beautiful night.'

'Good idea. Perhaps I can get you a drink, Mr Archery?'

'Thank you, no.' Archery found himself shaking hands, astonished because of his fantasy at the warmth of Ide's hand. 'I must go. I have to phone my wife.'

'I hope we shall see you again,' said Imogen Ide. 'I enjoyed our dance.' She took her husband's hand and they moved away into the centre of the floor, their bodies meeting, their steps following the intricate rhythm. Archery went upstairs to his bedroom. Earlier he had supposed that the music would annoy him but here in the violet-coloured dusk it was enchanting, disturbing, awakening in him forgotten, undefined longings. He stood at the window, looking at the sky with its long feathery scarves of cloud, rose pink as cyclamen petals but less substantial. The strains of the music had softened to match this tranquil sky and now they seemed to him like the opening bars of an overture to some pastoral opera.

Presently he sat down on the bed and put his hand to the telephone. It rested there immobile for some minutes. What was the point of ringing Mary when he had nothing to tell her, no plans even for what he would do in the morning? He felt a sudden distaste for Thringford and its small parochial doings. He had lived there so long, so narrowly, and outside all the time there had been a world of which he knew little.

From where he sat he could see nothing but sky, broken continents and islands on a sea of azure. 'Here will we sit and let the sound of music creep in our ears ...' He took his hand from the telephone and lay back, thinking of nothing.

Chapter 9

The words of his mouth were softer than butter,
having war in his heart: his words were smoother
than oil, and yet be they very swords.

Psalm 55, appointed for the Tenth Day.

'I suppose there isn't anything in it?'

'In what, Mike? Liz Crilling having some dark
secret her mother doesn't want extorted from her
under the third degree?'

Burden lowered the blinds against the brazen
morning sky.

'Those Crillings always make me uneasy,' he said.

'They're no more kinky than half our customers,'
Wexford said breezily. 'Liz'll turn up at the Assizes
all right. If not for any other reason simply because
Mrs Crilling doubts her ability to get a thousand
quid out of her brother-in-law, or whoever it is
supports them. And then if she's got something to
tell us, she'll tell us.'

Burden's expression, though apologetic, was obstin-
ate.

'I can't help feeling it's got some connection with
Painter,' he said.

Wexford had been leafing through a thick orange-
coloured trade directory. Now he dropped it on the
desk with a deliberate bang.

'By God, I won't have any more of this! What is it,
anyhow, some sort of conspiracy to prove I can't do
my job?'

'I'm sorry, sir, you know I didn't mean that.'

'I don't know a damn thing, Mike. I only know
the Painter case was an open and shut affair, and

nobody's got a hope in hell of showing he didn't do it.' He began to calm down slowly, and he spread his hands in two large implacable fans on the directory cover. 'Go and question Liz by all means. Or tell Archery to do it for you. He's a fast worker that one.'

'Is he? What makes you say so?'

'Never mind. I've got work to do if you haven't and ...' said Wexford, splendidly co-ordinating his metaphors, 'I'm fed up to my back teeth with having Painter rammed down my throat morning, noon and night.'

Archery had slept deeply and dreamlessly. It occurred to him that he had done all his dreaming while he was awake and there was none left for sleep. The telephone roused him. It was his wife.

'Sorry it's so early, darling, but I've had another letter from Charles.'

There was a cup of cold tea by the bed. Archery wondered how long it had been there. He found his watch and saw that it was nine.

'That's all right. How are you?'

'Not so bad. You sound as if you're still in bed.'

Archery grunted something.

'Now, listen. Charles is coming down tomorrow and he says he's coming straight over to Kingsmarkham.'

'Coming *down*?'

'Oh, it's all right, Henry. He's going to cut the last three days of term. Surely it can't matter much.'

'As long as it isn't the thin end of the wedge. Is he coming to the Olive?'

'Well, naturally. He's got to stay somewhere. I know it's expensive, darling, but he's got himself a job for August and September – something in a brewery. It sounds awful but he's going to get sixteen pounds a week and he says he'll pay you back.'

'I hadn't realised I made such an avaricious impression on my son.'

'You know he doesn't mean that. You *are* touchy this morning . . .'

After she had rung off he still held the receiver for some moments in his hand. He wondered why he hadn't asked her to join him as well. He had meant to last night and then . . . Of course, he had been so drowsy while she was speaking that he hardly knew what he was saying. The operator's voice broke in.

'Have you finished or did you want to make a call?'

'No thank you. I've finished.'

The little sandy houses in Glebe Road seemed to have been bleached and dried up by the sun. This morning they looked even more like desert dwellings, each surrounded by its own scanty oasis.

Burden went first to number a hundred and two. An old acquaintance of his lived there, a man with a long record and a nasty sense of humour called by some 'Monkey' Matthews. Burden thought it more than likely that he was responsible for the home-made bomb, a bizarre affair of sugar and weed killer stuffed into a whisky bottle that a blonde woman of easy virtue had received that morning through her letter box. The bomb had done no more than wreck the hall of her flat, she and her current lover being still in bed, but Burden thought it might amount to attempted murder just the same.

He knocked and rang but he was sure the bell didn't work. Then he went round the back and found himself ankle-deep in garbage, pram wheels, old clothes, newspapers and empty bottles. He looked through the kitchen window. There was a packet of weed killer – sodium chlorate crystals – on the window sill and the top had been torn off. How confident could you get, or how stupid? He went back up the street to a call box and told Bryant and Gates to pick up the occupant of a hundred and two Glebe Road.

Twenty-four was on the same side. Now he was so near there would be no harm in having a chat with Liz Crilling. The front door was closed but the latch was down. He coughed and walked in.

In the back room a plastic transistor was playing pop music. Elizabeth Crilling sat at the table reading the Situations Vacant in last week's local paper and she was wearing nothing but a slip, its broken shoulder strap held together with a safety pin.

'I don't remember inviting you in.'

Burden looked at her distastefully. 'D'you mind putting something on?' She made no move but kept her eyes on the paper. He glanced around the dismal, untidy room, and from the various miscellaneous heaps of clothes, selected something that might have been a dressing gown, a pink floppy thing whose flounces recalled withered petals. 'Here,' he said, and he wondered if she were not quite well, for she shuddered as she put the dressing gown round her. It was far too big, obviously not her own.

'Where's your mother?'

'I don't know. Gone out somewhere. I'm not her keeper.' She grinned suddenly, showing her beautiful teeth. 'Am I my mother's keeper? That's good, don't you think? Which reminds me . . .' The smile died and she exclaimed sharply, 'What's that clergyman doing here?'

Burden never answered a question if he could help it.

'Looking for a new post, are you?'

107

She gave a sulky pout. 'I phoned my firm yesterday when I got back from that bloody court and they gave me the push. I've got you lot to thank for that.' Burden inclined his head politely. 'Well, I've got to have a job, haven't I? They want girls at the raincoat factory and they say you can pick up twenty quid a week with overtime.'

Burden remembered her education, the expensive schools the Crilling relatives had paid for. She stared at him boldly.

'I may as well go and see them,' she said. 'What's the harm? Life's hell anyway.' She gave a strident laugh, walked to the mantelpiece and leaned against it, looking down at him. The open dressing gown, the tatty underclothes were provocative in a raw, basic way, that seemed to go with the hot weather and the dishevelled room. 'To what do I owe the honour of this visit? Are you lonely, Inspector? I hear your wife's away.' She took a cigarette and put it between her lips. Her forefinger was rusty with nicotine, the nail yellow, the cuticle bitten. 'Where the hell are the matches?'

There was something in the quick wary look she gave over her shoulder that impelled him to follow her to the kitchen. Once there, she turned to face him, grabbed a box of matches and stood as if barring his way. He felt a thrill of alarm. She thrust the matches into his hand.

'Light it for me, will you?'

He struck the match steadily. She came very close to him and as the flame shrivelled the tobacco, closed her fingers over his hand. For a split second he felt what his rather prudish nature told him was vile, then that nature, his duty and a swift suspicion took over. She was breathing hard, but not, he was certain, because of his nearness to her. From long practice he sidestepped neatly, freeing the long bare leg from between his own, and found himself confronting what she perhaps had hoped to hide from him.

The sink was crammed with dirty crocks, potato peelings, tea leaves, wet paper, but the Crillings were long past middle-class concealment of squalor.

'You could do with a few days off, I should think,' he said loudly. 'Get this place in some sort of order.'

She had begun to laugh. 'You know, you're not so bad-looking on the other side of a smoke-screen.'

'Been ill, have you?' He was looking at the empty pill bottles, the one that was half full and the syringe. 'Nerves, I daresay.'

She stopped laughing. 'They're hers.'

Burden read labels, saying nothing.

'She has them for her asthma. They're all the same.' As he put out his hand to find the hypodermic she seized his wrist. 'You've no business to turn things over. That amounts to searching and for searching you need a warrant.'

'True,' said Burden placidly. He followed her back to the living room and jumped when she shouted at him:

'You never answered my question about the clergyman.'

'He's come here because he knows Painter's daughter,' said Burden guardedly.

She went white and he thought she looked like her mother.

'Painter that killed the old woman?'

Burden nodded.

'That's funny,' she said. 'I'd like to see her again.' He had a queer feeling she was changing the subject, and yet her remark was not inconsequential. She turned her eyes towards the garden. But it wasn't, he thought, the nettles, the brambles and the mean wire fence she could see. 'I used to go over to the coach house and play with her,' she said. 'Mother never knew. She said Tess wasn't my class. I couldn't understand that. I thought, how can she have a class if she doesn't go to school?' She reached up and gave the birdcage a vicious push. 'Mother was always with the old woman – talk, talk, talk, I'll never forget it – and she used to send me into the garden to play. There wasn't anything to play with and one day I saw Tessie, mucking about with a heap of sand ... Why are you looking at me like that?'

'Am I?'

'Does she know about her father?' Burden nodded. 'Poor kid. What does she do for a living?'

'She's some kind of a student.'

'*Student?* My God, I was a student once.' She had begun to tremble. The long worm of ash broke from her cigarette and scattered down the pink flounces. Looking down at it, she flicked uselessly at old stains and burn marks. The movement suggested the uncontrollable jerking of chorea. She swung round on him, her hate and despair striking him like a flame. 'What are you trying to do to me?' she shouted. 'Get out! Get out!'

When he had gone she grabbed a torn sheet from a stack of unironed linen and flung it over the birdcage. The sudden movement and the gust of breeze it had caused fluttered the thing her mother called a negligee but that she had never feared until it touched her own skin. Why the hell did he have to come here and rake it all up again? Perhaps a drink would help. True, it hadn't done so the other day ... There never was a drink in this house, anyway.

Newspapers, old letters and unpaid bills, empty cigarette packets and a couple of old laddered stockings tumbled out when she opened the cupboard door. She rummaged in the back among dusty

110

vases, Christmas wrapping paper, playing cards with dog-eared corners. One vase had an encouraging shape. She pulled it out and found it was the cherry brandy Uncle had given her mother for her birthday. Filthy, sweet cherry brandy ... She squatted on the floor among the debris and poured some of it into a grimy glass. In a minute she felt a lot better, almost well enough to get dressed and do something about the bloody job. Now she had begun she might as well finish the bottle – it was wonderful how little it took to do the trick provided you started on an empty stomach.

The neck of the bottle rattled against the glass. She was concentrating on keeping her hand steady, not watching the liquid level rise and rise until it overbrimmed, spilt and streamed over the spread pink flounces.

Red everywhere. Good thing we're not house-proud, she thought, and then she looked down at herself, at red on pale pink ... Her fingers tore at the nylon until they were red and sticky too. O God, God! She trampled on it, shuddering as if it were slimy, alive, and threw herself on the sofa.

... You had nothing pretty on now, nothing to show to Tessie. She used to worry in case you got yourself dirty and one day when Mummy was indoors with Granny Rose and the man they called Roger she took you upstairs to see Auntie Rene and Uncle Bert, and Auntie Rene made you put an old apron on over your frock.

Uncle Bert and Roger. They were the only men you knew apart from Daddy who was always ill – 'ailing' Mummy called it. Uncle Bert was rough and big and once when you came upstairs quietly you heard him shouting at Auntie Rene and then you saw him hit her. But he was kind to you and he called you Lizzie. Roger never called you anything.

How could he when he never spoke to you, but looked at you as if he hated you?

It was in the autumn that Mummy said you ought to have a party frock. Funny really, because there weren't any parties to go to, but Mummy said you could wear it on Christmas Day. Pink it was, three layers of pale pink net over a pink petticoat, and it was the most beautiful dress you had ever seen in your life . . .

Elizabeth Crilling knew that once it had begun it would go on and on. Only one thing could stop it now. Keeping her eyes from the pink thing, all spattered with red, she stumbled out into the kitchen to find her temporary salvation.

Irene Kershaw's voice on the telephone sounded cold and distant. 'Your Charlie seems to have had a bit of a tiff with Tessie, Mr Archery. I don't know what it's all about, but I'm sure it can't be her fault. She worships the ground he treads on.'

'They're old enough to know what they're doing,' said Archery insincerely.

'She's coming home tomorrow and she must be upset if she's cutting the last days of term. All the people round here keep asking when the wedding is and I just don't know what to say. It puts me in a very awkward position.'

Respectability, always respectability.

'Did you ring me up about something special, Mr Archery, or was it just for a chat?'

'I wondered if you'd mind giving me your husband's business number?'

'If you two think you can get together,' she said more warmly, 'and have a go at patching things up, that would suit me down to the ground. I really can't contemplate the idea of my Tess being – well, thrown over.' Archery did not answer. 'The number's Uplands 62234,' she said.

Kershaw had an extension of his own and a bright cockney secretary.

'I want to write to Painter's commanding officer,' Archery said when the civilities had been exchanged.

Kershaw seemed to hesitate, then said in his usual eager, vital voice, 'Don't know the bloke's name, but it was the Duke of Babraham's Light Infantry he was in. Third Battalion. The War Office'll tell you.'

'The defence didn't call him at the trial, but it might help me if he could give Painter a good character.'

'If. I wonder why the defence didn't call him, Mr Archery?'

The War Office was helpful. The Third Battalion had been commanded by a Colonel Cosmo Plashet. He was an old man now and living in retirement in Westmorland. Archery made several attempts to write to Colonel Plashet. The final letter was not what he would have wished, but it would have to do. After lunch he went out to post it.

He strolled up towards the Post Office. Time hung heavy on his hands and he had no notion what to do next. Tomorrow Charles would come, full of ideas and extravagant plans, but comforting, an assistant. Or, knowing Charles, a director. He badly needed someone to direct him. Police work is for policemen, he thought, experts who are trained and have all the means for detection at their disposal.

Then he saw her. She was coming out of the florist's next door to the Post Office and her arms were full of white roses. They matched and mingled with the white pattern on her black dress so that you could not tell which were real and which a mere design on silk.

'Good afternoon, Mr Archery,' said Imogen Ide.

Until now he had hardly noticed the beauty of the day, the intense blue of the sky, the glory of perfect holiday weather. She smiled.

'Would you be very kind and open the car door for me?'

He jumped to do her bidding like a boy. The poodle, Dog, was sitting on the passenger seat and when Archery touched the door, he growled and showed his teeth.

'Don't be such a fool,' she said to the dog and dumped him on the back seat. 'I'm taking these up to Forby cemetery. My husband's ancestors have a sort of vault there. Very feudal. He's in town so I said I'd do it. It's an interesting old church. Have you seen much of the country round here yet?'

'Very little, I'm afraid.'

'Perhaps you don't care for clerestories and fonts and that sort of thing.'

'Quite the contrary, I assure you. I'll get the car and go over to Forby tonight if you think it's worth seeing.'

'Why not come now?'

He had meant her to ask him. He knew it and he was ashamed. Yet what was there to be ashamed about? In a way he was on holiday and holiday acquaintances were quickly made. He had met her husband and it was only by chance her husband was not with her now. In that case he would have accepted without a qualm. Besides, in these days there was no harm in a man going on a little excursion with a woman. How many times had he picked up Miss Baylis in Thringford village and driven her into Colchester to do her shopping? Imogen Ide was much farther removed from him in age than Miss Baylis. She couldn't be more than thirty. He was old enough to be her father. Suddenly he wished he hadn't thought of that, for it put things in an unpleasant perspective.

'It's very good of you,' he said. 'I'd like to.'

She was a good driver. For once he didn't mind being driven, didn't wish he was at the wheel. It was a beautiful car, a silver Lancia Flavia, and it purred along the winding roads. All was still and they passed only two other cars. The meadows were rich green or pale yellow where they had been shorn of hay, and between them and a dark ridge of woodland ran a glittering brown stream.

'That's the Kingsbrook,' she said, 'the same one that passes under the High Street. Isn't it strange? Man can do almost anything, move mountains, create seas, irrigate deserts, but he can't prevent the flow of water. He can dam it, channel it, pass it through pipes, make bridges over it . . .' He watched her, remembering with wonder that she had been a photographic model. Her lips were parted and the breeze blew her hair. 'But still it springs from the earth and finds its way to the sea.'

He said nothing and hoped she could sense if not see his nod. They were coming into a village. A dozen or so cottages and a couple of big houses surrounded a sprawling green; there was a little inn and through a mass of dark green foliage Archery could see the outlines of the church.

The entrance to the churchyard was by way of a kissing gate. He followed Imogen Ide and he carried the roses. The place was shady and cool but not well-tended and some of the older gravestones had tumbled over on their backs into the tangle of nettles and briars.

'This way,' she said, taking the left hand path. 'You mustn't go widdershins around a church. It's supposed to be unlucky.'

Yews and ilexes bordered the path. Underfoot it

was sandy, yet green with moss and the delicate tufts of arenaria. The church was very old and built of rough-hewn oaken logs. Its beauty lay in its antiquity.

'It's one of the oldest wooden churches in the country.'

'There's one like it in my county,' said Archery. 'At Greensted. I believe it's ninth century.'

'This one's nine something. Would you like to see the leper squint?'

They knelt down side by side and, bending forward, he peered through the small triangular gap at the base of the log wall. Although it was not the first of its kind he had seen, it pained him to think of the outcast, the unclean, who came to this tiny grille and listening to the Mass, received on his tongue the bread that some believe is the body of God. It made him think of Tess, herself an outcast, condemned like the leper to an undeserved disease. Within he could see a little stone aisle, wooden pews and a pulpit carved with saints' faces. He shivered and he felt her shiver beside him.

They were very close together under the yew boughs. He had a strange feeling that they were quite alone in the world and that they had been brought here for the working out of some destiny. He lifted his eyes, and turning to her, met hers. He expected her to smile but instead her face was grave, yet full of wonder and a kind of fear. He felt in himself, without analysing it, the emotion he saw in her eyes. The scent of the roses was intoxicating, fresh and unbearably sweet.

Then he got to his feet quickly, a little quelled by the stiffness of his knees. For a moment he had felt like a boy; his body betrayed him as bodies always do.

She said rather brightly, 'Have a look inside while I put these flowers on the grave. I won't be long.'

He went softly up the aisle and stood before the altar. Anyone watching him might have taken him for an atheist, so cool and appraising was his glance. Back again to look at the unassuming little font, the inscriptions on wall plaques. He put two half-crowns in the box and signed his name in the visitors' book. His hand was shaking so badly that the signature looked like that of an old man.

When he came out once more into the churchyard she was nowhere to be seen. The lettering on the older stones had been obliterated by time and weather. He walked into the new part, reading the last messages of relatives to their dead.

As he came to the end of the path where the hedge was and on the other side of the hedge a meadow, a name that seemed familiar caught his eye. Grace, John Grace. He reflected, searching his mind. It was not a common name and until quite recently he had associated it only with the great cricketer. Of course – a boy had lain dying in the road and that death and that boy's request had reminded Wexford of another, similar tragedy. Wexford had told him about it in the court. 'Must be all of twenty years . . .'

Archery looked to the engraved words for confirmation.

Sacred to the Memory of
John Grace
Who departed This Life
February 16th, 1945
In the Twenty-First Year
of His Age

Go, Shepherd, to your rest;
Your tale is told.

The Lamb of God takes
Shepherds to his fold.

A pleasant, if not brilliant, conceit, Archery thought. It was apparently a quotation, but he didn't recognise it. He looked round as Imogen Ide approached. The leaf shadows played on her face and made a pattern on her hair so that it looked as if it was covered by a veil of lace.

'Are you reminding yourself of your mortality?' she asked him gravely.

'I suppose so. It's an interesting place.'

'I'm glad to have had the opportunity of showing it to you. I'm very patriotic – if that's the word – about my county though it hasn't been mine for long.'

He was certain she was going to offer herself as his guide on some future occasion and he said quickly: 'My son is coming tomorrow. We'll have to explore together.' She smiled politely. 'He's twenty-one,' he added rather fatuously.

Simultaneously their eyes turned to the inscription on the stone.

'I'm ready to go if you are,' she said.

She dropped him outside the Olive and Dove. They said good-bye briskly and he noticed she said nothing about hoping to see him again. He didn't feel like tea and he went straight upstairs. Without knowing why he took out the photograph he had of Painter's daughter. Looking at the picture, he wondered why he had thought her so lovely. She was just a pretty girl with the prettiness of youth. Yet while he looked he seemed to realise for the first time why Charles longed so passionately to possess her. It was a strange feeling and it had little to do with Tess, with Tess's appearance or with Charles. In a way it was a universal diffused empathy, but it was selfish too and it came from his heart rather than from his mind.

Chapter 10

And if he hath not before disposed of his goods, let him be admonished to make his will . . . for the better discharging of his conscience and the quietness of his executors.

The Visitation of the Sick.

'You don't seem to have got very far,' said Charles. He sat down in an armchair and surveyed the pleasant lounge. The maid who was operating a floor polisher thought him very handsome with his rather long fair hair and his scornful expression. She decided to give the lounge a more than usually thorough do. 'The great thing is to be businesslike about it. We haven't got all that long. I start at the brewery on Monday week.' Archery was rather nettled. His own parochial duties were being over-looked. 'I'm sure there's something fishy about that fellow Primero, Roger Primero. I rang him up before I got here last night and I've got a date to see him this morning at half eleven.'

Archery looked at his watch. It was almost ten.

'You'd better get a move on, then. Where does he live?'

'You see? Now if I'd been in your shoes that's the first thing I'd have found out. He lives at Forby Hall. I suppose he fancies himself as the lord of the manor.' He glanced at his father and said quickly, 'Be all right if I have the car?'

'I suppose so. What are you going to tell him, Charles? He might have you thrown out.'

'I don't think he will,' Charles said thoughtfully. 'I've found out a bit about him and it seems he's mad

120

keen on publicity. Always trying to create an image.' He hesitated, then added boldly, 'I told him I was the top features man on the *Sunday Planet* and we were doing a series on tycoons. Rather good, don't you think?'

'It doesn't happen to be true,' said Archery.

Charles said rapidly, 'The end justifies the means. I thought I could put across a line about his early life being dogged by misfortune, father dying, grandmother murdered, no prospects – that sort of thing. And look at him now. You never know what will come out. He's supposed to be very forthcoming to the Press.'

'We'd better go and get the car out.'

It was as hot as ever, but more sultry. A thin mist covered the sun. Charles wore an open necked white shirt and rather tapering trousers. Archery thought he looked like a Regency duellist.

'You won't want to start yet,' he said. 'Forby's only about four miles away. Would you like to look round the place?'

They walked up the High Street and over the Kingsbrook bridge. Archery was proud to have his son beside him. He knew they were very much alike but he didn't for a moment deceive himself they might be taken for brothers. The heavy muggy weather had brought on a twinge of lumbago and today he had utterly forgotten what it felt like to be twenty-one.

'You're reading English,' he said to Charles. 'Tell me where this comes from.' His memory hadn't begun to fail, at any rate. He was word perfect in the little verse.

> ' "Go, Shepherd, to your rest;
> Your tale is told.
> The lamb of God takes

Shepherds to his fold." '

Charles shrugged. 'Sounds vaguely familiar, but I can't place it. Where did you see it?'

'On a gravestone in Forby churchyard.'

'You really are the end, Father. I thought you wanted to help me and Tess and all you've been doing is messing about in cemeteries.'

Archery controlled himself with difficulty. If Charles was going to take everything into his own hands there seemed no reason why he shouldn't just go back to Thringford. There was nothing to keep him in Kingsmarkham. He wondered why the prospect of returning to the vicarage seemed ineffably dull. Suddenly he stopped and nudged his son's arm.

'What's the matter?'

'That woman outside the butcher's, the one in the cape – it's that Mrs Crilling I told you about. I'd rather not come face to face with her.'

But it was too late. She had evidently seen them already, for with her cape flying, she came bearing down upon them like a galleon.

'Mr Archery! My dear friend!' She took both his hands in hers and swung them as if she were about to partner him in an eightsome reel. 'What a lovely surprise! I was only saying to my daughter this morning, I do hope I shall see that dear man again so that I can thank him for ministering to me in my wretched affliction.'

This was a new mood. She was like a dowager at a successful garden party. The cape was familiar but the dress she wore under it was an ordinary cotton frock, simple and dowdy, somewhat splashed with gravy stains on its front. She gave a broad, calm and gracious smile.

'This is my son, Charles,' Archery muttered. 'Charles, this is Mrs Crilling.'

To his surprise Charles took the outstretched, none-too-clean hand and half-bowed over it.

'How do you do?' Over her head he gave his father an angry glance. 'I've heard so much about you.'

'Nice things, I hope.' If it occurred to her that Archery had seen nothing nice about her to relate she gave no sign of it. She was quite sane, gay, even frivolous. 'Now, don't refuse to gratify my little whim. I want you both to come into the Carousel and take a wee cup of coffee with me. My treat, of course,' she added archly.

'Our time,' said Charles grandiloquently – absurdly, Archery thought, 'is quite at your disposal. Until eleven-fifteen, that is. Don't let us discuss anything so absurd as treats in the company of a lady.'

Evidently it was the right line to take with her. 'Isn't he *sweet*?' she gurgled. They went into the cafe. 'Children are such a blessing, don't you think? The crown of the tree of life. You must be proud of him, even though he quite puts you in the shade.'

Charles pulled out a chair for her. They were the only customers and for a while no one came to take their order. Mrs Crilling leant confidingly towards Archery.

'My baby has got herself a situation and she starts tomorrow. An operative in a ladies' wear establishment. I understand the prospects are excellent. With her intelligence there's no knowing how far she can go. The trouble is she's never had a real chance.' She had been speaking in a low genteel voice. Suddenly she turned her back on him, banged the sugar basin on the table and screamed loudly in the direction of the kitchen:

'Service!'

Charles jumped. Archery shot him a glance of triumph.

'Always having her hopes raised and then it comes to nothing,' she went on just as if the scream had never happened. 'Her father was just the same – struck down with T.B. in the flower of his age and dead within six months.' Archery flinched as she jerked away from him once more. 'Where the flaming hell are those bloody girls?' she shouted.

A woman in a green uniform with Manageress embroidered on the bodice came out from the kitchen. The look she gave Mrs Crilling was bored and withering.

'I asked you not to come in here again, Mrs Crilling, if you can't behave yourself.' She smiled frostily at Archery. 'What can I get you, sir?'

'Three coffees, please.'

'I'll have mine black,' said Charles.

'What was I talking about?'

'Your daughter,' said Archery hopefully.

'Oh, yes, my baby. It's funny really she should have had such a bad break because when she was a little tot it looked as if everything in the garden was lovely. I had a dear old friend, you see, who simply doted on my baby. And she was rolling in money, kept servants and all that kind of thing ...'

The coffee came. It was the espresso kind with foam on the top.

'You can bring me some white sugar,' said Mrs Crilling sulkily. 'I can't stomach that demerara muck.' The waitress flounced away, returned with another sugar bowl and banged it down on the table. Mrs Crilling gave a shrill little shriek as soon as she was out of earshot. 'Silly bitch!'

Then she returned to her theme. 'Very old my friend was and beyond being responsible for her actions. Senile, they call it. Over and over again she told me she wanted to do something for my baby. I passed it off, of course, having an absolute revulsion about stepping into dead men's shoes.' She stopped suddenly and dropped four heaped teaspoonfuls of sugar into her coffee.

'Naturally,' said Charles. 'The last thing anyone would call you is mercenary, Mrs Crilling.'

She smiled complacently and to Archery's intense amusement, leant across the table and patted Charles's cheek.

'You dear,' she said. 'You lovely, understanding dear.' After a deep breath she went on more practically, 'Still, you have to look after your own. I didn't press it, not till the doctor told me Mr Crilling had only got six months to live. No insurance, I thought in my despair, no pension. I pictured myself reduced to leaving my baby on the steps of an orphanage.'

For his part. Archery was unable to picture it. Elizabeth had been a sturdy youngster of five at the time.

'Do go on,' said Charles. 'It's most interesting.'

'You ought to make a will, I said to my friend. I'll pop down the road and get you a will form. A thousand or two would make all the difference to my baby. You know how she's gladdened your last years, and what have those grandchildren of yours ever done for you? Damn all, I thought.'

'But she didn't make a will?' Archery said.

'What do you know about it? You let me tell it in my own way. It was about a week before she died. I'd had the will form for weeks and weeks and all the time poor Mr Crilling was wasting away to a shadow. But would she fill it in? Not her, the old cow. I had to use all my most winning powers of persuasion. Every time I said a word that crazy old maid of hers would put her spoke in. Then that old maid – Flower, her name was – she got a bad cold and had to keep to her bed. "Have you thought any more about disposing of your temporal estates?" I said to my friend in a light-hearted, casual manner. "Maybe I should do something for Lizzie," she said and I knew my opportunity was at hand.

'Back across the road I flew. I didn't like to witness it myself, you know, on account of my baby being a beneficiary. Mrs White, my neighbour, came over and the lady who helped with her housework. They were only too delighted. You might say it brought a ray of sunshine into their humdrum lives.'

Archery wanted to say, 'But Mrs Primero died intestate.' He didn't dare. Any hint that he knew whom she was talking about and the whole narrative might be brought to a halt.

'Well, we got it all written out. I'm a great reader, Mr Archery, so I was able to put it in the right language. "Blood is thicker than water," said my old friend – she was wandering in her mind – but she only put the grandchildren down for five hundred a-piece. There was eight thousand for my baby and I was to have charge of it till she was twenty-one, and a bit left over for the Flower woman. My friend was crying bitterly. I reckon she realised how wicked she'd been in not doing it before.

'And that was that. I saw Mrs White and the other lady safely off the premises – more fool I, though I didn't know it at the time. I said I'd keep the will safe and I did. She wasn't to mention it to anybody. And – would you believe it? – a week later she met with her death.'

Charles said innocently, 'That was a good start for your daughter, Mrs Crilling, whatever misfortunes came afterwards.'

He started as she got up abruptly. Her face had

blanched to the whiteness it had worn in court and her eyes blazed.

'Any benefits she got,' she said in a choking voice, 'came from her dead father's people. Charity it was, cold charity. "Send me the school bills, Josie," her uncle'd say to me. "I'll pay them direct, and her auntie can go with her to get her uniform. If you think she needs treatment for her nerves her auntie can go with her to Harley Street, too."'

'But what about the will?'

'That bloody will!' Mrs Crilling shouted. 'It wasn't legal. I only found out after she was dead. I took it straight round to Quadrants, the solicitors that were in the High Street. Old Mr Quadrant was alive then. "What about these alterations?" he said. Well, I looked and, lo and behold, the old cow had scribbled in a lot of extra bits while I was at the front door with Mrs White. Scribbled in bits and scratched out bits too. "These invalidate the whole thing," said Mr Quadrant. "You have to get the witnesses to sign them, or have a codicil. You could fight it," he said, looking me up and down in a nasty way, knowing I hadn't got a bean. "But I wouldn't say much for your chances."'

To Archery's horror she broke into a stream of obscenities, many of which he had never heard before. The manageress came out and took her by the arm.

'Out you go. We can't have this in here.'

'My God,' said Charles, after she had been hustled away. 'I see what you mean.'

'I must confess her language shook me a bit.'

Charles chuckled. 'Not fit for your ears at all.'

'It was most enlightening, though. Are you going to bother with Primero now?'

'It can't do any harm.'

Archery had to wait a long time in the corridor outside Wexford's office. Just as he was beginning to think he would have to give up and try again later, the main entrance doors opened and a little bright-eyed man in working clothes came in between two uniformed policemen. He was plainly some sort of criminal, but everyone seemed to know him and find him a source of ironic amusement.

'I can't stand these contemporary-type nicks,' he said impudently to the station sergeant. Wexford came out of his office, ignoring Archery, and crossed to the desk. 'Give me the old-fashioned kind every time. I've got a slummy mind, that's my trouble.'

'I'm not interested in your views on interior decoration, Monkey,' said Wexford.

The little man turned to him and grinned.

'You've got a nasty tongue, you have. Your sense of humour's sunk as you've gone up. Pity, really.'

'Shut up!'

Archery listened in admiration. He wished that he had the power and the authority to talk like that to Mrs Crilling, or that such authority could be vested in Charles, enabling him to question Primero without the inhibitions of subterfuge. Wexford, talking silkily about bombs and attempted murder, ushered the little man into his office and the door closed on them. Such things did go on, Archery thought. Perhaps his own new-forming theories were not so far-fetched after all.

'If I could just see Inspector Burden for a moment,' he said more confidently to the station sergeant.

'I'll see if he's free, sir.'

Eventually Burden came out to him himself.

'Good morning, sir. Doesn't get any cooler, does it?'

'I've got something rather important to tell you. Can you spare me five minutes?'

'Surely.'

But he made no move to take him into a more private place. The station sergeant occupied himself with perusing a large book. Sitting on a ridiculous spoon-shaped chair outside Wexford's office, Archery felt like a school boy, who having waited a long time to see the headmaster, is compelled to confide in and perhaps take his punishment from an underling. Rather chastened, he told Burden briefly about Mrs Crilling.

'Most interesting. You mean that when Mrs Primero was murdered the Crilling woman thought the will was valid?'

'It amounts to that. She didn't mention the murder.'

'We can't do anything. You realise that?'

'I want you to tell me if I have sufficient grounds to write to the Home Secretary.'

A constable appeared from somewhere, tapped on Wexford's door and was admitted.

'You haven't any circumstantial evidence,' Burden said. 'I'm sure the Chief Inspector wouldn't encourage it.'

A roar of sardonic laughter sounded through the thin dividing wall. Archery felt unreasonably piqued.

'I think I shall write just the same.'

'You must do as you please, sir.' Burden got up. 'Been seeing much of the country round here?'

Archery swallowed his anger. If Burden intended to terminate the interview with small talk, small talk he should have. Hadn't he promised his old friend Griswold and, for that matter, the Chief Inspector, not to make trouble?

'I went to Forby yesterday,' he said. 'I was in the churchyard and I happened to notice the grave of that boy Mr Wexford was talking about in court the other day. His name was Grace. Do you remember?'

Burden's face was a polite blank but the station sergeant glanced up.

'I'm a Forby man myself, sir,' he said. 'We make a bit of a song and dance about John Grace at home. They'll tell you all about him in Forby for all it was twenty years ago.'

'All about him?'

'He fancied himself as a poet, poor kid, wrote plays too. Sort of religious mystic he was. In his day he used to try and sell his verses from door to door.'

'Like W.H. Davis,' said Archery.

'I daresay.'

'Was he a shepherd?'

'Not as far as I know. Baker's roundsman or something.'

Wexford's door swung open, the constable came out and said to Burden, 'Chief Inspector wants you, sir.'

Wexford's voice roared after him, 'You can come back in here, Gates, and take a statement from Guy Fawkes. And give him a cigarette. He won't blow up.'

'It seems I'm wanted, sir, so if you'll excuse me . . .'

Burden went with Archery to the entrance doors.

'You had your chat with Alice Flower just in time,' he said. 'If you had it, that is.'

'Yes, I talked to her. Why?'

'She died yesterday,' said Burden. 'It's all in the local rag.'

Archery found a newsagent. The *Kingsmarkham Chronicle* had come out that morning and fresh stacks of papers lay on the counter. He bought a copy and found the announcement at the bottom of the back page.

'Death of Miss A. Flower.'

He scanned it and took it back with him to the terrace of the hotel to read it properly.

'The death occurred today . . .' That meant yesterday, Archery thought, looking at the dateline. He read on. 'The death occurred today of Miss Alice Flower at Stowerton Infirmary. She was eighty-seven. Miss Flower, who had lived in the district for twenty-five years, will be best remembered for the part she played in the notorious Victor's Piece murder trial. She was for many years maid and trusted friend of Mrs Primero . . .'

There followed a brief account of the murder and the trial.

'The funeral will take place at Forby parish church on Monday. Mr Roger Primero has expressed a wish that the last rites may be celebrated quietly and that there will be no sightseers.'

Roger Primero, faithful to the end, Archery thought. He found himself hoping that Charles had done nothing to distress this kindly and dutiful man. So Alice Flower was dead at last, death had waited just long enough to let her tell him, Archery, all she knew. Again he seemed to feel the working of destiny. Well done, thou good and faithful servant. Enter thou into the joy of thy Lord!

He went in to lunch, feeling jaded and depressed. Where on earth was Charles? He had been gone more than two hours. By now Primero had probably seen through that absurd cover story and . . .

His imagination showing him his son being interrogated by Wexford at his nastiest, he was just picking at his fruit salad and warm ice-cream when Charles burst into the dining room, swinging the car keys.

'I was wondering where you'd got to.'

'I've had a most instructive morning. Anything happened here?'

'Nothing much. Alice Flower is dead.'

'You can't tell me anything about that. Primero was full of it. Apparently he was at her bedside for hours yesterday.' He threw himself into a chair next to his father's. 'God, it was hot in that car! As a matter of fact, her dying like that was a help if anything. Made it easier to get him on to the murder.'

'I didn't think you could be so callous,' said Archery distastefully.

'Oh, come off it, Father. She'd had her allotted span plus seventeen. She can't have wanted to live. Don't you want to hear what I got out of him?'

'Of course.'

'You don't want any coffee, do you? Let's go outside.'

There was no-one on the terrace. A yellow climbing rose had shed its petals all over the ground and the battered cane chairs. What residents there were had left possessions out here as if to reserve permanent perches, magazines, library books, a roll of blue knitting, a pair of glasses. Ruthlessly Charles cleared two chairs and blew away the rose petals. For the first time Archery noticed that he looked extremely happy.

'Well,' he said when they had sat down, 'the house first. It's quite a place, about ten times the size of Thringford Manor, and it's all built of grey stone with a kind of pediment thing over the front door. Mrs Primero lived there when she was a girl and Roger bought it when it came up for sale this spring. There's a park with deer in it and a vast drive coming up from a pillared entrance. You can't see the house from the road, only the cedars in the park.

'They've got an Italian butler – not so classy as an English one, d'you think? But I suppose they're a dying race. Anyway, this butler character let me in and kept me hanging about for about ten minutes in a hall the size of the ground floor of our house. I was a bit nervous because I kept thinking, suppose he's rung up the *Sunday Planet* and they've said they've never heard of me? But he hadn't and it was all right. He was in the library. Superb collection of books he's got and some of them looked quite worn, so I suppose someone reads them, though I shouldn't think he does.

'It was all furnished in leather, black leather. You know that rather sexy modern stuff. He asked me to sit down and have a drink . . .'

'A bit early, wasn't it?'

'People like that, they slosh it down all day. If they were working class they'd be alcoholics, but you can get away with anything when you've got a butler and about fifty thousand a year. Then his wife came in. Rather a nice-looking woman – a bit past it, of course – but magnificent clothes. Not that I'd want Tess to dress like that . . .' His face fell and Archery's heart moved with pity. 'If I ever get a say in what Tess wears,' he added dolefully.

'Go on.'

'We had our drinks. Mrs Primero wasn't very talkative, but her husband was most expansive. I didn't have to ask him much, so you needn't get all steamed up about your conscience, and he got on to the murder, quite naturally. He kept saying he wished he hadn't left Victor's Piece so early that Sunday evening. He could easily have stayed.

'"I was only going to meet a couple of chaps I knew at a pub in Sewingbury," he said. "And, as it happened, it was a dead loss because they never turned up. Or, at least, they did turn up but I got the wrong pub. So I waited about for an hour or so and then I went back to my lodgings. I wonder," he said, "how many times I've cursed myself for not staying at Victor's Piece."

'What d'you think of that? I thought it was fishy.'

'He didn't have to tell you,' Archery said. 'In any case the police must have questioned him.'

'Maybe they did and maybe they didn't. He didn't say.' Charles lounged back in his chair, and swinging his feet up poked them through the trellis. 'Then we got on to money,' he said. 'Money, I may add, is the mainspring of his existence.'

Inexplicably, Archery felt himself marked out as Primero's defender. Alice Flower had painted him in such glowing colours. 'I had the impression he was rather a nice sort of man,' he said.

'He's all right,' Charles said indifferently. 'He's very modest about his success and about his money.' He grinned. 'The kind of character who cries all the way to the bank. Anyway, now we come to the crux of the whole thing.

'Just before Mrs Primero was killed some mate of his asked him if he'd like to go into business with him. Importing or exporting. I don't quite know what it was but it doesn't matter. The friend was to put up ten thousand and so was Primero. Well, Primero hadn't got it, hadn't got a smell of it. As far as he was concerned it was hopeless. Then Mrs Primero died.'

'We know all this,' Archery objected. 'Alice Flower told me as much . . .'

'All right, wait for it. Alice Flower didn't know this bit. "That was the making of me," he said very breezily. "Not that I wasn't devastated by my grandmother's death," he added as a sort of hasty afterthought. His wife was sitting there all the time with a blank look on her face. He kept looking at her uneasily.

'"I put up the money and we were away," he said,

134

talking rather fast. "And since then I've never looked back."

'I was in a bit of a dilemma. Everything was going so smoothly and I didn't want to mess things up. I thought he was looking defiant and suddenly I realised why. *He didn't know how much I knew about Mrs Primero's money.* She'd died intestate, it was sixteen years ago, I was a newspaper reporter and for all he knew I was interested in him, not his grandmother.'

'A lot to read into a defiant look,' said Archery.

'Perhaps there was a bit of hindsight in that. But just wait a minute. Then I asked a question. It was a shot in the dark but it came off.

'"So you got your ten thousand just when you needed it?" I said casually. Primero didn't say anything, but his wife looked at me and said, "Just the exact sum after death duties. You should really be asking me. Roger's told me about it so often I know it better than he does."

'Well, I couldn't leave it there. I persisted. "I understand you've got two sisters, Mr Primero," I said. "I suppose they inherited similar amounts?" He began to look terribly suspicious. After all, it wasn't my business and it had nothing to do with the story I was supposed to be writing. "Are they successful in business too?" I asked, trying to justify myself. It was a stroke of genius. Sorry to be big-headed but it was. I could actually see him relax.

'"I really don't see much of them," he said. "Oh, Roger," said his wife, "you know we *never* see them." Primero gave her an icy look. "One's married," he said, "and the other has a job in London. They're much younger than I am." "It must be nice to inherit ten thousand pounds when you're still a child," I said. "I imagine it's always nice," he said, "but I've never had the pleasure of inheriting any more. Shall

135

we leave the subject and get on with the story of my life?"

'I pretended to take notes. I was doodling really but he thought it was shorthand. When we'd finished he got up and shook hands and said he'd keep his eye open for the *Sunday Planet*. I felt a bit awkward at that and I didn't quite know what to say but his wife saved me by asking me to lunch. So I accepted and we had a splendid lunch, smoked salmon and enormous steaks, great sides of oxen they were, and raspberries in framboise liqueur.'

'You've got a nerve,' said Archery in grudging admiration. He pulled himself up. 'It was very wrong of you. Most unethical.'

'All in a good cause. You do see the point, don't you?'

Why do one's children always think one senile yet childish, dully practical yet irrational, capable of supporting them but unintelligent to the point of imbecility?

'Of course I do,' Archery said irritably. 'Alice Flower and Mrs Crilling both said Mrs Primero had only ten thousand to leave, but apparently Roger Primero didn't get only a third of that, he got the whole ten thousand.'

Charles jerked round to face him, scattering more rose petals from the trellis. 'Now, why? There definitely wasn't a will. I've checked on that. And there were just the three heirs, Roger, Angela and Isabel. Mrs Primero hadn't another relative in the world and according to the law it should have been divided between the three grandchildren. But Roger got the lot.'

'I can't understand it.'

'Neither can I – yet. Maybe I shall when I've seen the sisters. I couldn't ask Roger where they lived, but Primero isn't a common name and the single one may be in the London phone directory. I haven't quite made up my mind about the line I'll take with them, but I've got the glimmerings of an idea I might say I've come from the Inland Revenue ...'

'*Facilis descensus Averni.*'

'In matters of this kind,' Charles said crisply, 'you have to be bloody, bold and resolute. Can I have the car again tomorrow?'

'If you must.'

'I thought you might like to go out to Victor's Piece,' Charles said in a hopeful tone, 'and just have a look round. See if you can see if Primero could have hidden himself anywhere, sneaked upstairs or something, instead of letting himself out of the front door that Sunday night.'

'Aren't you letting your imagination run away with you?'

'It's a family failing.' His eyes clouded suddenly and to Archery's dismay he put his head in his hands. Archery didn't know what to do. 'Tess hasn't spoken to me for two days,' the boy said. 'I can't lose her, I can't.' If he had been ten years younger his father would have taken him in his arms. But if he had been ten years younger the whole thing would never have happened.

'I don't give a damn,' Charles said, controlling himself, 'what her father was or what he did. I don't care if every one of her ancestors was hanged. But you do and she does and ... Oh, what's the use?' He got up. 'Sorry to make an exhibition of myself.' Still looking down, he scuffed his feet against the eddies of petals. 'You're doing all you can,' he said with a dreadful prim gravity, 'but you can't be expected to understand at your age.' Without looking at his father, he turned and went into the hotel.

Chapter 11

From fornication, and all other deadly sin; and from
all the deceits of the world, the flesh and the devil,
  Good Lord, deliver us.

The Litany.

Angela Primero lived in a flat at Oswestry Mansions,
Baron's Court. She was twenty-six years old and the
elder of Mrs Primero's granddaughters. That was all
Charles Archery knew about her – that and her
telephone number which he had easily found. He
rang her up and asked if he could see her on the
following morning. Thinking better of his original
plan, he said he represented the *Sunday Planet*, and
the death of Alice Flower having brought once more
into prominence Mrs Primero's murder, his newspaper were running a feature on the fate of the other
people concerned in the case. He was rather pleased
with that. It had the ring of verisimilitude.

Miss Primero had a grim voice for so young a
woman. It was gravelly, abrupt, almost masculine.
She would be glad to see him, but he did realise,
didn't he, that her recollection of her grandmother
was slight? Just a few childhood memories were
what he wanted, Miss Primero, little touches to add
colour to his story.

She opened the door to him so quickly that he
wondered if she had been waiting behind it. Her
appearance surprised him for he had kept a picture
of her brother in his mind and he had therefore
expected someone small and dark with regular
features. He had seen a photograph of the grandmother too, and though the old face was both

138

wizened and blurred by age, there were still to be seen vestiges of an aquiline beauty and a strong resemblance to Roger.

The girl whose flat this was had a strong plain face with bad skin and a big prognathous jaw. Her hair was a dull flat brown. She wore a neat dark blue frock bought at a chain store and her figure, though over-large, was good.

'Mr Bowman?'

Charles was pleased with the name he had invented for himself. He gave her a pleasant smile.

'How do you do, Miss Primero?'

She showed him into a small very sparsely furnished sitting room. He could not help adding to the mystery by contrasting this with the library at Forby Hall. Here there were no books, no flowers, and the only ornaments were framed photographs, half a dozen perhaps, of a young blonde girl and a baby.

She followed his gaze towards the studio portrait of the same girl that hung above the fireplace. 'My sister,' she said. Her ugly face softened and she smiled. As she spoke there came from the next room a thin wail and the murmur of a voice. 'She's in my bedroom now, changing the baby's napkin. She always comes over on Saturday mornings.'

Charles wondered what Angela Primero did for a living. A typist perhaps, or a clerk? The whole set-up seemed too scanty and poor. The furniture was brightly coloured but it looked cheap and flimsy. In front of the hearth was a rug woven out of woollen rags. Needy nothing trimmed in jollity . . .

'Please sit down,' said Angela Primero.

The little orange chair creaked as it took his weight. A far cry, he thought, from the brother's voluptuous black leather. From the floor above he could hear music playing and someone pushing a vacuum cleaner.

'What do you want me to tell you?'

There was a packet of Weights on the mantelpiece. She took one and handed them to him. He shook his head.

'First, what you remember of your grandmother.'

'Not much. I told you.' Her speech was brusque and rough. 'We went there to tea a few times. It was a big dark house and I remember I was afraid to go to the bathroom alone. The maid used to have to take me.' She gave a staccato, humourless laugh and it was an effort to remember she was only twenty-six. 'I never even saw Painter if that's what you mean. There was a child across the road we used to play with sometimes and I believe Painter had a daughter. I asked about her once but my grandmother said she was common, we weren't to have anything to do with her.'

Charles clenched his hands. He felt a sudden desperate longing for Tess, both for himself, and also to set her beside this girl who had been taught to despise her.

The door opened and the girl in the photographs came in. Angela Primero jumped up at once and took the baby from her arms. Charles's knowledge of babies was vague. He thought this one might be about six months old. It looked small and uninteresting.

'This is Mr Bowman, darling. My sister, Isabel Fairest.'

Mrs Fairest was only a year younger than her sister, but she looked no more than eighteen. She was very small and thin with a pinkish-white face and enormous pale blue eyes. Charles thought she looked like a pretty rabbit. Her hair was a bright gingery gold.

Roger's hair and eyes were black, Angela's hair brown and her eyes hazel. None of them was in the

140

least like either of the others. There was more to genetics than met the eye, Charles thought.

Mrs Fairest sat down. She didn't cross her legs but sat with her hands in her lap like a little girl. It was difficult to imagine her married, impossible to think of her as having given birth to a child.

Her sister scarcely took her eyes off her. When she did it was to coo at the baby. Mrs Fairest had a small soft voice, tinged with cockney.

'Don't let him tire you, darling. Put him down in his cot.'

'You know I love holding him, darling. Isn't he gorgeous? Have you got a smile for your auntie? You know your auntie, don't you, even if you haven't seen her for a whole week?'

Mrs Fairest got up and stood behind her sister's chair. They both gurgled over the baby, stroking its cheeks and curling its fingers round their own. It was obvious that they were devoted to each other, but whereas Angela's love was maternal to both sister and nephew, Isabel showed a clinging dependence on the older girl. Charles felt that they had forgotten he was there and he wondered how Mr Fairest fitted into the picture. He coughed.

'About your early life, Miss Primero . . . ?'

'Oh, yes. (Mustn't cry, sweetie. He's got wind, darling.) I really can't remember any more about my grandmother. My mother married again when I was sixteen. This is the sort of thing you want, is it?'

'Oh, yes.'

'Well, as I say, my mother married again and she and my stepfather wanted us to go out to Australia with them. (Up it comes! There, that's better.) But I didn't want to go. Isabel and I were still at school. My mother hung it out for a couple of years and then they went without us. Well, it was their life, wasn't it? I wanted to go to training college but I gave that

141

up. Isabel and I had the house, didn't we, darling? And we both went out to work. (Is he going to have a little sleep, then?)'

It was an ordinary enough tale, fragmentary and very clipped. Charles felt that there was far more to it. The hardship and the privation had been left out. Money might have changed it all but she had never mentioned money. She had never mentioned her brother either.

'Isabel got married two years ago. Her husband's in the Post Office. I'm a secretary in a newspaper office.' She raised her eyebrows, unsmiling. 'I'll have to ask them if they've ever heard of you.'

'Yes, do,' said Charles with a suavity he didn't feel. He must get on to the subject of the money but he didn't know how to. Mrs Fairest brought a carry-cot in from the other room, they placed the baby in it, bending tenderly over him and cooing. Although it was nearly noon neither of them had mentioned a drink or even coffee. Charles belonged to a generation that has accustomed itself to almost hourly snacks, cups of this, glasses of that, bits and pieces from the refrigerator. So, surely, did they. He thought wistfully of Roger's hospitality. Mrs Fairest glanced up and said softly:

'I do like coming here. It's so quiet.' Above them the vacuum cleaner continued to whirr. 'My husband and me, we've only got one room. It's nice and big but it's awfully noisy at weekends.'

Charles knew it was impertinent but he had to say it.

'I'm surprised your grandmother didn't leave you anything.'

Angelo Primero shrugged. She tucked the blanket round the baby and stood up. 'That's life,' she said in a hard voice.

'Shall I tell him, darling?' Isabel Fairest touched

her arm and looked timidly into her face, waiting for guidance.

'What's the point? It's of no interest to him.' She stared at Charles and then said intelligently, 'You can't put that sort of thing in newspapers. It's libel.'

Damn, damn, damn! Why hadn't he said he was from the Inland Revenue? Then they could have got on to money at once.

'But I think people ought to know,' said Mrs Fairest, showing more spirit than he had thought her capable of. 'I do, darling. I always have, ever since I understood about it. I think people ought to know how he's treated us.'

Charles put his notebook away ostentatiously.

'This is off the record, Mrs Fairest.'

'You see, darling? He won't say anything. I don't care if he does. People ought to know about Roger.'

The name was out. They were all breathing rather heavily. Charles was the first to get himself under control. He managed a calm smile.

'Well, I *will* tell you. If you put it in the paper and I have to go to prison for it, I don't care! Granny Rose left ten thousand pounds and we should all have had a share, but we didn't. Roger – that's our brother – he got it all. I don't quite know why but Angela knows the ins and outs of it. My mother had a friend who was a solicitor where Roger worked and he said we could try and fight it, but Mother wouldn't on account of it being awful to have a court case against your own son. We were just little kids, you see, and we didn't know anything about it. Mother said Roger would help us – it was his moral duty, even if it wasn't legally – but he never did. He kept putting it off and then Mother quarrelled with him. We've never seen him since I was ten and Angela was eleven. I wouldn't know him now if I saw him in the street.'

143

It was a puzzling story. They were all Mrs Primero's grandchildren, all equally entitled to inherit in the event of there being no will. And there had been no will.

'I don't want to see all this in your paper, you know,' Angela Primero said suddenly. She would have made a good teacher, he thought, reflecting on waste, for she was tender with little children, but stern when she had to be.

'I won't publish any of it,' Charles said with perfect truth.

'You'd better not, that's all. The fact is, we couldn't fight it. We wouldn't have stood a chance. In law Roger was perfectly entitled to it all. Mind you, it would have been another story if my grandmother had died a month later.'

'I don't quite follow you,' said Charles, by now unbearably excited.

'Have you ever seen my brother?'

Charles nodded, then changed it to a shake of the head. She looked at him suspiciously. Then she made a dramatic gesture. She took her sister by the shoulders and pushed her forward for his inspection.

'He's little and dark,' she said. 'Look at Isabel, look at me. We don't look alike, do we? We don't look like sisters because we aren't sisters and Roger isn't our brother. Oh, Roger is my parents' child all right and Mrs Primero was his grandmother. My mother couldn't have any more children. They waited eleven years and when they knew it was no good they adopted me. A year later they took Isabel as well.'

'But ... I ...' Charles stammered. 'You were legally adopted, weren't you?'

Angela Primero had recovered her composure. She put her arm round her sister who had begun to cry.

'We were legally adopted all right. That didn't make any difference. Adopted children can't inherit when the dead person has died without making a will – or they couldn't in September 1950. They can now. They were making this Act at the time and it became law on October 1st, 1950. Just our luck, wasn't it?'

The photograph in the estate agent's window made Victor's Piece look deceptively attractive. Perhaps the agent had long given up hope of its being sold for anything but its site value, for Archery, enquiring tentatively, was greeted with almost fawning exuberance. He emerged with an order to view, a bunch of keys and permission to go over the house whenever he chose.

No bus was in sight. He walked back to the stop by the Olive and Dove and waited in the shade. Presently he pulled the order to view out of his pocket and scanned it. 'Splendid property of character,' he read, 'that only needs an imaginative owner to give it a new lease of life . . .' There was no mention of the old tragedy, no hint that violent death had once been its tenant.

Two Sewingbury buses came and one marked Kingsmarkham Station. He was still reading, contrasting the agent's euphemisms with the description in his transcript, when the silver car pulled into the kerb.

'Mr Archery!'

He turned. The sun blazed back from the arched wings and the glittering screen. Imogen Ide's hair made an even brighter silver-gold flash against the dazzling metal.

'I'm on my way to Stowerton. Would you like a lift?'

He was suddenly ridiculously happy. Everything went, his pity for Charles, his grief for Alice Flower, his sense of helplessness against the juggernaut machinery of the law. An absurd dangerous joy possessed him and without stopping to analyse it, he went up to the car. Its bodywork was as hot as fire, a shivering silver blaze against his hand.

'My son took my car,' he said. 'I'm not going to Stowerton, just to a place this side of it, a house called Victor's Piece.'

She raised her eyebrows very slightly at this and he supposed she knew the story just as everyone else did, for she was looking at him strangely. He got in beside her, his heart beating. The continual rhythmic thudding in his left side was so intense as to be physically painful and he wished it would stop before it made him wince or press his hand to his breast.

'You haven't got Dog with you today,' he said.

She moved back into the traffic. 'Too hot for him,' she said. 'Surely you're not thinking of buying Victor's Piece?'

His heart had quietened. 'Why, do you know it?'

'It used to belong to a relative of my husband's.'

Ide, he thought, Ide. He couldn't remember hearing what had become of the house after Mrs Primero's death. Perhaps it had been owned by some Ides before it became an old people's home.

'I have a key and an order to view, but I'm certainly not going to buy. It's just – well . . .'

'Curiosity?' She could not look at him while she was driving but he felt her thoughts directed on him more powerfully than any eyes. 'Are you an amateur of crime?' It would have been natural to have used his name, to end the question with it. But she didn't. It seemed to him that she had omitted it because 'Mr Archery' had suddenly become too formal, his Christian name still too intimate. 'You know, I think I'll come over it with you,' she said. 'I don't have to

146

be in Stowerton until half-past twelve. Let me be your guide, may I?'

Imogen Ide will be my guide ... It was a stupid jingle and it tinkled in his ears on a minor key like an old, half-forgotten madrigal. He said nothing but she must have taken his silence for assent, for instead of dropping him at the entry she slowed and turned into the lane where dark gables showed between the trees.

Even on this bright morning the house looked dark and forbidding. Its yellow-brown bricks were crossed with fretted half-timbering and two of its windows were broken. The resemblance between it and the agent's photograph was as slight as that of a holiday postcard to the actual resort. The photographer had cunningly avoided or else subsequently removed the weeds, the brambles, the damp stains, the swinging rotted casements and the general air of decay. He had also succeeded in somehow minimising its rambling size. The gates were broken down and she drove straight through the gap, up the drive and stopped directly before the front door.

This moment should have been important to him, his first sight of the house where Tess's father had committed – or had not committed – his crime. His senses should have been alert to absorb atmosphere, to note details of place and distance that the police in their jaded knowledge had overlooked. Instead he was conscious of himself not as an observer, a note-taker, but only as a man living in the present, dwelling in the moment and discarding the past. He felt more alive than he had done for years and because of this he became almost unaware of his surroundings. Things could not affect him, not recorded fact. His emotions were all. He saw and experienced the house only as a deserted place into which he and this woman would soon go and would be alone.

As soon as he had thought this in so many words he knew that he should not go in. He could easily say that he only wanted to look at the grounds. She was getting out of the car now, looking up at the windows and wrinkling her eyelids against the light.

'Shall we go in?' she said.

He put the key in the lock and she was standing close beside him. He had expected a musty smell from the hall but he was hardly aware of it. Shafts of light crossed the place from various dusty windows and motes danced in the beams. There was an old runner on the tiled floor and catching her heel in it, she stumbled. Instinctively he put out his hand to steady her and as he did so he felt her right breast brush his arm.

'Mind how you go,' he said, not looking at her. Her shoe had sent up a little cloud of dust and she gave a nervous laugh. Perhaps it was just a normal laugh. He was beyond that kind of analysis, for he could still feel the soft weight against his arm as if she had not stepped quickly away.

'Terribly stuffy in here,' she said. 'It makes me cough. That's the room where the murder was committed – in there.' She pushed open a door and he saw a deal board floor, marble fireplace, great bleached patches on the walls where pictures had hung. 'The stairs are behind here and on the other side is the kitchen where poor old Alice was cooking the Sunday dinner.'

'I don't want to go upstairs,' he said quickly. 'It's too hot and dusty. You'll get your dress dirty.' He drew a deep breath and, moving far from her, stood against the mantelpiece. Here, just on this spot, Mrs Primero had felt the first blow of the axe; there the scuttle had stood, here, there, everywhere, the old blood had flowed. 'The scene of the crime,' he said fatuously.

Her eyes narrowed and she crossed to the window. The silence was terrible and he wanted to fill it with chatter. There was so much to say, so many remarks even mere acquaintances could make to each other on such a spot. The noonday sun cast her shadow in perfect proportion, neither too tall nor grossly dwarfed. It was like a cut-out in black tissue and he wanted to fall to his knees and touch it, knowing it was all he would get.

It was she who spoke first. He hardly knew what he had expected her to say, but not this – certainly not this.

'You are very like your son – or he's like you.'

The tension slackened. He felt cheated and peeved. 'I didn't know you'd met,' he said.

To this she made no reply. In her eyes was a tiny gleam of fun. 'You didn't tell me he worked for a newspaper.'

Archery's stomach turned. She must have been there, at the Primeros'. Was he expected to sustain Charles's lie?

'He's so very like you,' she said. 'It didn't really click, though, until after he'd gone. Then, taking his appearance and his name together – I suppose Bowman's his pseudonym on the *Planet*, is it? – I guessed. Roger hasn't realised.'

'I don't quite understand,' Archery began. He would have to explain. 'Mrs Ide . . .'

She started to laugh, stopped when she saw the dismay in his face. 'I think we've both been leading each other up the garden,' she said gently. 'Ide was my maiden name, the name I used for modelling.'

He turned away, pressing the hot palm of his hand against the marble. She took a step towards him and he smelt her scent. 'Mrs Primero was the relative who owned this house, the relative who's buried at Forby?' There was no need to wait for her answer. He sensed her nod. 'I don't understand how I can have been such a fool,' he said. Worse than a fool. What would she think tomorrow when the *Planet* came out? He offered up a stupid ashamed prayer that Charles had found out nothing from the woman who was her sister-in-law. 'Will you forgive me?'

'There's nothing to forgive, is there?' She sounded truly puzzled, as well she might. He had been asking pardon for future outrages. 'I'm just as much to blame as you. I don't know why I didn't tell you I was Imogen Primero.' She paused. 'There was no deceit in it,' she said. 'Just one of those things. We were dancing – something else came up . . . I don't know.'

He raised his head, gave himself a little shake. Then he walked away from her into the hall. 'You have to go to Stowerton, I think you said. It was kind of you to bring me.'

She was behind him now, her hand on his arm. 'Don't look like that. What are you supposed to have done? Nothing, nothing. It was just a – a social mistake.'

It was a little fragile hand but insistent. Not knowing why, perhaps because she too seemed in need of comfort, he covered it with his own. Instead of withdrawing it, she left her hand under his and as she sighed it trembled faintly. He turned to look at her, feeling shame that was as paralysing as a disease. Her face was a foot from his, then only inches, then no distance, no face but only a soft mouth.

The shame went in a wave of desire made the more terrible and the more exquisite because he had felt nothing like it for twenty years, perhaps not ever. Since coming down from Oxford he had never kissed any woman but Mary, scarcely been alone with any but the old, the sick or the dying. He did not know how to end the kiss, nor did he know whether this in itself was inexperience or the yearning to prolong something that was so much more, but not enough more, than touching a shadow.

She took herself out of his arms quite suddenly, but without pushing or struggling. There was nothing to struggle against. 'Oh, dear,' she said, but she didn't smile. Her face was very white.

There were words to explain that kind of thing away. 'I don't know what made me do that' or 'I was carried away, the impulse of the moment . . .' He was sick of even the suggestion of lying. Truth itself seemed even more compelling and urgent than his desire and he thought he would speak it even though tomorrow and in the days to come it too would appear to her as a lie.

'I love you. I think I must have loved you from the first moment I saw you. I think that's how it was.' He put his hands up to his forehead and his fingertips, though icy cold, seemed to burn just as snow can burn the skin. 'I'm married,' he said. 'You know that – I mean my wife is living – and I'm a clergyman. I've no right to love you and I promise I'll never be alone with you again.'

She was very surprised and her eyes widened, but which of his confessions had surprised her he had no idea. It even occurred to him that she might be amazed at hearing from him lucid speech, for up to now he had been almost incoherent. 'I mustn't suppose,' he said, for his last sentence seemed like vanity, 'that there's been any temptation for you.' She started to speak, but he went on in a hurry, 'Will you not say anything but just drive away?'

She nodded. In spite of his prohibition, he longed for her to approach him again, just touch him. It was

151

an impossible hunger that made him breathless. She made a little helpless gesture as if she too were in the grip of an overpowering emotion. Then she turned, her face held awkwardly away from him, ran down the hall and let herself out of the front door.

After she had gone it occurred to him that she had asked no questions as to his reasons for coming to the house. She had said little and he everything that mattered. He thought that he must be going mad, for he could not understand that twenty years of discipline could fall away like a lesson imparted to a bored child.

The house was as it had been described in the transcript of the trial. He noticed its layout without emotion or empathy, the long passage that ran from the front door to the door at the back where Painter's coat had hung, the kitchen, the narrow, wall-confined stairs. A kind of cerebral paralysis descended on him and he moved towards that back door, withdrawing the bolts numbly.

The garden was very still, overgrown, basking under a brazen sky. The light and the heat made him dizzy. At first he could not see the coach house at all. Then he realised he had been looking at it ever since he stepped into the garden, but what he had taken for a great quivering bush was in fact solid bricks and mortar hidden under a blanket of virginia creeper. He walked towards it, not interested, not in the least curious. He walked because it was something to do and because this house of a million faintly trembling leaves was at least a kind of goal.

The doors were fastened with a padlock. Archery was relieved. It deprived him of the need for any action. He leant against the wall and the leaves were cold and damp against his face. Presently he went down the drive and through the gateless entrance. Of course, the silver car would not be there. It wasn't. A

152

bus came almost immediately. He had quite forgotten that he had omitted to lock the back door of Victor's Piece.

Archery returned the keys to the estate agent and lingered for a while looking at the photograph of the house he had just come from. It was like looking at the portrait of a girl you had known only as an old woman, and he wondered if it had perhaps been taken thirty years before when Mrs Primero had bought the house. Then he turned and walked slowly back to the hotel.

Half-past four was usually a dead time at the Olive and Dove. But this was a Saturday and a glorious Saturday at that. The dining room was full of trippers, the lounge decorously crowded with old residents and new arrivals, taking their tea from silver trays. Archery's heart began to beat fast as he saw his son in conversation with a man and a woman. Their backs were towards him and he saw only that the woman had long fair hair and that the man's head was dark.

He made his way between the armchairs, growing hot with trepidation and weaving among beringed fingers holding tea-pots, little asthmatic dogs, pots of cress and pyramids of sandwiches. When the woman turned he should have felt relief. Instead bitter disappointment ran through him like a long thin knife. He put out his hand and clasped the warm fingers of Tess Kershaw.

Now he saw how stupid his first wild assumption had been. Kershaw was shaking hands with him now and the man's lively face, seamed all over with the wrinkles of animation, bore no resemblance at all to Roger Primero's waxen pallor. His hair was not really dark but thin and sprinkled with grey.

'Charles called in on us on his way back from

town,' Tess said. She was perhaps the worst dressed woman in the room in her white cotton blouse and navy serge skirt. As if explaining this, she said quickly, 'When we heard his news we dropped everything and came back with him.' She got up, threaded her way to the window and looked out into the bright hot afternoon. When she came back she said, 'It feels so strange. I must have walked past here lots of times when I was little, but I can't remember it at all.'

Hand in hand with Painter perhaps. And while they walked, the murderer and his child, had Painter watched the traffic go by and thought of the way he could become part of that traffic? Archery tried not to see in the fine pointed face opposite his own, the coarse crude features of the man Alice Flower had called Beast. But then they were here to prove it had not been that way at all.

'News?' he said to Charles and he heard the note of distaste creep into his voice.

Charles told him. 'And then we all went to Victor's Piece,' he said. 'We didn't think we'd be able to get in, but someone had left the back door unlocked. We went all over the house and we saw that Primero could easily have hidden himself.'

Archery turned away slightly. The name was now invested with many associations, mostly agonising.

'He said good-bye to Alice, opened and closed the front door without actually going out of it, then he slipped into the dining room – nobody used the dining room and it was dark. Alice went out and . . .' Charles hesitated, searching for a form of words to spare Tess. 'And, after the coal was brought in, he came out, put on the raincoat that was left hanging on the back door and – well, did the deed.'

'It's only a theory, Charlie,' said Kershaw, 'but it fits the facts.'

'I don't know . . .' Archery began.

'Look, Father, don't you want Tess's father cleared?'

Not, thought Archery, if it means incriminating *her* husband. Not that. I may already have done her an injury, but I can't do her *that* injury.

'This motive you mentioned,' he said dully.

Tess broke in excitedly, 'It's a marvellous motive, a *real* motive.' He knew exactly what she meant. Ten thousand pounds was real, solid, a true temptation, while two hundred pounds . . . Her eyes shone, then saddened. Was she thinking that to hang a man wrongfully was as bad as killing an old woman for a bag of notes? And would that too remain with her all her life? No matter which way things fell out, could she ever escape?

'Primero was working in a solicitor's office,' Charles was saying excitedly. 'He would have known the law, he had all the facilities for checking. Mrs Primero might not have known about it, not if she didn't read the papers. Who knows about all the various Acts of Parliament that are going to be passed anyway? Primero's boss probably had a query about it from a client, sent him to look it up, and there you are. Primero would have known that if his grandmother died intestate before October 1950 all the money would come to him. But if she died after the Act his sisters would get two-thirds of it. I've been looking it all up. This is known as the Great Adoption Act, the law that gave adopted children almost equal rights with natural ones. *Of course* Primero knew.'

'What are you going to do?'

'I've been on to the police but Wexford can't see me before two on Monday. He's away for the weekend. I'll bet the police never checked Primero's movements. Knowing them, I'd say it's likely that as soon as they got hold of Painter they didn't trouble with anyone else.' He looked at Tess and took her hand. 'You can say what you like about this being a free country,' he said hotly, 'but you know as well as I do that everyone has a subconscious feeling that "working class" and "criminal class" are more or less synonymous. Why bother with the respectable, well-connected solicitor's clerk when you've already got your hands on the chauffeur?'

Archery shrugged. From long experience he knew it was useless to argue with Charles when he was airing his quasi-communist ideals.

'Thank you for your enthusiastic reception,' Charles said sarcastically. 'What is there to look so miserable about?'

Archery could not tell him. A load of sorrow seemed to have descended on him and in order to answer his son, he sorted out from conflicting pain something he could express to them all.

'I was thinking of the children,' he said, 'the four little girls who have all suffered from this crime.' He smiled at Tess. 'Tess, of course,' he went on, 'those two sisters you saw – and Elizabeth Crilling.'

He did not add the name of the grown woman who would suffer more than any of them if Charles was right.

Chapter 12

Is it not lawful for me to do what I will with mine own?

The Gospel for Septuagesima Sunday.

The man who was shown into Wexford's office at nine on Monday morning was small and slender. The bones of his hands were particularly fine and with narrow delicate joints like a woman's. The dark grey suit he wore, very expensive looking and very sleek, made him look smaller than he actually was. He seemed to be surrounded, even so early in the morning and away from his own home, with a great many adjuncts of elegance. Wexford, who knew him well, was amused by the sapphire tie-pin, the two rings, the key chain with its heavy drop of chased – amber, was it? – the briefcase of some kind of reptile skin. How many years, he asked himself, was Roger Primero going to need to get used to wealth?

'Lovely morning,' said Wexford. 'I've just had a couple of days at Worthing and the sea was like a millpond. What can I do for you?'

'Catch a con man,' said Primero, 'a lousy little squirt posing as a journalist.' He unclipped the briefcase and flicked a Sunday newspaper across Wexford's desk. It slipped on the polished surface and fell to the floor. Raising his eyebrows, Wexford let it lie.

'Hell,' said Primero. 'There's nothing for you to see, anyway.' His glazed eyes had a sore look in the handsome expressionless face. The man's vanity had made him rebel against glasses at last, Wexford thought, blinking slightly behind his own heavy

157

tortoiseshell frames. 'Look here, Chief Inspector, I don't mind telling you, I'm hopping mad. This is how it was. Mind if I smoke?'

'Not at all.'

A gold cigarette case spilled out from his pocket, followed by a holder and a lighter in peculiar black and gold mosaic. Wexford watched this production of props, wondering when it was going to end. The man is furnished like a room, he thought.

'This is how it was,' he said again. 'Character rang me up on Thursday, said he was on the *Planet* and wanted to do an article about me. My early life. You get the picture? I said he could come along on Friday and he did. I gave him a hell of a long interview, all the dope and the upshot of it was my wife asked him to lunch.' He screwed up his mouth and nose like a man smelling something offensive. 'Hell,' he said, 'I don't suppose he's ever seen a lunch like that in all his life ...'

'But no article appeared and when you rang the *Planet* this morning they'd never heard of him.'

'How did you know?'

'It happens,' said Wexford dryly. 'I'm surprised at you, sir, a man of your experience. The time to ring the *Planet* was *Friday* morning.'

'It makes me feel such a frightful ass.'

Wexford said airily, 'No money passed, I daresay?'

'Hell, no!'

'Just the lunch, then, and you told him a lot of things you'd rather have left unsaid.'

'That's the thing.' His expression had been sulky, but suddenly he smiled and it was a likeable smile. Wexford had always rather liked him. 'Oh, hell's bells, Chief Inspector ...'

'Hell's bells, as you say. Still, you were wise to come to us, though I don't know that we can do anything unless he makes a move ...'

'A move? What d'you mean, a move?'

'Well, let me give you an example. Nothing personal, you understand. Just supposing a wealthy man, a man who is somewhat in the public eye, says something a shade indiscreet to a reputable journalist. Ten to one he can't use it because he's laying his paper open to libel action.' Wexford paused and gave the other man a penetrating look. 'But if he says those same indiscreet things to an impostor, a confidence trickster . . .' Primero had grown very pale. 'What's to stop the impostor following a few leads and ferreting out something really damaging. Most people, Mr Primero, even decent law-abiding people, have something in their pasts they'd rather not have known. You have to ask yourself, if he's not on the level, what's he up to? The answer is either he's after your money or else he's crazy.' He added more kindly, 'In my experience nine out of ten of them are just crazy. Still, if it'll help to set your mind at rest perhaps you could give us a description. I suppose he gave you his name?'

'It wouldn't be his real name.'

'Naturally not.'

Primero leant confidingly towards him. During the course of his long career Wexford had found it valuable to make himself *au fait* with perfumes and he noticed that Primero smelt of Lentheric's Onyx.

'He seemed nice enough,' Primero began. 'My wife was quite taken with him.' His eyes had begun to water and he put his fingers very cautiously up to them. Wexford was reminded of a weeping woman who dare not rub her eyes for fear of smudging mascara. 'I haven't told her about this, by the way. I passed it off. Wouldn't want to upset her. He was well-spoken, Oxford accent and all that. A tall fair fellow, said his name was Bowman, Charles Bowman.'

'A-ha!' said Wexford but not aloud.

'Chief Inspector?'

'Mr Primero?'

'I've just remembered something. He was – well, he was extraordinarily interested in my grandmother.'

Wexford almost laughed.

'From what you've told me I think I can assure you there won't be any serious repercussions.'

'You think he's a nut?'

'Harmless, anyway.'

'You've taken a load off my mind.' Primero got up, retrieved his briefcase and picked up the newspaper. He did it rather awkwardly as if he was unused to performing even so simple a service for himself. 'I'll be more careful in future.'

'An ounce of prevention, you know.'

'Well, I won't take up any more of your time.' He pulled a long, but possibly sincerely sad face. The watering eyes added to his look of melancholy. 'Off to a funeral, as a matter of fact. Poor old Alice.'

Wexford had noticed the black tie on which the sapphire glowed darkly. He showed Primero to the door. Throughout the interview he had kept a solemn face. Now he permitted himself the indulgence of gargantuan, though almost silent, laughter.

There was nothing to do until two o'clock except sight-seeing. Charles had been out early and bought a guide book. They sat in the lounge studying it.

'It says here,' said Tess, 'that Forby is the fifth prettiest village in England.'

'Poor Forby,' said Charles. 'Damned with faint praise.'

Kershaw began organising them.

'How about all piling into my car . . .' He stuck his

160

finger on the map '. . . and going down the Kings-brook Road to Forby – keep clear of Forby Hall, eh, Charlie? – have a quick look at the church, and then on to Pomfret. Pomfret Grange is open every week-day in the summer – we might have a look over it – and back into Kingsmarkham along the main road.'

'Lovely,' said Tess.

Kershaw drove and Archery sat beside him. They followed the same route he had taken with Imogen Ide when she had come to put flowers on old Mrs Primero's grave. As they came within sight of the Kingsbrook he remembered what she had said about the implacability of water and how, notwithstanding the efforts of man, it continues to spring from the earth and seek the sea.

Kershaw parked the car by the green with the duckpond. The village looked peaceful and serene. Summer was not as yet so far advanced as to dull the fresh green of the beech trees or hang the wild clematis with its frowsty greyish beard. Knots of cottages surrounded the green and on the church side was a row of Georgian houses with bow windows whose dark panes glistened, showing chintz and silver within. There were just three shops, a post office, a butcher's with a canopy and white colonnade, and a place selling souvenirs for tourists. The cottagers' Monday morning wash hung drying in the windless warm air.

They sat on the seat on the green and Tess fed the ducks from a packet of biscuits she had found on the shelf under the dashboard. Kershaw produced a camera and began taking photographs. Suddenly Archery knew he did not want to go any further with them. He almost shivered with distaste at the thought of trailing round the galleries of Pomfret Grange, gasping with false pleasure at the china and pretending to admire family portraits.

'Would you mind if I stayed here? I'd like to have another look at the church.'

Charles glared. 'We'll all go and look at the church.'

'I can't, darling,' said Tess. 'I can't go into a church in jeans.'

'Not in these trousers,' Kershaw quipped. He put away his camera. 'We'd better get moving if we're going to see the stately home.'

'I can easily go back on the bus,' said Archery.

'Well, for God's sake, don't be late, Father.'

If it was going to be any more than a sentimental journey, he too would need a guide. When the car had gone he made his way into the souvenir shop. A bell rang sweetly as he opened the door and a woman came out from a room at the back.

'We don't keep a guide to St Mary's, but you'll find them on sale inside the church door.'

Now he was here he ought to buy something. A postcard? A little brooch for Mary? That, he thought, would be the worst kind of infidelity, to commit adultery in your heart every time you saw your wife wearing a keepsake. He looked drearily at the horse brasses, the painted jugs, the trays of costume jewellery.

A small counter was devoted entirely to calendars, wooden plaques with words on them in pokerwork, framed verses. One of these, a little picture on a card, showing a haloed shepherd with a lamb, caught his eye because the words beneath the drawing were familiar.

'Go, Shepherd, to your rest . . .'

The woman was standing behind him.

'I see you're admiring the efforts of our local bard,' she said brightly. 'He was just a boy when he died and he's buried here.'

'I've seen his grave,' said Archery.

'Of course a lot of people who come here are under the impression he was a shepherd, you know. I always have to explain that at one time shepherd and poet meant the same thing.'

'Lycidas,' said Archery.

She ignored the interruption. 'Actually he was very well-educated. He'd been to High School and everyone said he should have gone to college. He was killed in a road accident. Would you like to see his photograph?'

She produced a stack of cheap framed photographs from a drawer beneath the counter. They were all identical and each bore the legend: John Grace, Bard of Forby. Those whom God loves, die young.

It was a fine ascetic face, sharp-featured and ultra-sensitive. It also, Archery considered, gave the impression that its owner suffered from pernicious anaemia. He had a curious feeling that he had seen it somewhere before.

'Was any of his work published?'

'One or two bits in magazines, that's all. I don't know the ins and outs of it because I've only been here ten years, but there was a publisher who had a week-end cottage here and he was very keen on making his poetry into a book when the poor boy died. Mrs Grace – his mother, you know – was all for it, but the thing was most of the stuff he'd written had disappeared. There were just these bits you see here. His mother said he'd written whole plays – they didn't rhyme, if you know what I mean, but they were kind of like Shakespeare. Anyway, they couldn't be found. Maybe he'd burnt them or given them away. It does seem a shame, though, doesn't it?'

Archery glanced out of the window towards the

little wooden church. 'Some mute inglorious Milton here may rest . . .' he murmured.

'That's right,' said the woman. 'You never know, they may turn up, like the Dead Sea Scrolls.'

Archery paid five and sixpence for the picture of the shepherd and the lamb and strolled up towards the church. He opened the kissing gate and, walking in a clockwise direction, made for the door. What was it she had said? 'You must never go widdershins around a church. It's unlucky.' He needed luck for Charles and for himself. The irony was that however things fell out, one of them would lose.

There was no music coming from the church, but as the door opened he saw that some sort of service was in progress. For a moment he stood, looking at the people and listening to the words.

'If after the manner of men I have fought with beasts at Ephesus, what advantageth it me, if the dead rise not?'

It was a funeral. They were almost exactly half way through the service for the burial of the dead.

'Let us eat and drink for tomorrow we die . . .'

The door gave a slight whine as he closed it. Now, as he turned, he could see the funeral cars, three of them, outside the other gate. He went to look again at Grace's grave, passed the newly dug trench where this latest coffin was to be laid, and finally sat down on a wooden seat in a shady corner. It was a quarter to twelve. Give it half an hour, he thought, and then he would have to go for his bus. Presently he dozed.

The sound of gentle footfalls awakened him. He opened his eyes and saw that they were carrying the coffin out of the church. It was supported by four bearers, but it was a small coffin, a child's perhaps or a short woman's. On it were a few bunches of flowers and a huge wreath of madonna lilies.

The bearers were followed by a dozen people, the procession being headed by a man and a woman walking side by side. Their backs were towards Archery and besides that the woman, dressed in a black coat, wore a large black hat whose brim curved about her face. But he would have known her anywhere. He would have known her if he were blind and deaf, by her presence and her essence. They could not see him, had no idea they were watched, these mourners who had come to bury Alice Flower.

The other followers were mostly old, friends of Alice's perhaps, and one woman looked as if she must be the matron of the Infirmary. They gathered at the graveside and the vicar began to speak the words that would finally commit the old servant to the ground. Primero bent down and, taking rather fastidiously a handful of black earth, cast it on to the coffin. His shoulders shook and a little hand in a black glove reached out and rested on his arm. Archery felt a savage stab of jealousy that took away his breath.

The vicar spoke the Collect and blessed them. Then Primero went a little way apart with him, they spoke together and shook hands. He took his wife's arm and they walked slowly towards the gate where the cars were. It was all over.

When they were out of sight Archery got up and approached the gradually filling grave. He could smell the lilies five yards off. A card was attached to them and on it someone had written simply: 'From Mr and Mrs Roger, with love.'

'Good day,' he said to the sexton.

'Good day, sir. Lovely day.'

It was gone a quarter past twelve. Archery hurried towards the kissing gate, wondering how often the buses ran. As he came out from under the arch of trees, he stopped suddenly. Charles was striding towards him up the sandy lane.

'Good thing you didn't come,' Charles called. 'The place was shut for redecorating. Can you beat it? We thought we might as well drift back and pick you up.'

'Where's the car?'

'Round the other side of the church.'

They would be gone by now. Just the same Archery wished he were safely back at the Olive and Dove eating cold beef and salad. As they rounded the yew hedge a black car passed them. He forced himself to look towards the gate. The Primeros were still there, talking to the matron. His throat grew suddenly dry.

'Let's cut across the green,' he said urgently.

'Mr Kershaw happens to be waiting on this side.'

They were now only a few yards from the Primeros. The matron shook hands and stepped into a hired limousine. Primero turned and his eyes met those of Charles.

He grew first white, then a curious vinegary purple. Charles went on walking towards him and then Primero too began to move. They were approaching each other menacingly, ridiculously, like two gunmen in a Western.

'Mr Bowman, of the *Sunday Planet*, I believe?'

Charles stopped and said coolly, 'You can believe what you like.'

She had been talking to the women in the car. Now she withdrew her head and the car began to move off. They were alone, the four of them, in the centre of the fifth prettiest village in England. She looked at Archery first with embarrassment, then with a warmth that conquered her awkwardness.

'Why, hallo, I . . .'

Primero snatched at her arm. 'Recognise him? I shall need you for a witness, Imogen.'

Charles glared. 'You what?'

'Charles!' said Archery sharply.

'Do you deny that you made your way into my home under false pretences?'

'Roger, Roger . . .' She was still smiling, but her smile had grown stiff. 'Don't you remember we met Mr Archery at the dance? This is his son. He's a journalist, but he uses a pseudonym, that's all. They're here on holiday.'

Charles said rigidly, 'I'm afraid that isn't quite true, Mrs Primero.' She blinked, her lashes fluttering like wings, and her gaze came to rest softly on Archery's face. 'My father and I came here with the express purpose of collecting certain information. That we have done. In order to do it we had to make our way into your confidence. Perhaps we have been unscrupulous, but we thought the end justified the means.'

'I'm afraid I don't understand.' Her eyes were still on Archery and he was unable to draw his own away. He knew that his face registered a tremendous plea for forgiveness, a disclaimer of Charles's statement, and also registered the agony of love. There was, however, no reason why she should read there anything but guilt. 'I don't understand at all. What information?'

'I'll tell you . . .' Charles began, but Primero interrupted him.

'Since you're so frank, you won't have any objection to coming down to the police station right now and laying your "information" before Chief Inspector Wexford.'

'None at all,' Charles drawled, 'except that it happens to be my lunchtime and in any case I have an appointment with the Chief Inspector already. At two sharp. I intend to tell him, Mr Primero, just how opportunely for you your grandmother died, how – oh, perfectly legally, I admit – you managed to cheat your sisters out of their inheritance, and how you concealed yourself in Victor's Piece on a certain evening in December sixteen years ago.'

'You're out of your mind!' Primero shouted.

Archery found his voice. 'That's enough, Charles.' He heard her speak, a tiny disembodied sound.

'It isn't true!' And then, terribly afraid, 'It isn't true, is it?'

'I'm damned if I'll argue it out in the street with this crook!'

'Of course it's true.'

'It was all above board.' Primero suddenly broke. They were all hot, standing there in the noon sun, but only Primero's face showed actual sweat, water drops on the cheesy sallow skin. 'Hell, it was a matter of law,' he blustered. 'What's it got to do with you, anyway? Who *are* you?'

Without taking her gaze from Archery, she took her husband's arm. All the gaiety had left her face and she looked almost old, a faded blonde who was effaced by her black clothes. Because she had become ugly she suddenly seemed for the first time within Archery's reach, yet she had never been farther from it. 'Let's go home, Roger.' Her mouth trembled and cobweb lines had appeared at its corners. 'In the course of your enquiries, Mr Archery,' she said, 'I hope you managed to combine pleasure with business.'

Then they were gone. Charles gave a great gasp.

'I must say I rather enjoyed that. I suppose by pleasure she meant the lunch they gave me. You can rely on these tycoons' wives to tot up every egg in

168

the caviare. Still it was hard on her. You needn't look so shattered, Father. It's awfully middle-class to have a phobia about scenes.'

Chapter 13

I deal with the thing that is lawful and right ... and all false ways I utterly abhor.

Psalm 119, appointed for the 26th Day.

'Public General Acts and Measures, 1950.' Wexford took the book – was it a White Paper? Archery was ashamed to confess that he did not know – and read the title aloud. 'There's something here you want me to look at?'

Charles found the page for him. 'Here.' Wexford began to read. The silence was tense, almost agonised. Archery looked surreptitiously at the others, Charles who was flushed with eagerness, Kershaw trying to sit casually, but whose bright darting eyes betrayed his anxiety, Tess who looked confident, serene. Was it her mother in whom she trusted so completely or was it Charles? A good deal of Charles's poise had deserted him when, on entering the office five minutes before, he had had to introduce Tess to the Chief Inspector.

'Miss Kershaw,' he had said, 'my ... the girl I'm going to marry. I ...'

'Ah, yes.' Wexford had been very urbane. 'Good afternoon, Miss Kershaw, Mr Kershaw. Won't you sit down? Heat wave's coming to an end at last, I'm afraid.'

And indeed a change had come over the bright blue un-English sky. It had begun just after lunch with the appearance of a cloud that was truly no bigger than a man's hand, and this cloud had been followed by more, driven by a sudden wind. Now, as Wexford, frowning a little, read steadily, Archery contemplated the window from which the yellow blind had been fully raised, and through it the lumpy blotchy mass of cumulus, hollowed and pock-marked with grey.

'Very interesting,' said Wexford, 'and new to me. I didn't know the Primero sisters were adopted. Convenient for Primero.'

'Convenient?' said Charles. Archery sighed within himself. He could always tell when his son was going to be rude or what Charles himself called forthright. 'Is that all you've got to say?'

'No,' said Wexford. Few people have the confidence and the restraint to say 'yes' or 'no' without qualification. Wexford was big and heavy and ugly; his suit had seen better days, too many wet ones and too many hot dusty ones, but he radiated strength. 'Before we go any further on this tack, Mr Archery,' he said to Charles, 'I'd like to say that I've had a complaint about you from Mr Primero.'

'Oh, that.'

'Yes, that. I've been aware for some days that your father had made the acquaintance of the Primeros. Perhaps it wasn't a bad idea and I'm sure it wasn't an unpleasant one to do so through Mrs Primero.' Archery knew his face had become white. He felt sick. 'And let me say in all fairness,' Wexford went on, 'that I told him it was all right as far as I was concerned to make contact with the people concerned in the Primero case.' He glanced briefly at Tess who didn't move. 'Make contact, I said, not make trouble. Your little escapade on Friday is what I call making trouble and that I won't have!'

Charles said sulkily, 'All right, I'm sorry.' Archery saw that he had to justify himself before Tess. 'You're not going to tell me that your people don't occasionally invent a cover story to get what they want.'

'My people,' Wexford snapped, 'happen to have

the law on their side.' He added grandiloquently, 'They *are* the law.' The frown thawed. 'Now we've got the lecture over you'd better tell me just what you and your father have found out.'

Charles told him. Wexford listened patiently, but as the evidence against Primero mounted, instead of surprise, his face registered a strange blankness. The heavy features had become brutish, like those of an old bull.

'Of course, you'll say he had an alibi,' said Charles. 'I realise your people would have checked his alibi and after all these years it's going to be difficult to crack, but ...'

'His alibi was not checked,' said Wexford.

'What did you say?'

'His alibi was not checked.'

'I don't understand.'

'Mr Archery ...' Wexford got up and rested his massive hands on the desk, but he didn't move away from behind it. 'I am quite happy to discuss this whole matter with you, answer any questions you may like to ask.' He paused. 'But not in the presence of Miss Kershaw. If I may say so, I think you were unwise to bring her with you.'

Now it was Charles's turn to get to his feet.

'Miss Kershaw is going to be my wife,' he said hotly. 'Anything you say to me you can say to her. I won't have any secrets from her in this.'

Casually Wexford sat down again. He drew a bunch of papers from a desk drawer and began to study them. Then he lifted his eyes slowly and said: 'I'm sorry this has been a fruitless interview for you. With a little co-operation I think I could have saved you a lot of useless enquiry. But, if you'll forgive me, I'm a very busy man so I'll say good afternoon.'

'No,' said Tess suddenly. 'I'll go. I'll wait in the car.'

'Tess!'

'Of course I'm going, darling. Don't you see? He can't talk about my father in front of me. Oh, darling, be your age!'

He is being his age, thought Archery miserably. Wexford knew something – something that was going to be horrible. But why was he playing this pouncing cat and mouse game with them all, why had he played it with Archery all along? Confidence and strength – but did it cover a fierce inverted snobbism, a fear that the Archeries might shake his authority and trouble the still waters of his district? And yet the man held such sway and was, beyond a doubt, a good, just man. He would never lie or even shift truth to cover a lapse. 'His alibi was not checked . . .' If only they would stop fencing!

Then, suddenly, Wexford stopped it.

'No need to leave the building, Miss Kershaw,' he said. 'If your – your father would care to take you upstairs – straight along the corridor and turn left when you come to the double doors – you'll find we've got quite a reasonable canteen, even for a lady. I suggest a cup of strong tea and an eccles cake.'

'Thanks.' Tess turned and just touched Kershaw's shoulder. He rose at once. Wexford closed the door after them.

Charles took a deep breath, and making a brave attempt to lounge casually in his chair, said, 'All right, then. What about this alibi that for some mysterious reason was never investigated?'

'The reason,' said Wexford, 'was not mysterious. Mrs Primero was killed between six-twenty-five and seven o'clock on the evening of Sunday, September 24th, 1950.' He paused to allow Charles's inevitable interruption of 'Yes, yes', uttered with fierce impatience. 'She was killed in Kingsmarkham and at six-

173

thirty Roger Primero was seen in Sewingbury five miles away.'

'Oh, he was seen, was he?' Charles scoffed, crossing his legs. 'What do you think, Father? Doesn't it seem remotely possible to you that he could have fixed it beforehand that he'd be "seen"? There's always some shifty mate who'll perjure himself and say he's seen you for twenty quid.'

'Some shifty mate, eh?' Wexford was now hardly bothering to conceal his amusement.

'Somebody saw him. All right. Who saw him?'

Wexford sighed and the smile was erased.

'I saw him,' he said.

It was a blow in the face. Archery's love for his son, dormant over the past days, rose within his breast in a hot tide. Charles said nothing, and Archery who had been doing this sort of thing rather a lot lately, tried hard not to hate Wexford. He had taken an unconscionable time coming to the point, but this, of course, was his revenge.

The big elbows rested on the desk, the fingers meeting and pressing together in an implacable pyramid of flesh. The law incarnate. If Wexford had seen Primero that night, there was no gainsaying it, for here was incorruptibility. It was almost as if God had seen him. Horrified, Archery pulled himself up in his chair and gave a dry painful cough.

'You?' said Charles at last.

'I,' said Wexford, 'with my little eye.'

'You might have told us before!'

'I would have,' said Wexford mildly and, oddly enough, believably, 'if I'd had the remotest idea you suspected him. Chatting up Primero about his grandmother was one thing, pinning murder on him quite another.'

Polite now, stiff and very formal, Charles asked, 'Would you mind telling us the details?'

Wexford's courtesy matched his. 'Not at all. I intend to. Before I do, however, I'd better say that there was no question of hindsight. I knew Primero. I'd seen him in court with his chief on a good many occasions. He used to go along with him to learn the ropes.' Charles nodded, his face set. Archery thought he knew what was going on in his mind. Loss was something he knew about, too.

'I was in Sewingbury on a job,' Wexford continued, 'and I'd got a date to meet a man who sometimes gave us a bit of information. What you might call a shifty mate, but we never got twenty quidsworth out of him. The appointment was for six at a pub called the Black Swan. Well, I had a word with my – my friend, and I was due back in Kingsmarkham at seven. I walked out of the public bar at just on half past six and ran slap bang into Primero.

'"Good evening, Inspector," he said, and I thought he looked a bit lost. As well he might. I found out afterwards that he'd been going to meet some pals, but he'd got the wrong pub. They were waiting for him at the Black Bull. "Are you on duty?" he said. "Or can I buy you a short snort?"'

Archery nearly smiled. Wexford had given a very fair imitation of the absurd slang Primero still affected after sixteen years of affluence.

'"Thanks all the same," I said, "but I'm late as it is." "Good night to you, then," he said and he went up to the bar. I'd only been in Kingsmarkham ten minutes when I got called out to Victor's Piece.'

Charles got up slowly and extended a stiff, mechanical hand.

'Thank you very much, Chief Inspector. I think that's all anyone can say on the subject, don't you?'

Wexford leaned across the desk and took his hand. A faint flash of compassion softened his features, weakened them, and was gone. 'I'm sorry I wasn't very polite just now,' Charles said.

'That's all right,' said Wexford. 'This is a police station, not a clerical garden party.' He hesitated and added, 'I'm sorry, too.' And Archery knew that the apology had nothing to do with Charles's ill manners.

Tess and Charles began to argue even before they had all got into the car. Certain that they had said it all or something very like it before, Archery listened to them indifferently. He had kept silent for half an hour and still there was nothing he could say.

'We have to be realistic about it,' Charles was saying. 'If I don't mind and Mother and Father don't mind, why can't we just get married and forget you ever had a father?'

'Who says they don't mind? That's not being realistic, anyway. I'm being realistic. One way and another I've had a lot of luck . . .' Tess flashed a quick watery smile at Kershaw. 'I've had more than anyone would have thought possible, but this is one bit I have to dip out on.'

'And what does that mean exactly?'

'Just that – well, it was ridiculous ever to imagine we could be married, you and I.'

'You and I? What about all the others who'll come along and fancy you? Are you going to go through the same melodrama with them or d'you think you'll weaken when the thirties rear their ugly heads?'

She winced at that. Archery thought Charles had almost forgotten they were not alone. He pushed her into the back seat of the car and banged the door.

'I'm curious, you see,' Charles went on, bitterly sarcastic. 'I'd just like to know if you've taken a vow

176

of perpetual chastity. O God, it's like a feature in the *Sunday Planet* – Condemned to lonely spinsterhood for father's crime! Just for the record, since I'm supposed to be so far above you morally, I'd like to know the qualifications the lucky man has to have. Give me a specification, will you?'

Her mother had built up her faith, but the Archery family with their doubts had knocked it down; still it had lived until Wexford had killed it. Her eyes were fixed on Kershaw who had given her reality. Archery was not surprised when she said hysterically:

'I suppose he'd have to have a murderer for a father.' She gasped, for she was admitting it to herself for the first time. 'Like me!'

Charles tapped Archery's back. 'Just nip out and knock someone off,' he said outrageously.

'Oh, shut up,' said Kershaw. 'Give it a rest, Charlie, will you?'

Archery touched his arm. 'I think I'll get out, if you don't mind. I need some air.'

'Me too,' said Tess. 'I can't stand being boxed up in here any longer and I've got a ghastly head. I want some aspirins.'

'Can't park here.'

'We'll walk back to the hotel, Daddy. If I don't get out I'll pass out.'

Then they were all three on the pavement, Charles's face as black as thunder. Tess swayed a little and Archery caught her arm to steady her. Several passers-by gave them curious looks.

'You said you wanted aspirins,' said Charles.

It was only a few yards to the nearest chemist's, but Tess was shivering in her thin clothes. The air was heavy and cloying. Archery noticed that all the shopkeepers had furled their sunblinds.

Charles seemed about to begin again but she gave him a pleading look. 'Don't let's talk about it any more. We've said it all. I needn't see you again till October, not then if we're careful ...'

He frowned silently, made a little gesture of repudiation. Archery held the shop door open for Tess to pass through.

There was no one inside but the assistant and Elizabeth Crilling.

She did not appear to be buying anything, just waiting and gossiping with the shopgirl. It was the middle of a weekday afternoon and here she was shopping. What had become of the job in the 'ladies' wear establishment'? Archery wondered if she would recognise him and how he could avoid this happening, for he did not want to have to introduce her to Tess. It gave him a little thrill of awe when he realised what was happening in this small town shop, a meeting after sixteen years of the child who was Painter's daughter and the child who had discovered Painter's crime.

While he hovered near the door. Tess went up to the counter. They were so close together that they were almost touching. Then Tess reached across in front of Liz Crilling to select one of the aspirin bottles, and in doing so brushed her sleeve.

'I beg your pardon.'

'That's O.K.'

Archery could see Tess had nothing smaller than a ten shilling note. His trepidation, his fears for the effect of illumination on Tess at this moment were so great, that he almost cried aloud, 'Never mind. Leave it! Only, please God, let us all get away and hide ourselves!'

'Haven't you anything smaller?'

'I'm sorry.'

'I'll just go and see if we've got any change.'

The two young women stood side by side in silence. Tess stared straight in front of her, but Liz

Crilling was playing nervously with two little scent bottles displayed on a glass shelf, moving them about as if they were chessmen.

Then the pharmacist in his white coat came out from the back.

'Is there a Miss Crilling waiting for a prescription?'

Tess turned, her face flooded with colour.

'This is a repeat prescription, but I'm afraid it's no longer valid ...'

'What d'you mean, no longer valid?'

'I mean that it can only be used six times. I can't let you have any more of these tablets without a fresh prescription. If your mother ...'

'The old cow,' said Liz Crilling slowly.

The swift animation on Tess's face died as if she had been struck. Without opening her purse she tumbled the change loose into her handbag and hurried out of the shop.

The old cow. It was her fault, everything bad that had ever happened to you was her fault – beginning with the beautiful pink dress.

She was making it for you and she worked at the sewing machine all day that cold wet Sunday. When it was finished you put it on and Mummy brushed your hair and put a ribbon in it.

'I'll just pop over and show you off to Granny Rose,' Mummy said and she popped over, but when she came back she was cross because Granny Rose was asleep and hadn't heard when she'd tapped on the window.

'Give it half an hour,' Daddy said, 'and maybe she'll be awake then.' He was half asleep himself, lying in bed, white and thin on the pillows. So Mummy had stayed upstairs with him, giving him his medicine and reading to him because he was too weak to hold a book.

'You stay in the sitting room, Baby, and mind you don't get that frock dirty.'

You had done as you were told but it made you cry just the same. Of course you didn't care about not seeing Granny Rose, but you knew that while she was talking to Mummy you could have slipped out into the passage and down the garden to show it to Tessie, now, while it was brand-new.

Well, why not? Why not put on a coat and run across the road? Mummy wouldn't come down for half an hour. But you would have to hurry, for Tessie always went to bed at half-past six. Auntie Rene was strict about that. 'Respectable working class,' Mummy said, whatever that meant, and although she might let you into Tessie's bedroom she wouldn't let you wake her up.

But why, why, why had you gone?

Elizabeth Crilling came out of the shop and walked blindly towards the Glebe Road turning, bumping into shoppers as she went. Such a long way to go, past the hateful little sand houses that were like desert tombs in this spectral form light, such a long long way . . . And there was only one thing left to do when you got to the end of the road.

Chapter 14

It is lawful for Christian men ... to wear weapons
and serve in the wars.

The Thirty-nine Articles.

The letter with the Kendal postmark was awaiting
Archery on the hall table when they got back to the
Olive and Dove. He glanced at it uncomprehend-
ingly, then remembered. Colonel Cosmo Plashet,
Painter's commanding officer.

'What now?' he said to Charles when Tess had
gone upstairs to lie down.

'I don't know. They're going back to Purley
tonight.'

'Do we go back to Thringford tonight?'

'I don't know, Father. I tell you I don't know.' He
paused, irritable, pink in the face, a lost child. 'I'll
have to go and apologise to Primero,' he said, the
child remembering its manners. 'It was a bloody
awful way to behave to him.'

Archery said it instinctively, without thinking. 'I'll
do that, if you like. I'll ring them.'

'Thanks. If he insists on seeing me I'll go. You've
talked to her before, haven't you? I gathered from
something Wexford said.'

'Yes, I've talked to her, but I didn't know who she
was.'

'That,' said Charles, severe again, 'is you all over.'

Was he really going to ring her up and apologise?
And why should he have the vanity to suppose that
she would even come to the phone? 'In the course of
your enquiries, Mr Archery, I hope you managed to
combine pleasure with business.' She was bound to

have told her husband what she had meant by that. How the middle-aged clergyman had suddenly gone sentimental on her. He could hear Primero's reply, his colloquialism, 'Didn't actually make the old pass, did he?' and her light dismissive laughter. His soul cringed. He went into the empty lounge and ripped open Colonel Plashet's letter.

It was handwritten on rough white vellum almost as thick as cartridge paper. By the occasional fading of the ink from deep black to pale grey Archery could tell that the writer had not used a fountain pen. An old man's hand, he thought, a military man's address, 'Srinagar', Church Street, Kendal . . .

Dear Mr Archery, he read,

I was interested to receive your letter and will do my best to provide you with what information I can on Private Herbert Arthur Painter. You may be aware that I was not called to give evidence as to character at Painter's trial, though I held myself in readiness to do so should it have been necessary. Fortunately I have retained in my possession certain notes I then made. I say fortunately, for you will appreciate that Private Painter's war service covered a period of from twenty-three to twenty years ago, and my memory is no longer what I should like it to be. Lest you should be under the impression, however, that I am the possessor of information sympathetic to Painter's relatives, I must reluctantly disabuse your mind. In deciding not to call me, Painter's defending counsel must have been aware that any statements I could truthfully have made would, instead of assisting their cause, have merely made the task of prosecution easier.

That was it, then. There would follow only another loathsome catalogue to Painter's propensities. Colonel Plashet's very idiosyncratic style and writing brought home to him more forcibly than the cold print of the transcript had done, the kind of man Charles was prepared to accept as a father-in-law. Curiosity, not hope, made him read on.

Painter had been serving with His Majesty's Forces for one year when he entered my regiment. This was shortly prior to our embarkation for Burma as part of the Fourteen Army. He was a most unsatisfactory soldier. We saw no action until we had been in Burma for three months, during which time Painter was twice put on a charge for being drunk and disorderly and sentenced to seven days' detention for gross insolence on an officer.

In action his manner and bearing improved considerably. He was a naturally pugnacious man, brave and aggressive. Soon after this, however, an incident occurred in the village in which we had our camp and a young Burmese woman was killed. A Court Martial was held before which Painter was charged with her manslaughter. He was found not guilty. I think I had better say no more on this matter.

In February 1945, six months before the cessation of hostilities in the Far East, Painter succumbed to a certain tropical affliction which manifests itself in severe ulceration of the legs, accelerated, I am told by his complete disregard of certain elementary hygienic precautions and his refusal to take a proper diet. He became seriously ill and responded badly to treatment. There was at this time a troopship lying off Calcutta, and as soon as Painter's condition allowed, he and certain other sick men were transported there by air. This troopship reached a United Kingdom port during the latter part of March, 1945.

I have no further information as to Painter's fate except that I believe he was shortly afterwards demobilised on health grounds.

If you have any other questions whatsoever to put to me regarding Painter's war service, you may be assured of my willingness to answer them to the best of my ability and discretion. You have my full permission to publish this letter. May I, however, ask your indulgence to an old man's whim, and request a copy of your book when it comes out?

Yours sincerely,

Cosmo Plashet

They all assumed he was writing a book. Archery smiled a little at the colonel's grandiose style, but there was nothing to smile at in the brief lines about the Burmese woman's death. The colonel's guarded, 'I think I had better say no more on this matter . . .' told him more than a page of explanations.

Nothing new, nothing vital. Why, then, did he have this urgent sensation of having missed something of importance? But no, he couldn't see it . . . He looked again, not knowing what he was looking for. Then, as he stared at the spidery loops and whorls, he was engulfed by a hot wave of trepidation and longing. He was afraid to speak to her, yet he longed to hear her voice.

He looked up, surprised to find how dark it had become. The summer afternoon sky simulated dusk with its covering of slate-coloured cloud. Over the housetops away to the east it was leaden tinged with angry purple and as Archery began to fold the letter, a vivid flash of lightning shocked across the room, flashing the words on the paper into relief and bleaching his hands livid white. The thunder followed it as he reached the stairs, and echoes were still curling and growling round the old building when he entered his bedroom.

She could only refuse to speak to him. She wouldn't even have to do that herself, for she could send the Italian butler. There was no question of her berating or reproaching him personally – she could do it with far more crushing effect by proxy.

'Forby Hall. Mr Primero's residence.'

It *was* the butler. The Italian accent distorted every word except the name to which it gave true Latin emphasis.

'I should like to speak to Mrs Primero.'

'What name shall I say, sir?'

'Henry Archery.'

Perhaps she would not be with her husband when the message came. People situated as they were in an enormous house of many rooms tended to live individual lives, he in the library, she in the drawing room. She would send the butler back with a message. As a foreigner the butler would be without that intimate feel for the nuances of English and that would give her scope. She could tell him to say something subtle and apparently polite and he would not appreciate the cutting sting that underlay the words. He heard footsteps, echoing footsteps across the big hall Charles had described. The phone crackled, perhaps because of the storm.

'Hallo?'

Out of a bone-dry throat he tried to speak. Why hadn't he rehearsed something? Because he had been so sure she wouldn't come?

'Hallo, are you still there?'

'Mrs Primero . . .'

'I thought you might have got fed-up with waiting. Mario took so long about it.'

'Of course I waited.' Rain burst against his window, smacking and sobbing at the glass. 'I want to apologise to you for this morning. It was unforgivable.'

'Oh, no,' she said. 'I've forgiven you – for this morning. You didn't really take any part in it, did you? It was the other times that seem so – well, not unforgivable, just incomprehensible.'

He could imagine her little helpless gesture, the white hands spreading out.

'One doesn't like to feel one's been used, you see. It's not that I'm hurt. I'm not likely to be hurt because I'm really very tough, much tougher than Roger. But I am a bit spoilt and I feel as if I've been kicked off my pedestal. Good for me, I expect.'

Archery said slowly, 'There's so much to explain. I thought I could explain on the phone, but now I find I can't.' And yet the violence of the storm made it easier for him. He could hardly hear his own words. 'I want to *see* you,' he said, forgetting his promise.

Apparently she had forgotten it too. 'You can't come here,' she said practically, 'because Roger's somewhere about and he might not look on your apology in the same light as I do. And I can't come to you because the Olive and Dove, being a respectable hostelry, doesn't allow visitors in residents' bedrooms.' He made an inarticulate murmur. 'That's the second cheap thing I've said to you today,' she said. 'Oh, my dear, you wouldn't want to talk in the lounge among all the fuddy-duddies, would you? I know, what about Victor's Piece?'

'It's locked,' he said, adding stupidly, 'and it's raining.'

'I've got a key. Roger's always kept one. Shall we say eight? The Olive will be only too happy if you have an early dinner.'

He dropped the receiver almost guiltily as Charles put his head round the door. And yet the telephone call had not been clandestine but made at Charles's instigation.

'I think I've made it all right with the Primeros,' he said, and he reflected on words from an unremembered source. God gave men tongues that they might conceal their thoughts.

But Charles, with the quixotry of youth, had lost interest. 'Tess and her father are just off,' he said.

'I'll come down.'

They were standing in the hall, waiting. For what? Archery wondered. The storm to cease? A miracle? Or just to say goodbye?

'I wish we hadn't seen Elizabeth Crilling,' Tess said. 'And yet now I wish I'd talked to her.'

'Just as well you didn't,' said Archery. 'You're worlds apart. The only thing you'd have in common is your age. You're both twenty-one.'

'Don't wish away my life,' Tess said oddly and he saw there were tears in her eyes. 'I'm not twenty-one till October.' She picked up the duffel bag that served her as a weekend case and held out her hand to Archery.

'We must love you and leave you,' said Kershaw. 'Doesn't seem anything more to be said, does there, Mr Archery? I know you hoped things would work out, but it wasn't to be.'

Charles was gazing at Tess. She kept her eyes averted.

'For God's sake say I can write to you.'

'What's the use?'

'It would give me pleasure,' he said tightly.

'I shan't be at home. I'm going to Torquay to stay with my aunt the day after tomorrow.'

'You won't be camping on the beach, will you? This aunt, doesn't she have an address?'

'I haven't got a piece of paper,' said Tess and Archery saw that she was near to tears. He felt in his pocket, pulled out first Colonel Plashet's letter – not that, not for Tess to see – then the illuminated card with the verse and the picture of the shepherd. Her eyes were misted and she scrawled the address quickly, handing it to Charles without a word.

'Come on, lovey,' said Kershaw. 'Home, and don't spare the horses.' He fished out his car keys. 'All fifteen of them,' he said, but no one smiled.

Chapter 15

If he hath offended any other . . . ask them forgiveness; and where he hath done injury or wrong to any man . . . make amends to the uttermost of his power.

The Visitation of the Sick.

It was raining so heavily that he had to dash from the car into the dilapidated porch and even there the rain caught him, blown by the gusty wind and tossed in icy droplets off the evergreens. He leant against the door and staggered because it gave with his weight and swung noisily open.

She must have arrived already. The Flavia was nowhere to be seen and he felt a shiver of self-disgust and trepidation when it occurred to him that she was being purposely discreet. She was well known in the district, she was married and she was having a secret meeting with a married man. So she had hidden her conspicuous car. Yes, it was cheap, cheap and sordid, and he, a priest of God, had engineered it.

Victor's Piece, dry and rotten in drought, smelt wet and rotten now the rain had come. It smelt of fungus and dead things. There were probably rats under these knotted flaking floorboards. He closed the door and walked a little way down the passage, wondering where she was and why she had not come out to him when she heard the door. Then he stopped, for he was facing the back door where Painter's raincoat had hung, and there was a raincoat hanging there now.

Certainly nothing had hung there on his previous

189

visit to the house. He moved up to the raincoat, fascinated and rather horrified.

Of course, it was obvious what had happened. Someone had bought the place at last, the workmen had been in and one of them had left his raincoat. Nothing to be alarmed about. His nerves must be very bad.

'Mrs Primero,' he said, and then, because you do not call women with whom you have secret assignations by their surnames, 'Imogen! Imogen!'

There was no answer. And yet he was sure he was not alone in the house. What about knowing her if you were deaf and blind, jeered a voice within him, what about knowing her by her essence? He opened the dining room door, then the drawing room. A damp cold smell came to meet him. Water had leaked under the window sill and formed a spreading pool, dark in colour, hideously evocative. This and the rusty veining on the marble of the fireplace recalled to him splashed blood. Who would buy this place? Who could bear it? But someone had bought it for there was a workman's coat hanging behind the door . . .

Here she had sat, the old woman, and bade Alice go to church. Here she had sat, her eyes closing easily into sleep, when Mrs Crilling had come tapping at the window. Then he had come, whoever he was, with his axe and perhaps she had still been sleeping, on and on over the threats and the demands, over the blows of the axe, on and on into endless sleep. Endless sleep? *Mors janua vitae.* If only the gateway to life had not been through an unspeakable passage of pain. He found himself praying for what he knew was impossible, that God should change history.

Then Mrs Crilling tapped on the window.

Archery gave a start so violent and galvanic that

he seemed to feel a hand squeeze his heart with slippery fingers. He gasped and forced himself to look.

'Sorry I'm late,' said Imogen Ide. 'What a ghastly night.'

She should have been on the inside, he thought, pulling himself together. But she had been outside, tapping, tapping, because she had seen him standing there like a lost soul. This way it altered the aspect of things, for she had not hidden the car. It stood on the gravel beside his own, wet, silver, glittering, like something alive and beautiful from the depths of the sea.

'How did you get in?' she said in the hall.

'The door was open.'

'Some workman.'

'I suppose so.'

She wore a tweed suit and her pale hair was wet. He had been silly enough – bad enough, he thought – to imagine that when they met she would run to him and embrace him. Instead she stood looking at him gravely, almost coldly, two little frown lines between her brows.

'The morning room, I think,' she said. 'There's furniture in there and besides it doesn't have – associations.'

The furniture consisted of two kitchen stools and a caneback chair. From the window, heavily encrusted with grime, he could see the conservatory to whose walls of cracked glass the tendrils of a dead vine still clung. He gave her the chair and sat down on one of the stools. He had a strange feeling – but a feeling not without a charm of its own – that they had come here to buy the house, he and she, had come early and were reduced to wait thus uncomfortably until the arrival of the agent who would show them round.

'This could be a study,' he would say. 'It must be lovely on a fine day.'

'Or we could eat in here. Nice and near the kitchen.'

'Will you be able to bear getting up in the morning to cook my breakfast?' (My love, my love . . .)

'You were going to explain,' she said, and of course, there would never be a shared bed or a shared breakfast or any future at all. This was their future, this interview in a damp morning room, looking at a dead vine.

He began to tell her about Charles and Tess, about Mrs Kershaw's belief. Her face grew even harder and colder when he came to the bit about the inheritance and before he had finished, she said:

'You really meant to pin the murder on Roger?'

'What could I do? I was torn between Charles,' he said, 'and you.' She shook her head quickly, the blood running into her face. 'I beg you to believe I didn't try to know you because you were his wife.'

'I believe you.'

'The money . . . his sisters . . . you didn't know about that?'

'I knew nothing. Only that they existed and that he never saw them. Oh God!' She screwed up her face, pushed her hands over her cheeks, across her eyes and up to the temples. 'We've been talking about it all day. He can't see that he was morally obliged to help them. Only one thing matters to him, that Wexford won't take it seriously as a motive for murder.'

'Wexford saw him himself that night at the crucial time in Sewingbury.'

'He doesn't know or he's forgotten. He's going to go through hell until he can pluck up courage to ring Wexford. Some people might say that's his punishment.' She sighed. 'Are his sisters very badly off?'

'One of them is. She lives in a single room with her husband and her baby.'

'I've got Roger to agree to let them have what they should have had in the first place, three thousand, three hundred odd each. I think I'd better go to see them myself. He won't even notice it's gone. It's funny, you know, I knew he was unscrupulous. You can't make that amount of money without being, but I didn't know he'd stoop to that.'

'It hasn't made you . . .?' He hesitated, wondering what he had destroyed.

'Never feel the same about him again? Oh, my dear, you are funny. Listen, I'll tell you something. Seven years ago it was and the month of June. My face was on the cover of six separate magazines that month. The most photographed girl in Britain.'

He nodded, puzzled and out of his depth.

'If you reach a peak there's nothing left but to go downhill. In June of the next year I had my face on one magazine. So I married Roger.'

'You didn't love him?'

'I liked him, you know. He saved me in a way and all the time I'm saving him.' Archery knew what she meant, recalling her soft tranquillity in the Olive dining room, her hand touching a mourner's trembling arm. He expected always from her calm serenity and he was shocked when she raged suddenly: 'How was I to know there was a middle-aged clergyman waiting for me – a clergyman with a wife and a son and a guilt complex as big as a mountain?'

'Imogen!'

'No, you're not to touch me! It was stupid to come here and I should never have done it. Oh God. How I hate these sentimental scenes!'

He got up and walked as far from her as the little room allowed. It had stopped raining but the sky was sludge-coloured and the vine was as dead as a doornail.

'What will they do now,' she said, 'your son and this girl?'

'I don't think they know themselves.'

'And you, what will you do?'

'"Go to the wife of my bosom,"' he quoted, '"the same as I ought to go."'

'Kipling!' She gave a hysterical laugh, and he was pained by the depths he was discovering too late. 'Kipling! That's all I need.'

'Good-bye,' he said.

'Good-bye, dear Henry Archery. I've never known what to call you. Do you know that?' She lifted his hand, kissed the palm.

'Perhaps it's not a name for dalliance,' he said ruefully.

'But it sounds well with Rev. in front of it.'

She went out, closing the door soundlessly behind her.

'Jenny kissed me,' he said to the vine. Jenny could just be short for Imogen. 'So what?'

Presently he came out into the hall and he wondered why the place seemed emptier and more lifeless than before. Perhaps it was his own fresh sense of loss. He turned towards the back door and then he saw. It was not an imagined but an actual diminishing. The raincoat had gone.

Had it ever been there or was his fancy, morbid and hypersensitive, creating hallucinations? It was a vision that might naturally come to someone involved as he was in Painter's story. But if the raincoat had never been there what would account for those penny-sized puddles on the floor, made surely by rain rivulets running from a sleeve?

He had no belief in the vulgar supernatural. But now as he stood looking at the hook where the raincoat had hung, he remembered how he had jumped at the tap on the window and had likened the marble veining to blood. It was not impossible that some evil hung over places such as this, fermenting the imagination and re-creating on the mind's retina images from a past tragedy.

The door was glazed in square panes. All were dirty yet all glinted faintly in the evening light – all but one. He peered, then smiled wryly at his absurd fancies. The glass had been completely removed from the frame nearest to the lock. An arm could have passed through it to turn the key and slide back the bolts.

It was unbolted now. He stepped out on to the flagged yard. Beyond, the garden lay enveloped in thin wet mist. The trees, the bushes, the lush blanket of weed sagged under their weight of water. Once he would have felt the responsible citizen's anxiety as to the whereabouts of whoever had broken that window, might even have considered going to the police. Now he was simply apathetic, indifferent.

Imogen filled his mind, but even on this subject, his thoughts were no longer passionate or ashamed. He would give her five more minutes to get away and then he would return to the Olive. Mechanically he stooped down and for something to do began carefully picking up the shards of broken glass, stacking them against the wall where no one, not even the burglar, might tread on them.

His nerves were bad, he knew that, but surely that was a foot-fall, the sound of indrawn breath.

She was coming back! But she must not – it was more than he could stand. The sight of her would be joy, but anything she said could only mean a fresh parting. He set his teeth, tightened the muscles of his hands and before he could stop himself his fingers had closed on a sliver of glass.

The blood came before the pain. He stood up, looking stupidly and aloud in that empty place, and he turned to meet the tap-tap of high heels.

Her scream burst in his face.

'Uncle Bert! Uncle Bert! Oh, my God!'

His hand was all bloody but he put it out, the hurt hand and the other, to catch Elizabeth Crilling as she fell.

'You ought to have it stitched,' she said. 'You'll get tetanus. You'll have an awful scar.'

He wrapped the handkerchief more tightly about the wound and sat grimly on the step, watching her. She had come round in seconds but her face was still white. A little gust of wind flicked through the tangled mass of green and showered them with water drops. Archery shivered.

'What are you doing here?' he asked.

She lay back in the chair he had fetched her from the morning room, her legs stretched out and limp. He noticed how thin they were, thin as the legs of an Oriental, the stockings wrinkled at the ankles.

'I've had a row with my mother,' she said.

He said nothing, waiting. For a moment she remained inert, then her body seemed to snap forwards, a trap with a steel spring. Instinctively, he shifted a little away from her, for she had brought her face towards his, her hands clutching each other between knees and breast. Her mouth moved before the words found sound.

'Oh Christ!' He kept still, controlling his inevitable reaction to the oath. 'I saw you with blood on you,' she said, 'and then you said it, what he said. "I've cut myself."' A great shudder rocked her as if she had been grasped and shaken by an invisible force. Amazed, he watched her slacken again and heard her say in cold contrast, 'Give me a cigarette.' She tossed her bag to him. 'Light it!' The flame guttered in the damp air and the tugging wind. She cupped her thin hands with their big knuckles around it. 'Always snooping, aren't you?' she said, drawing back. 'I don't know what you thought you'd find, but this is it.'

Bewildered, he found himself staring at the garden, up at the overhanging gables, down at the wet broken paving.

'Me, I mean,' she said with savage impatience. 'You've been telling tales to the police about me and you don't even know what it's all about.' Again she snapped forward and shamelessly – he was horrified – pulled up her skirt and exposed her thigh above her stocking top. The white skin was covered all over with needle punctures. 'Asthma, that's what it's about. Asthma tablets. You dissolve them in water – and that's a hell of a job on its own – and then you fill up a hypodermic.'

Archery did not think himself easily shocked. But he was shocked now. He felt the blood run into his face. Embarrassment silenced him, then gave place to pity for her and a kind of diffused indignation with humanity.

'Does it have any effect?' he asked as coolly as he could.

'It gives you a lift, if you follow me. Much the same as you get from singing psalms, I expect,' she jeered. 'There was this man I lived with, he put me on to it. I was in the right place for getting supplies, you see. Until you sent that bastard Burden down and he put the fear of God into my mother. She's got to get a new prescription every time she wants them now and she's got to collect them herself.'

'I see,' he said, and hope went. So that was what Mrs Crilling had meant. In prison there would be no tablets, no syringe, and because she had become

197

addicted to them she would have to reveal her addiction or . . .

'I don't think the police can do anything to you,' he said, not knowing whether they could or not.

'What would you know about it? I've got twenty left in a bottle so I came here. I've made myself a bed upstairs and . . .'

He interrupted her. 'It's your raincoat?'

The question surprised her, but only for a moment, then scorn returned to make her look twice her age.

'Sure it is,' she said scathingly. 'Whose did you think it was, Painter's? I went out for a bit to get something from my car, left the door on the latch and when I came back you were here with that tarty piece.' He kept his eyes on her, controlling himself. For the only time in his life he felt an urge to strike another person's face. 'I didn't dare come back for a bit,' she said, returning to the only other mood she had, a self-pitying childishness. 'But I had to get my raincoat – the tablets were in the pocket.'

She inhaled deeply and flung the cigarette away from her into the wet bushes.

'What the hell were you doing, returning to the scene of the crime? Trying to get under his skin?'

'Whose skin?' he whispered urgently.

'Painter's of course. Bert Painter's. My Uncle Bert.' She was defiant again, but her hand shook and her eyes glazed. It was coming now. He was like a man awaiting bad news, knowing it was inevitable, knowing even exactly what it was going to be, but still hoping that there would be some detail, some facet to mitigate it. 'That night,' she said, 'he stood there just like you. Only he was holding a piece of wood and there was blood on it and all over him. "I've cut myself," he said. "Don't look, Lizzie, I've cut myself." '

Chapter 16

When the unclean spirit is gone out of a man, he
walketh through dry places seeking rest and finding
none. He saith, I will return unto my house whence I
came out.

The Gospel for the Fourth Sunday in Lent.

She told it in the second person, 'You did this,' 'You
did that.' Archery realised he was hearing what no
parent and no psychiatrist had ever heard, and he
marvelled. The peculiar use of the pronoun seemed
to draw his own mind into the child's body so that
he could see with her eyes and feel with her
overweening terror.

She sat in the damp dusk on the spot where it had
all begun for her, utterly still now. Only her eyelids
moved. Sometimes, at agonising moments in the
narrative, she would close her eyes, then open them
again with a slow exhalation of breath. Archery had
never been to a seance – would indeed have
disapproved of such a thing as being theologically
untenable – but he had read of them. Elizabeth
Crilling's steady outpouring of terrible events told in
a flat monotone was reminiscent, he thought, of
mediumistic revelation. She was coming to the end
now and a weary relief crossed her face as of one
shedding a load.

. . . You put your coat on, your best coat because it
was your best frock, and you ran across the road,
down the sideway and past the greenhouse. Nobody
saw you because there was no one about. Or was
there? Surely that was the back door closing softly.

You came very quietly around the side of the

199

house and then you saw it was only Uncle Bert who had come out of the house into the garden.

'Uncle Bert, Uncle Bert! I've got my best frock on. Can I go and show it to Tessie?'

Suddenly you were very frightened, more frightened than you had ever been in all your life, because Uncle Bert was breathing in such a funny way, gasping and coughing like Daddy did when he had one of his attacks. Then he turned round and there was red stuff all over him, on his hands and all down the front of his coat.

'I've cut myself,' he said. 'Don't look, Lizzie. I've just cut myself.'

'I want Tessie! I want Tessie!'

'Don't you go up there!'

'You're not to touch me. I've got my new dress on. I'll tell my mummy.'

He just stood there with the red stuff on him and his face was like the face of a lion, big thick mouth, thick nose, curly tawny hair. Yes, it was like the lion in that picture book Mummy said you must not look at . . .

The red stuff had splashed on to his face and trickled to the corner of his mouth. He brought that dreadful face down close to yours and shouted right at you:

'You tell her, Lizzie Crilling, you stuck-up little snob, and d'you know what I'll do? Wherever I am – wherever, d'you hear me? – I'll find you and I'll give you what I gave the old girl.'

It was over. He could tell that by the way she came out of her trance, sat up and gave a kind of moan.

'But you went back,' Archery murmured. 'You went back with your mother?'

'My mother!' Weeping would not have surprised him. This violent bitter laughter did. On a high discordant peal, she stopped suddenly and rushed into her answer. 'I was only five, only a kid. I didn't know what he meant, not then. I was much more frightened of letting her know I'd been over there.' He noted that 'her' and knew intuitively she would not mention her mother by name again. 'You see, I didn't even know it was blood and I reckon I must have thought it was paint.'

'Then we went back. I wasn't afraid of the house and I didn't know what he meant by the old girl. I think when he said about giving me what he'd given the old girl I thought he meant his wife, Mrs Painter. He knew I'd seen him hit her. I found the body. You knew that? God, it was terrible. I didn't understand, you see. D'you know what I thought at first? I thought she'd sort of burst.'

'Don't,' said Archery.

'If you can't take it now, what d'you think it was like for me? I was *five*. Five, my Christ! They put me to bed and I was ill for weeks. Of course, they'd arrested Painter, but I didn't know that. You don't tell children that sort of thing. I didn't know what had happened at all, only that Granny Rose had burst open and he had made it happen and if I said I'd seen him he'd do the same to me.'

'But afterwards. Didn't you tell anyone then?'

She had talked about finding the body and said it was terrible, but then there had been affectation in her voice. A child finding a murdered woman, he thought. Yes, all the world would recoil in shock from that. Yet for her that had not been the worst. Now as he asked her about afterwards he saw the trance begin once more to mist her face as the spectre of Painter – Painter on this very spot – rose before it.

'He'd find you,' she mumbled. 'He'd find you wherever you were, wherever he was. You wanted to tell *her*, but she wouldn't listen to you. "Don't think about it, Baby, put it out of your mind." But it

201

wouldn't go *out* ...' Her features worked and the blank eyes flickered.

'Miss Crilling, let me take you home.'

She was standing up now, moving mechanically towards the house wall, a robot whose programming has failed. When her hands touched the bricks she stopped and spoke again, talking to him but into the house itself.

'It wouldn't go out. It went in and in, till it was just a little black wheel spinning and playing the same thing over and over again.'

Had she realised she was speaking in metaphor? He had thought of a medium's utterances, but now he knew it had been more like a discordant record, playing the same horror each time it was pricked by the stylus of association. He touched her arm and was surprised when she followed him meekly and limply back to the chair. They sat in silence for some minutes. She was the first to speak and she was almost her normal self.

'You know Tessie, don't you? She's going to marry your son?' He shrugged. 'I think she was the only real friend I ever had,' she said quietly. 'It was her birthday the next week. She was going to be five, and I thought I'd give her one of my old dresses. Sneak it round when *she* was with the old girl. Generous little beast, wasn't I? I never saw her again.'

Archery said gently, 'You saw her this afternoon in the chemist's.'

Her new tranquillity was very finely balanced. Had he pushed it too far?

'In the white blouse?' she said in a dead even voice, so low that he had to lean forward and strain to catch it. He nodded.

'That girl who hadn't got any change?'

'Yes.'

'She was standing beside me and I never knew.'

There was a long silence. The only sound was the faint rustling of wet bushes, water-loaded gleaming leaves on the coach-house walls. Then she tossed her head. 'I reckon I don't notice women much,' she said. 'I saw you all right and the boy that was with you. I remember I thought the talent's looking up in this dump.'

'The talent,' Archery said, 'is my son.'

'Her boy-friend? I never would have told you!' She gave a low cry of exasperation. 'And, my God, I never would have told her – not if you hadn't caught me out like that.'

'It was chance, coincidence. Perhaps it's better that I do know.'

'You!' she said. 'That's all you think about, you and your precious son. What about me?' She stood up, looked at him and moved towards the door with the broken pane. It was true, he thought, ashamed. He had been prepared to sacrifice all these other people to save Charles, the Crillings, Primero, even Imogen – but his quest had been doomed from the beginning because history could not be changed.

'What will they do to me?' Her face was turned away from him and she spoke softly. But there was such urgency and such fear in those six short words that their impact was as if she had shouted.

'Do to you?' He could do no more than get to his feet and stand helplessly behind her. 'Why should they do anything to you?' He remembered the dead man on the crossing and he remembered the needle punctures, but he said only, 'You've been more sinned against than sinning.'

'Oh, the Bible!' she cried. 'Don't quote the Bible to me.' He said nothing for he had not done so. 'I'm going upstairs now,' she said strangely. 'When you see Tess would you give her my love? I wish,' she said, 'I wish I could have given her something for her birthday.'

By the time he had found a doctor's house he felt all hand, nothing but hand, a throbbing thing that beat like a second heart. He recognised Dr Crocker at once and saw that he, too, was remembered.

'You must be enjoying your holiday,' Crocker said. He stitched the finger, filled a syringe with anti-tetanus serum. 'First that dead boy and now this. Sorry, but this may hurt. You've got thick skin.'

'Really?' Archery could not help smiling as he bared his upper arm. 'I want to ask you something.' Without stopping to explain he put the question that had been troubling him all the way from Victor's Piece. 'Is it possible?'

'Beginning of October?' Crocker looked closely and not unsympathetically at him. 'Look, how personal is this?'

Archery read his thoughts and managed a laugh. 'Not that personal,' he said. 'I am, as they say, enquiring for a friend.'

'Well, it's extremely unlikely.' Croker grinned. 'There have been cases, very few and far between. They make minor medical history.'

Nodding, Archery got up to go.

'I shall want to see that finger again,' the doctor said. 'Or your local G.P. will. You'll need another couple of injections. See to it when you get home, will you?'

Home ... yes, he would be home tomorrow. His stay in Kingsmarkham had not been a holiday, anything but that, yet he had that curious end-of-a-holiday feeling when the resort one has stayed in becomes more familiar than home.

He had walked along this High Street every day, more frequently even than he trod the main village street at Thringford. The order of the shops, chemist, grocer, draper, were as well known to him as to the housewives of Kingsmarkham. And the place was certainly pretty. Suddenly it seemed sad that he should hardly have noticed its prettiness – more than that really, for prettiness does not go with grace and dignity – but would associate it for ever with a lost love and a failed search.

Street lamps, some of them of ancient design and with wrought iron casings, showed him alleys winding between stone walls, coaching yards, flowers in a few cottage gardens. The weak yellow light bleached these flowers to a luminous pallor. Half an hour ago it had been just light enough to read print by; now the darkness had come down and lamps appeared in windows fronting the street. The sky had a rainy look and stars showed only in the crevices between bulbous bloated cloud. There was no moon.

The Olive and Dove was brightly lit and the car park full. Glass doors separated the hall from the cocktail bar and he saw that it was crowded. There were groups and pairs of young people, sitting on high stools, gathered round the small black oak tables. Archery thought he would give everything he possessed to see Charles among them, throwing back his head in laughter, his hand resting on the shoulder of a pretty girl. Not a beautiful, intellectual, tainted girl – just someone pretty and dull and uncomplicated. But Charles was not there. He found him alone in the lounge writing letters. Only a few hours had elapsed since his parting from Tess, but already he was writing . . .

'What on earth have you done to your hand and where have you been?'

'Hacking away at the past.'

'Don't be cryptic, Father. It doesn't suit you.' His tone was bitter and sullen. Archery wondered why people say that suffering improves the character, why indeed he had sometimes thoughtlessly said it to his own parishioners. He listened to his son's voice, carping, querulous and selfish. 'I've been wanting to address this envelope for the past two hours, but I couldn't because I don't know where Tess's aunt lives.' Charles gave him a sour accusing look. 'You wrote it down. Don't say you've lost it.'

'Here.' Archery took the card from his pocket and dropped it on the table. 'I'm going to phone your mother, tell her we'll be home in the morning.'

'I'll come up with you. This place goes dead at night.'

Dead? And the bar crowded with people, some of whom were surely as exacting as Charles. If Tess had been with them it would not have been dead. Quite suddenly Archery made up his mind that Charles must be made happy, and if happiness meant Tess, he should have Tess. Therefore the theory he was formulating would have to be made to work.

He paused on the threshold of his bedroom, put his hand to the light switch but did not press it. There in the darkness with Charles behind him there flashed across his brain a picture of himself and Wexford that first day at the police station. He had been firm then. 'Bitterly, bitterly against this marriage,' he had told the Chief Inspector. How utterly he had come round! But then he had not known what it was to crave for a voice and a smile. To understand all was not merely to forgive all, it was utter identification of the spirit and the flesh.

Over his shoulder Charles said, 'Can't you find the switch?' His hand came up and met his father's on the dry cold wall. The room flooded with light. 'Are you all right? You look worn-out.'

Perhaps it was the unaccustomed gentleness in his voice that did it. Archery knew how easy it is to be kind when one is happy, how nearly impossible to feel solicitude in the midst of one's own misery. He was suddenly filled with love, an overflowing diffused love that for the first time in days had no specific object but included his son – and his wife. Hoping unreasonably that her voice would be soft and kind, he moved towards the telephone.

'Well, you are a stranger,' were the first words he heard and they were sharp with resentment. 'I was beginning to wonder what had happened to you. Thought you must have eloped.'

'I wouldn't do that, darling,' he said, sick at heart. And then, because he had to set his foot back on the path of constancy, he took a grotesque echo, 'Kingsmarkham isn't conspicuous for its talent. I've missed you.' It was untrue and what he was going to say next would also be a lie. 'It'll be good to be home with you again.' That lie would have to be changed into truth. He clenched his hand till the hurt finger burned with pain, but as he did so he thought that he and time could make it true . . .

'You do use some extraordinary expressions,' Charles said when he had rung off. 'Talent, indeed. Very vulgar.' He was still holding the card, staring at it with utter absorption. A week ago Archery would have marvelled that a woman's address and a woman's handwriting could provide such fascination.

'You asked me on Saturday if I'd ever seen this before. You asked me if I'd heard it. Well, now I've *seen* it, it's rung a bell. It's part of a long religious verse play. Part of it's in prose but there are songs in it – hymns really – and this is the last verse of one of them.'

'Where did you see it? In Oxford? In a library?'

But Charles was not listening to him. He said as if he had been meaning to say it for the past half-hour,

'Where did you go tonight? Had it any connection with me and – and Tess?'

Must he tell him? Was he obliged to root out those last vestiges of hope before he had anything real and proven to put in their place?

'Just to have a last look at Victor's Piece.' Charles nodded. He appeared to accept this quite naturally. 'Elizabeth Crilling was there, hiding.' He told him about the drugs, the wretched attempts to secure more tablets, but he did not tell him everything.

Charles's reaction was unexpected. 'Hiding from what?'

'The police, I suppose, or her mother.'

'You didn't just leave her there?' Charles asked indignantly. 'A crazy kid like that? God knows what she might do. You don't know how many of those tablets would poison her. She might take them deliberately to that end. Have you thought of that?'

She had accused him of not considering her but even that taunt had not prompted him. It had simply not crossed his mind that he was doing something irresponsible in leaving a young girl alone in an empty house.

'I think we ought to go to Victor's Piece and try to get her to come home,' Charles said. Observing the sudden animation on his son's face, Archery wondered how sincere he was and how much of this spurt of energy was due to a desire to do something, anything, because he knew that if he went to bed he would not sleep. Charles put the card away in his pocket. 'You won't like this,' he said, 'but I think we ought to take the mother with us.'

'She's quarrelled with her mother. She behaves as if she hates her.'

'That's nothing. Have you ever seen them together?'

Only a glance across a courtroom, a glance of

indecipherable passion. He had never seen them together. He knew only that if Charles were alone somewhere and miserable, on the verge perhaps of taking his own life, he, Archery, would not want strangers to go to his succour.

'You can drive,' he said and he tossed the keys to his son.

The church clock was striking eleven. Archery wondered if Mrs Crilling would be in bed. Then it occurred to him for the first time that she might be worrying about her daughter. He had never attributed to the Crillings ordinary emotions. They were different from other people, the mother deranged, the girl delinquent. Was that why, instead of being merciful, he had merely used them? As they turned into Glebe Road he felt a new warmth stir within him. It was not too late – especially now she had found some release – to bring Elizabeth back, to heal that old wound, to retrieve something out of chaos.

Outwardly he was cold. He was coatless and the night was chilly. You expect a winter's night to be cold, he thought. There was something depressing and wrong about a cold summer night. November with flowers, a November wind that ruffled the ripe leaves of summer. He must not find omens in nature.

'What d'you call it,' he said to Charles, 'when you ascribe emotions to nature? What's the expression?'

'The Pathetic Fallacy,' Charles said. Archery shivered.

'This is the house,' he said. They got out. Number twenty-four was in darkness upstairs and down.

'She's probably in bed.'

'Then she'll have to get up,' said Charles and rang the bell. He rang again and again. 'Pointless,' he said. 'Can we get round the back?'

Archery said, 'Through here,' and led Charles through the sandy arch. It was like a cavern, he thought, touching the walls. He expected them to be clammy but they were dry and prickly to the touch. They emerged into a dark pool among patches of light which came from french windows all along the backs of houses. A yellow square segmented by black bars lay on each shadowed garden but none came from Mrs Crilling's window.

'She must be out,' said Archery as they opened the little gate in the wire fence. 'We know so little about them. We don't know where she'd go or who her friends are.'

Through the first window the kitchen and the hall showed dark and empty. To reach the french windows they had to push through a tangle of wet nettles which stung their hands.

'Pity we didn't bring a torch.'

'We haven't *got* a torch,' Archery objected. He peered in. 'I've got matches.' The first he struck showed him the room as he had seen it before, a muddle of flung-down clothes and stacked newspapers. The match died and he dropped it on wet concrete. By the light of a second he saw that on the table were the remains of a meal, cut bread still in its paper wrapping, a cup and saucer, a jam jar, a single plate coated with something yellow and congealed.

'We might as well go,' he said. 'She isn't here.'

'The door's not locked,' said Charles. He lifted the latch and opened it quietly. There came to them at once a peculiar and unidentifiable odour of fruit and of alcohol.

'You can't go in. There isn't the slightest justification for breaking in.'

'I haven't broken anything.' Charles's foot was over the threshold, but he stopped and said over his shoulder to his father, 'Don't you think there's something odd here? Don't you feel it?'

Archery shrugged. They were both in the room

210

now. The smell was very strong but they could see nothing but the dim outlines of cluttered furniture.

'The light switch is on the left by the door,' he said. 'I'll find it.' He had forgotten that his son was a man, that his son's adult sense of responsibility had brought them there. In that dark, evilly scented place, they were just a parent and his child. He must not do as Mrs Crilling had done and let the child go first. 'Wait there,' he said. He felt his way along the side of the table, pushed a small armchair out of his path, squeezed behind the sofa and felt for the switch. 'Wait there!' he cried again, much more sharply and in a spasm of real fear. Previously in his passage across the room his feet had come into contact with debris on the floor, a shoe, he thought, a book dropped face-downwards. Now the obstruction was larger and more solid. His scalp crept. Clothes, yes, and within those clothes something heavy and inert. He dropped to his knees, thrusting forward hands to palpate and fumble. 'Dear God . . . !'

'What is it? What the hell *is* it? Can't you find the light?'

Archery could not speak. He had withdrawn his hands and they were wet and sticky. Charles had crossed the room. Light pouring into and banishing that darkness was a physical pain. Archery closed his eyes. Above him he heard Charles make an inarticulate sound.

He opened his eyes and the first thing he saw was that his hands were red. Charles said, 'Don't look!' and he knew that his own lips had been trying to frame those words. They were not policemen, not used to sights such as this, and each had tried to save the other from seeing.

Each had to look. Mrs Crilling lay spread on the floor between the sofa and the wall and she was quite dead. The chill of her body came up to Archery's hands through the pink flounces that covered it from neck to ankles. He had seen that neck and at once had looked away from the stocking that made a ligature around it.

'But she's all over blood,' said Charles. 'It's as if – God! – as if someone had sprinkled her with it.'

Chapter 17

I held my tongue and spake nothing; I kept silence,
yea, even from good words; but it was pain and grief
to me.

Psalm 39. *The Burial of the Dead.*

'It isn't blood,' said Wexford. 'Don't you know what
it is? Couldn't you smell it?' He lifted the bottle
someone had found under the sideboard and held it
aloft. Archery sat on the sofa in Mrs Crilling's living
room, worn, tired, utterly spent. Doors banged and
footsteps sounded as Wexford's two men searched
the other room. The people upstairs had come in at
midnight, Saturday night happy, the man a little
drunk. The woman had had hysterics during Wexford's questioning.

They had taken the body away and Charles moved
his chair round so that he could not see the crimson
splashes of cherry brandy.

'But why? Why did it happen?' he whispered.

'Your father knows why.' Wexford stared at
Archery, his grey gimlet eyes deep and opaque. He
squatted opposite them on a low chair with wooden
arms. 'As for me, I don't know but I can guess. I can't
help feeling I've seen something like this before, a
long, long time ago. Sixteen years to be exact. A pink
frilly dress that a little girl could never wear again
because it was spoilt with blood.'

Outside the rain had begun again and water
lashed against the windows making them rattle. It
would be cold now inside Victor's Piece, cold and
eerie like a deserted castle in a wood of wet trees.
The Chief Inspector had an extra uncanny sense that

almost amounted to telepathy. Archery willed his
thoughts to alter course lest Wexford should divine
them, but the question came before he could rid his
mind of its pictures.

'Come on, Mr Archery, where is she?'

'Where is who?'

'The daughter.'

'What makes you think I know?'

'Listen to me,' said Wexford. 'The last person
we've talked to who saw her was a chemist in
Kingsmarkham. Oh, yes, we went to all the chemists
first naturally. This one remembers that when she
was in the shop there were two men and a girl there
too, a young man and an elder one, tall, fair,
obviously father and son.'

'I didn't speak to her then,' Archery said truthfully. The smell sickened him. He wanted nothing
but sleep and peace and to get out of this room
where Wexford had kept them since they had
telephoned him.

'Mrs Crilling's been dead six or seven hours. It's
ten to three now and you left the Olive at a quarter to
eight. The barman saw you come in at ten. Where
did you go, Mr Archery?'

He sat silent. Years and years ago – oh, centuries
ago! – it had been like this in school. You own up,
you betray someone, or everyone suffers. Funny,
once before he had thought of Wexford as a kind of
headmaster.

'You know where she is,' Wexford said. His voice
was loud, threatening, ominous. 'D'you want to be
an accessary? Is that what you want?'

Archery closed his eyes. Quite suddenly he knew
why he was prevaricating. He wanted the very thing
that Charles had warned him might happen and
although it was contrary to his religion, wicked even,
he wanted it with all his heart.

Charles said, 'Father . . .' and when he got no reply shrugged, turned his dull shocked eyes to Wexford. 'Oh, what the hell? She's at Victor's Piece.'

Archery realised that he had been holding his breath. He let it out in a deep sigh. 'In one of the bedrooms,' he said, 'looking at the coach house and dreaming of a heap of sand. She asked what they would do to her and I didn't understand. What will they do to her?'

Wexford got up. 'Well, sir . . .' Archery noted that 'sir' as one might notice the re-assuming of a velvet glove. 'You know as well as I do that it's no longer lawful to punish with death for certain . . .' His eyes flickered over the place where Mrs Crilling had lain. '. . . certain heinous and grievous offences.'

'Will you let us go now?' Charles asked.

'Until tomorrow,' said Wexford.

The rain met them at the front door like a wave or a wall of spray. For the past half hour it had been drumming on the roof of the car and seeping in through the half-open quarter light. There was water laying in a small pool at Archery's feet but he was too tired to notice or care.

Charles came with him into his bedroom.

'I shouldn't ask you now,' he said. 'It's almost morning and God knows what we'll have to go through tomorrow, but I have to know. I'd rather know. But what else did she tell you, that girl at Victor's Piece?'

Archery had heard of people pacing a room like caged beasts. He had never imagined himself so strung with tension that in spite of utter exhaustion he would have to find release by crossing and re-crossing a floor, picking up objects, replacing them, his hands shaking. Charles waited, too wretched even for impatience. His letter to Tess lay in its envelope on the dressing table and beside it the card

from the gift shop. Archery picked it up and
kneaded it in his hands, crumpling the deckle
edging. Then he went up to his son, put his hands
gently on his shoulders and looked into the eyes that
were young replicas of his own.

'What she told me,' he said, 'needn't matter to you.
It would be like – well, someone else's nightmare.'
Charles did not move. 'If you will only tell me where
you saw the verse that is printed on this card.'

The morning was grey and cool, such a morning as
occurs perhaps three hundred times a year out of the
three hundred and sixty-five, when there is neither
rain nor sun, frost nor fog. It was a limbo of a
morning. The policeman on the crossing had covered
his shirt sleeves with his dark jacket, the striped shop
blinds were rolled up and sluggish steps had grown
brisk.

Inspector Burden escorted Archery along the drying pavements to the police station. Archery was
ashamed to answer Burden's kindly question as to
how he had slept. He had slept heavily and soundly.
Perhaps he would also have slept dreamlessly had he
known what the inspector now told him, that
Elizabeth Crilling was alive.

'She came with us quite willingly,' Burden said
and added rather indiscreetly. 'To tell you the truth,
sir, I've never seen her so calm and sane and – well,
at peace, really.'

'You want to go home, I suppose,' Wexford said
when Burden had left them alone in the blue and
yellow office. 'You'll have to come back for the
inquest and the magistrates' court hearing. You
found the body.'

Archery sighed. 'Elizabeth found a body sixteen
years ago. If it hadn't been for her mother's self-
seeking vanity, greed for something she had no

claim to – that would never have happened. You might say that that greed reached out and destroyed long after its original purpose had been frustrated. Or you might say that Elizabeth bore her mother a grudge because Mrs Crilling would never let her talk about Painter and bring her terrors to the light of day.'

'You might,' said Wexford. 'It could be all those things. And it could be that when Liz left the chemist's she went back to Glebe Road, Mrs Crilling was afraid to ask for another prescription, so Liz, in the addict's frenzy, strangled her.'

'May I see her?'

'I'm afraid not. I'm beginning to guess just what she saw sixteen years ago and what she told you last night.'

'After I'd talked to her I went to see Dr Crocker. I want you to look at this.' Archery gave Wexford Colonel Plashet's letter, silently indicating the relevant passage with his bandaged finger. 'Poor Elizabeth,' he murmured. 'She wanted to give Tess a dress for her fifth birthday. Unless Tess has changed a lot it wouldn't have meant much to her.'

Wexford read, closed his eyes briefly and then gave a slight smile. 'I see,' he said slowly and restored the letter to its envelope.

'I am right, aren't I? I'm not juggling things, imagining things? You see, I can't trust my own judgment any more. I have to have an opinion from an expert in deduction. I've been to Forby, I've seen a photograph, I've got a letter and I've talked to a doctor. If you had the same clues would you have come to the same conclusions?'

'I'm sure you're very kind, Mr Archery.' Wexford gave a broad ironic grin. 'I get more complaints than compliments. Now, as to clues and conclusions, I would, but I'd have been on to it a whole lot sooner.

'You see, it all depends on what you're looking for and the fact is, sir, you didn't know what you *were* looking for. All the time you were trying to disprove something in the face of – well, you said it – expert deduction. What you've found now achieves the same result as the other thing would have. For you and your son, that is. But it hasn't changed what for justice is the *status quo*. We would have made sure we knew precisely what we were looking for at the start, the basic thing. When you come down to that, it doesn't matter a damn to you who committed the crime. But you were looking through a pair of spectacles that were too big for you.'

'A glass darkly,' said Archery.

'I can't say I envy you the coming interview.'

'Strange,' said Archery thoughtfully as he got up to go, 'that although we both held such opposing opinions in the end we were both right.'

Wexford had said he must come back. He would make his visits short, though, short and blind, his eyes opening only in the court he could see out of this window, his words mere evidence. He had read stories of people transported to strange places, blind-folded and in shuttered cars, so that they should not see the country through which they passed. In his case he would be prevented from seeing visions and associations with those visions, by the presence of those he was legitimately allowed to love. Mary should come with him and Charles and Tess to be his shutters and his hood. Certainly he would never see this room again. He turned to give it a last glance, but if he hoped to have the last word he was disappointed.

'Both right,' said Wexford, giving Archery's hand a gentle clasp. 'I by reason and you by faith. Which, taken all in all,' he added, 'is only what one might expect.'

She opened the door to them carefully, grudgingly, as if she expected to see gypsies or a brush salesman from a disreputable firm.

'I hope you'll forgive us, Mrs Kershaw,' Archery said with too loud heartiness. 'Charles wanted to see Tess and as we were coming this way . . .'

It is difficult to greet callers, even unwelcome callers, without some kind of a smile. Irene Kershaw did not smile, but she made muttering noises in which he caught the occasional word: 'very welcome, I'm sure,' 'unexpected . . .' and 'not really prepared . . .' They got into the hall, but it was an awkward manœuvre and it almost involved pushing past her. She had grown rather red and she said to Charles, now quite coherently:

'Tess has popped down to the shops to get a few last-minute things for her holiday.' Archery could see that she was angry and that she did not know how to vent her anger on people who were at the same time adults and from a different background from her own. 'You've quarrelled, haven't you?' she said. 'What are you trying to do, break her heart?' Apparently she was capable of emotion, but once she had shown it, not capable of control. Tears welled into her eyes. 'Oh dear . . . I didn't mean to say that.'

Archery had explained everything to Charles in the car. He was to find Tess, get her alone and tell her. Now he said, 'You might go down the hill, Charles, and see if you can meet her coming up. She'll be glad of a hand with her basket.'

Charles hesitated, possibly because he was at a loss to answer Mrs Kershaw's accusation and could not bring himself to echo so exaggerated an expression as 'a broken heart'. Then he said, 'I'm going to marry Tess. That's what I've always wanted.'

The colour died out of her face and now that there was no occasion for them the tears trickled down her cheeks. Archery would, under other circumstances, have been embarrassed. Now he realised that this mood of hers, tears, a lukewarm resentment that might be her nearest approach to passion, would make her receptive to what he had to say. A tired tigress apparently lurked under that dull suburban exterior, a mother beast capable of being roused only when its young was threatened.

Charles let himself out of the front door. Archery, left alone with her, wondered where the other children were and how soon Kershaw himself would return. Again he was finding himself, when in the sole company of this woman, at a loss for words. She made no effort to help him, but stood stiff and expressionless, dabbing at the tearmarks with the tips of her fingers.

'Perhaps we could sit down?' He made a vague gesture towards the glass door. 'I should like to have a talk, settle things, I . . .'

She was recovering fast, tunnelling back into the sanctuary of her respectability. 'You'd like some tea?'

The mood must not be allowed to peter out into small-talk over the cups. 'No,' he said, 'no, really . . .'

She went before him into the living room. There were the books, the Reader's Digests, the dictionaries and the works on deep sea fishing. The portrait of Jill on the easel was finished and Kershaw had made the amateur's mistake of not knowing when to stop, so that the likeness had been lost in last-minute touches. In the garden which was spread before him with the unreality and the garish colours of a cushion cover in gros point, the Paul Crampel geraniums burned so brightly that they hurt his eyes.

Mrs Kershaw sat down genteelly and crimped her skirt over her knees. Today, now that it was cold again, she wore a cotton dress. She was that kind of woman, Archery thought, who would wear her winter clothes on and on cautiously until she was sure a heat wave was fully established. Then, just as the hot weather was ending and the storm about to break, then at last the carefully laundered thin dress would be brought out.

The pearls had been restrung. She put her hand up to them and drew it away quickly, curbing temptation. Their eyes met and she gave a tiny nervous giggle, perhaps aware that he had noticed her tiny vice. He gave a small inner sigh, for all her emotion had gone and her face showed only the natural bewilderment of a hostess who does not know the purpose of a call and is too discreet to question the caller.

He must – he *must* – awaken something from behind that pale lined brow. All his carefully prepared openings died. In a moment she would begin on the weather or the desirability of white weddings. But she did not quite do that. He had forgotten the other stock remark that is so handy a conversation starter between strangers.

'And how did you enjoy your holiday?' said Irene Kershaw.

Very well. That would do as well as anything.

'Forby is your native village, I believe,' he said. 'I went to see a grave while I was there.'

She touched the pearls with the flat of her hand. 'A grave?' For an instant her voice was as raw as when she had talked of a broken heart, then all passionless Purley again as she added, 'Oh, yes, Mrs Primero is buried there, isn't she?'

'It wasn't her grave I saw.' Softly he quoted, '"Go, shepherd to your rest . . ." Tell me, why did you keep all the works he left behind him?'

That there would be reaction and that that reaction might be anger he had expected. He was prepared for a flouncing hauteur or even that damning, dulling response so dear to the heart of the Mrs Kershaws of this world: 'We needn't discuss that.' He had not thought she would be frightened and at the same time stricken with a kind of awe. She cowered a little in the armchair – if cowering is compatible with perfect stillness – and her eyes wide and glistening now, had the utter immobility of the dead.

Her fear had the effect of frightening him. It was as communicable as a yawn. Suppose she were to have a fit of hysterics? He went on very gently:

'Why did you keep them hidden away in the dark? They might have been published, they might have been acted. He could have had posthumous fame.'

She made no answer at all, but now he knew what to do, the answer came to him like a gift of God. He only had to go on talking, gently, mesmerically. The words tumbled out, platitudes and clichés, praise of work he had never seen and had no reason to suppose he would admire, assurances and unfounded promises he might never be able to honour. All the time, like a hypnotist, he kept his eyes on her, nodding when she nodded, breaking into a wide fatuous smile when for the first time a tiny vague one trembled on her lips.

'May I see them?' he dared. 'Will you show me the works of John Grace?'

He held his breath while with torturing slowness she mounted a stool and reached for the top of the book case. They were in a box, a large cardboard grocer's box that had apparently once contained a gross of tinned peaches. She handled it with a peculiar reverence, her care all concentrated on it, so that she let the magazines which had been stacked on it cascade to the floor.

There must have been a dozen of them but only one cover picture splashed at Archery like acid on the eyes. He blinked away from the beautiful photographed face, the pale hair under a hat of June roses. He had waited for Mrs Kershaw to speak now and her words pulled him out of shock and misery.

'I suppose Tess told you,' she whispered. 'It was supposed to be our secret.' She lifted the lid of the box so that he was able to read the writing on the topmost sheet of manuscript. *'The Fold. A Prayer in Dramatic Form* by John Grace.' 'If you'd told me before I would have shown them to you. Tess said I should show them to anyone who would be interested and would – would understand.'

Again their eyes met and Irene Kershaw's tremulous stare was caught and steadied in his strong one. He knew his face was mobile and expressive of his thoughts. She must have read them for she said, thrusting the box towards him, 'Here, have them. You can have them.' He drew away his hands and his body, horrified and ashamed. At once he had realised what she was doing, that she was trying to pay him off with her most precious material possession. 'Only don't ask me.' She gave a little thin cry. 'Don't ask me about him!'

Impulsively, because he could not bear those eyes, he covered his own with his hands. 'I've no right to be your inquisitor,' he murmured.

'Yes, yes . . . It's all right.' Her fingers touching his shoulder were firm with a new strength. 'But don't ask me about him. Mr Kershaw said you wanted to know about Painter – Bert Painter, my husband. I'll tell you everything I can remember, anything you want to know.'

Her inquisitor and her tormentor . . . Better a swift knife thrust than this interminable twisting on the rack. He clenched his hands till the only pain he could feel came from the wound where the glass had gone in and he faced her across the yellowing sheets of verse.

'I don't want to know about Painter any more,' he said. 'I'm not interested in him. I'm interested in Tess's father . . .' The moan she gave and the feel of those fingers scrabbling at his arm could not stop him now. 'And I've known since last night,' he whispered, 'that Painter *couldn't* have been her father.'

Chapter 18

She lay on the floor and wept. To Archery, standing by helpless, it was some measure of her total breakdown that she had come so far wide of her conventional limits as to lie there prone and shake with sobs. Archery had never in his life reached such a nadir of despair. He pitied with an anxiety that had something of panic in it this woman who cried as if the power to weep had long fallen into disuse, as if she were experimenting with some new and shattering exercise.

He did not know how long this abandonment to grief had lasted or would last. This room with all its apparatus for living what some call a 'full life' contained no clock and he had removed his watch to make room for the wrist anchorage of the bandage. Just as he was beginning to feel that she would never stop, she made a curious humping movement so that she rested like a flogged overburdened beast.

'Mrs Kershaw ...' he said. 'Mrs Kershaw, forgive me.'

She got up slowly, her breast still heaving. The cotton dress was creased into a faded rag. She said something but he could not hear her at all and he realised what had happened. She had utterly exhausted her voice.

'Can I get you a glass of water, some brandy?'

Her head shook as if it were not part of her body

225

but a separate thing quivering on a pivot. Her voice came in a hoarse croak. 'I don't drink.' Then he knew that nothing could fully pierce the layers of respectability. She fell into the chair from which his questions had prised her and let her arms hang limply over its sides. When he came back from the kitchen and gave her the glass of water she had recovered sufficiently to sip it and to rub with the old refinement at the corners of her lips. He was afraid to speak.

'Does she have to know?' The words had a hollow sound to them but the roughness had gone. 'My Tessie, does she have to know?'

He did not dare to tell her that Charles would have told her already. 'It's nothing these days,' he said, and shed with a word two thousand years' teaching of his faith. 'Nobody thinks anything of it any more.'

'Tell me what you know.' He knelt at her feet, praying that all his guesses would approximate to the truth and that there would be few gaps for her to fill. If only he could deal well with this last task and save her the shame of confession.

'You and John Grace,' he said, 'you lived close together in Forby. You were in love with each other, but he was killed . . .'

On an impulse he took the manuscript in his hands and laid it gently in her lap. She took it as a religious takes a talisman or a relic and she said softly:

'He was so clever. I couldn't understand the things he wrote, but they were beautiful. His teacher wanted him to go to college but his mother wouldn't let him. You see, his father had a bakery business and he had to go into that.' Let her go on, he prayed, edging away to squat on the edge of his chair. 'He still wrote his poems and his plays,' she said, 'and in the evenings he used to study for some exam. He wasn't strong enough to go into the forces, anaemia

226

or something he had.' Her fingers tightened on the manuscript but her eyes were dry and drained. Archery had a quick vision of the pale pointed face in the souvenir shop picture, only now it was blending into and becoming one with Tess's.

He let his eyes linger on Irene Kershaw for a brief moment with painful compassion. They had reached a point in this telling where she must, unless he could save her, touch on that which would humiliate her most.

'You were going to be married,' he said.

Perhaps she was afraid to hear the words he might choose. 'We never did anything wrong but the once,' she cried. 'Afterwards – well, he wasn't nasty like other boys, and he was just as ashamed as me.' Justifying herself, her head turned from him, she whispered, 'I've had two husbands and then there was John, but I've never been much for that side of things.' Her head swung back and her face was aflame. 'We were engaged, we were going to be married . . .'

Archery knew he must rush on with his conjectures. 'After he was killed you knew you were going to have a child?' She nodded, silent now with the enormity of her embarrassment. 'You had nowhere to go, you were afraid so you married Painter. Let me see, John Grace was killed in February 1945 and Painter got home from Burma at the end of March. You must have known him before,' he said, guessing, improvising. 'Perhaps he was stationed at Forby before he went to the Far East?' A tiny nod rewarded him and he was prepared to go on, drawing someone else's story out of an inspired imagination, out of a letter from Kendal, a photographed face, the bruises on a woman's arm. He lifted his eyes from her and clasped his hands tightly to stop the sound that might have been no more than a sigh. Even a sigh would tell her. At the open french window, against the blaze of red petals, Kershaw was standing, silent, still and powerfully alert. How long had he been there? How much had he heard? Archery, transfixed, sought momentarily in his expression for suffering or anger and saw a sweetness that brought a sudden strength to his heart.

Perhaps he was betraying this woman, perhaps he was doing the unforgivable. It was too late for such recriminations.

'Let me try to finish,' he said, and he had no idea whether he kept his voice on the same level he had used before. 'You were married and you let him think he was Tess's father. But he suspected and that was why he never loved her as a father loves his child? Why didn't you tell Mr Kershaw?'

She leant forward and he could tell she had not heard the man behind her move almost soundlessly into the room. 'He never asked me about my life with Bert,' she said. 'But I was so ashamed of it, of being married to a man like that. Mr Kershaw's so good – you don't know him – he never asked me, but I had to tell him some of it, didn't I?' She was suddenly eloquent. 'Think what I had to tell him, think what I had to bring him – nothing! People used to point to me out in the street like I was a freak. He had to take that on his shoulders – Mr Kershaw who'd never touched dirt in all his life. He said he'd take me away and give me a new life where no one'd know, he said I wasn't to blame, I was innocent. D'you think I was going to give up the one chance I'd ever had by telling him Tess was – was illegitimate?'

Archery gasped and staggered to his feet. By the power of his eyes and his will he had been trying to force the man behind her chair to retreat the way he had come. But Kershaw remained where he was, still, a man apparently without breath or heartbeats. His wife had been rapt, her own story dulling all outer stimuli, but now she seemed to sense the atmosphere in the room, the soundless passion of two other people whose sole desire was to help her. She twisted in her chair, sketched a strange little gesture of pleading and rose to confront her husband.

The scream Archery expected never came. She lurched a little, but whatever she was trying to gasp out was lost and muffled by Kershaw's strong embrace. He heard her say only, 'Oh, Tom, Oh, Tom!' but his energy was so drained that his brain was filled with just one foolish thought. It was the first time he had ever heard Kershaw's Christian name.

She did not come downstairs again for that time. Archery supposed that he would not see her again until they all met among flowers and bridesmaids and wedding cake. Tess sat pale-faced and almost shy, her hand clasped in that of Charles, the manuscript on her knees.

'I feel so strange,' she said. 'I feel I have a new identity. It's as if I had three fathers and the most remote of them was really my father ...'

Charles said tactlessly, 'Well, wouldn't you choose to have had this one, a man who could write like this?' But Tess lifted her eyes momentarily to the man Archery would have to learn to call Tom and he knew she had made her choice.

Then she thrust the heavy stack of paper towards Archery. 'What can we do with them?'

'I could show them to a publisher I know. I once wrote part of a book myself ...' He smiled. 'On Abyssinian cats. I do know someone who might be interested. Something I can do to make amends,' he said.

'You? You've got nothing to reproach yourself with.' Kershaw moved to stand between him and the lovers. Only marred one marriage to make another, Archery thought. 'Listen,' said Kershaw, his face scored with the lines of effort to make himself understood. 'You did nothing but what I should have done years ago, talked to her. I couldn't, you see. I wanted to get off on the right foot. Now I can see you can be too tactful, too damned diplomatic. Oh, there were a thousand little things, how she'd never cared for Painter but he'd been pestering her to marry him. I never asked her what made her change her mind when he came home from Burma. God help me, I thought it wasn't my business! She didn't want me to tell Tess about Painter and I went through agony trying to put that across to a kid of twelve.' Here, unafraid of sentimentality, he caught his stepdaughter's free hand and held it briefly. 'I remember I even got mad at Rene because she seemed to be contradicting every blessed word I said.'

Tess quoted softly, '"Never mind what Daddy says. Your father was no murderer."'

'And she was right but I turned a deaf ear. She'll talk to me now as she's never talked in all these years. She'll talk to you, Tess, if you'll go up to her now.'

Like a child she hesitated and her lips trembled into a nervous smile of indecision. But obedience – happy, reasonable obedience – was natural in that house. Archery had seen an instance of it before.

'I don't know what to say, how to begin,' she said, getting slowly to her feet. 'I'm so desperately afraid of hurting her.'

'Begin with your wedding, then,' Kershaw said

robustly. Archery watched him stoop to the floor where the magazines had fallen. 'Show her this and let her dream of seeing you in something like it.'

Tess was in jeans and a white shirt, an Olivia or a Rosalind finding her lost birthright and with it a new womanhood. She took the magazine from Kershaw and glanced at the cover picture, the hat that was a pyramid of flowers crowning the most photographed face in Britain.

'That's not for me,' she said, but she took it with her and Archery watched them depart together, Charles's flesh and blood love and his own, a paper fantasy. Not for me, not for me . . .

'We must go soon,' he said to his son. 'It's time we shared all this with your mother.'